The Fifth Goddess

The Fifth Goddess

by
Staci Backauskas

Jai Creations
1999

Library of Congress Catalog Card Number:
99-091249

Backauskas, Staci 1963-

This is a publication of Jai Creations and is designed for the reading pleasure of the general public. All characters and situations are fictional and in no way intended to depict actual persons or situations.

First Edition

ISBN: 0-9675259-0-X

$14.95 U.S./$20.95 Canada

Dedication

I dedicate this book to Joseph Stella, my Merlin, my friend, my legs, my heart. You have been with me since the dawn of time and if not for you, this book might have experienced a slow, torturous death withering in a dark drawer. Those who gain something from this work have you to thank. I love you.

Acknowledgements

No book reaches completion without the support, strength, and help of others. First, I thank God/dess without whom none of this would have been possible. My heartfelt thanks to my mother and father for their love, incredible support and belief in me. My mother's dedication in supporting this project is a big reason I was able to complete it—from paying for my registration to the Maui Writer's conference to brainstorming with me for the back cover copy. There are not words to express my gratitude. My father's pragmatic advice and the freedom to not take it are appreciated more than he knows. I'm able to fly because of the wings they gave me.

For providing light when I was stuck in dark caves of anxiety and doubt, I express appreciation to Eleanor, Gooch, Justin, Karen Z., Kathy, Kevin, Melanie, Meg, Sandy, Tanase, and Vicki. To my editor, Peggy Edmunds—I promise I'll establish my conventions prior to writing the sequel; Andrew Hershberger of O'Miley Ryan, who designed the cover; Christopher Moore for his time, suggestions and kindness; my copy heroes Colleen and Jim at Staples in Middletown, NJ; my typesetters, Angela Werner and Michael Höhne; Jennifer Henning, my guardian angel; all my friends and family who responded to my offer of advanced copies with checks of support; my colleagues on publish@onelist.com who willingly shared their knowledge and experiences; and the friends I've made through my many on-line Goddess and spirituality discussion lists; Jennifer Kahane and Melanie Engberg for proofreading : THANK YOU!

I also want to thank my dear friend, Olga Butterworth. She continually reminds me that I am always unfolding, as we all are. That all the knowledge we need is inside, if we are only brave enough to be still and listen. And, that if we're willing, we may all know the peace that comes with this stillness. Namaste.

Finally, I need to thank Billy and Bugsy—my spirit guides, my writing companions and, at times, my only connection to life—I am so grateful you are my roommates.

Cast of Voices

Erishkigal ~ Sumerian Goddess of the Underworld ~ is intimately familiar with the dark and hungry places of the Great Below, having lived most of her life there alone, feeling angry and resentful. The only bright spot in Erishkigal's life, her marriage to Gugalanna, quickly faded after his death. And once again, she was left alone. In Sumerian mythology she is the dark half of one being with Inanna, who represents light and is the third Goddess in Rena's story. But one is not good, and the other bad. Darkness is only that which has not yet seen the light. Erishkigal represents the aspect of Rena that is dominated by fear and self-criticism.

Kali ~ Hindu Goddess of Destruction ~ is a tri-tiered Goddess possessing three sets of arms, and is often depicted wearing a necklace of skulls and a belt of hands taken from the bodies of those who angered her. Kali murdered her husband and one true love, Siva, by dancing so powerfully after an argument that the world was almost destroyed. She is the part of Rena that is self-destructive but cleverly disguises it, convincing those around her that she acts the way she does merely because it feels good.

Inanna ~ Sumerian Goddess of Wisdom (a.k.a. Goddess of Heaven and Earth) ~ is Erishkigal's twin in Sumerian mythology and provides the balance of light to Erishkigal's dark. Inanna descends to the underworld to visit her sister under the pretext of attending Gugalanna's funeral. When she arrives, Erishkigal murders her in a jealous rage. After being resurrected and ascending back to earth, Inanna realizes she is stronger for having had the courage to make the journey. For Rena, Inanna represents the logical and pragmatic.

Kuan Yin ~ the Chinese Goddess of Compassion ~ was tortured and eventually murdered by her father for refusing to marry the suitor he chose for his daughter. She was in love with a simple physician, which her father found unacceptable. Through it all, Kuan Yin held to her truth of love and compassion, eventually being resurrected and made a Goddess because of her steadfast faith. She represents the part of Rena that knows that enlightenment is the only true path to happiness. And whatever pain accompanies the search will be more than worth it when enlightenment is achieved.

The Fifth Goddess

Erishkigal

The Fifth Goddess

I sat on my bed picking the hangnail on the side of my left middle finger. It was hard and sharp. The pain was deep, pleasurable, not the stinging of exposed skin that comes from a torn cuticle. Pulling, I twisted the piece of skin, playing with it to control the intensity of the pain. I knew it was wrong to enjoy it so much. But I did. The line between pleasure and pain blurred and my eyes floated in tears like the answer in a magic eight ball. I tried to pull it out by the root, but it was stubborn and wouldn't tear. I tapped the tip with my right index finger and felt the sharpness. Two kinds of pleasure. I went to the medicine cabinet and got the tweezers. Pinching the skin in the prongs, I tugged, ripping the whole piece out. I stuck the finger in my mouth and sucked. Iron and salt.

I pressed my thumb against the swollen surface and felt the warmth between my legs. Blood seeped into the nail bed. My bottom lip absorbed the heat as I brushed my finger across it. Hungry, I went to the kitchen to make macaroni and cheese.

After searching the cabinets, I remembered eating the last box yesterday. I ordered from Noodles on 28 and wondered if sitting home alone eating takeout instead of going to the party at my friend Maristel's made me a loser. A SoHo loft full of artistic hypocrites or House Special Lo Mein. No contest.

I sat smoking a joint watching *Desk Set* on American Movie Classics. Six hits was the magic number to make me sufficiently high and very horny. I retrieved a copy of *Cheri* from my underwear drawer and lay on the couch. I was used to this combination. Marijuana, orgasm, food. And always in that order.

Wanting immediate satisfaction, I stroked the smooth, wet place under my pubic hair while I looked at beautiful blonds sucking long hard cocks. I tried to block out Spencer Tracy and Katherine Hepburn's cheerful banter. I flipped the page, balancing the magazine on my stomach. I was close. It didn't take long when I was high. My middle finger pulsated from the earlier intrusion. I dumped the airbrushed lovers on the floor and closed my eyes, imagining a face for the nameless man on top of me.

The intercom buzzed as I finished. I sniffed my fingers like a curious dog. Handing the delivery boy money, I wondered if he could smell me. I carefully set a plate, silverware, and a cloth napkin on the dining room table. The steam from the barbecued shrimp made my mouth water. I spooned vegetables, shrimp, and Lo Mein onto my dish. While Katherine and Spence bickered, I crunched a water chestnut, then devoured a shrimp.

I put away the leftovers, collapsed on the couch and stared at the two fortune cookies resting on the coffee table. I cracked one open, popping half of it into my mouth. "You are going on a long journey." Not on my salary, I thought. I broke the other one, hoping for a better fortune. "You will live long and be happy." I passed out changing the channels.

I woke up disappointed that Richard hadn't called. The Manhattan morning was humid and overcast. I was usually at the office by eight, but I kept hitting the snooze button. Crossing 42nd street, I saw it was 8:20 on the Chemical Bank clock. My legs were lethargic as my calves yawned to stretch awake. Seven more blocks to go.

Joni, my boss, was volatile when things didn't go according to plan. And me showing up at eight-thirty was not part of the plan. I understood her being a little anal-retentive. It made her more organized and detail oriented. Maybe JC Communications thrived because Joni's parents had thrown her on the potty a little too early.

After two years at JC, I was stuck between wanting something different and not having the energy to leave my comfort zone. As Joni's right arm, I cajoled her out of bad moods, sympathized with her complaints and organized her life. Sometimes Joni let me write press releases or do small media buys, but my title was still Administrative Assistant. At 46th Street and Madison, I got caught at the light and had nowhere to go. If I'd have been smarter, I wouldn't have zigged and zagged so much.

The heat and humidity left me damp and drowsy. My inner thighs were already chafing from my pantyhose. I hated the women standing next to me who were thin enough to go without pantyhose in the summer, who had smooth tanned legs and colorful toenails. Perspiration dripped into my eyes. I should've remembered to bring a paper towel. Now my silk T-shirt had a stain at the neck and I could feel the sweat trickling down my back. Three blocks until air conditioning.

I fingered my limp hair in the ladies' room. It was hopeless. Each time I applied cover stick, it slid off my face and the powder kept clumping. I shook my jacket to get out the wrinkles and caught the mirrored reflection of my jiggling underarm flesh. I had no right to wear sleeves this short. Late and sweating and half made-up. Not a good way to start the day.

"Rena? Are you in there?" Joni called from the entry.

"Yes. Sorry I'm late. My cat …." I couldn't focus sufficiently to create a believable lie.

"I'm sorry about your cat, Rena, but the Jensen people are going to be here any minute for the presentation. There's no coffee and the VCR is jammed."

Jesus! The Jensen presentation. How could I have forgotten? Getting stoned last night certainly hadn't helped. "I'll be right there," I apologized. I could hear Joni's heels clicking on the miniature tiles as she angrily closed the door. I finished applying make-up and wriggled into my damp jacket.

I reattached a disconnected wire in back of the VCR and had coffee brewing before Joni found me again. "Did you remember to order Danish and bagels?" Joni's pale yellow silk suit hugged every curve on her petite frame. Her thick blond hair was swept into a French twist and the two-carat diamond stud earrings were tasteful without being flashy. Joni Crenshaw was the *Forbes Magazine* poster child for successful businesswomen.

Of course she'd had some help. A snip here, a tuck there. All essential to creating the illusion. Joni had gotten sick a year ago. A rare lymphatic illness that doctors were doing wonders with in South America. Goddamned FDA wouldn't give them approval to use the drugs in the States. Experimental, they said. Not enough clinical research. So Joni took a month off and flew to Argentina for treatment.

Everyone was nervous. Was she going to be OK? Where would we work if JC closed? When she returned, golden and glowing, everyone was quite relieved. Relieved enough to overlook the scars behind her ears and the missing wrinkles and the fuller lips. I wasn't that relieved. I didn't speak to her for days.

"The Danish and bagels will be here in a few minutes." I lied. After Joni returned to her office, I called Burke and Burke and ordered the food. If the Jensen people got here before it did, I'd blame it on the deli. I sat at my desk and flipped through my messages.

Maristel had called. I was sure at least one scandal had erupted last night. There was also a message from Nation's Bank. They were looking for money. My Visa bill was over the limit. As far as I was concerned, it was their fault for letting me do it. My mother had called at 8:25, and my grandmother's message said she'd try back later.

My grandmother was the sanest person in my family. Somehow she had escaped the lunacy that affected the rest of my relatives. My father's mother was the only one who had provided a modicum of normalcy in my childhood, especially after my parents' divorce. Since moving to New York five years ago, I had only seen her a couple of times a year, but she always called at least once a week so we could catch up. At sixty-eight my grandmother was still full of piss and vinegar.

Her bowling team had elected her captain and she volunteered at a local hospital twice a week, escorting patients to their X-rays and CAT scans. She still yelled at my father when he threw a cigarette butt out the car window. How she had managed to stay married to my grandfather, who sat home every night and wallowed in misery about his bookstore going bankrupt, was a mystery to me.

The receptionist buzzed the intercom to let me know the food had arrived. Walking out to the lobby to sign the bill, I wanted to be anyplace but 444 Madison Avenue. If I'd had the balls, I'd have strolled right past the deliveryman, down the elevator, taken the bus to the Cloisters and never come back. But I knew I didn't. I was taught to be responsible.

I was glad I still had some pot left, but when this bag was gone, I wasn't going to buy any more. It wasn't a problem, yet. But I knew that getting high every night was preventing me from seeing how miserable I really was. Right now my eyes stung from lack of sleep, and a Mary Jane hangover and I couldn't think about it.

"You have pen?" the immigrant delivery boy asked, smiling.

Always prepared, I pulled a Bic from behind my ear and signed the bill. On my desk, I found a note from Joni asking me to run across town and pick up a package. I grabbed a twenty from petty cash and left to hail a cab. By the time I'd returned the Jensen people were in the conference room with Joni and Harold Ramus, the agency's senior account executive. I was confident that Harold had been stuffed in a lot of lockers in junior high. As I was sorting through a stack of files, I opened my top right drawer and grabbed a handful of M&M's from under a pile of message pads. Popping two green ones in my mouth, I found Harold staring at me.

"Yes?" I said.

"Joni needs these changes made in the contract." I wondered if tugging his nasal hairs would alter his whiny voice. He thrust the papers at me, pushed his thick glasses up his long nose, turned on his heel, and returned to the meeting. The cheap spice of his drugstore cologne burned my nose. I'd contemplated getting a Harold voodoo doll to amuse myself, but hadn't been willing to travel to New Orleans. I was wondering where I could find one in New York when the phone rang. It was Richard.

"Hey, Ren! I found someone to buy a bag of weed from."

"Cool. When can you get it?"

"Well, that's the thing. She's working tonight and I've got plans with Tony tomorrow night, so I can't go. But you could."

"Where is it?"

"Brooklyn."

"I guess if I took your car, it wouldn't be too bad."

"I'm not letting you drive my brand new Camaro to Brooklyn to get drugs. What are you—crazy? What if you got busted? They'll impound my car."

"Nice."

"What?"

"Did it occur to you that if I get busted, I go to jail?"

"You can take the train. It's a straight shot on the F."

"I don't think so."

"Why won't you do this for me?"

"I'm not taking a train to some strange part of Brooklyn to go to some stranger's house to get drugs alone. I'm not doing it."

"What are you—afraid?"

"Yeah." That was only half-true. Part of me enjoyed these verbal duels with Richard. It made our relationship familiar. "I'm not going."

The boardroom in Rena's head was standing room only. Erishkigal knelt quietly while Kali paced, all six arms swinging furiously at her sides. "Watch it, sister!" Kali glared at Inanna, angry that her sister was unaware that she was in the way. Kuan Yin sat chanting in full lotus, her palms open on her knees.

"Doing drugs isn't very practical." Inanna stood between Erishkigal and Kali, lost in thought, twirling a long blond braid between her fingers. "And this trip would entail unnecessary risk."

"We, we need to go," stuttered Erishkigal, her raven hair knotted in a tight roll at the back of her head. "He's done so much for her."

"What has he done besides manipulate her?" argued Kali, her necklace of dried skulls rattling. "You're afraid of being alone after being stuck by yourself in the Great Below all those years. Don't put your shit on Rena."

"Richard does that because of his own insecurities." Kuan Yin felt obligated to enlighten her sisters. The Chinese goddess of mercy and compassion was serene as always.

"What are you—whacko?" Kali laughed and threw her head back. The dead infant earrings hanging from her ears swung back and forth.

"We need to have some understanding about where he's coming from." Kuan Yin's round face was peaceful, her almond eyes almost translucent. *"Rena has attracted him to her to break the patterns she's had with other important men in her life."* Although Rena was pushing thirty, Kuan Yin still thought of her as a child and was extremely protective.

"Sell that psychobabble bullshit to someone who'll buy it, Kuan Yin. Who cares where he's coming from? I just want to see him go." Kali showed no mercy. Just like when she stood over her husband Siva, blood dripping from her tongue, after she had slain him. Kali could be very un-goddess-like when her buttons were pushed.

"He's going to get mad," Erishkigal insisted. She couldn't let Richard leave Rena. She couldn't risk anything like that happening to Rena. *"It won't take long. We'll be home by nine."*

"Come on, Rena. It'll be fine," Richard soothed. "We'll get high this weekend, maybe go to the country. I'll even let you drive so I can suck your tits." His voice was low and husky.

My brain and clitoris waged an internal war. "Well, maybe." I caved. "But we'll have to do it next weekend. My mother's coming into town this Friday. Remember?"

"No. But you can get the bag to me before she gets here, right?"

"Meet me at lunch to give me the address and some cash."

"Well, that's the thing. I can't."

"Why?"

"Because I need the money I have left for tomorrow night. And I don't get paid until Wednesday."

"So, you expect me to pay for it as well as schlep all the way out there—by train—to get it? I don't think so."

"You just said you'd go!"

"I've changed my mind."

"You're almost out too, you know. Opportunities like this don't come along all the time."

"But I don't want to go alone," I whined.

"I wish I could go, but I can't." His buttery voice melted my anger. "You'd really be doing me a favor."

"I guess I could bribe a friend into going."

"That'd work." He paused and I heard someone talking to him. "Look, Rena, I gotta go. Thanks. I love you."

"I can't believe you're going to let her do this." Kali was furious.

"It's not that big a deal," Erishkigal argued. "I don't see what you're so upset about."

"He's gotten his way since they've known each other." Kali complained.

"What are you talking about?" Erishkigal had a convenient memory.

"She's right," Inanna chimed in. "And it's because Rena spent four years after college eating pizza and watching TV and getting as big as a house." Inanna puffed her cheeks up like a blowfish. "She didn't date anyone. The only reason she went out with him is because he was the first man who paid attention to her after she dropped some weight."

"The sex was great," Kali's smile turned evil. "But he always gets his way and it pisses me off." She stomped her foot and Erishkigal struggled to keep her balance.

"Don't you remember how Rena almost lost her job after their first date?" Inanna interrupted.

"I only remember her feeling wanted," Erishkigal's voice was soft. "He made her feel desirable and sexy."

"At what price?" Kali demanded. "Joni almost fired her ass. Don't you remember?"

Almost two years ago, I looked up from my computer to find a tall blond man with a goofy grin asking me where he could find Frank Renaldi. "I'm Frank's nephew, Richard, and I need to drop this off." He held up a manila envelope.

"He's the last office on the right." I pointed.

"Thanks," he smiled. "Thanks a lot." I admired his ass as he walked away and stored in my memory the fragments of his Obsession cologne that lingered around my desk. I was debating if I was horny because of him or Calvin Klein, when I heard Frank clapping his hand over Richard's back.

"Rena," Frank called. "Did you meet my nephew?"

"Not officially." I stood and extended my hand. "Rena Sutcliffe."

"Richard Renaldi." He took my hand and squeezed it. "Thanks for your help earlier."

"No problem." Our eyes were locked and he still held my hand. I broke the clasp to answer the phone. The rest of the girls were at lunch. "It's for you, Frank."

"Thanks, Rena," he shook Richard's hand walked toward his office. "Tell your mother I appreciate it. I'll call you," he yelled over his shoulder. "We'll go to a Knick's game."

"So, how long have you known my uncle?" Richard's blue eyes grazed my cleavage.

"Almost two years." He leaned over and pressed both hands on the edge of my desk. His long fingers drummed quietly. A few gold hairs lay placidly on the backs and a hint of blue tinged the slightly bulging veins. I imagined them running all over me.

"So, what do you do here, Rena Sutcliffe?" He smiled, his teeth white and perfectly aligned.

"I'm the President's assistant," I stuttered.

"You must have a lot of secrets." He winked.

"A few," I responded, playing with the papers on my desk.

"It was very nice meeting you Rena Sutcliffe. But I've got to get back to work." He took my hand and kissed it. "Have a wonderful afternoon." He glanced back at me from the elevator but I pretended to be on the phone. I felt like I was sitting in a puddle of lava, warm and sticky.

The next morning my phone rang around ten. "I'm looking for Frank Renaldi."

"This isn't his extension, but I can transfer you." I offered.

"Rena?"

"Yes."

"Hey, it's Richard. How about that? I got you instead of Uncle Frank. What are the odds?"

"About a million to one." I grinned.

"I've been thinking about you."

"Oh?"

"I just got out of the shower and I'm sitting here in a towel and for some reason I started thinking about you. Maybe that's why I got transferred to you by accident."

I squeezed my knees together hoping it would provide some relief.

"You're only wearing a towel right now?"

"Yep."

"Shouldn't you be at work?'

"I'm off today. When do you get off?"

"I get off plenty," I assured him. My cheeks were hot and I sucked the insides, searching for some moisture.

"I'm getting a little chilly," he sniffed. "Know how I can tell?"

"How?" I asked.

"My nipples are at attention." I swallowed hard.

"Guess what," he whispered.

"What?"

"It's my birthday next week."

"Really? How old are you going to be?" I asked.

"I'm ageless," I heard him smirk. "Why don't you take me out for a drink next week—for my birthday?" He told me he'd pick me up at the office around six the following Tuesday.

"You'd better wear something besides a towel," I joked.

"Why?" He laughed. "If I have my way, it'll end up coming off anyway."

The day of our date, I ran home at lunch and took a shower. At five to six he walked into the office wearing tight jeans and a white dress shirt. A few blond tufts peeked out from the open neck. "You look great!" he said, leaning on my desk.

"Thanks," I smiled, smoothing my flowered skirt. I had tied a pink blouse at my waist. We walked to a pub on 45th and he bought me a beer. "Hey, I'm supposed to buy you a drink," I argued. "It's your birthday."

"You can get the next one."

"Only if you open this." I handed him a card.

"You got me a card? That is so sweet." He ripped the envelope. On the front was a caricature of a woman who said, "I bought you the best present in the world. You're going to be so happy, you're going to get down on your hands and knees and thank me." He opened it to find "And while you're down there ...." His eyes moved slowly from the card to me. Then he leaned over and kissed me. As his tongue massaged my mouth, I combed my fingers through his silky hair.

We left ten minutes later. "I have an idea," he said as we walked up Madison. "Let's do it at your office. My uncle's always complaining about what a bitch Joni is. Let's do it on her desk!"

"You're out of your mind!"

"It's more fun with company." He reached over and tickled me until I was hysterical.

"OK, OK, you win!" The security guard made us sign in and we rode the elevator to the 21st floor. On the way, we couldn't keep our hands off of each other. I unlocked the door and we stumbled in, hands and tongues colliding. We made it to Joni's office and Richard swiped all the papers from her desk onto the floor. He pushed me onto the desk and fell on top of me. "I've always wanted to do it with a girl who's got meat on her bones," he whispered in my ear, untying my blouse.

The next morning Joni called me into her office. I thought I had carefully re-stacked all the files, but it looked messier than I remembered it. "Rena, were you in my office last night?"

"Why?"

"Because I'm missing the Food Emporium file." She stood and walked toward me, deciding at the last minute to lean her round ass on the desk. "Because my office looks like a hurricane swept through here last night." She crossed her legs. "And because when I got the security log I discovered that you and someone named 'Jim Beam' signed in at seven-thirty. Do you care to explain any of this?"

"No."

"You don't want to tell me what happened?"

"No."

"Then I'll use my imagination." She returned to her leather chair, swiveled it to face the window, and put her legs up on the sill. "My guess is that you and one of your boyfriends got a little too hot for your own good and couldn't bear the thought of a ten minute cab ride to your apartment." She had the tone of a district attorney trying to prove her case to a jury. "So you came back to the office and did God knows what. But why did you have to do it on my desk?" I couldn't tell if she was angry or amused. "I ought to fire you."

"Joni, I'm so sorry. It'll never happen again."

"You're damned right it won't. And if I don't have that missing file in my hands before lunch, Rena, I will fire you."

"We found the Food Emporium file. She didn't get fired." Erishkigal *said defensively.* "I don't see what the big deal is."

"The big deal is the fact that what Richard wants, Richard gets." Kali *jumped in.* "It doesn't matter what it could cost Rena."

"But he loves her. He wouldn't do anything intentionally to hurt her. Give him one more chance." Erishkigal *pleaded.*

"I don't like it." Kali *stomped her foot, rattling the necklace resting between her breasts.* "But it's still your call—for now."

I finished the changes on the Jensen file for Joni and knocked on the conference room door. "Thank you, darling." Joni waved me over to where she was sitting. I glanced around the room. Jonathan Jensen, the owner of Speedy Lube, sat at the head, surrounded by four drones in matching Brooks Brothers suits.

"That's all, sweetie." Joni dismissed me. As I closed the door, Joni and Mr. Jensen were laughing at a joke only they understood. Sometimes I believed this job would be much easier to deal with if I were stoned. I headed toward my desk wondering if I could talk Maristel into going to Brooklyn tomorrow night.

Break

Richard called later in the day to apologize and ask me out to dinner as a thank you for making the trip to Brooklyn. When I reminded him he had no money, he told me he'd charge it. Richard had recently taken a job with NEC, programming cash registers. When I'd met him, he was repairing them while his degree in computer science collected dust on his living room wall. I encouraged him to take the job with NEC, even though it meant a small pay cut, because I knew the return would be worth the sacrifice.

We sipped our margaritas, nibbling tortilla chips while a Mariachi band strolled through the Calliente Cab Company. I promised myself I wouldn't eat too many chips, but as the tequila floated around and numbed my insides, I began to lose count. I'd already blown it by eating the M&M's at work, so what the hell?

"Ready for another one?" Richard asked.

"No, thanks." I smiled. "I'm still working on this one."

"Aw—c'mon. Chug it!" He commanded. "Let's get wasted!" His hands were folded on the table, as his blue eyes pleaded with mine. "Whaddya say?"

"You've got a lot of fucking nerve, Richard Renaldi," I hissed through my teeth. "Do you know how many calories one of these has?" I held my glass close to his face. "You're the one telling me for months now that you're not attracted to me because I've gained weight." Droplets of my spittle landed on his hand, and the cigarette resting between his fingers sputtered. My weight had been an issue since I was seven. I gained and lost in large increments. I didn't have the delicate five-pound problems the women who wrote into *Shape* talked about.

"And you're always telling me how all of your friends say you can do better than me." I blinked back the tears. "I'm really trying here, Richard. Some support would be nice." The hair on the back of my neck tickled and I wanted to smack it to stop the itching.

"I know you're trying." Richard stared at the bowl of salsa. "But, let's face it, Rena, you've tried stuff before. You drop ten pounds right away, but you never stick to it. So, excuse me for not doing fuckin' cartwheels." He took a huge swallow from his salted glass. "And excuse me for wanting to have some fucking fun with my girlfriend."

Short of decking him with a right hook, I didn't know what my next move should be. "Yeah? Well, fuck you!" I picked up the margarita, pursed my lips around the straw, and sucked. The tang of lime and strawberry soothed the chilling burn of the tequila.

"Let's not fight." He looked tired. "We haven't been out in a long time. We'll have a few drinks, eat dinner, and maybe catch a movie or something. OK?"

It was a nice attempt, I thought, but as apologies go, it sucked. I knew that if I just lost some weight, everything between us would be fine. But I was still searching for the diet that would allow me to lose weight and still eat anything I wanted. "Yeah. Let's just have fun tonight." I squeezed his hand. "Maybe you'll even get lucky." I winked.

After dinner, numb and stuffed, we strolled through Greenwich Village. We sat on a stoop on Charles Street, smoked a joint and talked—about work, about how I wanted a bigger apartment, about his best friend Tony's latest conquest. "Let's go listen to some jazz," Richard suggested.

"I have an idea." I smiled, raising an eyebrow. I grabbed his hand and dragged him toward Bleeker. A street light painted an exaggerated portrait of us on the black tar—Richard tall and thin, me short and plump

"Where are we going?" Richard laughed.

"You'll see." We walked east on Bleeker, past the antique shops, coffee bars and card stores. We giggled at the buff boys in muscle shirts flirting with each other and the butch lesbians with their arms wrapped around their lipsticked dates. We pretended to be part of a German tour group gathered around the Army Navy Store and failed miserably to translate the guide's description of the Village.

When we reached MacDougal, I spread my arms wide in front of The Village Comedy club like I was finishing a big Broadway number. "This is where we're going?" Richard asked, slightly amused.

"They're having a variety show tonight! I read about it in the *Village Voice*. Singers, jugglers, comedians! Won't it be cool?" I felt like a two-year-old.

"Sure. Let's try. How bad can it be?" He grabbed me, spun me around and kissed me.

Richard paid and we tiptoed down a long, dark hallway with me leading the way. "I feel like we're headed to Oz." I skipped and started singing "We're Off to See the Wizard." Richard squeezed my waist from behind, tickling me, and shouted, "I'll get you my pretty!" I squealed as he pushed me up against the wall, kissing my neck and running his hands underneath my blouse.

I caressed his back and allowed my hand to cup his rear end. A group of college boys roared down the corridor, their laughter exploding around us. I stiffened. "We really shouldn't be doing this here." I straightened my blouse, tucked it back into my long flower print skirt, and combed my fingers through my curls.

"What the hell just happened?" Richard stood a few feet away. "We were having a great time."

"Nothing." I couldn't admit that I was terrified that the college boys would make a remark about me and then Richard would feel compelled to defend me and the whole night would be ruined. I may have poured a little water on the fire, but the flames could be fanned later. "I just think we should get a table, that's all."

The hallway emptied into a small room with a bar, a tiny platform stage, and dozens of round black Formica tables big enough for two. There was a handful of people already sitting in the black vinyl banquet chairs. "Where do you want to sit?" Richard asked. "There's a table right up front."

"*Absolutely not!*" *ordered Erishkigal, trembling.* "*We are not sitting up front so some guy who thinks he's a comedian can do a whole routine of fat jokes.*" *Her olive skin was flushed.*

"*You're such a wimp,*" *Kali argued, loosening her bronze belt.* "*And you've made Rena so uptight. Where's the spontaneity? You are so paranoid.*"

"*I don't care. We're not doing it.*"

"*Inanna, help me out here,*" *Kali begged, fingering the rows of metal layered like crocodile skin around her waist.* "*Talk some sense into our Queen of the Underworld.*"

"*I don't know, Kali.*" *Inanna was calm, but neutral. Her blond hair was plaited into three braids that hung like silk ropes halfway down her back.* "*Comics can be mean when they're dying on stage. Sitting up front at a club like this entails risk.*" *She paused and wrapped a few golden strands around her index finger.* "*Remember when I almost died?*"

"*What does that have to do with anything?*" *Kali demanded.*

"*Patience, sister. I'm going somewhere with this.*" *Inanna retied the knot on one leather sandal.* "*After the Euphrates flooded, I wanted nothing more than to save that sacred Hullupu tree. I stumbled over rocks and twigs and got soaked to my fanny because I wanted nothing more than to rescue that tree.*" *Kali sighed loudly, but Inanna continued.*

"*The water had ripped its roots from the ground and it was almost dead. Remember?*" *Inanna tossed a braid over her shoulder and adjusted the crown on her head.* "*But I got it home and took care of it and it grew into a magnificent tree. And I haven't missed a wink of sleep since I used its branches to make my bed. So you see, Erishkigal, risks can pay off. I say yes.*"

"*You conveniently forgot about the serpent that was nested in the branches, Inanna. One drop of poison from its fangs and you'd have been history." Erishkigal was distraught, her eyes tearing at the thought of Rena being humiliated. "I say no."*

"You can't let her live in fear for the rest of her life." Kali insisted. "It's not fair."

"But what if someone says something? She'll be embarrassed in front of Richard." Erishkigal paused. "She couldn't take it."

"This is a perfect opportunity for her to face her fear. Can't you see that?" Kuan Yin looked deeply into Erishkigal's eyes, knowing it was time for Rena's enlightenment to begin. "It's the only way Rena's going to grow."

"Yeah!" smirked Kali. "What KY said."

"OK. But just this once." Erishkigal acquiesced to end the argument.

Richard and I sat at a tiny table in front of the stage. I didn't want to know what was making my feet stick to the floor. And it reeked of stale beer and smoke. I pinched my nose. "This place smells like an old porno theater." I grinned. "When do the lap dancers start?"

"And how would you know what a porn theater smells like?" His brows were knitted together, no gap above his nose.

"Don't you remember going to that one in Chicago when we were there last year?" I looked down at the ashtray and gradually raised my eyes toward him, attempting to convey my lust. We'd had a pretty kinky time squeezed into a little booth shoving quarters into a video machine so we could watch naked men and women going at it.

"Oh, yeah." Richard smiled and reached into a pocket for his wallet. "I forgot about that. What do you want to drink?"

"Absolut and tonic." It was noisy and I noticed the rowdy college kids who had passed us in the hall in the back left corner. The rest of the tables were filled with young couples and groups of friends laughing and drinking.

A tiny man in ripped jeans jumped onto the stage and introduced himself as Flip Budski. He told a few lame jokes and then brought out the first comic, who opened his routine with how much he enjoyed getting pussy in the shower. "You look like you enjoy pussy!" he said to one of the guys sitting behind Richard. The man, tastefully dressed and slightly effeminate, forced a laugh and shifted in his chair. His eyes darted nervously around the crowd, finally landing on his male companion. Left hanging on stage, with no response, the comedian moved in for the kill. "Or maybe you prefer an old tomcat."

Part of me was relieved. I was much more comfortable with gay jokes than with fat jokes. But after a while, even I was squirming. The next comic, openly gay, joked about how much easier it is for gay men to get laid. "When you're straight, you've got to take your date out for drinks, then dinner—maybe a movie. Me? All I've got to do is go to the bookstore." While the crowd was laughing, he zoned in on the man behind Richard. "Maybe that's where I know you from!" The audience found it hysterical. The man folded his hands and tapped his index fingers together, staring at the crusty candle in the center of the table.

Flip Budski strutted back onto the stage, a guitar slung over his shoulder. He coerced the audience into participating in a song he had written. Richard and I communicated mentally, wondering why we were glued to our chairs for this train wreck. When Flip finished, he introduced the evening's first singer.

A teenage boy, wearing jeans and flannel shirt, bounded onto the stage and the melody of Frank Sinatra's "My Way" strained to be heard through the club's tired woofers. Within seconds, the crowd was howling with laughter. Oblivious, the boy continued: "Ehnd thwew it awhl, I did it myahh way." I couldn't decide if it was a joke, if he was a really bad singer or if he was deaf.

I averted my eyes, staring at the track lighting until I saw stars. I tried to stifle my laughter, but it erupted in sporadic giggles and snorts. Richard's jaw hung open as he stared at the stage. The college kids in the back were whooping and hollering for the boy to stop singing, screaming "You suck!" and "Frankie's gonna sue!"

Finally, it was over and the boy spoke. "My name is Jeffrey Rollins and I'm fifteen years old." He shoved his hands deep into his pockets. "I know I'm not the best singer in the world, but I love Frank Sinatra. I appreciate you letting me sing. Thank you." The audience burst into applause. A smile spread across the kid's face, almost touching his ears. Flip Budski climbed onto the stage and shook his hand.

"This is our chance to escape." Richard whispered across the table. He held out his hand and I took it. I waited for a bomb to drop as we were walking out. Some remark like, "Guess he's got to get started early. She's a lot of woman." Or "How do you fuck a fat girl? Why would you want to?"

"What a trip!" Richard pinched the bone between his eyebrows as we hit the lobby. "Just remember, this was your idea."

"And I know you're never going to let me forget it, are you?" I laughed. "At least it was an adventure."

"You could say that." We walked uptown through Washington Square Park. There were two police cars at the fountain. A black man in handcuffs leaned against one of them while an NYPD officer frisked him. I had a joint in my purse. What if they stopped me and searched my bag?

"Do you want to take a cab?" I asked.

"No. Why would you want to? It's only fifteen blocks or so to your place." It wasn't like me to let the fear slip out. But there it was like a murky trail of something spoiled trickling out of aluminum foil on the bottom of the fridge.

"No reason. It's just that this park used to be a lot more quiet."

"Are you scared?" Richard talked to me in a baby voice.

"No. It's just that it's hot." Good save, I thought. I'd never admit that I was freaked out about the police. Or that my feet were tired and swollen from walking around all day. Or that I was really hoping Richard would spend the night and I didn't want him to see how much I sweated on the walk home. Or that I knew I'd be huffing and puffing after the first few blocks.

We continued up University Place, passing the old buildings that housed part of NYU and the fancy shops that sold flowers and lingerie and clothes I couldn't fit into. We cut through Union Square Park and headed up Park Avenue, the sidewalks filled with people out for an evening of food and flirting. In front of my building, Richard leaned over and kissed me on the cheek.

"I'll talk to you tomorrow."

"You're not coming in?" I tried to figure out a way to get him to change his mind.

"I've got to get up early for work. I'll call you after my meeting."

The fear of Richard rejecting me gripped me around the throat. "Come on. I'll make a pot of coffee."

"Really, Ren. I can't."

"Why are you doing this?"

"Doing what?"

"Letting me think everything is OK between us and then dumping me at the door." I turned to put the key in the door. "Fine."

"What are you talking about?"

"You know exactly what I'm talking about. I'm trying to lose weight, but you still find me so unappealing you kiss me on the cheek and take off? Whatever—just go."

"Rena, I just have get up early tomorrow."

"We can't let him leave." Erishkigal's longing for companionship was endless. She was so lonely in the Underworld. No friends, no husband since Gugalanna had died. And her desire for sex was insatiable. She needed to experience it through Rena.

"Let him go," Kali snorted, her brows furrowed over her third eye. "He's a fucking loser." She knew she was almost strong enough to take control from Erishkigal. And when she did, there would be plenty of sex. Rena didn't need to beg for it.

"Can't you see how desperate she feels?" asked Kuan Yin. "How can you encourage that, Erishkigal?" Kuan Yin was a firm believer that taking care of yourself would be rewarded.

"And you're no stranger to desperation, Kuan Yin. We all know your story." Erishkigal's face was twisted and mean. "Your father was so angry that his precious princess wouldn't go through with the marriage he'd arranged that he tried to burn you alive in front of the whole village. You must have felt pretty damned desperate then."

"You're right, I did." Kuan Yin brushed a tear from her cheek. "I loved a man my father didn't think was worthy of our family because he wasn't royalty, only an ordinary physician. But I stood my ground and I spoke my truth. And the spirit gods protected me. I transcended the fear. Rena can too. She needs to let him go home. Enough!"

"No!" screamed Erishkigal. "He needs to prove he loves her."

"And that would be accomplished by him staying the night?" asked Kuan Yin.

"Yes," responded Erishkigal. "Rena needs him."

"You didn't hear a word I said," Kuan Yin sighed.

I turned toward Richard. "Look, I know that you're not feeling attracted to me right now. But there are plenty of guys out there who would be." I stuck out my chin, steeling myself. "Maybe this isn't going to work."

"You're a fucking loon! Yeah, we're having some problems right now, but I don't want to break up with you. You think that since I want to go home because I have to get up early that I want out?"

"Well, don't you?" I braced myself.

"Would it mean that much if I came in for a while?" His voice was softer.

"Yes," I said to the stoop.

"OK. But I really can't stay long."

"That's fine. I'll just make half a pot." I smiled to myself as I turned the key.

Break

"So, where is it we're going?" Maristel asked, gathering her long black hair into a rubber band as we crossed Sixth Avenue. Her features were tiny, like a China doll.

"6201 Bay Parkway in the beautiful hamlet of Bensonhurst," I answered.

"I have cousins who live out there," Maristel said. "It's not a bad neighborhood, unless you don't like pasta." We laughed jogging down the steps to the subway to buy tokens.

"I hate that noise!" Maristel screamed, grinding her teeth as the train screeched into the station. We pushed into the crowded car and leaned against the doors. The air conditioning was welcome relief after standing on the sweltering platform.

At the Bay Parkway stop, we got off the train and climbed down the steps from the elevated platform. A breeze brushed our faces, drying the perspiration. As we ran against the "Don't Walk" sign, I noticed gravestones on each side of the highway. The streetlights cast a silvery glow on the headstones closest to the sidewalk. Hundreds more, like marble dominoes, faded into the blackness. I stopped at the metal fence, staring at the names in the first row.

"Want to hear something gruesome?" Maristel asked joining me. "In the sixties, all of these graves were dug up and reburied to make room for Bay Parkway."

"How do you know that?

"My cousin Paulo works for the city." She looked at me knowingly.

"That's sick. How did they get the relatives to go along with it?"

"They paid them off. How does anything get done in New York?" she laughed.

We strolled past the brick and aluminum-sided row houses that stretched into the heart of Bensonhurst. Neon lights from the bodegas and pizza joints illuminated the street. Four teenaged boys stood in front of a tiny Italian restaurant named Gino's checking out the action. As Maristel and I approached, one of them called out, "Well, well, well. What do we have here? A goddess and her fat friend."

"Why don't we cross to the other side of the street." Maristel stepped off the sidewalk.

"No. That's OK." I tugged at my curls and silently begged any god who might be listening to make the boys disappear. I felt sweat at the top of my neck and my stomach gurgled. I held my head up and continued toward them.

"Hey lady." A ponytailed Guido walked toward Maristel. "You are soooo beautiful. Don't fat chicks cramp your style, sweetheart?" he laughed, his young muscles hard under his white T-shirt. My heart beat rapidly. There was no escape now.

"Soooo-weeee!! Here piggy piggy!" The boy in the white T-shirt snorted and held his arms wide, waddling around in a circle. "Think I'd break the bathroom scale?" The boys started arguing about how much I weighed, calling out numbers and debating who was right.

"Why don't you assholes shut the fuck up and mind your own business?" Maristel glared at them.

"Why don't you come over here and suck my dick?" The boy in the T-shirt was apparently the leader.

"You're disgusting," Maristel retorted. "I think I hear your Mama calling. She says it's past your bedtime. Maybe if you're lucky, she'll give you a bath. It'll be the only way your dick's gonna get any attention tonight."

"She's feisty," said one of the boys. "Bet she gives great head."

"Ignore them," Maristel commanded. We were a half a block away when one of the teens called out.

"If you can dump your fat friend, it'll be the best night you ever had."

"I can't believe those guys. I think we should go to the police station. No one has the right to harass you like that," Maristel looked at me for the first time in several minutes. "Are you OK?"

"What?" Maristel's words echoed, but didn't penetrate.

"They were rude—a bunch of bored Guidos looking to start trouble. You shouldn't take what they said seriously."

"Oh, no. I didn't." I lied, cutting her off.

"We'll just pretend it never happened," Erishkigal muttered. She sat rocking back and forth with her arms circled around her shins, the tops of her knees touching her chin.

"Well, I can't." Kali was furious. "It was humiliating."

"People can be cruel." Inanna piped in. "Those boys didn't mean anything by it. Sometimes Rena's an easy target."

"You're a pain in my ass." Kali snapped at Inanna. "And I don't give a shit if she is an easy target. It was mean. It would've been one thing for them to have made a comment and been done." Kali winced. "But it was a nightmare."

"Maristel didn't care." Erishkigal tried to convince herself. "It's not that big a deal."

"I beg to differ," Kali sneered. "It's a huge deal." Inanna scratched her head and scanned the floor.

"Have any of you seen my crown? I had it this morning."

"What's the apartment number?" Maristel asked when we arrived at the address that Richard had given me. I let her take control. We climbed the three floors and knocked on the door. I was winded. A black woman with shaky hands and glazed eyes answered.

"You Richard's friend?" Her short, wiry hair was slicked back into a tiny knot.

I told her who I was and she opened the door to let us in. Two black guys in ripped jeans sat on the couch. I pulled the cash out of my pocket and handed it to her. "I'll be right back," she said.

Maristel and I stood against the door. The men stared at us. I had neglected to ask Richard how the hell he knew this woman when he gave me the address. Three milk crates were tied together with twine and topped with a piece of plywood. A bong rested in the middle. A couple of mismatched couches partially covered a huge stain on the red carpet. The furniture was scattered, like the person who moved it in suddenly got tired. The two men kept staring and not talking as I nervously tapped my foot to the Janet Jackson song on the stereo. The woman reappeared holding a baggie.

"You wanna smoke?" It was customary to sit with your dealer to smoke a joint and check the quality before you actually bought it, but I just wanted to get the hell out of there. From the way Maristel looked at me, she felt the same way.

"I'd really like to, but I've got a friend waiting downstairs."

"Richard told me you'd have to take the train."

"My boyfriend drove us." Maristel explained. "I don't want to keep him waiting." She opened the door. I took the baggie, stuffed it in my bag and said my good-byes. Richard owed me big.

"That was beyond weird. Let's go back to my place and smoke one," Maristel grinned once we were outside. "We could both use it." On the way back to the subway, we walked down the other side of the street.

We climbed the steps to Maristel's Broome Street studio after arriving back in Manhattan. An easel stood in one corner, the edge of an unfinished canvas peeking out from under a blue sheet. The apartment smelled warm and fresh from the cinnamon candles and apple potpourri that she had strategically placed around the room. Maristel sat cross-legged on the floor, a street light beaming through the six foot casement windows, cleaning a bud.

"I'm glad we're back." Maristel said. She passed me a joint and smiled apologetically.

"Yeah. But I don't think I'll be doing it again any time soon." I wanted to forget what had happened and I certainly didn't need her pity. I took a deep drag and stared at the colorful bolts of silk and velvet piled on the floor. I exhaled upward, allowing the ceiling fan's blades to slice the smoke into fine ribbons.

"Tell me again why Richard couldn't lend you his car."

I almost felt the need to tell the truth. "He had to get his car inspected and the only time he could drop it off was tonight." I got up and went to the kitchen. "Do you want something to drink?"

"That sounds pretty lame to me." Maristel pulled the curtains together causing shadows from the flickering candles to bounce and wobble on the wall. "Get me a Coke?"

I returned with a bottle of Coke and two glasses of ice. Coke always tasted better when I was high. I loved the thick, syrupy sweetness and the bubbles tickling my nose. "There's something you're not telling me, isn't there?" Maristel asked.

"Rena cannot tell her the truth," Erishkigal begged, tightly wrapping her red satin robe around her. *"Maristel won't understand."*

"Understand what?" Kali asked snidely. *"That Rena allows Richard to manipulate her? That she does whatever he wants because she's afraid he'll leave her? He's left her twice before and she's survived."* Kali's life had taught her not to rely on anyone.

"No. That she loves him." Erishkigal sat, resting on her heels.

"I'd rather her be alone than anywhere near him after that trip to Bensonhurst," Inanna chimed in.

"That wasn't Richard's fault," Erishkigal was protective of relationships, no matter what the quality since losing Gugalanna.

"The hell it wasn't. He cajoled her into going." Kali's distaste for Richard was as strong as her fondness for blood. *"Sister, you are in serious denial."* Kali glared at Erishkigal. *"It's time to do something about her weight. She's got to choose another drug besides food. Get her stomach stapled, exercise, something. She cannot live like this anymore."*

"You're the one being cruel now," Kuan Yin admonished, fanning herself with the willow branches in her left hand. *"There are a lot of reasons Rena eats, most of which she is not even yet aware. This is part of her process, Kali. You are being as judgmental as those boys were tonight. When Rena gets to a point where she doesn't want to live this way anymore, she will do something."*

"But it's our job to help her get there." Kali removed her sword from the leather sheath on her waist with one of her six hands and planted it in between Kuan Yin's feet.

"We are." Kuan Yin quietly removed the sword and handed it back to Kali. *"You must have faith, even if you can't see where the road is going."*

"Bullshit. Rena needs to get some discipline in her life." Kali slipped the weapon between her black silk sheath and the belt, which was made from the hands of people who had angered her.

"I don't know why you two are arguing. Everything is fine." Erishkigal rose from her corner and smoothed the sheer cloth covering her twig-like body. *"Richard got what he wanted. Rena's having a nice time with Maristel. And next weekend she and Richard will spend*

time together because he loves her. We need to forget what happened tonight. It's over."

I avoided Maristel's question about Richard and refocused the conversation on the costumes she was working on for the SoHo Theater. Excited, she showed me the patterns she had designed, then removed two cigar boxes from under the futon and pulled out dozens of antique buttons and several pairs of rhinestone earrings. "Aren't they fabulous?" Her blue eyes sparkled and she swiped stray black hairs out of her eyes as she dug through the box.

"I found them all at an estate sale in Queens last week." She grabbed one of the bolts, draped the silk around her slender frame and held two of the buttons in between her breasts. "They're perfect!" She whirled around in her bare feet, clanking the buttons together like cymbals. "Hopefully, I'll be finished by next month."

The bolt thudded to the floor as Maristel gracefully returned to her cross-legged position. The events in Brooklyn seemed to have evaporated, except for a shallow tension that swam underneath us, tickling our toes. "How's work going?" Maristel asked, leaning against her futon, which also served as a bed.

"Same shit, different day," I complained.

"That blows," Maristel sipped her Coke and looked at me. "Why the hell are you still there?" The right cross hit me square in the jaw.

"I don't know. She treats me OK." I dug around for a cigarette.

"You're always making excuses for her."

"I am not." My voice was sing-songy.

"She treats you like a second-class citizen and, for some reason, you don't want to see it. You're too smart to be her lackey forever." Maristel stood up. "I have to pee. Need anything?"

"No." I leaned back against the futon and accidentally grazed her leg as I stretched my arms. It was firm and tight. "There's an opening in account services," I called to Maristel, offering evidence that I wasn't going to be under Joni's thumb forever.

"Are you going for it?" Maristel asked from the bathroom.

"Yeah. I think so." I wasn't convinced.

"Do you really think you have a chance?"

"I don't see why not. It's going to cost her a lot more money to bring someone in from the outside."

"The question is, will she ever see you as anything besides her assistant?"

"I guess we'll see." I stood up to go. I'd had enough honesty for one night. "It's late. I've got to get up early tomorrow."

"Don't be mad." Maristel pouted, sticking out her plump bottom lip.

"Who said I was mad?" I threw the pot and my cigarettes in my backpack. "But, I finally have some hope of moving out of this job and you can't even be happy for me. You've had some pretty crappy jobs and I've always supported you. You're not even happy where you are now. And you've got the stones to imply I can't get this job?"

"That's not what I said. You get so defensive." She sipped her Coke.

"Thanks for going with me," I squeaked as I opened the front door.

"No problem." Maristel hesitated. "If you want to talk about what happened tonight, we can."

"It's no big deal. Just some crazy Brooklyn kids." I opened my backpack and pretended to search for something. "I'll give you a call later in the week."

"If you're sure." The pity in Maristel's smile made my cheeks hot. I pressed the elevator button as the deadbolt turned.

Break

The rain and my apprehension collected in a puddle at my feet. Stuck without an umbrella, I shivered in a T-shirt. It wasn't cold, but the dampness raised gooseflesh on my forearms and my nipples were hard. I don't know why I bothered to blow dry my hair since it was now wet and stuck to my forehead and cheeks. Standing across from Penn Station, I searched for someone peddling umbrellas. The cheap ones would be seven dollars instead of four because of the storm. But I didn't dare meet my mother's train without one.

Three different forecasts that morning said sun all day. What a job—making lots of money telling people whether to schlep a coat or galoshes or a scarf. And if you worked on the radio, no one could hold you accountable because no one knew what you looked like. Where could I find a job like that?

The white walk sign flashed and I started across Seventh Avenue. The wind shifted and a wall of french fry grease and donuts stopped me cold. I didn't understand the motivation behind putting Roy Rogers, Dunkin Donuts, and Nathan's under one roof. Some things were better kept separate, like my mother and me. I had spoken to my grandmother earlier and had been warned that my mother and Raymond, her boyfriend, appeared to be having problems again. I didn't have too many details, mainly that Raymond had been traveling on business for nearly three weeks now and my mother was more than a little moody.

I spied an old black man in a tattered trench coat selling umbrellas near Peppermint Park. I parted the yellow sea of taxis and grabbed a ten out of my pocket.

"How much?"

"For you pretty lady, ten dollars."

"Ten dollars? You've got to be joking."

"It's awful wet out here." He leered at my chest, crumbs hanging from his matted gray beard. "And it looks like you're a little cold."

"I'll give you five."

"No nee-goe-she-ay-shun, honey." His bloodshot eyes tried to focus. "But I'll tell you what Maxie'll do. You give me a little kiss, right here." Maxie's leathery index finger touched his left cheek. "And I'll let you have it."

"For free?"

Maxie nodded. Droplets of water dripped from my nose. My Knick's T-shirt clung to me, showing the world the rolls of flesh around my waist and hanging over my bra that I tried so hard to hide. I stared at the clouds for a second. The digital clock read 3:45. My mother's train arrived in six minutes.

I turned my head to the side and inhaled deeply, trying to guard myself against the assault of Maxie's body odor. Quickly kissing his cheek, I grabbed the umbrella and fled. I ignored his lecherous chuckle about me being a good girl.

I got to the platform as the train opened its doors. I went through a period as a teen when I called my mother by her first name because I thought it was cool. "Faith," I'd say, "pass the ketchup." Or, "Faith, I need twenty dollars." Faith didn't like it and it didn't last long.

There she was, striding toward me in a camel hair pantsuit and three-inch heels, pulling a little suitcase behind her. Everything about her appearance was perfect—the highlighted hair, the Adrien Arpel makeover face, the tasteful pearl studs. She saw me and waved. I could tell she'd been drinking.

My mother has a fondness for gin, preferring Tanqueray, but accepting any kind in a pinch. That had been part of the reason my parents split.

That and the fact that my father couldn't keep his fly zipped. It was one of those chicken-and-egg conundrums. Which came first? Faith's drinking or Michael's cheating? I accused her once of drinking too much. Her eyes scanned me from head to toe and then she said, "Liquor's easier to hide on the hips."

"Hello, darling." She leaned over and kissed the air next to my cheek. "I'm so relieved to be off of that dreadful train. I wouldn't have even considered it except for your grandmother telling me what a peaceful way it is to travel. But ten hours on an Amtrak is cruel. Like keeping a boa constrictor in a fish tank." She pulled a Kent III out of a leather case and fired up her silver monogrammed lighter.

"You can't smoke in here!" I scolded. "We'll get arrested." She looked at me like a child who's Barbie Dream House had just been demolished by an earthquake.

"Really?"

"Really. Put it out now." She flattened the cigarette with the toe of her Pappagallo pump.

"You can't smoke anywhere anymore. It's a crime."

"Other than that, Mrs. Lincoln, how did you like the play?"

"Excuse me?"

"Nothing. Do you want to drop your things off at my apartment before we go anywhere?"

"That would be fine." We rode the escalator up to the street.

"You can light up now." I granted permission. She rummaged in her purse for the case, quickly muffling the clinking from the airplane bottles of gin. I stepped off the curb and hailed a cab.

My oasis on the island of Manhattan was a small one-bedroom apartment on the ground floor of a building on 24th Street between Park Avenue South and Lexington. The front door opened onto a small hardwood landing with a wrought iron railing. Five steps led down into an eight-by-ten-foot living room. The first time Maristel saw the apartment after I had moved in, she stood on the landing, arms spread wide and sang, "Who can turn the world on with her smile?"

The kitchen was barely big enough to turn around in, but that was OK since my idea of dinner was ordering out. My queen-sized bed touched two of the bedroom walls, and I kept my dresser in the hall. The bathroom was standard size and tiled in ivory. The saving grace was the courtyard out back that I shared with my neighbors. Last summer, I was so excited about having outdoor space I spent a hundred dollars decorating it with green outdoor carpet and white resin furniture.

I spent all day at the farmer's market at Union Square, buying ivy and flowers to spruce it up. I bought soil and planters and dug out back for hours, repotting the plants. I placed window boxes full of ivy and morning glories at the back fence, twisting the vines around the chicken wire hoping they would grow up the fence and enclose me in a cool green veil. It was a cheaper escape from the steamy urban summer than doing a summer share in the Hamptons or Fire Island.

But the courtyard didn't get enough light and the morning glories died on the vine, their unopened buds shriveled from lack of sunlight. This summer, I didn't have the energy to redo everything and the courtyard looked abandoned. Brown plants stood leafless in pretty pink pots and cigarette butts thrown off the decks from the apartments above me littered the green carpet. Looking out the window while my mother was in the bathroom, I wished I had cleaned it up a bit before she arrived. If she made a comment, I'd blame it on the new neighbors. They were always having parties out there anyway. It didn't even feel like my space anymore.

We had dinner at Rungsit on 23rd and she enlightened me over Pad Thai about what was wrong with my job and my relationship with Richard. I called it a night at nine and retreated to my room to read the latest Lawrence Block novel.

We both woke early the next morning. I pressed my ass against the kitchen wall so I had enough room to open the refrigerator door to get some juice. "Let's go shopping," my mother said as if it were a foregone conclusion and not a suggestion. I know my mother loved me, but I also knew that she felt my strengths didn't include style or fashion. And it wasn't too difficult to tell that this embarrassed her.

I wore prairie skirts that had gone out of style in the eighties. And big blousy tops. And granny boots. It's what made me comfortable. Elastic is a good friend when you're carrying around a few extra pounds—or fifty. I knew Faith thought she could help, so I managed a weak smile. "Unless you don't want to, dear." She extracted a cigarette from her leather case and lit it. "I have to get out of this apartment, Rena. It's cute, but Jesus, it's small. I'm tripping over myself."

My disappointment sailed around the apartment like a popped balloon. "If that's what you want to do, that's fine." I mentally kicked myself. Shopping was not a sport like tennis or soccer, although I knew my mother thought it was. It did require stamina and the more bags acquired, the bigger the win. But it certainly wasn't something I did for pleasure.

I shopped only when there was a purpose, like a party or a vacation. Why would I subject myself to tiny dressing rooms and a four-way mirror unless I had to? The last time I had gone shopping was to buy an outfit for the Christmas party at JC. Trying on skirt after blouse after dress made me sweat as I twisted and tugged, battling to remove each item until piles of clothes were scattered on the floor. Limp and damp and inside out, they were a bitter testimony to my lack of physical fitness. The shock absorbers of denial began to rust when I shopped.

"How long will it take you to get ready?" Faith walked the six steps into the kitchen and placed her coffee cup in the sink. The smoke from her Kent III burned off the fog of Jean Naté trailing behind her. "Let's start at Bendels. Or should we start at Saks and work our way uptown?" Acid burned my stomach and I fought the panic I felt around shopping at a store like Bendels. As a child, I had worn clothes from Woolworth's and Grant's. Responsible people didn't spend hundreds of dollars on a scarf and more than a paycheck on one pair of shoes.

Raymond's money was the one benefit left in my mother's relationship. Faith had three Master Cards, two Visas, a platinum American Express, and Diner's Club. I suspected that as long as she acquiesced in the bedroom, not a word was said about how much she spent. Wearing Chanel, Ferragamo and Escada were the foundation of her suit of mail.

"I only have one token, Mom, but I have some change." I called from the bedroom. "We can take the bus up Madison and walk over."

"Don't be silly, we'll just take a cab." I hated my mother's inability to acknowledge that money needed to be earned, not just spent. So did my father. "Faith," he lectured her once, "I don't work my ass off so you can piss money away." "It's not all right for me to buy a new dress," she countered, "but it's OK for you to charge jewelry on our credit card for your floozies." Checkmate.

"Why don't we just take the bus? It won't take long."

"Why pay to ride with the riffraff when we can have our own car?"

"Maybe we should just rent a car and a driver for the day," I said sarcastically.

"What a wonderful idea!" Faith exclaimed, grabbing the phone from the coffee table and dialing information. "Yes, I'd like the number of a car service please."

"What are you doing?" I stomped into the room.

"Oh, hold on honey, I'm getting us a car."

Faith stared at the wisps of smoke from the ashtray. "Isn't there a Manhattan Car Company or something?"

"Mother, why are you calling information? It's fifty cents a call. That's why we have phone books."

"Don't be so stingy. I'll write you a check for Christ's sake." The operator must have hung up on her because Faith sat on my futon looking stunned. "I guess we'll have to take a taxi. She couldn't give me a number."

"You're such a pretentious bitch," I mumbled under my breath on the way to the bathroom.

"What did you say to me?" She stood outside the half-closed door, silk wrapped fingernails clasping her bony left hip like a claw. "I'm still your mother and I deserve some respect."

"You have to earn respect; you can't demand it," I said mockingly. "Isn't that what you always tell me?"

Tears stood at the ready in my mother's eyes. She waited to discharge them until she was confident in their ability to push me over the edge and send me crashing into a bottomless pit of guilt. "What have I done to deserve you speaking to me like this?" she demanded. I stood over the sink, clutching a hairbrush, my fingertips purple from lack of circulation.

"Are you going to answer me?" Faith lit another cigarette and anxiously puffed. I was sure she was stifling the urge to drag me out of the bathroom.

Looking at myself in the mirror, I questioned my sanity. All my mother wanted was to take me shopping and I had come dangerously close to spoiling the entire weekend. I splashed cold water on my face and composed myself. "Sister, you're a big old mess," I said to my reflection without making eye contact. "I'll be out in a minute." I called to my mother. "Let's have lunch at Fellisimo—my treat."

Reapplying her lipstick, Faith smiled. "I only want to help, Rena. I'm glad you changed your mind. And lunch at Fellisimo would be lovely."

Faith was plastered to the seat of the cab as it careened up Park Avenue, her fingers gripping the edge of the driver's vinyl seat. We perused the jewelry and make-up counters at Saks, stopping occasionally to admire a ring or splash on some perfume. I couldn't believe I was enjoying myself. "Honey, why don't we get you a make over?" Faith asked.

"Are you saying I need one?" I answered defensively.

"Truth be known, dear, it wouldn't hurt." I felt the acid burn my esophagus.

"Well, Mother, no one else seems to think so."

"That's because no one looks out for you the way I do. I mean, really Rena, how do you ever expect to get a job that will allow you to move out of that matchbox as long as you look like that?" I wanted to curl up on the cold tile floor, enveloped in the scents of a hundred colognes, and go to sleep.

"Don't be angry," Faith cajoled. "It's for your own good. And I'm offering to pay for it. It'll be an early birthday present." I didn't have the strength to fight. She grabbed my arm and shuffled me toward the Chanel counter. "My daughter needs a complete make-over." Faith smiled at the perfectly coifed woman in the black smock.

"Maybe she's right," said Inanna, her bronze breastplate glowing from the incandescent lights over the Chanel counter. "How is she ever going to make any money looking like a drifter from the East Village?"

"If we don't go along with her, she'll be angry," Erishkigal whimpered, grateful for Faith's company, even if it made Rena unhappy. "I don't want her to be angry."

"Fuck her," whispered Kali. "She's a manipulative bitch who's only doing it because she has to be in control." Kali didn't recognize the similarities she shared with Faith. She ignored the fact that Rena's resistance was as much about Rena's need to control as it was about Faith's need to proceed.

"Faith is Rena's mother," Kuan Yin piped in. "We need to love her, regardless of her faults."

"She's not my mother," sneered Kali. "Let her go to a shelter and find a real charity case. We don't need her help." She inspected her reflection in the round mirror next to the Prescriptive's counter.

"It might be fun," decided Erishkigal. "And Inanna is right. Joni's never going to take Rena seriously unless she fits in."

A blond woman sponged foundation over my skin. It was cold and gooey. "You could be so beautiful with just the right make-up," she cooed.

"I told you," Faith nodded, one eyebrow raised. I sat perfectly still, afraid a pencil or mascara brush would blind me if I moved. The Chanel woman, whose name tag pronounced her Clarice, used the back of her hand as a palette, mixing and matching eyeshadows and blushers. She continued to speak and I saw her lips moving, but heard nothing.

Clarice and Faith continued to chat about the best colors to bring out my green eyes and how to accentuate my cheekbones, which according to them were still hidden under baby fat. I remembered sitting like this when I was six as a friend of my mother's pierced my ears with a darning needle. The two women discussed me—my weight, my progress in school, my propensity for infections—as if I were a statue, not a child who had water trickling down her neck from the ice cube numbing her lobes. After a while, I had fallen into a zone where I heard nothing, even though I was acutely aware of the activity around me.

"Voila!" Clarice exclaimed. Startled, I blinked and looked around. Bottles, tubes, brushes and small compacts covered the glass counter. Clarice's white, capped teeth shined at me as she held out a mirror. "Smile darling; you're a new woman."

"We'll take everything you used!" Faith bubbled. "And throw in an extra lipstick." Taking the mirror from Clarice, I gasped. I vacillated between repulsion and curiosity. The face staring back at me certainly didn't belong with my body or clothes, yet I was unable to put the mirror down.

Faith signed the receipt and we headed to the elevator. On the 2nd floor we browsed through racks of expensive clothes. I loved running my fingers over soft things: silk, satin, stuffed animals. A saleswoman appeared from behind a mannequin. Faith explained to her how she was providing a make-over for her dear, but slightly fashion impaired, daughter.

The woman tugged at her expensive gold hoop, an upside-down smile staring at my ample frame with concern. "Well, we might be able to find a few things that would fit." She breezed around the floor, choosing elastic waist bands and stretch knits. "The dressing room is right here," she pointed. The hangers clicked as I hung them on the hooks. They left me in the tiny room alone with clothes they all knew wouldn't fit. I chose the largest dress and slid it over my head. It was part Lycra, so I managed to pull it all the way down, but the large orange flowers printed on the shiny black fabric made me feel like a bad Halloween joke.

"Come out, honey." Faith called. "We want to see!" I was trapped, surrounded by full-length mirrors.

"In a minute," I answered, wanting to evaporate. I gingerly opened the dressing room door and stepped barefoot onto the plush carpet in the hallway. Faith's eyes grew wide and she suddenly didn't know what to do with her hands. The saleswoman stifled a gasp as I stood in front of them, face like a cover girl and flesh bulging in all the wrong places, out of a three-hundred dollar Dani Max. "I'm sorry, Miss," said the woman. "I think you'd be better off looking on nine. That's where the big—I mean the *women's* sizes are. You'll have more luck there." She looked Faith in the eye. "I'm sorry." And she vanished, leaving a faint trail of Youth Dew in the cool, conditioned air.

"I want to go home," I said, slamming the dressing room door.

"I warned you," Kali self-righteously pointed three left index fingers at Erishkigal.

"Faith is going to be angry," Erishkigal said, hiding behind Inanna. She was just trying to help."

"Faith needs to take her Chanel make-up and her designer clothes and get her skinny butt on the next plane home to that sado-masochistic loser, Raymond," Kali screeched. "And then she needs to get out and stay out of Rena's life. Period."

"Maybe it would be better if Rena took a break from Faith," Inanna said, fingering her earlobe thoughtfully. "Where are my earrings?" Inanna panicked, realizing her topaz studs were missing. "Did one of you take them?" She scoured the dressing room carpet, but found nothing. "First my crown, now my earrings—what's the deal?"

"It's time to go home!" pronounced Erishkigal, ignoring Inanna's missing jewelry.

I unlocked the front door and pushed it open so Faith had to walk in front of me to get in. "I think I should go." Faith was indignant as she folded her jacket and placed it in the suitcase.

"Do whatever you want. You always do."

"I only wanted to help"

"Well you didn't." I went into my bedroom and closed the door. I lay on the bed and turned on the television. A few minutes later there was a soft knock. "I'm leaving, Rena." I couldn't respond. "I'll call you when I get home."

I banged my head against the wall, the throbbing a welcome distraction. I couldn't control the tears. They erupted like a broken fire hydrant, forceful and endless.

The pain multiplied inside me like bacteria, doubling and tripling until it enveloped me entirely. I almost vomited into my pillow. When the sobbing was over, I stumbled into the bathroom and looked in horror at my reflection. The glamorous make-over was all there, but not the way Clarice had arranged it. Mascara on my cheeks, streaks of blush on my forehead, eyeshadow on my chin. I scrubbed my face until it hurt and then I took off my clothes and went to bed.

"I was only trying to help," Erishkigal whispered, her eyes fixed on Kuan Yin. Enveloping Erishkigal in her arms, Kuan Yin stroked her hair and quietly hummed her an ancient melody.

"I wanted Rena to look nice so Richard and Faith would see how wonderful she is," Erishkigal insisted.

"Ah, sister," Kuan Yin said, "motive is everything. Rena deciding to get a make-over to please Faith was a recipe for disaster. Had she done it because she wanted to improve her appearance for herself, well, that would have been a different story."

"Enough of the 'enlightened' point of view." Kali's lip curled in a nasty scowl. "What do we do now?"

"Sleep," answered Erishkigal, starting to doze on Kuan Yin's shoulder.

Break

The dance floor of the Spectrum resembled the album cover from *Saturday Night Fever*. I watched men in tight jeans and gold chains thrusting their pelvises at skinny women wearing short skirts and plunging necklines. Hundreds of dancers sweated on the lit floor that flashed checkerboards of red, yellow and white. The onlookers' faces made tiny screens for the jagged reflections from the silver disco ball spinning beyond the edge of the dance floor. Richard and I stood on the periphery.

I knew Richard wanted to be inside the crowd, but I willed him not to move for fear of what people would think of us dancing together. I had meticulously blow-dried the curls out of my hair and had worn the bright coral lipstick that was left from my mother's early birthday present. But I knew that other people wondered what someone good looking like Richard was doing with a fat girl like me.

We had come with some of Richard's friends, who, according to Richard, were always telling him that he could do better than me. He felt compelled, in the name of honesty he told me, to share their comments with me. Then he couldn't understand why I didn't want to spend any time with them.

As I watched the dancers, Sammy, one of Richard's friends, approached us with three beers. "Hey, come on guys, the party's out back." His leather jacket crunched as he handed Richard a beer. "Let's go get stoned." He stood grinning, his thinning hair revealing a shiny patch of scalp.

I felt conspicuous enough without the paranoia that engulfed me when I was high in public. "Richie, can't we just sit and have a drink?"

"Oh come on, Rena," Sammy snickered. "Let the guy have some fun. Don't be such an uptight bitch."

Richard stood motionless, his hand clamped around the beer bottle like a life preserver. I waited in vain for him to defend me. "Fuck off, Sammy. Richard's a big boy; he can do what he wants," I said.

"A big girl for a big boy." Sammy smirked. "Well, you two can do whatever the fuck you want. But I'm goin' outside to catch a buzz." He disappeared in the crowd.

"Rena, I'm gonna go with Sammy," Richard announced. "You comin' or do you wanna stay here?"

"I guess I'll go with you," I relented. Turning around, I noticed two women, laughing and flirting with a couple of guys at the bar. I wished I could sit at a bar by myself, chatting casually with the bartender, coyly smoking a cigarette. If I could scrape up some confidence and pretend that I didn't care what the world thought, I wouldn't need Richard or his Neanderthal friends.

Trailing Richard and Sammy, I snaked in and out of the throng. I squeezed through fleshy tight spots, between backs and buttocks, chests and legs. "Excuse me!" I screamed over the pulsing beat of the music, but there seemed no way to avoid contact. We pushed past a group at the back bar and up a flight of stairs.

Fresh air washed over me as we neared the door. The patio was surrounded by a picket fence and several old kitchen chairs were scattered on the concrete. A mix of gay and straight clubbers stood in cliques smoking huge joints. I was amazed that they were getting high so openly.

"There's Mark and Rob," Sammy yelled over the music that was blasting from the dance floor through two four-foot speakers. "I know they brought a bag with them."

Grinning, he took off through the crowd toward his friends. I stood behind Richard, perspiring. I wiped my damp palms up and down my dress.

"You want to get high?" Richard asked me.

"I don't know. What if we get busted?"

"Don't be so paranoid. There are a hundred people out here. You think you're so special the cops'll come and arrest just you?"

"I don't want to." I crossed my arms over my chest.

"You know, Rena, I try." Richard shook his head. "I get shit from my friends all the time for being with you. But do I quit? No. Then you go and act like a bitch in front of Sammy. Why'd you do that? You know he's over there telling Jeff and Rob you told him to fuck off." Richard pinched the bridge of his nose, rubbed his eyes and pushed back his blond hair. "How does that make me look? And now you won't even come get high with us. What the hell is your problem?"

"I'm sorry, Richie," my voice quivered. "I didn't mean to be bitchy to Sammy. But when you told me yesterday that he said I wore so much perfume last weekend that I smelled like a float at the Puerto Rican Day Parade, it pissed me off."

"That's just Sammy, Rena. He didn't mean anything by it. You're way too sensitive." He stifled a smile. "And you did go a little heavy on the perfume that day."

"He's an asshole." I picked at my cuticle. I was trapped. Trapped in the middle of Brooklyn at midnight, with no idea how to get home by subway and five dollars in my pocket. I forced a smile. "But I know he's your friend. I'll try to be nicer."

Richard put his arm around my waist. "Let's go smoke one."

The last time Kali had been this angry, she'd danced so feverishly the world had almost been destroyed. "I can't believe what fucking pussies you all are!"

"What am I supposed to do? Get us killed in the middle of nowhere?" trembled Erishkigal, opting to stay where she was uncomfortable rather than venture out.

"I wouldn't let that happen." Kali shouted, nose to nose with Erishkigal.

"You can't guarantee that." Erishkigal preferred to keep her head in the sand.

"I can guaran-damn-tee we have absolutely no dignity standing out here partying with these assholes." Kali waved all six arms at the patio like a game show hostess, her long hair piled underneath a bright red headdress.

"Enough!" shouted Kuan Yin, her thousands of years of patience expired. *"Can't you two ever compromise? Do you always have to be at each other's throats? We'll never get her out of here this way."*

"We need to be reasonable about this," Inanna piped in, reminding them of her wisdom, one of the many gifts bestowed by her grandfather, Enki. The fact that Enki was also Erishkigal's father made Erishkigal her sister in the world of mythology. But Inanna always considered herself to be better, smarter and more clever than Erishkigal. After all, she had wangled her way out of spending any time in the Underworld.

"We have five dollars cash, fifteen in the bank and payday isn't for another four days. I think it's best we stay put," Inanna insisted.

"You're the biggest pussy of them all!" Kali glared at her. *"How can you let her stand out here with people who hate her and make fun of her behind her back? You make me sick."* Kali's tolerance for people who were abusive was as thin as the robe she wore. She had killed for less.

"Now see here," Inanna defended herself, grabbing at Kali's necklace and breaking a nail. *"Damn!"* She frowned at the chip. *"I'm only trying to be sensible about this. Even if we could find a bank machine, none of them lets you take out less than twenty dollars anymore. And a cab back to the city's going to cost between twenty and twenty-five. How do we get around that, Miss Know-It-All?"* Inanna finished smugly.

"I'll tell you how." Kali cracked the knuckles on her middle set of hands. *"As a peace offering, Rena tells Richard she'll go get beers for the cavemen. She bats her eyelashes, flashes a smile and sweetly asks for a twenty. Then she walks through this tired dump, past the bar and right on out of here. It's not that tough."*

"Richard will be furious," Erishkigal piped in.

"Who cares?" Kali answered. *"He's a moron. He treats her like shit and his friends are the founding members of the Beer-Swilling-Ball Scratching-*

Cigar-Chomping-He-Man Club. We don't need any of them." She posed, warrior-like, with her sword in the air, ready for battle.

"But Rena loves him," said Erishkigal, not wanting her to be alone. "Besides, it's not like Rena's got guys lining up at her front door. There's a lid for every pot and Richard's her lid."

"I think she may be right," Inanna agreed, filing her nail. "Who wants to dive headfirst into the dating pool again? It's tough enough if you're pretty and a perfect size eight. Rena's not Quasimoto, but she's no Playboy Bunny either."

"Christ! You're all spineless," Kali was through with the conversation. "I can't stand to watch this scene anymore. But you are all going to regret it. Trust me."

The night air was cool and comforting. Maybe I did need to be nicer to Richard's friends. You got what you gave, right? I didn't want to end up like my mother, screaming like a shrew at my husband through a locked door because he had sought comfort elsewhere. "Honey," I turned to Richard, "you guys look like you're almost dry. The waitress hasn't been around for days. Let me get you guys a few cold ones."

"Really?" Richard was surprised.

"Yeah, really. I know I've been moody. I'm just overwhelmed right now. My Mom's visit was a nightmare. Work has been hell. I'm always broke. I'm sorry if I've been taking it out on you."

"That's OK, honey," Richard said, handing me a twenty. "Get yourself something, too." I placed my hand on his butt and kissed his cheek.

"I'll be right back." Pushing my way back through the crowd didn't seem as awful as before. I nudged and prodded until I was against the bar. "Four Budweisers." The bartender turned to get them from the cooler. I could stiff the bartender, take the twenty and get a cab. I could be home in bed and away from Richard and his buddies in fifteen minutes.

I gathered the bottles and headed toward the patio. Stoned, Richard and his friends were grateful for cold beers. "You're not so bad after all," said Sammy.

"Yeah!" cheered Jeff, raising his Bud. "Here's to Rena." They all clinked their bottles in salute. Richard smiled.

"See. They don't hate you."

I couldn't believe I had considered taking Richard's twenty and leaving. "I'm glad we came," I whispered to Richard, sliding my fingers through his hair.

"Damn!" said Kali.

Break

"I don't understand you, Rena!" Richard yelled. "I finally get the guys to include you and now you don't want to go to Great Adventure with us tomorrow. Remind me why I keep trying."

I couldn't handle another argument with him, but something I couldn't touch wrapped its fingers around my throat and I was unable to speak. "OK." I finally whispered. "I'll go." I hated amusement parks. Being buckled into a space designed to fit Barbie's ass wasn't what I would call fun. But Richard was making an effort. The least I could do was meet him halfway.

I felt the panic making its journey from my belly to my brain, but I cut it off midway with several slices of pepperoni pizza and a brownie. Maybe going tomorrow wouldn't turn out so bad. I did have a good time a few weeks ago with all of them. Richard was right; I needed to relax.

The morning was sunny and clear and I sat in a cloud of smoke, waiting for Richard and Tony to pick me up. I stubbed out the cigarette and went to check my make-up for the third time. The bottle of perfume called to me from the vanity, but I resisted. Sammy's comment still stung. I didn't appreciate being accused of smelling like some cheap floozy.

Years ago, I had gone with some friends to the Houlihan's in Station Square on Pittsburgh's South Side. I had maneuvered my way up to the bar for a refill and wrinkled my nose at the cheap extra sweet scent worn by the woman standing next to me. I was about to make a comment to my friend who had sneaked up behind me when I recognized the voice of her male companion. I turned my head in time to see my father lean over and kiss her neck.

"Dad?"

"God! Rena!" He shoved the girl away from him. "What are you doing here?" He and my mother had been discussing divorce when they thought I was out of hearing range, but nothing was official yet.

"I'm looking for the same thing you've already found." I snapped on my way back to my table. He came running after me, explanations and excuses tripping off his tongue. I let him catch me and politely listened while I sucked the vodka out of every ice cube. Then I told him to fuck off.

Richard rang the buzzer as I fluffed my hair. He waited for me in the lobby and walked me to the car. Tony was in the front seat with Richard. I didn't want to be relegated to the back seat, but I knew that starting the day with a scene wouldn't be a good thing. I jumped in the back, smiled and offered an overly chipper "Good morning!"

"Hey, Rena!" Tony grinned. "Do you want the front seat?"

"No, that's OK." I was proud of myself for being cool.

"Hey, baby." Richard smiled in the rear view mirror. "Guess what Sammy's got?"

"A big fat joint, I hope."

"Better."

"I don't know." I stared out the window.

"Guess!" Richard was annoyed that I didn't want to play his game.

"It better not be coke, Richie."

"Mushrooms." Richard nearly giggled with delight.

"Acid?" I wasn't into hard-core drugs. All I required was enough to get a pleasant buzz.

"Don't freak." Tony laughed. "It's mild. Everything seems brighter, clearer. You'll laugh a lot. That's all."

Sammy was waiting on his stoop, his white T-shirt tucked into Levis and a pack of Marlboro's rolled up in the sleeve. Typical Jersey asshole, I thought. How the hell do I make myself like him? His tight, hard little body bounced into the seat next to me. "Hey, Rena." He waved a baggie full of dried mushrooms in front of me. "Ready for a trip to Great Adventure?" he laughed at his joke.

"We need to wait 'til we get there." Richard said. "They don't last real long. No sense wasting them on the ride." He began laughing, quietly at first and then louder until he was almost doubled over. "Waste them—get it?" He was hysterical.

"I can't believe you got high before you picked me up!" I crossed my arms and flung myself against the back of the seat.

"Jesus. Chill out." Sammy waved his hands like an umpire declaring a runner safe. "So he smoked a little pot without you? What the hell's the problem?"

"The problem is you're a fucking asshole," Kali screamed, wanting to wrap all six of her hands around Sammy's throat. "How can anyone stand being around this John Travolta wannabe?"

"Rena is overreacting just a bit," said Inanna indignantly. "Look at me. I've lost my crown and my earrings, but you don't see me having a hissy fit."

"Why's it always gotta be about you, Inanna?" Kali retorted. "Richard's an insensitive bastard and I don't understand why we haven't made her dump his sorry white ass." She stomped her feet until the ground shook.

"Rena never told Richard she was uncomfortable with this." Kuan Yin was almost whispering. "How is he supposed to know?"

"He just should," Kali answered. "I'm telling you, we should've left him at the Spectrum—walked out and never looked back." Kali enjoyed having the ammunition to be self-righteous.

"You can't expect people to know how you feel, Kali, unless you're willing to take the risk and express yourself," Kuan Yin piped up again. Sometimes she got tired trying to convince her sisters that truth was the only way.

"Bullshit. When you love someone, they know these things." Kali was adamant. When Siva hadn't understood her need to control their empire, she killed him. No one was going to fuck with her. "You've been quiet, Erishkigal. Don't you want to get your two cents in?"

After a small pause, she said, "If Rena tells Richard how she feels, he's going to make fun of her. He's always telling her she's too sensitive."

"Exactly my point," Kali nodded. "He's always criticizing her. Trust me, this isn't going to be a good day."

The four of us sat in the car in the parking lot of Great Adventure, methodically chewing mushrooms coated in dried dung. "These taste like shit," I complained.

"Of course they do, stupid," Sammy laughed. "They grow in cow manure." He winked at Richard.

"Well, why don't they wash them first?"

"Look, princess, this is how they come. Quit bitching and chew." I scrunched my face, but continued to eat.

"I don't feel anything," I said.

"Patience, princess." Sammy rolled his eyes and opened the car door. We bought our admission tickets and went through the turnstiles. I had to turn sideways. Standing inside, we discussed what rides we wanted to go on and where we should start. They all wanted to ride the ferris wheel and the Pirate Ship. I agreed to go on the ferris wheel, but bowed out of the Pirate ride after watching the ship gather momentum and turn its riders completely upside down.

We got stuck at the top of the ferris wheel so passengers could get out of the bottom car and I felt my heart race. Last summer, Richard and Tony and I went to Coney Island and they talked me into going on the Zipper, a ride similar to the ferris wheel. But when it reached a certain position, the car suddenly swung out to the edge of its track and it felt like you were going to fly into the Atlantic. Hyperventilating and shaking, I begged to get off. I guess I was a little dramatic because Richard and Tony became hysterical. It hadn't helped that we were all stoned. I swore I'd never go to another amusement park.

Now, a hundred feet above ground, we could see the entire park. I was a little anxious, but nothing like last summer. The guys got in line for the Pirate Ship, and I went to get beers for them. I waited until they made it inside and then went for a walk, not realizing how the mushrooms were starting to take effect.

Wandering into a little garden, I began to see things as if I was at the eye doctor and he was sliding different lenses in front of me, asking which one was better. Everything became clearer the longer I looked. All the flowers had a defined edge and the colors were exaggerated, brilliant and almost painful. The gravel crunched under my feet and the noise was so loud, I turned around to see if anyone else had heard it.

I stared at a bed of lilies. After standing there a while, I felt the flowers sucking in air through their stamens. I ran a hand through my hair and realized I was sweating, cold and damp in the ninety-degree sun. Richard had said the effect didn't last long, but my skin felt like it was going to explode and spray my image all over the Oriental Garden at Six Flags Great Adventure.

"Rena!" I heard Tony calling me. I looked around, panicked from being in this acid-induced solitude. A hand touched my shoulder and my scream pierced the quiet. "Jesus! It's just me." Tony jumped back. "We're done with Captain Ron's Pirate Ship. Richard and Sammy went to take a leak." He grinned and then looked at me staring at him, like I didn't recognize him. "Are you OK?"

"Me? Yeah. Fine."

"It's the mushrooms, huh?"

"No, I'm fine."

"I don't think we got to feel the full effect because we were having the shit scared out of us. But apparently, you got your money's worth." He laughed.

"No, really. I'm fine."

"All right, Miss Fine. Let's go get a Coke or something while we wait for those guys." We sat at a picnic table, me still in a mushroom zone. Richard and Sammy returned with nachos and climbed onto the benches, offering some to Tony and me.

"Miss Rena now knows what it's like to do acid," Tony joked. "I found her in the garden communing with nature."

"Really?" Richard sounded impressed. "Did you like it?"

"No." I was exhausted. "It flipped me out. I've never experienced anything like that. I wanted to jump out of my skin."

"That's my boy Chuck." Sammy beamed. "Never steered me wrong in all the years he's been my dealer."

"I really don't feel good, Richard."

"So, what does that mean? You want to go home? Come on—suck it up. It can't be that bad." I only half listened to their plans for the next few rides. They wanted to ride the new Batman roller coaster, but I knew my stomach and its contents would end up all over the ground. They talked me into the parachute ride after explaining that we'd sit on a bench and be pulled up by a wire to the height of the ferris wheel. When they released the tension on the wire, it would feel like skydiving as we floated to the ground because there was a parachute attached to each bench.

As we passed the Batman ride, I watched the people harnessed in upright, weaving in and out of steel loops at sixty miles an hour. I was grateful the line was a few hundred people long so that Richard wasn't tempted to change his mind. We got to the parachute ride and walked through the maze to the back of the line. As we got closer, I saw a sign that blared, "Maximum weight 350 pounds." The gate dropped on my throat again. I knew Richard had put on some weight and was over 175 pounds. I hadn't been on a scale in years.

"Get her the hell out of this line, now!" Kali shouted, all six hands waving frantically. Her eyes were bloodshot.

"There's no way to do it without making a scene," Erishkigal hushed her, pulling the thin cloth of her robe around her tightly. She was naked underneath except for a thong made out of leaves. "We'll just have to pray it'll be all right." Shuddering, she placed her palms together and started mumbling a prayer to the goddess Ninmar, the Mesopotamian mother and guardian.

"It's not going to be all right," Kali argued. "When are you going to see that?"

"I'm not going to embarrass her," Erishkigal finished her prayer.

"We can make her throw up. Twist her ankle. Trip over something. Anything. You cannot let her go through with this." Kali panicked.

"It will be fine."

"Kali is right," added Inanna, doing a quick calculation in her head. "The numbers don't lie. They're not going to make it."

"They probably just say that," Erishkigal referred to the sign, ignoring Inanna's crisis. "I'm sure it will hold the two of them."

Sammy and Tony ran for the bench that had the smallest parachute, screaming that it would make them fall faster. Richard and I headed to a bench and allowed the ticket taker to strap us in. All the benches were full and Richard put his hand on my leg. "Ready?" he asked. I winced. "I'm so glad you decided to come with us today." We sat quietly, anticipating the climb to the top. A bell sounded and we waited for our bench to move. I opened my eyes to find the ticket taker standing next to Richard.

"I'm sorry you guys, but between the two of you, you exceed the maximum weight limit."

"You sniveling coward!" Kali hovered over Erishkigal as she hugged her knees.

"This is because of you."

"Leave her alone Kali," interjected Kuan Yin. *"Everything is unfolding the way it's supposed to. Remember what I said about trusting?"*

"Fuck trusting—Rena needs a diet!" sneered Kali.

"We'll have to make sure nothing like that occurs ever again," Inanna said definitively, stroking her neck.

"Anger isn't going to get you anywhere Kali," Kuan Yin reminded her sister.

"Jeez!" cried Inanna, feeling her naked neck. "Not my lapis beads now! What the hell is going on?"

I shuffled like a zombie off the bench and through the exit line, past the line of people waiting to get on wondering what the holdup was. "Are you OK?" Richard asked me when we got outside the gate.

"Sure. Why wouldn't I be?" I answered defensively.

"Well, it was kind of embarrassing. I just wanted to make sure you were OK."

"Don't worry about me. I'm fine." The wall came up, the armor went on and the pain was pushed down until it was manageable. I stood there, numb, not allowing myself to cry. Tony and Sammy ran over, their fall to earth completed.

"What happened?" asked Tony.

"I felt sick," Richard said.

"You don't have to lie, Richard." My smile was pinched. "The two of us together were too heavy for it to go up."

"Really?" Sammy started to laugh, but caught a look from Richard that stopped him cold.

"Well, what do you want to do next?" Tony changed the subject. "I really want to shoot some hoops and see if I can win something."

"Let's go," I said.

We wandered around the arcade, spraying water at ducks, throwing pennies at frogs and attempting to shoot basketballs through hoops that were too far away. Tony won two stuffed animals and a Swiss army knife.

"Let's go on the log jammer ride," suggested Richard. "It's been a long day and we're all really hot."

"Yeah and hopefully the line won't be too long," Sammy said.

We walked to the other end of the park and found the line was short, but still crowded enough that all four of us were forced to get into one log. "God," I prayed, "if you let this thing get up this ramp with all of us in it, I swear I'll do something about my weight. Just please, please, don't let us get stuck half way up." The log shaped car grunted and squeaked, struggling to the top. It hurtled over the crest and careened down the other side, Sammy, Tony and Richard shrieking with delight.

"Thank you," I whispered as the log flew down the last slide, soaking all of us.

Break

I approached St. Nicholas' Episcopalian Church like a sapling facing its first storm, ungrounded and weak. Two large women cautiously made their way down the crumbling stone steps. I stood on 22nd Street searching for an excuse to go home.

Last Sunday, I was returning a video to Blockbuster and I noticed a sign in front of St. Nicholas'. "Are You On A Roller Coaster Ride To Hell?" screamed the message. I had no interest in attending The Very Reverend Jonathan Wyclef's sermon, but the small words at the bottom caught my attention. "Do you have problems with food? Can't stop eating, but want to? Join our support group: M-F at 7 PM" It had taken all week, but now I was here.

I stood on the top step, a voice in my head whispering that being around a bunch of fat people couldn't possibly help me lose weight. Inside the church basement were a couple of dozen folding chairs, the metal seats as inviting to me as the parachute ride at Great Adventure. Several people, mostly women, milled around, some talking, others silent, engrossed in their own thoughts. A woman wearing a smile approached, but I dodged her and headed for the bathroom.

I locked myself in a cubicle and squatted, fully clothed on the toilet. I heard the door open and someone entered the stall beside me. There was grunting and heavy breathing as the woman settled in. I sat very still, lulled by my own heartbeat. Curious, I leaned over my knees to peek at the legs of my neighbor. Pale, unshaven and doughy, they were covered to mid-shin in a loud floral print. The woman sighed as she hit the porcelain with a thud.

I wanted to disappear as I listened to the explosive diarrhea. The air became soggy and I held my nose. It didn't occur to me that after I ate a medium pizza, a bowl of pasta and half a coffee cake that that's exactly what happened to me in the bathroom. I thought I heard a sniffle. "Damn!" came an exasperated voice. I looked down and saw a roll of toilet paper on the floor. It was trapped on the border between the two stalls, a small white tail surrendering to me, hoping to be saved from a gruesome death. I stifled a giggle. "Why doesn't she pick it up?" I wondered. The common wall shook as the woman heaved herself off the toilet and I could see her bright orange fingernails wiggling at the roll, commanding it to come closer. If I helped, the woman would know I had heard her bowel symphony. But watching her struggle was agony. Before I could think anymore, I bent over, picked up the roll and with my wrist braced on the bottom of the metal wall, offered it to the stranger. "Thank you," whispered the woman. "You're welcome," I said quietly, as I grabbed my bag and hurried out of the bathroom. Most of the seats in the meeting room had been filled. The people in them were all sizes, from extremely overweight to slim. I was insulted by the handful of slender women, unaware that people came to these meetings not just to lose weight, but also to hold onto their sanity.

There was one chair behind the circle that was empty. I sat. A woman in her early thirties, the one who had tried to talk to me earlier, spoke. "Hi. My name is Karen and I have a problem with food."

"What does Rena think she's going to accomplish with this bunch of losers?" Erishkigal asked, denying her own ambivalence. She wanted to be included in something and yet was embarrassed by Rena's weight problem.

"She needs help, you ninny." Kali touched the tip of her sword to Erishkigal's aquiline nose. "Things haven't really been going too well with you in charge, in case you hadn't noticed." Kali wanted to slice Erishkigal in half for acting like a quivering field mouse.

"This is stupid," Erishkigal insisted batting away Kali's sword. "Being with a bunch of losers sitting around a church basement on a Friday night is pathetic."

"And getting thrown off an amusement park ride with your boyfriend isn't?" Kali retorted.

"What could she possibly learn here?" Erishkigal tightened the flax belt around her tiny waist.

"Maybe through some miracle, she'll be able to see that her life is not working."

"Kali, do you really think this could work?" Inanna asked, always open to options. "Maybe a diet doctor or Weight Watchers would be better."

"Rena's eating issues are about much more than food," Kuan Yin said, folding her stocky legs into half lotus. "I think this could be helpful." She knew her own enlightenment should afford her understanding of her sisters' fears and their need to control. But they drained her energy.

"I think we should leave," Erishkigal insisted.

"You lose this time." Kali smirked.

I listened as Karen spent fifteen minutes telling her story. "I've had a problem with food my entire life," she began. "My mother shoved whatever was lying around the kitchen into my mouth to shut me up. I was pretty hyper as a kid and cookies and crackers put me in kind of a food coma—after the sugar high wore off." Karen smiled. "I managed to stay a size eight until I was a senior in high school by throwing up three times a day."

I listened intently, even though I had nothing in common with Karen. I had never stuck my finger down my throat.

"When I was seventeen, my best friend committed suicide and it had a pretty dramatic effect on me. I started binging two or three times a day and I couldn't make myself vomit enough to keep the weight off. I tried laxatives, but ended up being rushed to the hospital for intestinal bleeding. My parents checked me into a rehabilitation center for food addicts." She paused, as if deciding whether or not to share her next thought.

"It didn't work. I was miserable and as soon as I got out, I was binging again. I stopped purging, though, so I put on a lot of weight. My top weight was two hundred and five pounds."

"Eeesha!" I gasped. I sheepishly looked around, hoping no one had heard—hoping no one noticed how close I was to that number. Everyone was absorbed in her story. Karen continued, talking about her college years where she alternated among food, pot and cocaine. "I enrolled in law school after graduation, having achieved straight A's, and placed in the top five of my class."

Fidgeting in my chair, I tuned Karen out for a minute and observed the rest of the group. There were ten people in the room besides me. Seven women and three men. I had never been good at guessing other people's weight. What I saw in the mirror wasn't what others saw. The three men ranged in age from early thirties to one who appeared to be fifty or so. They were all normal size and the younger one was handsome in a blue-collar way, wearing jeans and a T-shirt, a large key chain dangling from his belt loop.

"I applied to the top law firm in my home town and all of my professors told me it was a lock. I was in like Flynn." Karen shook her head and laughed sadly. "I had six interviews over two weeks. It was more grueling than sitting for the bar."

An enormous woman took a tissue out of her purse and blew her nose. The sound was familiar. I recognized the woman's brightly flowered caftan and how her ankles rolled over her sandal straps. Droplets of sweat rolled down her face leaving white streaks in her caked on blush. Her cheeks looked like Fruit Stripe gum. She placed the dirty tissue back in her bag and removed knitting needles and yarn from a plastic tote.

Karen continued. "One of my professors called me in for a meeting and told me I wasn't hired because I didn't fit the firm's image. I was devastated. I had spent three hundred dollars on a suit. My make-up was perfect; my nails, manicured. I bought new shoes and a briefcase. I had done everything I could. My professor apologized for hurting my feelings, but said he told me because he felt it might help in some way." I shifted in my seat, and closed my blazer around me.

"I went on an unprecedented month-long food and drug binge. I was lying in my house one day, watching an old movie, and not having showered for three days. Empty pizza, cereal, and cookie boxes were strewn around my living room. And I just cried. I cried and cried into the night until finally, I fell asleep from sheer exhaustion. It was horrible, but it got me to meetings and this has saved my life. I've lost seventy-two pounds and kept it off for five years." Karen finished, sitting back in her metal folding chair on the gold-flecked linoleum floor and crossed her legs. I applauded with the rest of the group. Maybe there was something to this.

For the next forty minutes, others shared about their struggles with food. Curiously, listening to other people talk about their problems with eating made me feel better. Some of the people had lost weight and kept it off. Others, like the woman in the flowered caftan, seemed miserable.

"I can't stop eating," the woman who introduced herself as Melissa whispered. Her hands operated autonomously, her swollen fingers wrapped around long needles as she knitted. She occasionally loosened the purple yarn from the bag that rested between her thick legs. "I go to work. I have a responsible job. But my boss treats me like shit and I go back for more—

every day. I've worked there fifteen years. I do everything for him. I even picked out his wife's birthday gift last month. But I know I'm not his friend." She sniffled into her tissue. "He asks me for favors all the time, but when I need a day off or want to call in sick, there's hell to pay. And then I go home, alone, to my apartment, and eat until the sugar numbs my brain and I pass out."

"You could find another job," I offered.

"Shhh!" The woman next to me hissed at me.

"I'm sorry; I don't think I know your name," Karen said to me.

"Rena." My face was hot.

"Rena, one of the rules we have at these meetings is to not respond while someone else is talking. We're here to share our experiences and our feelings and to work through what's bothering us. One of the principles we adhere to is not to give advice."

"I'm sorry." My eyes were locked on my shoes.

"It's OK." Karen smiled. "You wouldn't have known. Go ahead, Melissa."

Melissa stared at me for a moment. I squirmed in my chair. "I don't want to take care of myself anymore," she continued. "I have to force myself to take a shower. All I want to do is eat or sleep." The knitting needles clicked furiously and soon a furry purple fountain poured into her giant lap. The tears started again and they swam down her face in thin lines and dropped off her chin into the purple lake.

Someone signaled Melissa that her time was up. She thanked everyone for being there. Then someone else began to talk.

"She's disgusting." Erishkigal wrinkled her nose thinking of Melissa. "Rena is nothing like that. She's clean. Her hair's not greasy. These people are sick." She circled her wrist with her thumb and index finger to make sure they still touched. "You guys are crazy making her sit through this." Melissa's underworld was a little too close to home for Erishkigal.

"Excuse me, but I can remember plenty of weekends where Rena couldn't get out of bed, didn't shower, couldn't even brush her teeth." Kali shivered. "Where she did nothing but order in food." Kali couldn't understand why Rena couldn't take charge. When Kali wanted something, she went out and got it. When she had an urge or an impulse, she followed it. Consequences be damned.

"Rena's got a lot in common with this woman." The ruby in the middle of Kuan Yin's forehead shone in the fluorescent light. *"That's why you can't stomach her, Erishkigal. She's done some of the things Melissa talked about. You can't deny it."* She was careful not to divulge more than she believed Erishkigal could handle.

"But I can deny she looks like that. Melissa must weigh more than three hundred pounds." Erishkigal defended her position, afraid that being around people like this would start Rena on a descent that wouldn't easily be reversed.

"That's where Rena's headed if she doesn't get some discipline and control," Kali argued.

"It's about so much more than that," Kuan Yin pleaded. *"Let her take the time to discover what caused the problem."* Once again, her sisters ignored her words of compassion.

"I can deal with that crap later." Kali placed her bottom set of hands firmly on her hips. *"Now it's about dropping forty or fifty pounds. And then telling Richard to take a hike because she'll be able to get any man she wants."*

"Rena would be lost without him. I'll agree to support you with her losing weight, but Richard stays. He can help her with this." Erishkigal was confident.

"I think you're delusional," Kali grinned. *"But it's a start."*

I ducked out that night as soon as the meeting was over. Holding hands and saying a prayer felt too much like being a Hare Krishna. On my way, I grabbed a few pamphlets lying on a table by the door. That night, I sat in my apartment, surrounded by eggplant parmesan and garlic bread from Pasta Pronto, the brochures resting on top of the Sunday *Times*. I made a salad, convincing myself that would counteract the calories from the bread and cheese. I inhaled everything, barely tasting it.

An hour later I was starving and fixed a bowl of popcorn. I loved the salty kernels at the bottom. My mother had warned me for years that I could chip a tooth eating them, but there was something satisfying about crunching down hard and pulverizing that little seed. The popcorn woke my sweet tooth up and I polished off the rest of the mint-chip ice cream in the freezer. I passed out around nine and when I woke up the next morning, I felt like shit. I retrieved the pamphlets from the trash pile and answered the questionnaire, trying to determine if I was a food addict. I answered yes to nine of the ten questions.

The next few times I went to St. Nicholas, I took my seat behind the circle and listened. Each time, I heard something that touched a spot in the soft place under my belly. At my fifth meeting, Karen approached me again and I didn't run.

"I've noticed you coming the last couple of weeks, Rena." She smiled, her eyes scrutinizing me. "Have you found coming here helpful?" Karen's straight brown hair was pulled into a tight bun at the crown of her head. She was wearing a tasteful pinstripe suit with a silk bow wrapped around the neck of her button-down shirt. A neutral shade barely blushed her lips and her only jewelry was a pair of pearl earrings and a plain gold wedding band.

This time there was no pepperoni pizza to stuff it back down. No brownies to placate me into the delusion that everything in my life was good. "I've heard some interesting things," I admitted.

"Well, something must keep you coming back." Karen waited for a response. I had none. "Do you have any questions?"

"Will you be my sponsor?" I was surprised the words came out of my mouth.

Karen hesitated. "I would love to Rena, but I already have a sponsee and I lead two meetings a week." Karen looked me in the eye. "I'm sorry, but I have a difficult job and I only got married three months ago. I just don't know if it's possible."

My face burned. When I was four, I proudly showed my mother how I had tied my own shoes. The laces were knotted and hung limply over the edge of my saddle shoes and there wasn't a bow in sight, but I had done it myself. She scolded me because she broke a nail trying to undo the knots. Suddenly, I was four. "Never mind." I turned to leave. "I shouldn't have asked."

"Wait." Karen reached into her bag and scribbled something on a scrap of paper. "Rena, take my number. I'll be an interim sponsor for you—until you find one who has the time to make a full commitment. Call me later tonight and we'll get you started." Karen watched as I folded the paper into tiny squares.

"What do you mean?" I asked.

"You need a food plan," Karen took control. "We'll arrange a time for you to call me every day so that you can commit to me what you're going to eat that day. I'll teach you how to keep a food journal so you can see what foods trigger you to binge." Karen continued explaining, but the word "binge" ricocheted in my head like an escaped pinball, searching for a bumper to put it back in play. I didn't binge. Yeah, sometimes I ate too much, but binging made me too much like the other people in this room. And I was supposed to choose what I was going to eat for the day before it began and not deviate? And then call Karen and tell her? That was insanity.

"No. Insanity is sitting alone in your apartment eating three Big Macs." Kali patted the head of the cobra resting on her shoulders. *"Or not answering the phone for two days because you want to eat undisturbed, but secretly hoping someone will express concern. That's insanity."*

"You're always talking about the control Richard has over her." Erishkigal began her case. *"How's this going to be any different? Telling someone what you're going to eat? That's crazy! How will she do that?"*

"I'm not sure," Kali answered. *"But we've done it your way long enough."*

What if I really was a food addict? All I knew was that I wasn't happy. I flew into Karen's hands, trusting her blindly, like a baby bird, more afraid to open its eyes than to not. During our first conversation, I committed to attend ninety meetings in ninety days. Upon Karen's recommendation, I eliminated refined sugar and white flour from my diet. I faithfully called every morning at six forty-five and told her what I was going to eat for the day. Slowly, I began to feel better, the structure providing the comfort food once had. I was determined to make this work.

In a month, I lost ten pounds. Nobody noticed. I wanted to shout from the rooftops of New York that I, Rena Sutcliffe, had lost ten pounds. But I was afraid it would jinx everything. I decided it was better to just let people notice. I didn't tell Richard because I wanted to surprise him. I avoided seeing him for a couple of weeks keeping myself busy with work and going to a meeting every day. I figured the longer in between us seeing each other the more likely he would be to notice me getting smaller. But he didn't.

I gave Karen just enough information about myself so she thought I was really working hard. It seemed to pacify her. After thirty days without binging, I qualified to share my story the way Karen had at my first meeting. I was elated, sitting in front of the room, telling everyone how I'd finally found the answer. I was sure of myself like I had never been before. And I really was OK with eating only three times a day and giving up my secret stash of M&M's in my drawer at work.

A few of us went out for coffee after the meeting. Lee, the nice looking blue-collar guy came with us and I found myself flirting. Seven of us sat at the Lyric Diner on Third Avenue as I sipped a cup of peppermint tea and tried not to judge what everyone else was having. Melissa had pot roast and mashed potatoes, and Lee had apple pie and coffee.

I went home that night and ordered enough Chinese food for ten people. I ate most of it. When I woke up the next morning, I threw the rest of it out and vowed that it would never happen again. I didn't tell Karen.

I continued going to meetings and as far as I was concerned the Chinese food massacre had never occurred. I enjoyed having people look to me for answers. I couldn't disappoint them. People liked me. I was actually pretty funny. And I was just honest enough to make people believe I was sharing everything. What I wasn't saying was that I was there only to drop forty pounds. Once I had done that, I was out of there.

There was nothing wrong with me that a little discipline couldn't cure. I hadn't had the best childhood, but I certainly wasn't abused. My mother was pretty much of a pain-in-the-ass, but I know she did what she did because she loved me. My father provided the best he could and I never went hungry growing up. I had recently remembered keeping a stash of pretzels and crackers in the desk in my room when I was a child. Sometimes when I'd get up to go to the bathroom I would grab a handful and eat them laying in bed, being careful to get rid of the crumbs the next morning. I still ate in the middle of the night sometimes but it wasn't a big deal. I just ate less the next day.

I also hadn't been molested the way I heard some of the women talk about during their shares. And sometimes I wondered if they were making it up as a way to explain why they were fat. They got so upset and angry while they were talking. It was scary.

I decided that calling Karen every day was a good thing for now. And if I pushed the envelope a little bit here and there I was OK with that as long as I continued to lose weight. An occasional cookie or bag of chips wasn't going to kill me. These people went overboard with the deprivation thing. After three months, I was down almost twenty-two pounds. I had discovered step aerobics and body conditioning at the New York Sports Club across from the office. I spent a lot of time alone, but I knew that's what I needed to do. Richard had gotten a promotion so we didn't spend a lot of time together. Several newcomers called me and asked me to sponsor them. I cheerfully shared my happiness and how I'd obtained "it." But most of them seemed more insane to me without food than if they'd have been binging their brains out. I knew I was different. When I'd lost enough weight, I'd stop going.

Break

I especially liked the meeting on Friday night that was on Food, Intimacy and Relationships and went every week. One night, after the meeting, the leader, Alison, told me she was being transferred to Chicago by her company and asked if I'd be willing to take over leading the meeting. I said yes.

I called Karen to give her the good news. "Do you think you're ready?" she asked. "Why wouldn't I be?"

"You've only been coming for a few months, Rena. And that's a pretty heavy topic. Do you feel confident enough in your relationship with food to take that on?"

"So you're saying you don't think I can handle the responsibility?"

"I'm asking if you believe you can."

"I don't see why not. I've got a lot to learn, but I can share what I've learned so far, right?" The couple of times a week I got up and ate in the middle of the night certainly didn't mean anything. I was capable of handling this meeting.

"Well, if you're sure." She didn't sound enthusiastic .

"I'm quite sure. And I've really got to run. I'll talk to you tomorrow." I hung up the phone and turned on the television. I was hungry. I couldn't decide what I wanted, so I ordered a burger and fries from the diner. I knew it would be twenty minutes or so before they got there and I needed something to eat now. I rummaged through the cabinets and found a box of garlic croutons. I poured myself a diet soda and plopped on the couch, munching and drinking until the doorbell rang.

I told Karen that morning I was going to have a chicken breast and a salad for dinner, but I was bored with chicken. One cheeseburger never killed anyone. A couple of months ago, Karen told me as we were going over my food journal that she thought potatoes were a trigger food for me. But I knew I could eat french fries every once in a while and not have a problem.

I finished dinner and sat on the couch, bored, watching another episode of *Seinfeld*. Around ten, Richard called from San Francisco. NEC was grooming him for management and he was traveling a couple of times a month now. "Hey, Rena. What's going on?"

"Not much." I flipped the channels during the commercial.

"It's beautiful out here. I could live in California with no problem."

"That's nice."

"Is there something wrong?" He seemed concerned.

"No. What makes you say that?"

"You just sound, I don't know, different."

"No. Everything's fine." I popped an ice cube into my mouth.

"How's work?"

"The same."

"If you don't want to talk to me, that's fine." He sounded insulted.

"What makes you say that?"

"You seem involved with something else. Is this a bad time?"

"Actually, it's a really good time, Richard. Alison is getting transferred to Chicago and asked me to lead the meeting she started on Friday nights on Food and Relationships."

"Do you think you're ready for that?" I saw his eyebrows go up.

"You sound just like Karen." I was irritated. "Why wouldn't I be ready?"

"I didn't mean it the way it came out."

"What other way could you mean it?"

"Look, Rena. I care about you, that's all. It just seems like that's a big responsibility."

"I'm perfectly capable of handling it, Richard. And I don't need your doubting Thomas attitude."

"I don't doubt you, Rena," he sighed. "But sometimes you rush things. Patience has never been your strong suit."

"I really have to go." I slowly increased the volume on *Seinfeld*. "When are you going to be back?"

"I'm taking the red-eye tomorrow night. I'll be in early Saturday morning. What are you doing this weekend?"

"I may have to go to the office Saturday. And I want to get to a meeting. Other than that, nothing. Why?"

"Maybe we could have dinner Saturday night?" I laughed silently at Kramer's modeling escapades.

"Call me."

"OK. Sleep well."

"You, too." I got up to place the phone in the cradle and continued into the kitchen. I wanted something sweet. I hadn't had sugar in a few months and I didn't have anything in the house that would satisfy my craving. I threw on my coat and walked to the deli. Standing in front of boxes of Entemann's and rows of miniature apple pies and coffeecakes, I couldn't decide.

"We can't let her do this," cried Kuan Yin.

"Why not. She'll just have to work out harder tomorrow," answered Kali, licking her lips, eyeing the Louisiana Crunch Cake.

"It'll make her feel better," Erishkigal explained. "No one is supporting her right now. She needs some comfort."

"That's my whole point." Kuan Yin raised her voice, frustrated and annoyed. "Rena has got to find a way to comfort herself without food. She'll feel ten times worse in the morning if she eats this crap."

"Look, oh compassionate goddess sister of mine," Kali swept her hands around her body and bowed to Kuan Yin. "She's got this eating thing under control. They even respect her enough to ask her to lead one of their little meetings. Let her have a treat."

"You don't understand, do you?" Kuan Yin shifted her eyes between Erishkigal and Kali. "Rena is obsessed with food. It'll be one little thing now. And then tomorrow or the next day, it'll be half a box." She ran the stack of wire bracelets up and down her arm.

"And then next week, the whole box. That's the way addiction goes. You are kidding yourselves to think it's OK for her to have "one" of anything like this."

"You, my little Asian friend, are a reactionary. Everything is fine." Kali whispered condescendingly.

"She's been lying to Karen. She certainly isn't sober around food by the group's guidelines. And now she's going to lead a meeting because it fills the void of being needed. Things are anything but fine."

"Erishkigal and I have it covered, don't we, E?" Kali raised an eyebrow at Erishkigal and winked.

"She's right," Erishkigal nodded. "There's nothing to worry about, Kuan Yin."

I handed the cashier a dollar for my Hostess coconut cream pie. I made a cup of coffee when I got home and put the pie on a plate. I savored every sweet, creamy bite. Then I took a shower and went to bed. I was tired of nobody having any faith in me.

In between typing and answering the phone the next day, I struggled to come up with a good topic for the meeting that night. I left the office at five and went home to change. I wasn't really nervous, just a bit anxious. I arrived fifteen minutes early to set up the chairs. I'd heard that in some of the other support meetings they had at St. Nicholas' that coffee and cookies were served. Well, the cookie thing probably wasn't a good idea, but tea or coffee might be nice. I made a mental note to bring that up to the group.

"Hi, my name is Rena and I have a problem with food." I looked out at the dozen faces staring at me. I recognized some of them. "Tonight's meeting topic is about food and relationships. I'll share for five or ten minutes and then we'll open it up." There were a few butterflies in my stomach, but they got stuck in coconut cream pie.

"I'd like to start by saying how grateful I am to Alison for asking me to lead this meeting. I was such a mess when I first walked into this room almost four months ago. I knew I had a problem, but I didn't know how to admit it or where to go for help." A lot of the heads nodded in silent understanding.

"These meetings have become very important to me. They've taught me how to take back control of my life. And in thinking about what I wanted to talk about tonight, I realized that the most fundamental relationship that I need to deal with is the one I have with food." I noticed Melissa remove the knitting needles from her bag. The yarn was blue.

"I started eating too much at a very early age and was criticized for it by everyone. My mother constantly told me that I'd be miserable if I wasn't the perfect size six. The kids at school called me all kinds of names." I took a breath. "I ate all through high school and although I had some friends, food was my best friend. On Saturday night when everybody was on a date, I was intimately involved with Mr. Frito Lay." A young blond woman chuckled out loud. "College was much of the same, but I had more freedom. I graduated to relationships with Burger King and McDonald's and made my own selections at the grocery store without worrying about my mother's digs. And my roommate was always sleeping in her boyfriend's room, so that was a bonus." Everyone laughed.

Melissa's blue yarn took on a life of its own and the abstract form covered the tops of her legs. "The relationship I need to work on the hardest is the one I have with food. I can no longer expect it to hold my hand. To comfort me and keep me company. It's very painful to talk about, but I'm turning to people at these meetings for the things I used to get from food." Again, I watched the heads bobbing in agreement.

"When I feel stressed out now, I pick up the phone and call my sponsor or someone else from the meetings." Most of the time. "I no longer feel tempted to run out to the deli at ten o'clock because I just have to have something." Most of the time. "I love the feeling of freedom that gives me. I no longer feel like food is my best friend or my worst enemy. It's something I need to survive, to fuel my body. It's exhilarating."

I paused for a second, the slightest twinges of hypocrisy gnawing at my stomach. "There are times I hate food and wish I didn't have to deal with it ever again. Sometimes it's so hard. But as long as I'm clean and steering clear of my trigger foods, everything is OK." That would be true if it were true. "My relationship with food has changed. And with the grace of the meetings, it will continue to change. Thank you for letting me share."

The room broke into applause. The blond woman who had laughed raised her hand. I called on her and then gave her the responsibility of selecting the next person to share. My obligation for the evening was over.

"Hi, my name is Lucy and I have problems with food." The others responded with a joint "Hi, Lucy."

"I want to thank you, Rena, for your honesty. Listening to other people's truth is the only way I'm going to break out of this vicious cycle of binging and purging." I crossed my legs. Then I uncrossed my legs. "My relationship with food is very similar to yours. Listening to you gives me hope that I can get to where you are with it. You're an inspiration. Thank you." Lucy looked at the hands waving and pointed at Melissa.

"Thank you for picking me, Lucy," Melissa smiled, her eyes barely visible, sunken behind her bloated cheeks. "My name is Melissa and I have a big problem with food." The group gave a rousing "hello." I searched my purse for a piece of gum.

"Thank you so much, Rena. I don't know how you've managed to accomplish what you have in the short time you've been here. I've been coming for almost a year and I'm no where near close to you in the evolution of my relationship with food." She played with the blue puddle in her lap. "I have to admit I'm a bit jealous." She twirled a piece of yarn through her fingers.

"It seems no matter how hard I try, I just can't stop eating. I wake up each morning with the best of intentions, but by the end of the day, there I am in my apartment with a bag from the Food Emporium, watching television and systematically consuming everything I've purchased. I don't know how to stop." A tear leaked out of her left eye. "I just don't know why I'm the only one who can't seem to get it." The room was still. I accidentally cracked my gum. Melissa was crying. Her hips and thighs spilled over the edges of the card chair because her knees wouldn't touch.

"I'm sorry," she whispered. She coughed and sniffled, one seeming to cause the other. "I feel so lost." Lucy handed Melissa tissue. "Thank you all for listening."

"Why don't we pass the gift basket?" I interrupted, grateful for the sound of my voice. I explained the tradition of collecting donations and started the basket around the room. When it had made its way back to me, I asked Melissa to call on someone else.

"Hi, my name is Lee and I've been abstinent for eighty days." The room applauded. Lee smiled and I recognized him as the man I thought was cute at the first meeting I attended. "I've been coming to these meetings for several years and I lost my sobriety with food five months ago. It was a real struggle to get it back. I appreciate your honesty, Rena. Like Lucy said, the only way I'm going to stay clean is to hear everyone else's story. And I appreciate your sense of humor. It makes the whole damn thing seem a little less painful." He looked at me with chocolate bullets. "I don't know how you've managed to get it so quickly, but keep it. You're a gem. Thank you."

He called on the next person and twenty minutes later the meeting was over. They all came up to me after and told me how glad they were that

Alison had asked me to take over. I started refolding the chairs and putting them against the wall. I felt good about the meeting. Everyone seemed to get a lot out of it—and wasn't that the point? I turned around to find Lee holding two chairs. "Thanks," I said.

"No problem," he smiled. "I can see I'm going to have to make this meeting a standing appointment." He had dark brown hair and was wearing tight Levi's and a gray T-shirt. His cheeks had a slight blush and his teeth were straight and white. "Hey, what are you doing for dinner? There's a great Chinese place right around the corner." He paused. "Or if that doesn't work with your food plan, we could try something else."

"Chinese sounds great." Was this a date? "Let me put the rest of these chairs away." He helped me finish and we walked around the block to Third. The place was deserted, except for two old Chinese men cleaning peapods at a back table. Fluorescent lights showed the stains on the green carpet. The tables were dressed with white linen and each black bamboo chair had a fire-breathing dragon embossed on the seat cover. Red and gold fringe dangled from the sconces on the walls and it smelled of steamed rice and pickled cabbage.

We ordered chicken and broccoli and hot and sour soup. Lee pushed the fried noodles and the gooey orange sauce off to the side. I devoured the entire bowl in my head. I debated whether it was all right for me to eat some of them in front of him. I was glad Richard was still in San Francisco.

"So, what made you start coming to meetings?" Lee asked. I held my plate in the air as he scooped chicken onto it.

"I wasn't happy and I saw the sign walking down 22nd Street one Sunday so I decided to check it out."

"Yeah, I know how you felt." He took a sip of tea. "Let's change the subject—enough of that for one night. So, what do you do for a living?"

"I work at an advertising agency." His eyes grew wide. "It's a lot less glamorous than it sounds," I grinned. "What do you do?"

"My old man has a construction company. I run the crews for him. It's fairly mundane, but I know what I'm doing." Through a mouthful of Chinese food he said, "I'm comfortable."

"Is there something else you'd like to do?" I speared a piece of broccoli.

"I've always wanted to be a photographer."

"What's stopping you? Your father?"

"You sound like my girlfriend." I chewed the broccoli, pulverizing it into baby food. I still couldn't swallow. "She's always telling me I need to take a class or find a job with a photographer. I know she's trying to help me, but I just feel worse after we discuss it."

"I can understand that." I attempted to collect myself from the various parts of the room to which I'd spread after the girlfriend revelation.

"Susan's an alcoholic. Sometimes she's a bit pious in her sobriety. She makes it sound like it would be so easy to leave the family business. She doesn't get it."

"It sounds like she only wants what's best for you."

"But I have a responsibility to my family. The business has been around since my father's grandfather. I can't walk out. They'd flip." His hands rested between the plate and the edge of the table. They were strong and sexy, callused, with small wisps of dark hair on the knuckles. He rolled his thumbs over one another.

"What's the alternative?" Lee dropped his fork on the china and the clink reverberated in the empty restaurant.

"I really just wanted to have a nice dinner. I don't want to talk about all of this stuff. No one knows the pressure I feel. No one understands that my family would excommunicate me if I walked away from the business. It's my decision and I don't want to discuss it anymore." He threw his napkin on the vacant seat next to him. "Excuse me. I need to go to the lav."

He pushed his chair away from the table and walked to the back of the restaurant in search of the 'lav.' I sneaked a couple of fried noodles.

"That's great. He pretends he likes her. She thinks he interested, and then he drops the girlfriend bomb." Kali's hands rested on her sword. *"Lying scumbag."*

"What the hell are you talking about?" Inanna asked, her skin glowing in the dim light of the restaurant. *"He asked her to get a bite to eat. He didn't propose."*

"It sounds like he's not happy with his girlfriend," Erishkigal said quietly, wrapping her cloak around herself. *"Maybe she still has a chance."*

"If she's interested in leaving Richard, why can't she find someone who's available?" Kuan Yin questioned.

"Yeah. Fuck him." Kali withdrew her sword. *"He's got 'issues,' as Kuan Yin would say. Can you imagine being too chicken to tell your Father you don't want to slop in the mud for the rest of your life?"*

"He's comfortable," Erishkigal said. "He even admitted that. What's wrong with being comfortable?"

"Comfortable and happy aren't the same thing." Kuan Yin stood and placed her left foot against the inside of her right knee in the Tree Asana. She pressed her palms against one another and raised them over her head. "Lee is a mirror of Rena's unhappiness with her life." She closed her eyes.

"You've come up with some far fetched notions before, Kuan Yin, but now you're off the deep end." Kali held the point of her sword an inch from the tip of Kuan Yin's nose, waiting to see how long it would take for her to notice.

"Rena likes him. And he likes her," Erishkigal was oblivious to the duel going on beside her. "If we try to help him, he'll see that she deserves a chance. He's a nice guy. He just needs a little encouragement."

"She needs to help herself." Inanna batted the sword away from Kuan Yin's nose.

"Maybe they can help each other." Erishkigal fingered the soft leather thongs from her sandals. "This thing with Richard isn't going to last much longer. I don't want to be alone."

"Hey, I'm sorry." Lee pulled himself up to the table. "I'm a little sensitive about that particular subject."

"No problem." I was fortified with fried noodles and sweet and sour sauce. "We don't have to talk about it."

"I actually have to get home soon. I need to be up early."

"Where do you live?"

"Brooklyn." He motioned to the waiter for the check. "Bensonhurst."

"I've been to Bensonhurst."

"Really? When?"

"My friend Maristel has a cousin who lives out there," I lied.

"I like it, but it's a pain to commute into the city."

"Do you have your own place?"

"No. I have the apartment over the garage of my parents' house." He placed a Visa inside the check. A busboy brought us an orange cut in four. We each took a slice. "I don't want to live there forever, but I'm trying to save money and they don't charge me much rent."

"Don't even talk about the rent thing. It's outrageous to have an apartment in Manhattan."

"You ought to think about Brooklyn. You know someone who lives there now." He smiled. "Well, besides your friend's cousin."

We stood on 23rd and Lexington. "I'm going to walk over to Sixth and catch the F Train." He ran his left thumbnail under the nail of his right index finger, extracting a string of orange. "I really had a nice time, Rena. I hope we can do this again sometime."

"I'd like that." He leaned over, took my hand and kissed me on the cheek. "I'll see you next Friday, then."

"You will." I wanted to kiss him. "Get home safe."

"You too. You're not going far, right?"

"No, just up the block. I'll be fine."

"Well, good night then." He let go of my hand and crossed the street. I watched him until the crowds of students from Baruch and The School of Visual Arts wiped him out of my sight.

Break

I ordered breakfast and sat at my desk feeling sorry for myself. Joni had been pushing off my promotion for three months. She always had a logical explanation as to why it wasn't a good time. In the middle of typing, the phone rang. "JC Communications, Joni Crenshaw's office. This is Rena; can I help you?"

"Hi, honey. It's Granma." The voice on the other end soothed my frayed nerves.

"Hey, Granma. How are you?"

"Better than you sound. What's wrong?"

"Nothing new," I sighed.

"Work stuff or men stuff?"

"A little of both. What's new with you?"

"Not much. Your grandfather's in Chicago for the week visiting his sister, so I'm playing single. I thought I might fly up to visit since he's not getting home until Sunday."

"Really?" I was surprised. She had never come to visit me in New York. I had assumed a city this big scared her. "That'd be great!"

"Wonderful. I'll book the ticket this morning. I'll call you and let you know what time I get in."

"Why don't you come up Thursday?" I suggested. "I could use a break from this place and I have some vacation time left. I'll take Friday off."

"Are you sure, honey? That would be great! We'll go to a show, maybe a museum. It'll be fun." We said good-bye and I returned to my typing, smiling.

After lunch, things quieted down. Joni was at a meeting across town and wasn't coming back. As I was preparing Joni's itinerary for her trip to California, I opened my drawer and dug under the message pads for a carrot. It was better than chocolate. The phone rang and I swallowed a half-eaten carrot before answering.

"Rena?" An unfamiliar voice addressed me.

"Yes?"

"This is Melissa—from the meetings at St. Nicholas'?" I cringed. I had placed my phone number in the "Sharing is Caring" book that got passed around at the end of the meeting, but no one had ever called before.

"Oh, hi. How are you?"

"Actually, I'm pretty good. I got so much out of what you shared in the meeting the other night. You know, about how horrible it feels to be isolated. And my therapist suggested I call someone from the group and invite them to dinner."

I tried to think quickly. Did I really want to have dinner with someone from St. Nicholas'? It was painless to talk for five minutes and walk out. This way I got the benefits with no real contact. My phone calls to Karen had dwindled to a couple a week. Karen had mentioned something a few times, but I made excuses about work and Richard. After two weeks, Karen stopped asking. I was relieved.

I had preserved most of my secrets, sharing enough with the group so that I felt I had the right to attend the meetings. But I was careful not to divulge any information that would breed intimacy. I still thought most of the people who went were whacko.

"I don't know, Melissa. It's kind of hectic at work," I lied.

"I've bought a chicken and salad. You can eat that can't you?" Melissa wasn't giving up.

The guilt set in. "Sure, Melissa, that'd be great." As soon as I agreed, I tried to figure out a way to cancel. We agreed to meet on Madison and 78th Street because Melissa had a doctor's appointment there at four-thirty. Then we could walk to her apartment on Park and 80th. I decided I'd be home before eight.

The bus was crowded and I stood, smashed between an Indian man with a luggage carrier holding a computer and a woman with several Duane Reade bags. As I got off the bus, I saw Melissa on the corner. I didn't know how old she was, but my guess was around forty. She was wearing a black tent dress and a long scarf, patterned in pink and green geometric shapes, was wrapped around her ample neck. Her lipstick matched the pink in the scarf and her hair was clean, pulled back in a green barrette.

"Hi, Rena!" Melissa waved as I crossed the street and I noticed her nail polish was the same color as her lipstick. "I'm glad you came." She held up a bakery box wrapped in red string. "I picked up a little something for dessert. But you don't have to worry. It's a fruit tart—no sugar!"

"Sounds good." I fought the disgust I felt at the sight of Melissa waddling down the street, mounds of flesh, one on top of the other, jiggling under the loose dress. "Who says black is slimming?" I thought to myself.

"I hope you don't mind, I have to pick up my laundry. It's on the way."

"Sure. No problem." I noticed how slowly Melissa walked and her breathing became labored after a few steps. Melissa was wheezing by the time we got to Park Avenue. Inside Carlton Cleaners, Melissa removed a ticket from her Winnie the Pooh tote bag and handed it to the Asian man behind the counter.

"Ah, yes, Miss Francis," the man took the ticket and ducked behind the movable racks of dry cleaning. He returned with a large blue and white striped laundry bag and set it on the floor at the end of the counter. "I afraid we have problem, Miss Francis." He peered over his half glasses. Several gray hairs stuck straight out from the top of his head.

"What's the matter?" Melissa was concerned. "Did something get ruined?"

The man shifted uncomfortably. "Miss Francis, I afraid we can no longer do laundry," he looked at her nervously, "for you."

"Why not?" Melissa was confused. I felt a bomb coming. I was an expert at detecting an impending explosion.

"I sorry. But workers say can't do Miss Francis clothes." He pinched his nose and scrunched his mouth into a scowl. "Stinky." His other hand, gnarled with age, grasped the ticket.

Melissa's face fell. "Besides," the man continued, "it cost too much money to dry." He held his arms open, "Clothes big, take long time to dry. Maybe cross street do for you. I sorry." He ducked back under the plastic hanging from the rack.

I didn't move. Melissa leaned against the counter, a twenty-dollar bill in her pudgy hand. Everything moved in slow motion; Melissa placed the money back in her bag. I reached for the laundry and the two of us left the store. I struggled with the heavy bag and my briefcase, but Melissa seemed not to notice. At the entrance to her building, Melissa turned to me. Her mascara had run, streaking her cheeks with black. "If you want to go, I'll understand."

I wanted to run.

"Well, at least Rena knows there are people more miserable than her," joked Kali, fingering her girdle of hands.

"I think we should go," said Erishkigal quietly, believing it was easier to run.

"Hell, no!" exclaimed Kali. "This will show her what will happen if she doesn't get this food thing under control."

"That's not the reason," Kuan Yin was shocked at Kali's callousness. *"This woman needs love and understanding, not someone who's grateful she's not in the same position. You're impossible, Kali."* Kuan Yin struggled to understand her sister.

"Fuck that," Kali sneered at Kuan Yin. *"You and your bleeding heart. Now I know why your father did what he did."*

"That was mean," interrupted Inanna. *"I agree with Erishkigal. We should go."*

"No way. Rena needs to be taught a lesson. We're staying," Kali grinned.

"Let me help you get this upstairs," I said.

"Really, you don't have to," Melissa sniffled. "I understand. You probably want to go home."

"Don't be silly." I pressed the button for the elevator.

"Thank you." She placed the key in the door. "I left the chicken cooking when I went to the doctor. It should be done by now." The warmth of rosemary and basil caressed my nose. "You can put that in the living room," Melissa instructed.

Melissa's living room was smaller than mine. I didn't think that was possible. In it were a couch and a loveseat, each in a different loud floral print, and an armoire. Two area rugs overlapped under a square coffee table. A cat reclined on the loveseat, his large white belly staring at the ceiling. I placed the laundry next to the armoire and sat down.

"It's almost done," Melissa called from the kitchen. "It just needs to cool before I cut it."

"That's fine." I leaned over and rubbed the cat's stomach. He purred and stretched his front paws over his head.

"I see you've met Jester." Melissa stood in the doorway of the kitchen, a heel of French bread in her fist. I stared at the bread. "I tried the 'no white flour' thing," Melissa explained. "But I just can't do it." She turned and walked down the hall, toward the bedroom. "I'll be back in a second."

I went to the kitchen to get a glass of water. On the counter was the chicken, a drumstick ripped off. The bag from the bread lay empty on a mountain of crumbs in the sink. I opened a cabinet, searching for a glass. The contact paper was filthy, sticky from grease. Dirty dishes were piled next to the microwave. I wasn't thirsty anymore. Escape was the only thing on my mind. But I didn't feel right walking out now.

I was sitting on the couch when Melissa returned wearing a green sweat suit. "I have low fat salad dressing," she announced. Crumbs had collected in the corner of her mouth and I wanted to scream at her to wipe them away. "I hope you don't mind eating off of TV trays. I don't have room for a dining table in this place."

"No, that's fine." I wasn't hungry. "Could I use the bathroom?"

"Sure. First door on the right," Melissa pointed down the hall. "I'll get the dishes."

I shut the door behind me and collapsed. I sat on the furry leopard toilet lid, my head hanging between my legs. A strong sour smell burned the inside of my nose. I looked up and noticed a black wicker hamper across from me. A half a dozen shampoo bottles peeked out from behind a jungle print shower curtain. On the sink were three colors of liquid make-up, compacts of powder and blush and several cases of eye shadow. A toothbrush was suspended in a metal holder and a small crack in the mirror of the medicine cabinet was surrounded by dried hairspray. I stared at my reflection as I washed my hands. I needed to leave.

I found her in the kitchen, breaking lettuce into two bowls. "I'm sorry, but I'm not feeling well. I need to go."

"That's an original excuse."

"Excuse me?"

"You heard me. Why should I have expected you to be any different?"

"Different from what?" I was defensive.

"From anyone."

"I don't know what you're talking about." I picked at my cuticles.

"Just go." I heard her sniffling. My shoes seemed glued to the floor. Maybe it was just the fact that the tile hadn't been mopped in fifty years.

"You are so full of shit." She whirled around and waved the paring knife at me.

"Put the knife down, Melissa." It was definitely time to go. She faced me, her cheeks flushed.

"You sit there in those meetings and talk about how hard it is to be alone. How difficult it is to have people treat you like you're from another planet because you're not a size ten." A piece of lettuce clung to the sweatshirt above her left breast.

"I assumed you understood what it was like to see someone's eyes beg you not to sit next to them on the bus." Melissa walked over to the refrigerator and pulled two carrots out of the vegetable crisper. "But you risk their contempt because your feet ache. So you squeeze in while everyone around watches. And you know they're thinking 'What the hell is she doing?'"

"They can't stand to feel your flesh touch theirs as your hips spill into their seat. And they squirm, pulling a jacket around them, hoping it will create more room." She pushed her sleeves up to her elbows and reached to the back of the bottom shelf, eventually retrieving an onion in a Ziplock bag. I held my breath. "Finally, if you're lucky, another seat becomes available and they run to it, grateful to get away from you. And you stumble between relief and anger and denial."

She turned toward the sink and threw the knife and carrots onto the empty bread bag. She unzipped the baggie and took out the onion. She opened a cabinet and brought down a cutting board. She began peeling the brown skin from the onion. "I thought you understood. But you don't. So go."

"Look, Melissa ...." I began.

"Don't apologize." She minced the onion. The knife made clicking sounds on the plastic cutting board. "Just go."

"I wasn't going to apologize." My fingernails cut my palm as I clenched my fists. "I wanted to say that I don't know anyone who could've dealt with what happened tonight and not had some sort of reaction. I tried; I really did. But I have to go now."

"Good-bye." Melissa faced the sink, having moved onto the task of peeling the carrots. Guilt sucked me into its vortex and I changed my mind. "Why don't I stay for dinner? You've worked so hard."

"Don't do me any fucking favors." Melissa turned on her heel and glared at me, her eyes flaming like burning coal. My cheeks burned. "I don't need your do-gooder attitude. You don't want to be here. I don't want you here. Go."

I slammed the door to her apartment and stabbed the elevator button until the doors opened. When I got home, I kicked my shoes off under the futon and retrieved the message from Richard on the answering machine. I called him back, but he wasn't home. I couldn't remember if I'd told him I was having dinner with Melissa. I grabbed my keys and walked to the deli on the corner.

The phone was ringing as I unlocked the door. "Hey, Ren. What's going on?" I could see Richard sitting on his couch, pushing his hair back, trying to cover the bald spot that was growing on the top of his head.

I told him about the episode with Melissa.

"Why do you hang around with those losers?" He sounded confused.

"You know, in case you haven't noticed, hanging around those losers has helped me lose twenty-five pounds. Not that you'd notice or say anything."

"C'mon Rena, that's not fair," he said. "I never know where you're going to be with it. Sometimes you want to talk about it and sometimes I ask you a question and you act like I'm a Russian spy trying to get a national secret. I can't predict your moods. It's just easier not to say anything."

"Who asked you to predict my moods?" I plucked a shoe with my toes from under the futon and flung it across the room. "I want you to tell me I look good, that it's paying off, anything."

"Sorry."

"That's all you have to say?"

"I don't know what to say anymore, Ren."

"That's just fucking great. I try to do something nice for Melissa and I witness probably the most humiliating experience of her life. I'm trapped in her house while she's binging her brains out and when I tell her I'm leaving, she attacks me. And now you tell me you don't know what to say. Well, I know what to say." I slammed the phone into the receiver. "Fuck him! Fuck her, too!" I yelled to my empty apartment. "Who needs this shit?"

The phone rang. I stared at it for a moment and picked it up. "Richard, I don't want to talk to you."

"That's fine, but it's Maristel." She had been leaving messages since the trip to Brooklyn and I had been returning them during the day when she wouldn't be home, initiating an endless game of phone tag.

"Sorry for the way I answered the phone," I mumbled.

"It's OK. I was calling to see if you were all right."

"Yeah, I'm fine." I ran my feet under the rug.

"Why haven't you called me back?" Maristel sounded hurt.

"I've been so busy. Work's been crazy."

"Did you get the promotion?" she asked excitedly.

"They haven't decided yet," I lied.

"I hope you get it, if you still want it."

"Yeah, me too. Look, I really have to go."

"Are you sure you're OK?"

"Yeah, I'll call you later."

"Promise?"

"Sure. Bye."

I stared at the bag of food sitting on the floor.

"She can't do this," Kali whispered, hands on her sword.

"She's had a rough night," argued Erishkigal, playing with her bone hairpin.

"Did it occur to either of you that Melissa was embarrassed tonight? That she genuinely likes Rena?" asked Kuan Yin. "That she appreciates what she shares in the meetings?"

"Rena did the right thing getting out when she did," Inanna said rubbing her blue eyes. "It was the only logical thing to do after what happened."

"Besides, Melissa only invited Rena to dinner because she felt sorry for her," added Erishkigal.

"You're sure of that?" Kuan Yin sighed. "It's not because Rena smiles or wishes her a good day when she sees her?"

"Melissa asked her because she knew Rena would feel too guilty to say no." Erishkigal removed and reinserted the hairpin at the nape of her neck.

"But the eating thing doesn't feel good anymore." Kali stomped her foot. "There's no pleasure, no satisfaction. Not like there used to be."

"It's the last time, I promise." Erishkigal grew quiet, nervously trying to figure how Rena could soothe herself without food.

Opening a bag of corn chips, I flipped on the television.

Break

Richard offered to let me borrow his car to pick up my grandmother from the airport, but not before he lectured me on the proper way to change lanes. I drove to Newark to get her and didn't get lost because Richard had made me take three dry runs the first time he ever let me keep the car when he went out of town. I think he was afraid I wouldn't pick him up.

While we sat at the Holland Tunnel for a half-hour, my grandmother filled me in on the current family dysfunction. Faith and Raymond were definitely having trouble. A friend of hers had seen him at a restaurant with another woman. I almost felt sorry for her. Then I remembered she had created the whole mess. My grandfather's sister was in the hospital getting a knee replaced. And my father's new marriage to a twenty-four-year-old graduate student was still in the honeymoon stage. He'd get sick of her too, eventually.

We were forty minutes late getting to Pete's Tavern to meet Richard. He was sitting at the O. Henry booth up front, sipping a beer. I could tell he was pissed, but the whole population of New Jersey simultaneously deciding to go into Manhattan wasn't my fault.

"Hey," he stood to kiss my grandmother on the cheek. "Where have you guys been? I was getting worried."

Granma took off her fedora and waited for Richard to help her with her wrap. "It's so lovely to see you, Richard. Thank you for letting Rena borrow your car to fetch me." He uncloaked her and wadded the black felt into a ball. I grabbed it from him before she noticed and hung it on the hook next to the booth.

"What can I get you?" The aproned waiter hovered over us.

"I'll have a Manhattan," my grandmother said.

I raised my eyebrows. I wasn't accustomed to her drinking liquor. I don't think I'd ever seen her have a beer or a glass of wine. "Absolut and tonic with lime, please." The waiter looked at Richard.

"Oh, I'm OK," he dismissed the waiter. "I can't stay, remember, Rena? I have to meet Tony at eight. I thought you guys were going to be here almost an hour ago."

"Well, the traffic wasn't my fault, Richard. Can't you stay a little longer?"

"I wish I could." I knew he was lying. My grandmother and he weren't the best of friends. Part of me believed it was because she'd never think that anyone was good enough for her only granddaughter. But I knew she didn't like him.

We had gone to Pittsburgh for Thanksgiving last year and we fought the whole drive. By the time we arrived for dinner, we were barely speaking. He had been sullen and critical, eyeing everything I put into my mouth. It was Thanksgiving. I didn't think about dieting on the holidays. I know she noticed. He didn't offer to help clean up and opted to sit in the living room watching a *Star Trek* marathon.

My grandmother was old fashioned. She didn't believe in sex before marriage and was furious with my mother for letting Richard and me sleep in the same room. When we all went out to dinner that Friday night, he didn't even offer to pick up part of the check. In her subtle atomic bomb way, she asked him how his job was going and if he found the money satisfactory. I don't think Richard caught on, but I knew exactly what she was doing.

The waiter returned with our drinks. "Can I get the keys, Ren?" Richard asked.

"You're sure you can't stay just a little bit?" My grandmother asked. "I'm sure your friend will understand." She smiled at him, her green eyes like lasers. "I know it would mean a lot to Rena."

"I would love to, Mrs. Sutcliffe, but I can't." He gulped the rest of the bottle.

"Should you be driving if you've been drinking, Richard? I hear on the news all the time about these drunk driving accidents."

"I'm taking a cab, Mrs. Sutcliffe. I need the keys for tomorrow."

I sat there, sipping my drink, watching him squirm and not wanting to stop it. "Let him go, Granma. He and Tony have had these plans for weeks." I placed the keys on the table. "Have a good time."

"Yeah, thanks." He grabbed his leather bomber jacket from beside him and leaned over to kiss me on the cheek. "It was nice seeing you again, Mrs.

Sutcliffe. I hope you have a nice visit." He extended his arm to shake her hand.

"I won't be seeing you again?" She quizzed.

"I'm real busy at work right now. I don't know if I can. But if I don't see you, have a safe trip back." He took the keys and made his way through the crowd and out the door. I got up and switched to the other side of the booth.

"Look, Granma. We've been having some problems lately. He probably feels uncomfortable."

"Honey, whatever makes you happy is fine with me."

We ordered dinner and talked about what we were going to do for the next two days. There was a Richard Avedon exhibit at the Museum of Modern Art. And we both wanted to see *Victor/Victoria*. We caught a cab to my apartment and I was nervous about her reaction. "This is adorable, Rena!" she exclaimed on the landing. "A real single gal's New York apartment. And you've decorated it so beautifully!" I felt ten feet high.

The next morning, we went to my cheap little diner on 28th and Lexington for eggs and pancakes. My grandmother was a small woman and I'd never seen her struggle with her weight. She never wore pants and had a flair for placing a scarf or a pin in the right place. Over coffee I told her about my mother's last visit.

"I'm sorry, Rena. Faith means well," she poured cream into her decaf. "But sometimes she doesn't think about the consequences. She can be selfish that way. But you could've spoken up. You could've told her you didn't feel comfortable and suggested something else to do. You can't blame this entirely on her."

I was stunned. She was actually sticking up for my mother. "I'm not defending her actions." She read my mind. "All I'm saying is you have a tendency to blame her for everything without looking at how you reacted. Am I right?"

I didn't like this line of questioning. "You know how she can be, Granma. She sweeps into New York, complains about my apartment, refuses to take public transportation and any time I disagree with her, it's a fight. I wasn't up for it."

"So, instead, you subjected yourself to a make-over and trying on clothes that didn't fit you?" She sipped her coffee. "By the way, you look very good, Rena. I meant to tell you last night, but my old bones were begging for sleep and I forgot to mention it. What have you been doing?"

I told her about the support group. I was never afraid to be honest with her. I told her that I was thinking of not going back because I'd lost almost all the weight I wanted to and I didn't see the point.

"You've always chosen food to handle your problems, Rena. Ever since you were a little girl. Faith uses booze. Your father can't keep his hands off a pretty woman. But you've always used food." I wasn't prepared for this kind of honesty from her. It was weird and uncomfortable.

"I can remember finding you in the kitchen with your hand in the cookie jar on more than one occasion. I tried to talk to Faith about it, but she wouldn't, or maybe couldn't, listen." She pulled a lipstick out of her bag and opened a little mirror. "I don't think it would be wise to stop going just because you've lost weight. You need to figure out why you do it or you're just going to start doing it again."

"What are you talking about? I've lost almost thirty-five pounds. And I'm telling you, some of these people are insane."

"You need to do what you feel comfortable doing, honey. All I'm saying is that we don't do things without a reason. Whatever you decide is fine with me." She smiled at me, her eyes sparkling through the wrinkles. She had let her hair go gray and it was stunning on her. I hoped I looked that good in my seventies. We paid the check and headed to the museum.

"Rena's grandmother doesn't know what she's talking about," cried Erishkigal.

"Who the hell does she think she is telling Rena what to do?" Kali agreed. "She doesn't know anything about her. She hasn't seen her in almost a year."

"What she's saying makes a lot of sense, Kali, if you would listen." Kuan Yin silently chided herself for getting snippy. Dealing with Kali was one test after another.

"After that scene at Melissa's, I think she ought to run from those people." Kali argued.

"I told you going there wasn't a good idea," Erishkigal whimpered.

"Enough bickering!" Inanna raised her hands to the heavens. "You two are going to drive me insane. Rena's grandmother is the only person in her life who's been vaguely supportive. Maybe we ought to listen."

"No fucking way. She's lost the weight. It's time to go. Buh - bye!" From
deep in her throat, Kali laughed, raspy and evil.

We spent the next two days running around New York. We even took
the Grayline bus tour. My grandmother was pretty fit for someone her age
and we didn't stop the entire time. The last night she was here, we went to
Canastel's, one of my favorite Grammercy Park Italian restaurants. Before
we left the house, Richard called to say he needed the car the next morning, so he couldn't let me borrow it to drive her to the airport. I was furious.

"I'll be honest, Granma. I've been thinking of breaking up with him anyway. I just don't feel the same way about him as I used to. Things have
changed."

"How do you mean?" We were walking down Park Avenue to the restaurant.

"He hasn't been supportive about these meetings—or the fact that I want
to lose weight. He complains about it enough, but then when I do something he suddenly becomes mute."

"He's scared, Rena."

"What the hell are you talking about?"

"He's afraid that if you lose weight and other men become interested in
you, you'll leave him."

"That's total bull… crap." I couldn't swear in front of my grandmother.

"I don't think so. Maybe you should talk to him."

"I know you don't like him. Why are you defending him?"

"I'm not doing it for him, Rena. I'm concerned about you. Make sure it's
really what you want before you do it. It's hard to take something like that
back."

We shared a bottle of wine and were a little tipsy walking home. We giggled like schoolgirls about the scene at the bar. It was hysterical watching
the middle-aged men trying to pick up girls in their twenties. It was easier to
joke about it than to think about how one of them could've been my father.

The next morning I carried my grandmother's suitcase outside and hailed
her a cab. I was teary as I said good-bye. "Rena, I just want you to be happy.
You deserve to be happy. And you need to do whatever it is that's going to
make you feel that way." She held my face in her gloved hands. "I love you,

sweetheart." She kissed me on the forehead and climbed into the cab. I had never felt so sad.

Later that day, I called Richard. I knew I should probably do it in person, but I wanted it be over. Being with him didn't make me happy anymore and my grandmother was right. I deserved to be happy.

"Richard?" I chewed the inside of my mouth. "I need to talk to you."

"Does it have to be right now?" I heard voices in the background. "I'm kind of busy."

"Yes, it does have to be right now."

"OK, make it quick."

What a perfect out. I took a deep breath. "I don't think we should see each other anymore."

"What the fuck are you talking about?" he screamed. "Hold on, hold on." I heard a door shut.

"I'm not happy, Richard. I want out."

"You're fucking insane. I swear to Christ, Rena. Where do you get this shit?"

"I'm not the one who's insane, Richard. You never listen to anything I say. You constantly criticize me. I don't need your shit anymore. Good-bye." I resisted the urge to slam the phone, but stomped my foot on the floor. I felt good. I was in control of my life. My stomach growled. It was almost five and I hadn't eaten since breakfast. It was reasonable that I should be hungry. I couldn't decide what I wanted, so I figured I'd get a little of everything that appealed to me and save the rest for lunch the next day.

I had enough time to get high and take a shower before the delivery boy showed up. I sat on the floor with a mountain of food from the diner. I was sure I could eat half the cheeseburger, a piece of the Reuben and a bite of the chocolate cake. How I ended up with nothing but empty Styrofoam was a mystery. My stomach felt like it was going to explode. I considered sticking my finger down my throat, but vetoed that idea because I didn't want to deal with the mess. I'd have to eat carrots and celery for the next three days to make up for this. Usually, just one day of starving was enough to keep the weight from coming back. I thought I might feel better if I went for a walk, so I got dressed and was in the lobby when I saw Richard at the front door.

I was trapped. He had a key. I tried to run back into my apartment, but he was faster than me and he grabbed my arm. "What the hell is going on?"

"I'm not going to argue with you in the hall, Richard. In fact, I don't want to talk to you at all."

"We've been together for almost four years, Rena. And I'm supposed to accept you calling me out of the blue and telling me you don't want to see me anymore? What the fuck is wrong with you?"

"You're what's wrong with me." I screamed, my temper getting the best of me.

"Let's take this inside." He put his key in my door.

"No!" All of the empty diner cartons were on the floor. He turned the lock and shoved me inside. He stood on the top step, me behind him on the landing, and stared at the mess in front of the couch. The open jars of ketchup and mayonnaise were on the coffee table. I started to cry.

"What the hell is going on?" He walked down the steps and over to the pile of trash, disgust registered on his face as he picked up each container. "You're crazy, Rena. I don't understand you. How could you have eaten all of this? How?"

"It's none of your business." I didn't owe him an explanation.

"My friends were right about you. I didn't believe them. They all said that you couldn't be as big as you are, were, only eating what I saw you eat. You do this all the time don't you?"

"I hadn't eaten all day. I was hungry."

"You've got a problem, man, a real problem. You're sick. You know what? This break up idea is looking better and better." He stepped backward into one of the boxes, splashing ketchup on the floor. "I can't deal with this." He walked toward the steps, tracking the ketchup all over the floor.

"Look what you're doing!" I yelled. "You're getting ketchup all over the place."

"That's the least of your problems, Rena."

"I'm sorry I disgust you. But I guess that's par for the course, lately."

"No, it's been par for the course for a long time. I felt sorry for you. That's the only reason I've stayed with you. I knew you had no other friends and would have nobody if it weren't for me." His face was set and hard. "But I'm sure you and your delivery boy from the diner will have a great life. I'm out of here." He brushed past me on the landing, his eyes drenching me in a fog of loathing. "You just lost the best thing that ever happened to you." The door slammed and I was alone.

"How could you have done that, Kali?" Erishkigal flailed her arms at her dark sister, striking her repeatedly on the arm.

"Well, it's not the way I intended to end it, but at least it's done." Kali was satisfied. She brushed Erishkigal's slaps away as if she were chasing a gnat.

"Rena is devastated," Kuan Yin wept. "This is really what you wanted?"

"Look, Kuan Yin," Inanna interrupted. "Kali's right. This may not have been the best way, but at least he's out of her life now. He dragged her down. She'll be better off without him." Inanna suddenly felt Rena's pain and began to cry. "Eventually." She pounded her knuckles against her heart but heard nothing but a dull thud. "Hey! Where's my breastplate?"

"You're evil, Kali." Erishkigal shouted, ignoring Inanna's crisis. "You caused all of this. This is all your fault." She began tugging at her hair, ripping it out in clumps.

"She'll get over it. It'll teach her not to fuck around with food again. And Richard is gone. That's all that matters."

I cleaned up the mess in my apartment. I should've listened to my grandmother, but I couldn't take it back now. I was totally alone, except for those losers at St. Nicholas'. I laid on the couch watching some ridiculous made-for-cable movie. And I cried. I thought losing weight was supposed to make me happy.

If my grandmother had been right about this, maybe she was right about the group. I decided not to quit right away. I had to be sure before I did, because I couldn't face going back there after I left.

Break

The morning after Richard had stormed out I woke up hoarse. My eyes burned from all the crying and I had to plead with them to stay open. I argued with myself about calling in sick. After inventing several believable scenarios in my head, I settled on cramps. No one ever wanted details about that. Or diarrhea. But I had used that one last time.

I moped around the apartment all day watching people attack each other on *Ricki Lake* and *Jerry Springer*. I couldn't bring myself to eat after Richard's tirade, even though my stomach was screaming. I contemplated suicide. I was way too chicken to cut myself, but pills of some sort seemed appealing. I would go to sleep and never wake up. Never have to deal with seeing Richard—or any of his cavemen. I wouldn't have to listen to one more excuse about why Joni couldn't promote me. My mother might finally understand how her "help" ate away at me. I didn't care that the church wouldn't bury me because I had committed a mortal sin.

Then I thought of my grandmother. But she wasn't going to be alive for much longer and I'd see her wherever it was that dead people went. I put on my robe and got my mail, hoping my new issue of *Entertainment Weekly* was there. Instead, I found a solitary envelope, lonely and thin, in the little steel box. It was from Maristel. I ripped it open in the lobby and read it in my bedroom slippers.

> Dear Rena,
>
> I don't understand why you won't talk to me. I thought we were friends. I've tried so hard to be there for you, but you won't let me. I know what happened that night in Brooklyn couldn't have been easy for you, but you've completely shut me out. I'm not perfect, but your behavior is hurtful and unforgivable. I try to help and all you do is get defensive and mean. I can't deal with it anymore. I hope you find what it is you're looking for. I really do. But you're going to have to do it without me. I hope you make other friends who care about you as much as I did.
>
> Maristel

I retreated into my empty apartment, the last nail firmly in place. Another two hours of transvestites, gothic punks, and cheating spouses and I was done feeling sorry for myself. I was fairly attractive—thinner—funny. Fuck Richard. Fuck Maristel. Fuck my mother. There had to be something better out there for me. Maybe I wasn't ready to quit just yet.

After showering, a major task considering my exhaustion, I was invigorated. I went to St. Nicholas' and prayed that I could bring myself to talk about some of this. Maybe they were right about keeping it bottled up never helping. Sitting in the hard metal chair, I felt a hand on my shoulder. It was Melissa. I hadn't seen her since that night. For a couple of months, I avoided this meeting so I wouldn't run into her. And here she was, looming over me, large and intimidating.

"Hello, Rena." Her voice was sweet and thick, like Coca-Cola syrup.

"Hi, Melissa. How are you?"

"Fine now that I've found another place to do my laundry and realized what a hypocrite you are." I had tried to be nice, tried to be a decent human being and she was twisting everything around to make me look like an asshole. I wondered who in the group she had told.

"Look, Melissa. Just because you can't get your food thing under control, don't fucking take it out on me."

"You're pathetic." A piece of her spit landed on my cheek and I rubbed it off with the back of my hand. "You have no right to be here. Your food thing is no more under control than mine. Who do you think you are preaching to me? You think you're better than me because you've lost a few pounds?"

"That would be almost forty pounds, Melissa. And yes, as a matter of fact, I do. At least I can fit into a bus seat now." She waddled away and sat in a chair near the leader. Melissa was the first one to share after the main speaker and she had her eyes glued to me as she started.

"I hesitated about whether to share this with the group, because it's so humiliating, but something happened a while ago that I feel compelled to talk about." I couldn't believe she was going down this road. "I tried to put myself out there, even though it's so difficult for me, and I invited a member to my house for dinner. Something embarrassing happened on the way to my place and instead of being supportive and understanding, this person ran away, leaving me alone and mortified. I was so hurt."

I couldn't listen anymore. My heart was racing and I didn't want to attract attention by leaving, but I couldn't sit there and listen to her spin her yarn in front of the people that I, too, wanted help from tonight. I slid out of my chair and sneaked out, knowing I would never come back. Once I was through the door, I bolted through the entryway and smacked into a woman coming out another door.

"Ay!" she yelled as I connected with her shoulder.

"I am so sorry." I rubbed my arm.

"Me too," she smiled, massaging hers. "I just had to get out of that meeting. All of these people talking about their wives leaving them and having beer for breakfast and losing their jobs because they were drunk all the time. Holy Jesus!"

"You were at a meeting?"

"Yeah. For people who have problems with alcohol." She rolled her head when she said "problem." "I felt like I was on the *Titanic* or something for Christ's sake. And I'm not gonna let all those crazy motherfuckers take me down with them." We stood on the top step outside and she lit a Newport. She looked Puerto Rican, her caramel skin smooth and unblemished and her black eyes smoldering. My shoulder ached. For someone who was barely five feet tall and a hundred pounds soaking wet, she packed a serious wallop.

"Celia E." She laughed and held out her hand. "I guess I can say Estevez—sorry, old habit."

"Rena."

"How 'bout we blow this Popsicle stand mommie and go have a drink?"

"I thought you were at a meeting for people who had trouble with drinking."

"So?"

"Sure. A drink would be great."

We went to Cavanaugh's on Third Avenue and claimed a booth in the back. Over vodka and cigarettes we shared life stories. I told her about Richard and my job and losing weight and what had happened with Melissa.

"That's fucked up, chica. You don't need no fat sorry ass pullin' you down. You've done what you needed to and she can't. That's why she's so mean to you."

"I thought maybe I really was an asshole."

"That's the problem with goin' to these meetings." Celia searched for a place in the butt-loaded ashtray to stub out her cigarette. "They don't tell you at the beginnin' that everyone who's in those rooms is just as fucked up as you are. And you're so desperate for help that you listen to what everyone says without questioning it. It's dangerous, man. I'm tellin' you. Who needs advice from the admittedly insane?"

"But I did lose weight. It did help."

"Sure, but look at you now. You tried to be nice and you got bent over the kitchen sink. Trust me—leave it alone. You dropped the pounds. You're fine."

I hesitated. "Why do you go?"

"I have to. It's part of my probation."

"Probation?"

"Yeah. My boss at the plumbing shop caught me taking a hundred dollars out of petty cash. Stupid bleeding-heart liberal, he convinced the judge to give me probation as long as I went to three meetings a week. I'd rather be in jail than sit through that shit." She laughed. "The funny thing is, he fired me two months later."

"So why'd you leave tonight?'"

"My sponsor didn't show up. I'll just tell her I was there. I heard enough to make her believe I stayed the whole time—like who the speaker was and shit. Not a problem." We ordered another round of drinks. Drunk and unable to breathe from all the cigarettes, I left around eleven. As I was going, Celia climbed onto a bar stool, her short black skirt riding up her ass, and started flirting with a tall, dreadlocked Jamaican. I wondered what her boyfriend, Carlos, would say. I told myself it was none of my business.

"Finally, someone who can tell the bullshit from the bullshit!" Kali smirked, dancing a little jig on the edge of Erishkigal's sheath.

"Kali, I don't know about this." Inanna wanted Rena to be thin and happy as much as her sister, but Celia seemed a little too dangerous. "Celia goes with what feels good without thinking about the consequences. And there are always consequences."

"Doesn't anyone care what I think?" Erishkigal whined.

"Not particularly," Kali laughed. "Where have you gotten Rena so far?"

"Don't judge her," Kuan Yin interrupted, lightly patting Erishkigal's shoulder. "We each have a purpose, Kali."

"And mine is to take control from Little Miss Scaredy Cat here." The corner of Kali's mouth reached for her nose.

"That's not it at all," Kuan Yin scolded.

"Then what is it?" Erishkigal questioned meekly. "None of this is my fault."

"Rena needs all of us if she is to evolve. It's time for Kali to provide a different perspective." Kuan Yin looked peaceful, her long lashes touching her eyebrows.

"What if I don't let go?" Erishkigal asked.

"I'll beat your ass," Kali threatened, raising her fists toward Erishkigal.

"Fine. Have it your way." Erishkigal squeaked, huddled behind Kuan Yin. "But I'm not responsible anymore."

I walked home. Still drunk, I threw my clothes on the floor and fell into bed without taking my make-up off.

Kali

The Fifth Goddess

Celia called the following Wednesday and we met at McGuire's on Third and 19th. "I've been thinking," she said sipping her beer. "You've lost a whole person, chica! It's time for a Celia Estevez make-over! Especial!"

"What are you talking about?" I didn't know whether to be flattered or insulted.

"Leave those long skirts to the Little House on the fuckin' Prairie. You have a figure now, girlfriend. Let the world see it."

"I don't know, Celia."

"It's like you're a butterfly waiting to take flight," she fluttered her fingers around her face. "But you're stuck in your Chrysler."

"I think you mean chrysalis."

"Whatever. C'mon, we'll go to Astor Place and get those curls buzzed. They make you look old. Maybe a new color." She reached across the table and fingered my hair. "Black. I see you in black."

"My hair?"

"Sí. Like the night. Maybe a couple of lines cut in over your ears. It'll show off your cheeks."

"I don't know."

"Think about it." She lit a cigarette. "In the meantime, you need to start working out."

"I already do." I wanted to melt into the booth.

"Could've fooled me." Smoke rings drifted up to the tin ceiling. "My trainer, José, is the man!" She snapped her fingers. "He'll whip your ass into shape so quick you won't recognize yourself." She studied me for a minute. "Chica, don't take this the wrong way. I see how hard you've worked. I want to speed the process up, that's all. Don't be offended." She waved the waitress over and ordered two more beers and some mozzarella sticks.

"I'm not offended," I offered. "A little caught off guard maybe."

"Don't be. We'll be struttin' our stuff on St. Mark's before you can say 'Gracias.'"

Maybe she was right. Change would be good. A whole new Rena. No Richard to criticize. "OK."

"Cool. I'll call José tonight and set up a session for you." The waitress put the mozzarella and the beers in front of us. "So you've been working out? What have you been doing?"

"Walking mostly. I have a few aerobics tapes. And I bought weights a few weeks ago."

"You don't belong to a gym?"

"No. I have no desire to a part of that whole scene." I'd belonged to New York Sports Club for a year. I never wanted to see Lycra leotards again.

"What scene? I go to the Y on 23rd Street. Honey, there's no scene. It's not like going to Crunch or the Health and Racquet Club where everyone's there just to get laid." Marinara sauce dribbled down her chin. "It's just sweat and muscle, baby." She pushed her long bangs away from her mouth. I munched a celery stick.

"I don't picture myself doing squats in a thong."

"You will!" she laughed. "Once José gets his hands on you. I'll call you tonight and let you know what time to meet us tomorrow."

I agreed, reluctant, but excited. After we paid the check, we walked down Third, peering in the windows of the furniture and framing stores. We stopped at Staghorn for Celia to get a birthday card for Carlos. Celia caught the bus to go home and I went home and did laundry.

I walked into the YMCA on Thursday at five-thirty after work. It reminded me of being in high school. The gray flecked tile was shiny, but scuffed. A security guard stood by the elevator. Bright colored papers hung on the bulletin board advertising Summer Camp, swimming lessons, and babysitting services. Three black teens stood by the soda machine, jeans hanging loosely around their slender male hips, their heads covered with knit caps even though it was sixty degrees outside. Two women talked near a door while they rocked their babies back and forth in strollers.

I wore black leggings, a baggy T-shirt, and a windbreaker. I had bought new sneakers at lunchtime, blue and white Reebock's. Their fresh rubber smell bounced off the old sweat and clean towels stacked on the registration desk. Celia was working until five at Tootsie La Frock, a funky vintage clothing store on 11th Street. I sat on a bench under the directory of departments. "Can I help you?" The security guard asked.

"No, I'm waiting for a friend." I smiled.

"You a member?"

"Thinking about it." Celia bounded in the door.

"Ay, chica. I am so sorry." She handed a laminated card to the buff man at the registration desk. "And she's my guest."

"Do you have a pass?" His baritone voice was like molasses, thick and rich.

"I must have one in here somewhere." Celia hefted her gym bag onto the counter and started pulling things out of it—a jog bra, leopard thong, shampoo, deodorant, "I know it's in here." The bag was bottomless. She continued piling items on the counter.

A hand started putting Celia's things back into her bag. "It's OK," he smiled plastically, his patience expired. "Remember it next time." He handed us each a towel and we got on the elevator. When the doors closed, Celia burst into a fit of laughter.

"It works every time!"

"You mean you didn't have a guest pass for me?" I was appalled.

"Somewhere—probably in my apartment—under the couch or in the magazine rack." She was still laughing.

"What if he wouldn't have let me in?"

"He did, didn't he? Relax."

"But what if he didn't?"

"He did. We don't need to worry about it." She slung her bag over her shoulder. "This is us."

We walked into the women's locker room. The odor of dirty towels was part of the sweet soapy mist emanating from the showers. Women of all sizes walked around in various phases of naked and an emaciated blond stretched on a worn red vinyl mat. I threw my things in a locker and went to the bathroom. When I returned, Celia was reapplying lipstick.

"We're going to work out," I said, confused. "Why are you putting on lipstick?"

"José's still a man, honey." She blew a kiss to her reflection in the mirror, twirled the bright red wax down into its cylinder and snapped on the lid. "Ready?"

"This is so cool!" Kali shook her hips. "I can't wait for her to wear some tight jeans and skimpy blouses."

"She's petrified." Erishkigal pointed a finger at Kali. "And it's all your fault. She doesn't belong here with all these sweaty obsessed people."

"*You're touched.*" *Kali swirled an index finger at her temple.* "*This is exactly where she belongs. With people who want to look good.*"

"*I want her to look good, too. But why does she need to let the world see her lumps and bulges while she struggles on these contraptions?*" *Erishkigal eyed the Gravitron.*

"*She's wearing a big shirt. No one can see anything.*" *Inanna said, blousing her robe over her belt.* "*I think it's a good idea for her to get fit physically. It'll give her a purpose—some focus.*"

"*What about in the locker room?*" *The distressed tone in Erishkigal's voice hung in the air.* "*You have to get naked to take a shower. Those little washrags they call towels won't go all the way around her body!*" *She shivered.* "*It's too soon for Rena to be here.*"

"*She can bring her own towel next time.*" *Inanna reasoned.* "*This will be good for her. And it'll give her a chance to meet some new people.*"

"*It'll also help reduce her stress level,*" *added Kuan Yin, her flat nose pressed against the glass of the aerobics room.*

"*So there.*" *Kali flicked her black tongue at Erishkigal.*

We climbed the two flights of stairs to the weight room. I was puffing by the time we reached the top. I had never seen so many firm biceps, ripped abs, and squat necks in my life. Most of them were men, but a few women stared at themselves in a wall length mirror as they lifted free weights. "Hey, José, honey." Celia squealed.

"Hey mommie!" José swaggered toward us, his enormous tanned arms swinging from his shoulders like a gorilla's. He had on shiny turquoise bike shorts and a torn tank that said "NYU Fitness Department—XXXX LARGE." Celia threw her arms around his neck and he patted her butt.

"This is my friend, Rena." She turned toward me. "Rena—José." He extended his hand and I shook it. It was large and damp.

"Nice to meet you." His black eyes gulped Celia down like lemonade in her hot pink Lycra. "Celia, why don't you get started and let me talk to Rena about what her goals are. Sí, chica?"

"OK." She pouted.

"So, Rena, what is it you want to accomplish?" His eyes were glued to Celia's ass as she sashayed toward a machine designed to work the inner and outer thighs.

I clapped my hands and José's head snapped toward me. "I've lost almost forty pounds and Celia and I were talking and thought it might be a good time for me to get serious about working out." He gave me his full attention, his dark eyes penetrating and serious. "I really want to be leaner and more toned. I feel so flabby." José nodded. Then I noticed Celia winking as she rhythmically opened and closed her legs to the beat of "Holiday" by Madonna. I turned around and there she was again in the mirror.

"Busted, I know." José grinned, looking at his feet. "I'm sorry, Rena. She gets under my skin. Let's go out here." We walked into another room filled with weight benches and very large men. He got an index card from the filing cabinet in the corner and started writing. Twenty minutes later he had designed a routine for me. "I'll walk you through it a couple of times, but it's simple enough to do on your own," he explained.

We started on the stationery bike. After ten minutes my heart was racing, my cheeks were pink and I was sucking wind. "Alright, you should be warmed up now." José walked over to the rowing machine. He demonstrated the proper way to use it and stuck me on it for ten minutes. My legs were like jelly. He headed toward the Nordic Track and waved for me to follow. He recommended I only do the leg part the first few times until I got used to how it felt. I still almost fell off.

Back in the room with the weight machines, he explained that I shouldn't use resistance training on the same muscle group two days in a row. We started with upper body. He tentatively held my fleshy hips while I attempted chin-ups. Then we did a few sets of bicep curls, tricep extensions, pushups, pectoral stretches, and sit-ups. I collapsed on the mat, knees in the air, drenched. Celia bounced over, not a drop of sweat on her face or one dark spot on her pink leotard. And her lipstick looked fresh.

"How are you, chica?"

"I can't move."

"Sure you can." She pressed her feet against mine and reached out her hands. I grabbed them and she leaned back, pulling me up. I was lightheaded. Cold sweat dripped down my back. "What you need is a good hot steam and a shower." We walked, well she jogged, and I hobbled, down the steps to the locker room. "Isn't that José fine?"

"He's nice looking." I agreed. "You seem to have quite an effect on him."

"We flirt. But I love Carlos." Celia peeled off her clothes and stood naked in front of her locker. Her caramel skin was smooth and stretch-mark-free. Her breasts were small, but full, with enormous burgundy nipples. There was a faint line of hair stretching from her belly button to the base of her triangle. "Ready for that steam?"

"I have to be naked?"

"It's the only way, honey." She threw a towel around her and padded toward the steam room. "Hurry, your muscles are getting colder the longer you stand there."

I gingerly removed my shirt and shorts. My stomach flesh rolled over and touched the tops of my thighs. I placed one of the tiny towels over my breasts and crotch and held it together with my hand behind my back.

I opened the door to the steam room and was relieved it was empty. "Over here," Celia called. I walked toward the voice and sat on my towel on the tile bench. I let the hot moist droplets wash over me. Soon, I was sweating again. I spun around and lay down, not caring that part of my ass fell off the seat.

Forty minutes later, Celia and I were at McGuires' having a beer. "You did good!" she exclaimed, raising her Coors.

"Thank you." Our glasses clinked.

"Are you going to go back?"

"If I can move tomorrow."

"You need to go. You'll feel so much better." She had a white foam mustache. "Give it a few weeks and see if there's a difference. Then we'll go clothes shopping. And if you'll let me, we'll dye your hair black." I thought about St. Nicholas'. And Lee. And Melissa.

"It's a date." I agreed popping a peanut into my mouth.

I could barely get out of bed the next morning, but I promised José I'd be at the Y by six. And I needed to get there early to join. I was glad they took credit cards. Over the next few weeks, I took aerobics in the morning before work then went at night to lift weights. The regulars helped me, spotting me and pushing me to do just one more set. In a month, I went down an entire dress size.

One Saturday morning in May, I met Celia to have my hair cut. I stood outside the barbershop smoking a cigarette and drinking a cup of coffee. Astor Place is famous for their cheap punk haircuts. The kids coming out had twelve-inch spikes sticking out of their heads and the colors ranged from fuchsia to chartreuse to bright blue. Celia arrived, ten minutes late, and couldn't stop talking about the great morning sex she and Carlos had just had. As someone who hadn't had sex in quite some time, I politely told her to shut up.

Two of the stylists waved to Celia when we walked in. "You've gotta have Olga do your hair," she ordered. I discovered that many of the people cutting hair were from Russia or Czechoslovakia. The place was crowded, all the chairs filled and electric razors buzzing. Two black boys were having their initials carved in the backs of their heads. A girl with a nose ring sat in Olga's chair getting the final touches on an asymmetrical cut that left one side of her head shaved and pink, and the other side blue and hanging in her eyes.

Punk music blared from the speakers hanging from the ceiling and a small Mexican man ran around feverishly sweeping up clumps of hair.

"You get cut?" Olga looked at Celia.

"No, my friend Rena." Olga stared at me, her platinum hair erect with gel.

"OK." Rainbow girl vacated the seat and Olga grabbed my shoulder and plunged me into it. She ran her hands roughly through my hair. "What we do?"

Celia jumped in. "I think she should go short—real short." Olga nodded. "Not quite a buzz cut," Celia continued, "but maybe a couple of lines over the ears?"

"Fine." Olga was short and squat, with hands like a man's. She pulled a pair of scissors from the pocket of her white lab coat and grabbed a comb from the jar of blue water on the counter. The mirror I looked into was edged in photographs with handwritten notes praising Olga's styling ability. The fluorescent lights made her sallow skin pale. I couldn't tell where the circles under eyes ended and the mascara began.

She began cutting and I whimpered as my curls tumbled to the dirty white tile. Celia stood next to the chair, advising Olga as she chopped. After a few minutes, Olga reached in front of me to get the electric razor. Her body odor assaulted my senses, watering my eyes and organizing my nose hairs into a mass revolt. She flicked it on and shaved two angled lines over my ears.

"Gel it!" Celia yelled, excited. Olga obeyed and rubbed men's pomade in between her thick hands, warming it up, and then massaged my scalp. She pulled my hair up from the roots. It had no choice but to stand straight up.

"Finish." Olga said and wrote out a ticket. Celia grabbed it from her.

"My treat."

"No, Celia, that's not necessary."

"I want to. Don't look a gift horse in the mouth, chica. Sí?" We walked to the front where an old man sat like an ancient gargoyle protecting the cash. The register looked to be the same age, proudly displaying yellowed keys in dollar increments. He wore a musty brown sweater on which were pinned dozens of buttons with sayings like "Wake up Barbie, Ken is Gay" and "Jesus Saves. He shops double coupon day at Acme." Celia ran back to Olga, shoved a few dollars in her pocket, and kissed her cheek. Olga was already shaving the next victim.

"So, you like?" Celia circled me, her fingernails combing my spikes.

"I guess." My hair had never been so short.

"Wait until we color it. It'll be fabulous." We headed toward Third. "Are you hungry? I'm starving." We agreed on a slice at Stromboli's and stood at the counter watching the traffic on First Avenue. When we were done, we headed down St. Mark's Place in search of a new wardrobe.

The first place we stopped was a store called MOD. A headless mannequin in the window wore a skintight pink velvet mini-skirt and a sheer ivory halter barely covering its erect nipples. A pink feather boa was tied in a bow around the neck. "This place has really hip stuff," Celia grabbed my elbow and dragged me inside.

"Leather, velvet, and feathers!" whooped Kali dancing around her sisters. "You gotta love it!"

"Rena can't wear clothes like that." Erishkigal was appalled.

"Why not?"

"She'll look ridiculous! These clothes are for kids, college students. People who go to the School for the Visual Arts—not a responsible working woman." Erishkigal peeked through the spaces between her fingers covering her eyes.

"She doesn't have to wear them to work." Inanna said. "But they could be fun for a night out."

"No!" Erishkigal was shaking. "The salesgirls are going to laugh at her trying to fit into mini-skirts and tight blouses. She'll be a laughingstock. I won't allow it."

"First of all, they're not going to laugh." Kali giggled at her sister's paranoia. "Secondly, who the fuck cares if they do? And last, but certainly not least, it's not your decision. Now, where's the dressing room?"

"How about this?" Celia held up a Lycra black dress with no back.

"My stomach will pooch." She put it back on the rack and pulled out a sheer maroon skirt with an overlay of velvet flowers.

"That I like." I smiled. I tried on skirt after dress after blouse. Two hundred dollars later, we walked out and headed over to Tootsie's. Because the clothes were vintage, basically used, they were less expensive. And Celia got a twenty percent discount because she worked there.

The store was tiny and filled with zoot suits, fur-trimmed sweaters, and bell-bottoms. They hung from huge hooks on the wall and were jammed on freestanding garment racks. A tall, skinny Asian man with thick black glasses and orange hair sat in an armchair reading the *Times*. He looked up and uncrossed his legs when we entered. He saw it was Celia and went back to his paper.

"A great black bomber jacket came in yesterday and I know it'll fit you," she whispered. "I stashed it in the back." She swept aside the zebra striped drapes and disappeared into the office. "How about this?" She nodded at me with a cockeyed grin. "And it's only forty bucks!" I tried it on and it fit like a glove. I bought a few shirts and a couple of purses and spent less than seventy-five dollars.

"I'm tapped out for now." I said as we left.

"That's OK, chica. Let's get the hair color and go back to your apartment. You have better weed than me!"

An hour later, I sat in an old T-shirt, my hair soaked with black goo, smoking a bong. "What about my eyebrows?" I asked. "Isn't that going to look strange?"

"Yeah, it will." Celia took a hit from the bong. She got off the couch and I heard her digging around in the bathroom. She emerged with four Q-Tips. She dipped the end of one in my hair and commanded me to sit still. I felt the wet cotton across my brow and got a vision of Groucho Marx.

"Do you know what you're doing?" I giggled.

"Don't move." She sounded a bit panicked.

"Is everything OK?"

"Fine, Sí. Just don't move." She dipped the other end in the gel and dyed my other eyebrow. "Now we wait." She returned to the couch and lit a cigarette. We watched *Bewitched*, laughing like hyenas at Samantha's pathetic efforts to extricate Darren from the trouble she'd caused. "OK, it's time." Celia escorted me into the kitchen and dunked my head in the sink.

Rubbing my head with a dark towel after she'd rinsed and washed my hair, she said, "I hope you like it. Black is a bitch to lighten."

I stood in front of the mirror in my bathroom. Celia had dried and moussed my hair and applied eyeliner and bright red lipstick. "Thanks." I ran into the bedroom and put on one of the outfits I had bought. I threw on the black leather jacket and paraded through the tiny living room, pirouetting on my toes when I reached a corner.

"Bravo, bravo!" Celia applauded.

After she left, I dug through my makeup bag and threw out the rest of the cosmetics from my adventure to Saks.

Pause

I sauntered down St. Mark's Place with Celia. I loved how my short black hair made my cheekbones appear higher and my skin whiter. Four holes in my left ear were filled with dangling gold earrings, none of which matched. Two holes in the right ear were secured with cubic zirconium studs.

The neon light from a bar flickered and buzzed in the cool October air. Across the street, Tompkin's Square Park was pulsing. Homeless Bowery bums guzzled booze out of brown paper bags, tattered clothes, and homemade barrel fires their only warmth on the cool fall night. A small group of protesters in the southwest corner picketed against the impending reconstruction of the park. College kids hid in dark corners, smoking pot, snorting coke, and drinking beer. It was Saturday at midnight in the East Village.

We were dressed alike: black combat boots, black tights, short black skirts, and black leather jackets. Only the bright red of our lipstick was a contrast. We'd smoked a joint at Celia's apartment around the corner and were on the prowl for the night. Our first stop was The Alcatraz, a tiny bar on the corner of St. Mark's and Avenue A.

We crossed First Avenue, passing the Chemical Bank where I had been held up at the ATM machine a few weeks ago. The thief was a nervous young black kid, who didn't seem to have much experience in robbing people. But I panicked and handed him the $100 I had taken out of my checking account.

"What the fuck are you doin?!" Celia yelled at me, shock registered on her pretty round face. "This nigger don't know nothin' bout robbin' nobody." She turned to the boy. "So you think you gonna steal money from us? I don't think so."

"He's got a knife," I whispered. "Don't be stupid."

"He's the one who's bein' stoo-pidt." Celia reached over and grabbed my money from the boy's hand. "Now get the fuck out of here." I gaped at her, my mouth open and silent. The boy stared at Celia. She had her hand on one hip and an overstuffed DKNY bag on the other. Her dark brown hair cascaded in ringlets from a clip secured at the top of her head. She pointed a two-inch black fingernail at his eyes and glared into them. "I said get out of here, motherfucker, before I pull my piece from this bag." She moved her left arm slowly toward the purse. He kicked the wall and slammed out the door, muttering about bad luck and some stupid crazy spic bitch.

"Do you really have a gun?" I had asked.

"Hell, no. I don't believe in violence." Celia said. "Here's your money." Celia took no shit from anyone, but she sure could dish it out. I wanted to be like her.

"Rena, do you have any butts?" asked Celia, as we approached Avenue A.

"No, I'm out. We should stop and get some." Celia squeezed her hands over her ears as an ambulance sped past, the earsplitting whine of its siren piercing the air.

"Jesus Christ! Why do they have to be so fucking loud?" She screamed. "Like people aren't gonna see the red light whirlin' around? Pah-leese." She twisted and waved her wrist, then flattened her palm like a crossing guard stopping traffic. "P-shh! They're probably just chasin' some lowlife drug dealer anyway. And they gotta make me go deaf becaus'a his sorry ass." I loved Celia's ethnic urbanness. It made me feel like a participant instead of an observer in the world below 14th Street.

The blare of the siren dissipated as the police car sped down Avenue A. We walked into the bodega for cigarettes. Three older Latino men sat in the back, smoking cigars and drinking from a bottle of Jack Daniels. "Ayy chica!" They called to Celia from the table. "Come sit on my lap, mommie."

"None of you is enough man for me," she joked. "You'd all be asleep in an hour."

"I keep you up ahhhll niiight lohhng, mommie." The youngest one raised his shot glass toward her.

"So would gas." Celia retorted. "And you probably wouldn't be as exciting."

We got our cigarettes, stepped outside, and headed back toward The Alcatraz.

A bus tooted its horn at us as we crossed the street. "Someone you know?" I asked and giggled.

"I didn't get a good look at him," she smirked, "but probably." Celia was an admitted bus troll. On nights when she was horny and didn't have a date, she'd take the bus home from work instead of the train. It usually took three or four buses before she found a driver who matched her criteria: tall, muscular, and wearing no more than three tasteful pieces of jewelry.

Celia had given me the whole lesson. She got his attention with seductive glances while placing her token in the machine. Then she'd strut down the aisle, knowing he was eyeing her ass in the rearview mirror. Celia told me that the motor was like a low voltage vibrator if you sat the right way in the last row. She'd allow her eye to catch his a few times and then move toward the front, a few seats at a time. "What's your last stop?" she'd inquire, sitting in the first seat and slowly crossing her legs.

Only Celia never left the bus. She'd send him to a nearby deli for coffee and when he returned, she'd be lying across the back bench in a teddy and a garter. "The bus seat is just the right height to give a great blowjob, if he's tall enough," she explained. "And I never have to pay to get home the next time I see him."

I watched people watching Celia in the crisp air. Men and women stared at her as they passed. Celia was oblivious to it. She continued to blather on about a guy at the office she wanted to have sex with and thought out loud as she developed her strategy. I had always wanted to believe I could have any man I wanted, but I didn't.

The music coming from The Alcatraz blared at us before we opened the door. The bar area was packed with spiked hair, leather, and tattoos. Members of The Cycle Sluts from Hell, a local band, were serving beers and shots to thirsty kids rocking back and forth to Metallica. "What do you want?" Celia screamed.

"Molsen," I yelled back, relieved. Even though I had lost forty pounds, I still felt panic when I had to squeeze through crowds. I was much more comfortable making a little space for myself near the jukebox. "I have a dollar if you pick," I heard from over my shoulder. Turning around, I looked up into the eyes of a dark skinned man with a sexy five o'clock shadow. A tuft of black hair was peaking out from the top of his T-shirt.

"Sure," I heard myself say. He put the bill into the machine.

"I love Bob Marley," he said.

"Me too."

"I like Nirvana."

"They're OK." I couldn't believe I wasn't agreeing with him. This wasn't the way I'd been taught to snag a man. "But I like REM better."

"I'm Miguel."

"Rena." Inside I was hysterical. This beautiful man was interested, apparently, in me. Maybe he'd seen Celia and me come in together and was killing time with me until Celia got back with the beers.

Celia walked toward me carrying two Molsens. I almost wished she'd stay near the bar. I was sure Miguel's attentiveness would end once he got another look at Celia.

"Who's your friend?" Celia asked with a "you're gonna get lucky tonight" expression.

"Celia, this is Miguel." He smiled, but didn't drool. That was a good sign.

"Nice to meet you." Celia held out her hand. "I just came to drop off this beer to Rena." Miguel was staring at me. "I saw some friends at the bar. I'll catch up with you later, chica. Sí?"

"Sure." I answered, my eyes locked with Miguel's. I wanted to attack him, taste his warm, tender neck; bury my face in his hairy chest. He was talking about how he moved to New York last spring. I listened with half an ear while I argued with myself about the potential consequences of this conversation.

"Absolutely not!" Erishkigal absently stroked the back of her hand. "First of all, he's just being nice until Celia comes back. Secondly, he'll have to see her naked. Absolutely not!"

"Buckle up tight, baby, because I'm in charge now and we're in for a long, bumpy ride!" hooted Kali, her necklace of skulls clattering as she danced.

"You'll regret this," warned Erishkigal.

"But it'll feel so–o–o good," Kali groaned, pumping her hips toward Erishkigal. "He's probably hung like a horse. Look at him. Let her have some fun."

"I want to go on record as opposing this." Erishkigal stated emphatically.

"Duly noted," grinned Kali.

"Let's get out of here." Miguel said lightly touching my cheek. "It's hard to hear in here."

We started for the door. "Let me say good-bye to my friend," I said. "I'll meet you outside." I pushed my way to the front of the bar, not caring who I stepped on or bumped. Celia was sitting on a barstool, flirting with a stocky black man. "Celia!" I screamed. "I'm leaving. I'll call you tomorrow."

"Yes, you will," she replied, smiling. "Have fun."

"I will." I was glowing, my cheeks flushed.

"Be safe," Celia called after me.

I went out the front door and rounded the corner to meet Miguel at the other exit. His butt was high and firm in his jeans and he was built the way I liked men, with broad shoulders and a narrow waist. I squeezed my vaginal walls together, enjoying the lingering sensation. I skipped up behind him. "I'm ready."

"For what?" he laughed.

"Anything and everything," I smiled.

We walked, hand in hand, down St. Mark's Place. It was alive with hundreds of people. The gift stands selling silver jewelry, sunglasses, hats, and gloves were still open. College students spilled onto the street from various bars, talking and laughing loudly. African men sold books from card tables on the sidewalk. And tiny restaurants, offering ethnic delicacies from falafel to pizza, were doing brisk business from wasted bar patrons succumbing to an attack of the munchies.

Ordinarily, I would have been uncomfortable, fearing someone would call out to me, making me the focus of attention. I was convinced the only time people paid attention to me was when I had done something wrong, like gaining weight or wearing too much perfume or talking too loudly.

"Let me walk you home," Miguel said.

"That'd be great. I don't live too far from here."

My palms were sweating. I hadn't been with a man since Richard and I split six months ago. Would I remember what to do? Where things went? How to do it? We strolled up Second Avenue toward 24th Street, chatting about our jobs and how we planned to escape someday.

"Here we are." I raised my eyes to meet his. "Would you like to come in for coffee?" I smiled, thinking of Celia's bus driver ploy.

"What's so funny?"

"Nothing," I laughed quietly. "I have a cappuccino maker."

"I'm a sucker for steamed milk," he said, his voice husky.

"I'll teach you how to make it, if you want." I unlocked the front door and walked through my apartment, turning on lamps as I went. "Let me take your coat."

"This is nice," he said. "Twice the size of mine."

"You've got to be kidding! Can you turn around in your place?" I called from the bedroom. I stepped out of the closet to find Miguel standing in the middle of the room. He held out his hand and pulled me close.

"I want to make love to you," he whispered.

I knew that it wouldn't be making love. It would just be fucking. But that was OK. I liked him and if he called again, fine. If not, I'd survive. I lifted my mouth to meet his lips and shivered when his tongue touched mine. I picked up his hands and flattened my palms against them. I drew his right hand to my mouth and swallowed his long index finger.

He broke my grasp on his left hand and leaned over to unbutton my shirt. I continued to suck his fingers, one by one. My nipples were already erect with anticipation. "I want to fuck you," he whispered in my ear.

"Not half as much as I want you to," I gasped, my mouth nibbling his earlobe. His other hand, now free, reached behind me to unclasp my black satin bra. His lips moved from my breasts to my mouth, and as his tongue danced with mine, his hands slid under my skirt.

We fell onto the bed, tearing at each other's clothes. Miguel's body was hard and smooth, except for the hair on his chest. Our limbs intertwined, as we explored each other hungrily. I couldn't bring myself to give him a blowjob. I just wanted him to give me an orgasm. I stroked his huge dick with my hand until it was firm and twitching. "I want to fuck you. Now." Miguel panted. "Turn over."

I hesitated. Did he want anal sex? That was a little too weird for me. "What's wrong?" he panted.

"Nothing." I was embarrassed at my naiveté. Would it hurt? What if I liked it?

"Don't you enjoy doing it doggy-style?"

"Oh! Sure!" I laughed, relieved that he only wanted to fuck me from behind, not in my behind. "Woof!" I got on all fours and waited. After a minute or two of feeling him poke around, I sat up on my knees. "What's wrong?"

"Either you're too short or I'm too tall." His hair was sticking up at various angles and the perspiration sheen on his body made him seem sexier. "Do you have more pillows?"

I got out of bed and retrieved four pillows from the couch. "Hurry!" he called. Placing them under my knees raised me sufficiently for us to be on an even playing field. The first few minutes were wonderful, but after forty minutes of feeling like I'd been riding a seesaw, I was covered in sweat. I laid on my back, knees pointing toward the ceiling as Miguel moaned and groaned, concentrating solely on pleasuring himself. The alarm clock read 3:10. Mentally, I rifled through my to do list for Sunday: pick up tights at Lord and Taylor, send a check to the phone company. Oh, and call my aunt who'd had surgery last week.

The sound of Miguel's thighs slapping my rump returned me to the present. "Oooh baby, I'm almost there." And I was nowhere near it. He hadn't touched me in almost an hour except for pumping me like he was trying to unclog a drain. I wanted him to run his hands over my body, kiss my neck, lick my nipples. But he was too busy trying to make himself come. Ten minutes later, I'd had enough.

"Miguel, you seem like a nice guy and everything, but this just isn't working," I said, sliding away from him.

Miguel and his rapidly fading erection gaped at me. "But I didn't even come," he pleaded. "Five more minutes?"

"I don't think so." I got out of bed, wrapped myself in an old flannel robe, and went to the kitchen. "Do you want a Coke?"

"I don't fucking believe you!" he screamed. "You invited me up here." He hobbled out of the bedroom, pulling up his pants. "What the fuck is your problem?"

"My problem is an arrogant asshole who thinks that my pussy exists solely to provide him with a place to stick his dick. Didn't you notice that I wasn't moving? Wasn't making a sound?" I sipped my Coke. "What would it have taken to make you notice? I feel like a blow-up doll with a pulse." He looked at me in disbelief. "The bars don't close for a half hour," I continued. "I'm sure you could at least find someone to give you a blowjob. If you're lucky, maybe she'll let you come in her mouth. Now get the hell out of my apartment."

Miguel slammed the front door. I put on a Johnny Coltrane CD and drew a bath, grateful I had picked up a pack of batteries at the drug store earlier that day. I grabbed a pint of Chunky Monkey from the freezer and set it on the edge of the tub as I slid into the bubbles.

Pause

I sat at my desk, temples throbbing, trying to focus on typing the reports Joni wanted finished by the end of the week. I had taken advantage of her being in Chicago since Monday, enjoying long lunches and arriving late. The extra hour of sleep in the morning was useful since I rarely got home before two or three. But now I had an enormous stack of work that I should've been doing all week instead of goofing off. I sipped my coffee and let the caffeine move my fingers across the keyboard.

"Rena!" Harold Ramus stood at my desk, waving a manila file folder at my face. "Have you lost your mind?" His gold-framed bifocals rested on the tip of his nose.

"What the hell are you talking about, Harold?" I whispered, hoping he would catch the drift and lower his voice.

"The figures for the Jensen budget are all wrong!" His ruddy complexion was beet red and his fingers nails were white from squeezing the file.

"I typed exactly what you gave me, Harold," I said defensively. "So if there's a mistake, it's yours, not mine."

"Nice try," he threw the folder on my desk and opened it, thrusting a stubby finger onto the numbers at the bottom of the page. "The budget is one million, two hundred thousand, four hundred seventy. Not two million one hundred thousand, four hundred seventy!" He pulled his handwritten sheet from behind the report. "And I didn't appreciate getting a call from Jonathon Jensen this morning, accusing me of inflating the budget and trying to sneak it past him. This is your fuck-up, Rena."

"I'm sorry," I stuttered. "I don't know how it happened." Harold loomed over me, his requisite Armani suit creased in all the right places. His wiry brown hair had begun to recede and his scalp was shiny and red.

"I'll tell you how it happened," he lectured me in a nasal Long Island accent. "You haven't been paying attention at all lately. You're too busy trying to capture the title of Miss East Village."

"What the fuck are you talking about?" I stood and looked him squarely in the eye.

"You know exactly what I'm talking about Rena." He slid his hands into his pants pocket and leaned back, a satisfied look on his face. "You drop a few pounds, get a haircut and all of a sudden you're coming in late and fucking up. This isn't the first mistake you've made over the last few months." He removed his hands and grabbed the file from my desk. "I've covered your ass a couple of times, although I have no idea why." He stared into space, tapping the edge of the file on his palm. "And I can't hide it from Joni anymore. I've got to tell her about this before Jonathon calls her Monday."

"Please don't tell her," I heard myself begging. "I'll call Jonathon and tell him it was my mistake."

"Like he's going to believe that," he snickered. "Why don't I blame it on a temp. That would be just as believable."

"I've known him for a long time. He'll believe me," I argued.

"The jig is up, Rena. Have a good weekend." He sauntered away and I sat there stunned, trying to figure a way out.

"This is great!" Inanna paced back and forth, fingering her braid.

"No problem," insisted Kali. "Rena can call Jonathon and that way it'll be all taken care of by the time Joni gets back. Let Harold tell Joni. If the problem is solved it won't be a big deal."

"It's risky," Inanna shook her head. "What if he doesn't believe her?"

"He's not going to," whimpered Erishkigal. "I told you," she glared at Kali. "She's been too busy doing drugs and fucking to be awake at work. This is all your fault.""

"We need to work together if she's going to get out of this," declared Inanna. "We need all of our energy to devise a strategy. Let's all put our thinking caps on. I'm sure we can come up with something by the end of the day."

I wandered aimlessly at lunchtime, concocting a way to pacify Joni when Harold told her what I did. I considered telling her I would take a pay cut, but I was already a month behind on my credit card bills and had just paid NYNEX eighty dollars to restore my phone service because I hadn't paid my bill. I decided to offer her ten extra hours a week for a few months to make up for my blunder. She was so cheap, I was sure she'd go for it. I'd come in an hour earlier and leave an hour later. Pleased that I'd concocted a punishment that I was content with, I walked into the Wendy's on Lexington and ordered a cheeseburger and fries.

I sat at the window, watching people rushing with pizza boxes, paper bags, and plastic salad bar containers. A one-legged man leaned on crutches against the entrance of the building across the street, a cardboard sign was suspended around his neck with twine. "Served the US in Vietnam. Change appreciated" was written in blue marker. He jangled a coffee stained cup with a bright red apple on it. For most of the pedestrians who walked past, he evaporated into the scenery. An occasional tourist tossed in a dime or a quarter. I finished my lunch, went back to the counter to get a Frosty for dessert and strolled back to the office, grateful I had a job and both legs.

The phone was ringing as I got to my desk. "Rena!" Joni sounded distraught.

"Hey, what's up?" Something was definitely wrong. Joni didn't panic. "Why did you schedule my flight to San Francisco for Saturday instead of today?"

"I didn't," I replied, hurriedly flipping through my calendar, looking for the information I scribbled from the airline. "I booked it for the 15th," I said, triumphant at locating it.

"Today's the 14th," she hissed. "How could you have done this? Now I'm going to be stuck in Chicago tonight and my kids are in San Francisco with my mother. Dammit, Rena!"

"Oh my God, Joni. I am so sorry." I was doing a lot of apologizing today. "Let me call the airline and see what I can do about getting you out of there."

"I've already tried. There's only one more flight going to San Francisco today and it's booked." I could see the steam rising out of her French twist.

"Give me the number where you are and I'll call you back in twenty minutes. I'll see what I can do." I called United and got her on a flight to Seattle and a connection to San Francisco. She wouldn't arrive until two in the morning, but at least she'd be there. I dialed the pay phone number in Chicago.

"Yes?" Joni answered.

"Good news," I explained what I had done.

"This does not make me happy, Rena. We will have a conversation about this Monday when I get back." I pictured her pointing a manicured nail at the receiver.

"I made a mistake, Joni. I'm sorry."

"How's everything else?" She glided over my apology.

"Fine," I lied.

"OK. I'll see you Monday. That is, if you booked me a flight for this Sunday and not next week." The line went dead. I wasn't sure that even an extra fifteen hours a week would get me out of this mess. I couldn't wait to meet Celia at the Holiday. I flew out of the office at five on the dot, avoiding Harold and anyone else who might have discovered a mistake I made.

I got a quick shower, gelled my hair, and selected a bright purple lipstick to match the shiny vintage shirt I wore under my leather jacket. I walked into the Holiday on St. Mark's Place around seven. I didn't see Celia, so I claimed a barstool and ordered a vodka tonic. Jerome, the bartender, was at least sixty-five and leered at my cleavage as he placed my drink on the scratched wood. "How are ya tonight, Rena?"

"I've had better weeks, Jerome," I squeezed the lime into the bubbles. "How are you tonight?"

"Same old, same old," he wheezed, flicking the ash from his Camel into the glass ashtray on the bar. "Cops were in here today looking for Ralph. I told them it was his day off, but they searched the place anyway. It took me three hours to put everything back proper." He hacked for a minute, eventually placing a fist to his mouth to catch the spit. "What're you gonna do? Right?" He shuffled to the end of the bar to take an order from the new waitress who impatiently tapped her tray on the bar. I lit a cigarette and admired my reflection in the smoky mirror.

The shelves behind the bar were lined mostly with liquor brands I didn't recognize, an occasional Tanqueray or Absolut bottle sprinkled in. Several signs were taped to the glass, discouraging pregnant women from consuming alcohol and warning the underaged that serving them would result in spending the night in the tombs downtown. A ragged piece of tinsel looped over the top of the cash register, a remnant from last Christmas.

"Hey, chica!" I heard Celia behind me. She hopped on the stool next to me and banged her palm on the surface to get Jerome's attention. She wore knee-high leather boots and a micro-mini skirt that barely covered her round ass. On top of her curls lay a turquoise satin hat with matching netting. "Like my chapeau?" she asked, straightening the bow.

"It's different," I laughed.

"Don't make fun of me!" She playfully smacked my arm. "It came into the store today and I decided I had to have it."

"It's lovely," I kidded. "You could be Joan Crawford's sister."

"Fuck you," she turned her back toward me and talked to the man with the green hair sitting next to her. I ordered another drink and stared out the window, dread about Monday morning dripping into my stomach like rain through a cracked roof. I felt a hand on my shoulder.

"Rena, is that you?" I spun the stool around and found myself eye to eye with Richard. "God, you look great." His crystal blue eyes smiled at me. "How've you been?"

"Fine," I straightened my back and crossed my legs. "How are you?"

"Good, good." He ordered a beer from Jerome. "I went for a walk to clear my head after work and couldn't resist stopping in for a drink." He laid a five-dollar bill on the bar and grabbed the bottle. "I haven't been here in months."

"Rena," I heard Celia call me. "Oh, I'm sorry. I didn't realize you were occupied," she winked.

"Celia, this is Richard," I introduced her. "Richard, Celia."

"Ay!" She scooted to the edge of her seat. "So, you're Richard." She jumped off, her heels clicking on the black linoleum. "Take a load off. I need to go to the little girl's room anyway." She adjusted her hat and sashayed toward the restroom. "Nice meeting you, Richard," she called over her shoulder.

"I don't remember her," Richard leaned against the vacant stool.

"That's because I didn't know her when you and I broke up." I swirled the ice in my drink with the red cocktail straw.

"You know, Rena. I'm really sorry how it ended up that last time I saw you." His eyes fixed on my knees.

"So am I."

"I couldn't handle it. I didn't know what to do." He swigged his beer. "I felt like I was in a lose-lose situation. No matter what I did, it kept getting worse. I'm sorry." He held the bottle up and touched my glass. "Here's to remembering the good stuff."

"What do you want Richard?"

"There's no need to get an attitude with me, Rena. I didn't plan on seeing you tonight. I'm just trying to take advantage of the situation and apologize for being a jerk, OK?" I uncrossed my legs and faced the bar, staring at the shreds of lime floating in the vodka. I couldn't admit that I was just as responsible for that disastrous night as he was.

"Look, Richard. You really hurt me." I felt the moisture in my eyes. "I don't know what to say."

"Then let me talk for a while." He slid onto the stool and placed a foot over his knee. "If it makes you feel any better, I don't talk to Tony or Sammy anymore." I perked up.

"Why?"

"Well, it's a little embarrassing." He reached over and took a cigarette out of my pack, flipped the butt toward me, and raised it to my lips. Then he took one for himself and lit them. "I was dating this girl, Carrie. I liked her, but I knew it probably wasn't going anywhere. I moved down to Park and 29th after you and I split and Tony was around a lot because it was convenient. I was happy he got along with Carrie after the way he and Sammy treated you."

"Can I get youse anything?" Jerome appeared before us, wiping his hands on a dirty dishtowel. We ordered another round.

"Anyway, a few months after Carrie and I started going out, I come home one night and find Tony and her going at it on my couch. I blew a gasket. I'm not quite sure why. Principle mainly. I liked her, but I certainly wasn't going to marry her. And Tony obviously liked her. I just wish he'd have said something to me before doing anything about it." I resisted laughing aloud.

"So I threw both of them out and haven't talked to him since. That was five months ago. And Sammy, turncoat that he is, took Tony's side. I haven't heard from him either."

"That's a shame," I stifled a giggle.

"Yeah, right," he leaned over and tickled me. "You're so full of shit. You could've pretended to be upset for me. Just a little anyway."

"Sorry. I'm not that good of an actress." I removed his hands from my waist and placed them in his lap. "They were vicious to me, Richard. I'm not the least bit sorry." He swallowed the rest of his beer and gently placed the empty bottle down.

"How's work going? JC still the same?"

"It's going great," I lied. "Joni has finally recognized that I'm an important part of the company and promoted me to a junior account executive."

"Really? That's wonderful." He beamed like a proud parent. "You certainly put your time in there. It's nice to see that she acknowledged it after all these years." He waved Jerome over. "Two shots of peppermint schnapps, my man. And make 'em large." He leaned over and kissed my cheek. "Congratulations, Rena. I'm really happy for you." Jerome placed two shot glasses in front of us and held the schnapps bottle a good two feet above the glasses, pouring the clear liquid in a long stream without splashing a drop. Richard passed him a ten.

"I know you don't like doing shots of hard liquor, but you always had a weakness for peppermint schnapps." He smiled and lifted his glass. I raised mine to meet it, clinking the edge. "To successful careers." I tossed the shot back, enjoying the burning mint as it glided down my throat. My hands and feet were suddenly warm.

"Speaking of careers," I asked, "how's yours?"

"Can't complain." He pursed his lips around his teeth and sucked in. "That stuff is pretty minty." Grabbing a fresh bottle of beer, he took a swig and swooshed it around in his mouth. "They promoted me to district manager about the same time Tony and Carrie decided to make a fool of me. So it was good timing. I threw myself into the job and I'm actually pretty happy."

"I'm happy for you. You really started at the bottom there." I felt his hand on my knee.

"I'm so glad I ran into you, Rena. I've been thinking about you a lot lately."

"Richard," I was melting from his stare. "I, I don't know what you want from me. It took me a long time to get over you."

"Go out with me tomorrow night." His hand moved slowly up my thigh. I let the vodka wash away my fear.

"OK," I agreed.

"You won't regret it. I promise." He put more money on the bar. "I don't want to ruin your night out with Celia. I'll pick you up at seven." He kissed my neck. I watched him walk up the steps to the sidewalk and disappear into the Friday night crowd. I sat at the bar, numb and confused. On my way to the ladies' room I found Celia, butt in the air, playing pinball.

"C'mon, you fucker. How could you eat two of my balls?" She battered the buttons attached to the flippers

"I don't know, but I'd pay to see her do that!" A dark man in dreadlocks and a Hawaiian print shirt joked to his friend.

"Damn!" She slammed the glass. "This machine is broken. Jerome," she screamed to be heard over "Mesopotamia" by the B-52's. "I want my money back."

"Celia," I grabbed her arm on my way past. "I need to talk to you."

"You look like you've seen a ghost, chica. What's wrong?"

"I just agreed to go out to dinner with Richard tomorrow night."

"You what?"

"You heard me."

"Are you insane?" She followed me to the bathroom. "After the way he treated you? After the way he let his friends treat you? Have you lost your mind?"

"He doesn't even talk to them anymore," I defended him. "He's totally into his job. He's really changed. He apologized and everything."

"And that matters? That he said he was sorry? That was the least he could fucking do." We were squeezed in the tiny bathroom, me seated in the stall while she primped in the cracked mirror. I flushed and bumped her out of the way to wash my hands. Dripping, I searched for a paper towel.

"This is the Holiday," she laughed. "Use your skirt." I shook the water off my hands. Leaning over the sink, I pulled lipstick out of my purse and traced my lips. The door opened and an NYU student in jeans and a sweatshirt walked in and retreated into the stall. Celia leaned against the closed door, blocking her in. "It's your life, chica, but I think you're nuts. My mother always says a leopard never changes its spots." She threw her hands up in the air. "Ay, ay ay!"

"He seems so different." I smacked my lips together.

"So does a chamomile when it changes colors. But underneath it's still an ugly, scaly lizard, right?"

"You mean chameleon?" I rolled my eyes.

"Whatever. The point's the same."

"I'll be careful," I promised. "I know enough to recognize the signs of him being the same asshole he was before. Trust me." Celia moved toward the door, releasing the NYU student from the stall.

"Just remember," she warned throwing open the door, "I told you so."

"He seems genuine," Erishkigal was hopeful, her brown eyes wide. "I don't see anything wrong with her having dinner with him."

"I don't know," Inanna shook her head. "She's worked really hard to get over him. I'm not sure it's such a good idea."

"Is she really over him?" Kuan Yin asked, wrapping her robe tightly around her full body.

"Who cares?" Kali was lost in thought. "I say we go out with him and then humiliate him the way he did Rena."

"What are you talking about?" Erishkigal was horrified.

"Was I speaking Greek?" She threw Erishkigal an annoyed look. "I say we go out tomorrow, play along like she's interested all night and then dump him for good."

"That's cruel," Kuan Yin murmured.

"That's life," laughed Kali, flicking the ruby in the center of Kuan Yin's forehead.

I anxiously lit a cigarette as I removed the electric rollers. My hair had gotten long enough for me to use them on the top, but it grew so fast that I had to buy a can of aerosol hair paint to touch up the short hair over my ears and my eyebrows. It was becoming more of a pain in the ass than it was worth. But I had tried to color over the black with auburn and ended up with red roots and black tips. I had to let it grow out and used a black rinse every other week to cover the roots in the meantime. I wasn't into high maintenance hair.

The phone rang. "Hi, Rena, is this a bad time?" It was my grandmother.

"I'm getting ready to go out, but I can talk for a minute." I cradled the phone between my ear and shoulder while I fastened the clasp of my necklace. "How are you?"

"I'm fine, honey. I just wanted to say hi. It's been so long since we've talked," she coughed for a minute.

"Are you OK?"

"Fine, just a cold. How's the group going?" I squeezed toothpaste onto my brush.

"Fine," I fibbed. "It's going fine."

"Have you met a new fellow yet?" She pretended she wasn't happy about my breakup with Richard, but I knew she was.

"Actually, I have a date tonight." I scrubbed my teeth, holding the phone up toward my forehead. She didn't need to know it was Richard.

"Good, honey. I worry about you sometimes." She coughed again.

"No need to worry, Granma," I spit into the sink. "I'm fine."

"As long as you're OK. That's all I care about." The buzzer rang and I shoved the rollers under the sink. "He's here, Granma. I've got to go. I love you." I criticized myself in the full-length mirror for a minute, wondering if my clothes were too tight.

Richard and I walked up Lexington, past all of the Indian restaurants and shops. The night was mild, but the ever-present curry spiced the air raising the temperature by several degrees. "Where are we going?" I asked crossing 25th Street.

"La Petite Auberge," he answered. "I know how you love escargot."

"I don't think I've been there since we split," I admitted. "Snails and butter, mmm." I felt the tights I was wearing roll over my stomach. I refused to buy a bigger size. I was still a good thirty pounds lighter than the night Richard discovered the remnants of my food orgy.

I slid my hands under my jacket and subtly tried to pull the elastic back up around my waist. I needed the support from the Lycra to keep my stomach from pooching in the skirt I was wearing. The band kept slipping out of my hands and I didn't want to draw his attention to what I was doing, so I gave up. As soon as we entered the restaurant I made a beeline for the ladies room.

I returned to find a glass of Merlot at my place setting, a bottle on the corner of the table. "You still drink red?" Richard asked.

"Sure, thanks." I went to sit down and he jumped up to pull out my chair. "You never did that when we were together," I remarked.

"I took a lot of stuff for granted," he said wistfully. "I need to use the loo. Be back in a minute." I watched him walk away. I didn't recognize any of the clothes he wore. The tan herringbone pants hung nicely over his long legs. He had chosen an olive silk shirt, opting not to wear a tie, the unbuttoned collar revealing a few stray hairs. His hair had definitely thinned, but he kept it long in the back and I detected no gray. I sipped my wine and looked around the tiny dining room.

The immigrant busboys scurried in and out of the tight spaces replenishing empty water glasses and crumbing tables. Most of the tables were filled with other couples, gay and straight. The light from the votive on each table gave the room a pale glow. I tore a piece from the baguette next to the wine bottle and stabbed a pat of butter with my knife. I was wiping fragments of crust from my blue cashmere sweater when I noticed Richard returning. I brushed quickly, not wanting to evoke any reminders of that last night.

"What looks good?" He squinted at the menu in the candlelight.

"I haven't even looked." I scanned the selections. "The frog's legs were excellent if I remember correctly." He shuddered. "Kermit?"

"Don't knock it 'til you try it," I joked. "It tastes like chicken."

"That's what someone told me about alligator once." I loved the way his eyes narrowed when he grinned. "I'm not falling for that again."

"So what are you going to get?" I gently kicked his foot under the table. "The chateaubriand." He closed the menu. "And their french onion soup." He ordered for me and we nibbled bread and drank wine listening to old French music while we waited for the appetizers. "Do you recognize this song?" Richard cocked his head to hear more clearly over the din.

"'Ma Pomme,'" I answered, flooded with memories. One night after having dinner at La Petite Auberge, I commented on the walk home how I couldn't get that song out of my head. A couple of days later, Richard surprised me with a "Songs From France" CD that included Maurice Chevalier's rendition of "Ma Pomme." We'd had wicked sweaty sex for hours.

As we laid in my bed panting, he told me that I couldn't accompany him to his company's Christmas party. His boss' daughter was coming home from Stanford over the holidays and Chuck wanted Richard to take her. Richard couldn't understand why I resented a beautiful co-ed being his date at the Rainbow Room when I had been his girlfriend for over a year.

He insisted he'd rather take me, but needed to make Chuck happy if he wanted to move up in the ranks. A few weeks later at his apartment, after seeing pictures from the party, I informed him that having a tall thin blond attached to his hip while he drank champagne didn't qualify him for martyrdom. We didn't speak for almost a week.

"It wasn't all bad." He smiled as he buttered a piece of bread.

"No," I admitted. "Just most of it." I sipped my wine and lit a cigarette from the candle.

"Why did you have to do that?" He impatiently smeared hard butter onto his bread, shredding the doughy white center. "We were getting along great. Leave it to you to find a way to fuck it up." He dropped his knife and it clattered on his plate.

"I was only stating a fact," I replied, taken aback by his attitude.

"Whatever." He swallowed the rest of his wine and emptied the bottle into his glass.

"No, thank you. I don't want any more right now," I said sarcastically. His long fingers, wrapped around the green bottle, held it suspended in midair over the table. He set it down hard on the tablecloth.

"Maybe I should've listened to my friends about you. I'm crazier than you are for asking you out and thinking things had changed."

"Some friends. Hello! The one fucked your girlfriend while you were sweating your balls off to make the money that you were going to spend on her. And Sammy, there's a winner. He's the only man in the history of New Jersey to flunk out of GED school. I can understand why you have such high regard for their opinions," is what I wanted to say. "You're right, I'm sorry," is what I actually said. "It was nice of you to ask me out and treat me to dinner. I'm sorry I was such a bitch."

"That's OK," he relaxed. "I guess we're both a little tense." He lifted the wine bottle and dribbled the remains into my glass. "Let me order another." We drank two more bottles of Merlot and devoured our food. It was ten by the time we finished and he paid the check. As we left, Richard tripped and skittered down the one step in front of the restaurant.

"Are you all right?" I asked grabbing his arm, trying to balance him. He sunk his forehead into a large hand.

"I'm so embarrassed," he recovered quickly, straightening and combing his fingers through his blond hair. "Must be the wine."

"Probably." I had diluted mine with water when he wasn't looking.

"I'm OK now." He took a deep breath and exhaled loudly. "Where to now?"

"I haven't seen your new apartment," I returned my hand to his arm.

"Really?" He looked as if he didn't believe me at first, then touched my cheek and smiled. "OK. We can pick up a bottle of Grand Marnier on the way and I can make some coffee. You still like a shot on the side?"

"That sounds yummy." I leaned into him as we headed up Lexington. We walked to Third to buy the Grand Marnier then made our way over to Park. His apartment was much bigger than mine and had a sliding glass door that led onto a small balcony. There was an exposed brick wall with a fireplace in the living room where a black leather couch rested on the polished hardwood floor. I was surprised to see he had a framed print of Van Gogh's *Night Café* hanging over the sofa. When we were together the walls had been naked except for an occasional poster of the B-52's or Rolling Stones.

"I see you've taken a few steps up in the world of interior decorating." I couldn't resist the jibe. He looked offended.

"What's that supposed to mean?"

"When we dated you had a plaid thrift store couch and a rug that was so worn, you could see the floor through it."

"Well, this is what happens when you make more money." The hair on the back of his neck was up. "Didn't you get a raise with the promotion?"

"Of course. But I'm saving it for a trip to Europe this fall." I plopped onto the soft leather. "Nice couch. Must have been expensive."

"What is with you?"

"What are you talking about?" I smiled sweetly. "I'm happy for you that you're making enough money to finally afford nice things." He sat a carafe of coffee and the bottle of Grand Marnier on the wrought iron table in front of the couch and put a Charlie Christian CD on the stereo.

"I can't believe you're here," he remarked pouring coffee. He disappeared into the kitchen and returned with two shot glasses. I cracked the seal off the dense glass bottle and poured some amber syrup into each one, putting a little more in his. Before he could make a toast, I dumped mine in my coffee and swirled it around with my finger. I slowly drew my finger out of the steaming cup and licked it like an ice cream cone.

"You're making me nuts," he whispered, leaning over and sniffing my hair. "You always smelled so good." I tossed my head back, allowing a throaty laugh to percolate above my Adam's apple. I let him kiss my neck and nibble my ear. I ran my nails over his scalp and down the back of his neck, under his shirt. He pushed me onto my back and lay on top of me, his face buried in the hollow under my chin. His hands, occasionally sticking to the leather, caressed my back and buttocks.

He sat up, straddling me, and unbuttoned his shirt. Then he leaned over and cupped my breasts. I grabbed his forearms and pulled him toward me, sticking out my tongue to meet his. He pulled off my sweater and unclasped my bra. I massaged around his zipper, up and down, feeling him grow with each stroke. He slid my skirt up to my hips and traced around the outline of my underwear. I was moaning in spite of myself.

"I'm going to the bathroom for a minute," he whispered. His voice had the burnt edge of Grand Marnier. Emitting noises that fell somewhere between a yelp and a groan, he hobbled down the hall. I sat up, caught my breath and stood up; inching my skirt down until it ended just above my knees. I fastened my bra and put on my sweater. I fluffed my hair in the reflection from the glass around the Van Gogh and retrieved my coat.

Richard stepped out of the bathroom holding his now erect penis in one hand and a Trojan in the other. "What the hell is going on?" he asked, seeing me fully dressed in the doorway of the kitchen.

"You're lucky I'm leaving now." I stifled a laugh, watching him stand there naked, his manhood hard and exposed

"What the fuck are you talking about?"

"If I really wanted to repay you for the shitty way you treated me, I would've sat on that couch until you returned. Then I'd have given you the blowjob of your life." I strutted toward him running my tongue over my lips. "Sucking and licking until you were on the edge of exploding. Then," I growled at him like a rabid Pomeranian and snapped my teeth together a few inches from his face, "your dick would've become dessert." I yanked his withering erection and turned my back on him. Stepping through the doorway, I smiled. Celia would be proud.

"Go on, girl!" Kali pranced around, waving all six hands in the air. "Finally, that asshole got what he deserved!"

"That wasn't very nice," Kuan Yin chided.

"Compassion is your bag, baby, not mine," she laughed, head thrown back to the heavens, enjoying the fresh taste of blood on her black tongue.

"Now she's alone again," whimpered Erishkigal. "Why do you have to be so vicious?"

"Me? What about all the shit he put her through?" She stomped a foot. "Why am I always made out to be the bad guy?"

"Maybe it's because you're a bitch," Inanna chimed in.

"No," Kali insisted, shaking her head. "It's because I'm the only one with the balls to tell it like it is. And I'm the only one not afraid to retaliate."

"And where did it get her?" Kuan Yin asked.

"Even." Kali howled with delight.

Pause

My nose burned as the cooling numbness spread over my body. Celia's boyfriend, Carlos, had convinced us to come to this party for moral support because it was an opportunity for him to network. A couple dozen people milled around, drinking beers and getting high. They were all good looking and adorned in Armani and Calvin Klein. I nodded to a question Celia asked without knowing what I was agreeing to. Resting against the arm of the couch, I closed my eyes and tried to think.

The music was loud, the stereo blasting Deep Purple. I rocked along to "Smoke on the Water," thankful for something to focus on besides my job. Joni had been furious when Harold blabbed about the budget mistake on the Jensen account. I spent the entire week sucking up and working late. And who knew how much longer I'd have to keep my nose buried in Joni's ass until my penance was complete.

A hand on my shoulder broke the spell. "Want another line?" A man with a graying beard and mustache asked. He held a mirror in his left hand and a razor blade in the other. I didn't know who he was, but I accepted the offer. I placed the tiny gold straw inside my left nostril, plugged the right one with my index finger and snorted. I made sure I removed the mirror from under my nose before I exhaled, having made that faux pas the first time I ever got wired.

The white powder had been blown all over the floor as I gagged from the bitter sensation of cocaine and mucous sliding down the back of my throat. The four witnesses had scrounged on the floor like dogs, sniffing the rug and dipping their fingers in its fibers, rubbing the residue on their gums in an attempt to avert a three hundred-dollar disaster. I hadn't been the most popular person at that party, but I had gotten wasted.

I passed the mirror back to the man and he smiled. "I don't think we've met." He placed the mirror on the coffee table and extended his hand. "I'm Dennis."

"Hello, Dennis." My hand met his. "I'm Rena."

"You'll probably think this is a bit forward." He averted his eyes for a moment, then stared straight at me. "I think you're beautiful."

Compliments made me nervous, but I was working on it. "Thank you," I said, looking him in the eye. Dennis continued the conversation, asking how I had been invited, what I did for a living, and if I was involved with anyone. My mouth wouldn't stop moving and I divulged more information than Dennis probably wanted to know.

"I have some stuff that's better than this," he invited. "We can go into my office." The party was in a floor-through loft on the Bowery, and Dennis, it turned out, was the owner. He gently placed his arm on my back and escorted me down the dark, quiet hall into his studio.

"Would you mind if my friend, Celia, came?" I asked, feeling vulnerable.

"I'd really like to get to know you," Dennis murmured into my neck.

"What the hell?" I thought. I was only going to do a few lines. What could possibly happen? I allowed him to open the door for me. He flipped a switch and a dim light revealed a striped love seat crouched in front of six-foot casement windows. The shutters were partly open, exposing a breathtaking view of the World Trade Center.

An antique roll top desk was angled in the corner and dozens of blue prints were scattered around it. Dennis walked over to a small table and I noticed a blue lava lamp. It bubbled and glowed, large silver globs floating in turquoise liquid. He opened a drawer in the desk and removed an amber vial.

"I save the best stuff for good company," he grinned. He retrieved a beveled mirror from a shelf above the table and sat on the small couch, patting his hand on the empty cushion. I sat next to him and watched fascinated, as he dumped a small white rock on the glass and began pulverizing it with an Exacto knife. "You really enjoy it, don't you?" He didn't wait for a response. "Those guys out there are doing stuff that's only about fifty percent. This stuff is almost pure." He sniffed in anticipation.

"This is nice of you." I ran through a dozen things to say in my mind, none of which made sense. I wasn't used to having to search for words. Conversation came easily to me. I looked around the room as he continued cutting. A Frank Lloyd Wright print hung to the left of the door. The wood floor wore a polished sheen and was partially covered by a green woven area rug. A wrought iron coffee table held the mirror that Dennis worked on.

"Why don't you put on some music?" Dennis pointed to a stereo in another corner of the room. It appeared to be suspended in air, held in place by thin wires screwed into the ceiling. I flipped through his CD collection underneath and chose a Billie Holiday disc. I pretended to know how to work the stereo, but after a few minutes, I felt Dennis behind me, his arms extended above my shoulders.

"Ain't Nobody's Business" echoed in the room. He took my hand and led me to the couch. Dennis watched intently as I snorted two lines and passed the mirror to him. Six lines remained and I had been careful to do the thinnest ones first. I immediately felt numb. I needed a cigarette desperately and started toward the door to get my purse from the living room.

"Where are you going?" I noticed a tense tone in his voice.

"I need a cigarette."

"Here, I have a pack in the desk." He held up a pack of Marlboro Lights and a lighter. "I could use one too."

I was nervous and couldn't distinguish if it was the cocaine or if I had a reason to feel that way around Dennis. I sat back down and the words flowed. We talked and gossiped and laughed like old friends. Dennis was an interior architect and had been divorced for three months. According to Dennis, his ex-wife was a total buzz kill and didn't like to party at all. He had avoided it at all costs while he was with her, but now that she was history, the party had begun.

"So," Dennis rubbed his gums. "What do you do?"

"I work for an ad agency," I flicked my cigarette in the crystal ashtray.

"Doing what?"

"A little bit of everything." I didn't want to talk about work. Harold had told everyone about the budget faux pas so the entire office gossiped about it for a week. Even though it turned out to not be that big a deal once Joni batted her eyelashes and allowed Jonathon Jensen a peek at her perpetually tanned cleavage.

We continued snorting in spurts, slowing the pace, not wanting to get too wasted too quickly. He showed me drawings and photos of the condo he had recently designed for Al Pacino and some office sketches he was working on for a prominent plastic surgeon. "I could probably get you a discount, if you ever wanted anything done." He stopped. I wanted him to suck the words back into his mouth. "Not that you need anything done."

Wired and chatty, I laughed. "Well, you never know. I may decide at some point that a little nip and tuck wouldn't hurt." When the last of the coke was gone, Dennis leaned over and tried to kiss me. He was handsome, I thought, and he'd been so nice to me, sharing his stash. I responded, gliding my tongue into his mouth. It felt swollen and numb from the cocaine and I couldn't stifle the giggles as he kissed me.

"What's so funny?" He leaned back looking slightly hurt, but curious.

"My tongue is completely numb." I put my hand over my mouth. "I'm so sorry, but it feels like it does at the dentist. I'm afraid I'm going to start drooling."

"Drool away." He put his arm around me and pulled me toward him.

"What the hell is going on here?" Erishkigal had stepped up onto her self-righteous soapbox.

"Fun!" Whooped Kali. "I bet doing cocaine is a blast. I used to smoke opium, but it made me too mellow."

"Fun is not doing drugs all night with a strange man and then letting him stick his tongue down your throat." Erishkigal shivered.

"Maybe not for you—but then you wouldn't know, would you? Because you're too much of a pussy to ever give something like that a whirl!" Kali *was thrilled.* *"Look, Erishkigal, your reign is over. I proved that when I dumped Richard. I proved it again when I picked up that guy at the Alcatraz and then booted his sorry ass out of bed for being so fucking insensitive."* She held up a third finger. *"And let's not forget Richard's withering erection when Rena walked out on him."*

"You won't be in charge forever." Erishkigal retaliated.

"Says who?" taunted Kali. *"Relax. Rena is finally enjoying herself. Don't you dare make her feel afraid. There's nothing to worry about."*

"I really need something to drink." I'd even have a beer if there was nothing else.

"Sure—OK." Dennis stood up and held out his hand. "I guess I should take a head count anyway." We sauntered down the hall, arms wrapped around each other.

A smoky wall of jasmine stung my eyes halfway down the hall. The music had changed from driving rock to an eerie Pink Floyd tune. When we reached the doorway, I wished the wall of incense had been made of brick. Celia sat on the couch in her bikini underwear and no bra. She held Carlos's dick in her mouth while one hand stroked another man into arousal. Carlos pushed her head further into his crotch and stared up at the ceiling, his eyes glazed and unfocused.

Under the window, the red warning lights from the twin towers blinking in the distance, two naked girls knelt on the floor giving a blowjob to a GQ-ish man who was desperately reaching for the one girl's breasts. I was titillated and disgusted. "Yeah, man!" said Dennis. "Finally, a little action." He turned to me. "Ready for some real fun?"

"I, I, I can't do this." I stuttered.

"Sure you can, baby." Dennis grabbed my hand and placed it on his zipper.

"Group sex!" hooted Kali. *"Finally! I've always wanted to know what it felt like to have two guys at once."*

"This is revolting," Erishkigal *sniffed, ignoring the warmth between her legs.*

"You might get a nosebleed that high up on your soapbox," Kali giggled. "It's not funny, Kali," Inanna chided, at the ready with statistics on STDs. "No one is using condoms. It's not safe."

"Rubbers schmubbers." Kali waved her hands. "It's a new experience. You've been hanging around Erishkigal too much."

"Kali," said Kuan Yin quietly, "this really isn't what Rena needs. She likes Dennis. She was hoping he might ask for her number, go on a date, see where things led. This doesn't have to be a stop on her path." She had seen disastrous results from succumbing to an animal urge.

"Says you." Kali accused. "I say it could be fun—acquiescing to lust—for a little while—experience it—see what happens."

Inanna was serious. "This is like opening Pandora's box. It's going to free emotions and feelings Rena's not prepared for. She doesn't need the distraction."

"You guys are all a bunch of ninnies." Kali was frustrated. "So she'll have a few orgasms. She'll give a few orgasms. It'll feel good. What's the big deal?"

I jerked my hand away. "Give into it, baby." Dennis whispered. "You know you want to." He kissed me, his hard tongue probing my mouth, while his hands pulled my shirt out of my jeans. Guilt and pleasure fought for control. He pinched my nipples and nibbled my neck. My hands involuntarily caressed his back and surprised me by travelling to his belt buckle. We staggered toward a sofa and fell on it, arms and legs entwined. Mouths glued. I came up for air and saw Celia bent over the couch, arms taut against the back of it while Carlos entered her from behind. The other man stood in front of her, stroking himself and gently slapping her face with his erection.

The trio in the corner had switched positions and one woman straddled the model, her hands pushing on his thighs as she pumped. The other woman squatted over his mouth, moaning. The one bouncing on the model's stiff penis caught me staring and climbed off. She walked toward Dennis and me, smiling. Her blond hair was slightly damp and she cupped her big tits in her hands. I lay on the couch, bare-chested and nervous.

Dennis was mesmerized watching the blond approach. Jealousy knocked me upside the head until the woman sat next to me and began playing with my breasts. Dennis unbuttoned my jeans and slid them off. He kissed my feet, working his way up my legs until his tongue traced the outline of my underwear. At least I'd had a bikini wax yesterday. The blond tweaked my other nipple and plunged her tongue into my mouth.

I tried to block out the sight of the skin around my waist bunched up like Pillsbury dinner rolls. Dennis ripped my panties off and dove in between my legs. I tried to remember if I'd taken a shower, fighting the orgasm Dennis was trying so hard to give me. The blond took my hand and forced it onto her shaved lips. I had never felt another woman's slickness before. I had cringed when I learned my neighbor Liz was a lesbian. And here I was, rubbing the blond's button with my thumb and thrusting three fingers into her. Wetness spread onto my palm as the woman shuddered and yelped.

Dennis loomed over me, his cock purple and erect, sticking out like a peg to hang keys on. "Blow me," he commanded. I sat up and wrapped my mouth around him. He ran his fingers through my hair, softly at first and then roughly as he became more aroused. Having climaxed, the blond climbed off my hand, and knelt behind Carlos. She spat on her index finger and poked it up his rectum. He grunted, Celia's cries mixing with his.

I continued licking and sucking Dennis until I sensed he was about to come. I didn't want him doing it in my mouth. The last time I'd let a guy come in my mouth, I had puked all over him. I didn't need a repeat performance, so I grasped his arms as I removed my mouth and signaled him silently to enter me. We fucked from every angle, completely oblivious to the activity going on around us. Spent, we collapsed in a heap on the couch, our buzz sweated away.

I surveyed the room and noticed that the model and his cunnilingus partner had split. Carlos and Celia were curled up in one corner of the couch while the blond continued sucking the dick of the man Celia had previously been working on.

"I need a line." Dennis licked his parched lips. He got off the couch, his limp dick bobbing as he made his way toward the mirror on the coffee table. I was overcome with guilt and repulsion. How could I have done this? Fucked this guy in front of six other people? Fingered a strange woman? It was the drugs, I reasoned. There was no way I would have participated in something like this sober. I struggled to make it OK in my head.

A loud gagging snapped me back to the present. The blond had puked all over the carpet after the dick slapper came in her mouth. "Aw, man!" Dennis addressed the naked man with vomit on his feet. "Don't you know you got to shove it far enough down her throat so that she doesn't taste it? Jesus!".

"Sorry, man." He grabbed the arm cover from the couch and began mopping up the vomit. He turned to the blond. "Where'd you learn to give head? A lesbian convention?" She started crying, looking to me for comfort. Black tears ran down her face from the cheap mascara and she wiped her mouth with the back of her hand. Celia and Carlos woke up, dazed and hung over. They scrambled off the couch and hurriedly dressed, disgust clearly expressed on their bewildered faces as they watched Dennis clean the rug.

"You ready to leave, Rena?" Celia asked, buttoning her shirt. "We'll drop you off." I felt sorry for the woman who had enjoyed the pleasure of my fingers earlier. The blond's pale skin, so appealing before, looked ashen and I noticed the pock marks on her back as she sobbed into the carpet.

"Everyone out." Dennis shouted. "Party's over." He gingerly picked up the vomit-soaked arm cover and ran into the kitchen, his white ass exposed like a light bulb without a shade. I wondered how I could manipulate him into letting me spend the night. I didn't want to be alone.

"Are you coming with us or not?" Celia had grown impatient.

I waited for Dennis to return. Celia glanced angrily at the kitchen. "What? You think you're gonna spend the night here? Get real—it's over. We did a few lines, had some good sex. It's time to go home, Rena."

"But we were having such a good time before." I was defensive. "We spent two hours talking in his office. It's not what you think." I knew it was more. It had to be. It wasn't possible.

"Are you guys still here?" Dennis was clearly annoyed. He stood naked from the waist up in a fresh pair of jeans.

"I thought ..." I started.

"Don't do it, Ren." Celia cut me off. "Trust me."

Ignoring her, I continued. "You never finished giving me advice on how to redo my apartment." I smiled at him and picked my finger. "I could really use your help."

"Oh well. Some other time maybe." He gathered empty beer bottles and wineglasses and retreated to the kitchen. I covered my nakedness with the Indian throw from the couch as I fumbled for my clothes. The wool itched as I pulled it behind me and I stormed into the bathroom to get dressed.

Celia and Carlos were waiting at the door when I emerged. "Where's Dennis?" I asked, timidly.

"He went to bed." Celia answered. "I told you, chica. You should've listened to me. I was only trying to protect you."

"Who the fuck asked you?" I ran ahead down the steps and into the early morning blackness. My head pounded and I was afraid no amount of food or booze or coke would make it stop.

"Who cares if he doesn't want her phone number?" Kali snickered. "At least the sex was great!"

"This is your fault!" Inanna raised her foot to kick Kali. "Hey! Who took my sandals?"

Pause

I'd had enough. Enough of the bars and the drugs and the wildness of the East Village. It had been more than a month since the debacle with Dennis and I was tired of lying in bed while some guy I'd just slept with skulked off at four in the morning. I wanted to go to the movies. I wanted to see a play. I wanted to be taken out for dinner. Convinced I could find my soul mate in eight-point type, I flipped to the classifieds of the *Village Voice* and scoured the personal ads.

"SWM 34 ISO INDEPENDENT BUSTY FEMALE IN NEED OF RELIEF. NO RECIPROCITY REQUIRED. LUNCHTIME RENDEZVOUS OK." He wouldn't be my soul mate, but it wouldn't hurt to have an outlet for sex while I was looking. I took a sip of coffee and circled it in red.

I kept reading, using my red pen when something caught my attention. A date with any of these guys was one night, I reminded myself. If I didn't like him, I never had to see him again. But what if I liked him and he didn't like me?

"This is the stupidest thing she's ever done!" Kali squawked.

"At least she'll have a chance to talk to these guys before she meets them," Inanna shot back. "Not like your method of spear fishing men in some dingy bar."

"You can tell a lot more from looking at someone than you can from hearing their voice over the phone," argued Kali.

"She shouldn't be doing this at all," Erishkigal added. "It's dangerous."

"Nothing wrong with living a little dangerously," Kali laughed from deep in her throat and tossed her long hair behind her shoulders. "In fact, you'd probably be a whole lot happier if you could muster the courage to try it."

"She could put an ad in herself," suggested Erishkigal. "At least that way she'd have control over who she responded to."

"Not a bad idea," smiled Inanna. "Let's give it a try this way first, but that's not a bad idea at all."

"Hi, my name is Rena Sutcliffe and I'm responding to your ad in the April 5th *Village Voice*," I read from the script I'd prepared. "I'm 31 years old and work in advertising. I have curly brown hair and green eyes and a great sense of humor. I enjoy movies, music and theater and love going for long drives. You can reach me at 555-2659. I look forward to hearing from you." I left four messages at $1.99 per minute.

I purposely forgot to mention my weight. I considered saying I was a size fourteen because men have no idea what it means. The ads I responded to were all looking for Rubenesque or full-figured women. Well, that I was. I somehow had replaced over half the fifty pounds I lost going to the support group.

Over the next two days, all of the men whose ads I responded to called me back. The first guy left a message about whisking me off to Italy for our first date and proposing to me on the Piazza del Sol. Then he pontificated about what beautiful children we'd have together. I hit delete. Mr. No Reciprocity actually sounded normal and so did some guy named Vince. The fourth one had such an accent I couldn't understand him, so I deleted him too.

I poured a glass of wine after work that night and stared at the phone. It had been a while since I'd had sex, but did I really want to enlist some stranger from a personal ad to give me an orgasm? "Is Jeremy there?" I took a big swallow of Merlot.

"Speaking."

"Hi, this is Rena." It felt like I had twelve cotton balls stuffed in my mouth. "I answered your ad in the *Voice*."

"Oh, yeah. Hey. How are you?"

"I'm good, thanks. How about you?"

"Fine, fine. Kind of a rough day at work, but it's over."

"What do you do?" I lit a cigarette wondering if it was appropriate to be asking someone who wanted nothing more from me than to stick his face in between my legs what his day at work was like.

"I sell real estate."

"That sounds stressful."

"It can be. That's why I put that ad in the paper. It helps me relax."

"The ad?"

"Making a woman moan with pleasure."

"Oh."

"So, what made you respond?"

I had to make a quick decision. Lie or tell the truth. "Orgasms are the key to life. But I don't really want a relationship right now." A little of both. Not a bad choice.

"Well, I can help you find the key."

"How do I know that?"

"Meet me tomorrow for lunch and find out."

"Sure," I heard myself say. "Where?" The call waiting beeped in. "Can you hold on one second?" I pressed the receiver. "Hello."

"Is Rena there?"

"May I ask who's calling?"

"Vince."

"Oh, hi. This is Rena."

"I got your message. Is this a bad time?"

"I'm on the other line, but I'm getting off. Can you hold on a minute?"

"Sure."

I switched back to Jeremy. "Sorry about that. Where were we?"

"Deciding where we could meet that would be soundproof so no one can hear your screams of ecstasy."

I was terrified and turned on. "Why don't we meet at Pete's Tavern on Irving for a drink first."

"Perfect. If we like each other, my place isn't far. I'll meet you there at twelve."

"How will I know you?" I asked.

"How will I know you?" He countered.

"I'll have a copy of the *Voice* with me at the bar."

"But what do you look like?"

Vince was still hanging on the other line. "I guess you'll have to wait until tomorrow. I've really got to go. See you at Pete's." I took a deep breath. "Hey, Vince. I'm really sorry."

"That's OK. How're you doing tonight?"

"Pretty good, pretty good."

"She's not fine," moaned Erishkigal. "She's just made a date for some man she's never met to lick her pussy." The tips of her ears were red. "But she's having a drink with him first, so it's much more civilized than it sounds, right Kali?"

Kali stood motionless, staring at her sister. "You, Little Miss Prim and Proper, using the word 'pussy?' You're killin' me!" She erupted in a fit of laughter that shook the ground.

"It's not funny, Kali." Inanna chided. "It could be dangerous.

"Both of you need to chill the hell out. Relax." Her grin had a grinch-like twist. "It'll be fine, trust me."

"How are you?" I asked.

"Excited about calling you. I really liked your message. You sounded so down to earth. A lot of the responses I've gotten are from women who seemed a bit too pretentious for me."

"Thank you, Vince. That's very nice of you to say." Wow. He sounded like he didn't have a drinking problem or a dog collar in his underwear drawer. We talked for an hour. He was a teacher for physically challenged kids and his favorite thing was jumping in the car and seeing where he ended up. I loved that.

We both enjoyed a lot of the same music and movies. He had an excellent sense of humor and had an interesting perspective on life. I didn't remember laughing that hard in forever. He asked me out for Friday night. I hesitated because of my scheduled romp with Jeremy that afternoon, but I figured I'd at least be relaxed.

"Sure, Friday night would be good."

"Rena, before you say yes, there's something I've got to tell you." Oh, no, there was a dog collar under the boxers. "I'm in a wheelchair."

"Oh, that's not a big deal."

"Who the hell said that?" Kali demanded.

"It's the right thing to do. She likes him." Kuan Yin defended. "Just because he's in a wheelchair doesn't mean she can't have a good time with him."

"You're insane." Kali waved the fingers from her three left hands under Kuan Yin's nose. "She's never known anyone in a wheelchair. She's going to be uncomfortable. And it's going to be even worse if she does like him because then she's going to feel guilty for being uncomfortable."

"That's not true, Kali." Kuan Yin sat and folded her legs under her. "It's important for Rena to have compassion for those who don't have all of the advantages she does."

"I agree with you, to a point," Inanna admitted. "But I don't think Rena is ready for this." She turned toward Kali. "Anymore than I think she's ready to meet some man she doesn't know so he can perform cunnilingus on her."

"Cunnilingus?" Kali snickered. "Where'd you get that?" She began giggling and soon was snorting and slapping her thigh.

"What's so funny?" Inanna looked hurt. "That's what it's called."

"Only when you've never experienced it." Kali laughed. "When you've been on the receiving end, you don't call it that."

"What do you call it then, Miss Smarty Pants?"

"Muff diving, beaver poaching, getting a good tongue thrashing." Kali was having trouble breathing.

"I'm glad I've amused you. But we have more important matters at hand."

"OK, I'll let her go on both dates because you gave me a good laugh." Kali placed a hand on Inanna's shoulder and wiped the tears from her eyes with another. "At least she's done with the bars and the drugs."

"OK, Kali. But I'm watching."

"You don't need to remind me." Kali winced.

I dressed meticulously that morning in a short black skirt and an oversized lavender shirt, hoping that if I covered my stomach he wouldn't notice the rolls of flesh above him as his tongue was buried in my snatch. I used a half a bar of Dove in the shower and prayed the temperature stayed fairly cool. After warning Joni I might be back late from lunch because of a doctor's appointment I took a cab down to Pete's. I passed a messenger on the corner, puffing a joint, the acrid smoke titillating my memory. I was tempted to ask him for a hit.

I walked into the bar at eleven forty-five and it was empty. I slid onto a stool and ordered an Absolut and tonic. I never drank this early, but the only place in my body that had no moisture was my mouth.

What if I really liked him? What if he thought I was too fat? What if I wanted to kiss him? What the hell was I doing? I was a ten-minute walk from my apartment. I was ready to pack up when I felt a hand on my shoulder. Damn, I'd left the *Voice* sitting next to my cigarettes on the bar. "Rena?"

I slowly turned around and found myself looking into blue eyes magnified to the size of walnuts by a pair of very thick glasses. "I'm Jeremy." He was dressed in a cheap short-sleeved shirt and polyester pants and he had a Bic pen sticking out of his shirt pocket. He did have sexy hands, though, and they were rather large. "You're very pretty."

"Thank you." I picked up my sweaty glass and took a sip.

"I could make you very happy," he whispered into my ear. "I can already tell you taste like honey." The vodka slid down the back of my throat. "Why don't you finish that and we'll get out of here." I swallowed the rest of the drink, left a five on the bar, and followed him out. We didn't speak walking down 18th Street and headed downtown after we crossed Third Avenue. On 16th Street, we entered a luxury building where the doorman winked at Jeremy in a way that was a tad too familiar.

Still silent, we entered the elevator and Jeremy pushed the button for the 17th floor. He stood facing the doors and I studied him. He really wasn't bad looking, just a little fashion deprived. He appeared to have some solid muscles under his inexpensive clothes. I was so turned on by the danger, I thought I was going to come right there. "Stand in front of me," he said.

"Excuse me?"

"Stand in front of me."

"Why?"

"Please?" I slid in front of him. He held out his hands and caressed the air around my neck and shoulders. He slowly moved them around me until his left hand lingered in front of my crotch and his right one hung in front of my breasts. He never touched me. "Do you like your breasts licked?" He whispered with his eyes closed, the mist from his breath dampening my skin.

"Yes," I squeaked.

"Maybe we can make that a part of the experience." The doors opened and he gently shoved me into the hallway. We walked into a beautiful apartment with a view of the East River. There was a black leather couch and a coffee table in the living room. A huge stereo sat on the floor against the wall across from the couch. There was no other furniture and the walls were bare. A small hallway was off to the right, darkened by two closed doors.

"Make yourself comfortable. I'll be back in a minute." He disappeared behind one of the doors. I sat on the couch, wondering if I should get undressed or run. I removed my tights and tucked them in my bag. I felt exposed from the sunlight pouring in. He came back into the room and walked over to the sliding glass doors and pulled the verticals. The light seeped through the two-inch blinds, casting shadows like bars across the white walls.

He knelt in front of me and rubbed his hands over my shins and calves. He looked up at me with those huge magnified eyes, like some sort of nuclear cricket and I shivered. "I haven't even started yet," he smiled. I closed my eyes.

He spread my legs apart and rubbed his index finger along my lips through my underwear. He kissed my inner thighs and slipped my lace panties over my ankles. He gradually worked his tongue up into me, licking and sucking until I moaned. I opened my eyes and looked down. All I could see was his brown hair sliding out from under my short black skirt. After a while, he emerged, his lips glistening from my wetness. "Unbutton your shirt."

I did as I was told and he pulled my breasts from my bra and pinched and licked my nipples until I was bucking against him like a rodeo cowboy. Just when I could bear no more, he re-entered the cave under my skirt and sucked on my clit while his fingers thrashed in and out of my hole. Silver and blue bursts of light bounced off the naked walls, drenching me in their explosions. I sagged on the couch, breathing heavily and sweating. "I'll be back in a minute." He left, but I didn't care. I couldn't move.

After fifteen minutes or so, and I'm guessing because there was no clock that I could see anywhere in the apartment, I became curious. I hoisted myself off the couch, surprised to find that I was sore all over. I tiptoed down the hall, listening to see if I could tell where he was. Finally, I called out his name. Nothing. I stood in front of one of the closed doors and I thought I heard grunting. "Jeremy," I called again. "Are you OK?" I stood in decision paralysis, trying to imagine what was going on. I felt the wetness on my thighs as I pressed my legs together, reacting to the fact that my bladder was now in immediate need of emptying. I couldn't tell whether I was imagining the groans and grunts; if he was jerking off or if he was ill.

I hesitantly turned the knob on the one door and peered in through a tiny slot. Sitting naked on the tile floor, his back against the tub, was Jeremy. In his left hand, he was holding what looked like a large plastic vagina, complete with a big blond bush. He was stroking it up and down his very large, erect penis, a half-squeezed tube of KY jelly collapsed near his right foot. His right hand massaged his balls and his face was screwed up in a disturbing grimace. I couldn't tell whether he was coming or crying.

"Well, you've done it now, Kali," Inanna accused. "That's the last time I listen to you. What a disaster."

"Felt pretty damned good to me," Kali licked her lips. "And she didn't even have to put out."

"You're disgusting," Erishkigal said, squished her eyes together to block out the memory. "He was masturbating in there. That's not normal. Rena was sitting on his couch and he chose to fuck a piece of plastic."

"So what? Rena got some pleasure and didn't have to pay for it."

"How can you say that?" asked Kuan Yin. "She's going to pay for this for a while. That guy chose a rubber vagina over Rena. She paid plenty."

"I agree," nodded Inanna, "It was completely illogical and hedonistic. Rena is ready to move on. It's time for her to realize that the desire for physical pleasures are sometimes in conflict with what is logical."

"Or spiritual," added Kuan Yin.

"Whatever," Inanna rolled her eyes. "We'll see how spiritual she's ready to be after the date with the guy in the wheelchair." She smoothed her palms down the front of her robe. "Where the hell is my belt? None of you has owned up to taking my crown or my jewelry either. And what about my breast plate and shoes?" She moved among the other goddesses, examining

their necks and ears, peeking under their robes. Hands on her hips, she demanded "Where is my belt?"

I went home and took a shower. I wanted to collapse. I stood in front of the refrigerator, naked, searching for something to eat because I was starving. I hadn't had lunch. I needed food.

I called Joni and told her I'd had some tests at the doctor's that made me woozy and I couldn't come back today. She was as sympathetic as she was capable of being and told me to feel better. I called Noodles on 28 and ordered sesame noodles and Kung Pao chicken and flipped on the television to watch the last half-hour of *All My Children*. Erica Kane had nothing on me today.

I contemplated canceling on Vince, but I knew he'd think I'd done it because of the wheelchair thing. And maybe it would've been. I decided if I ate and took a nap, I'd be OK by seven. I was wrong. I ate everything the delivery boy brought, including the three fortune cookies and orange slices and passed out. I woke up with an MSG hangover, bloated and strung out. I felt like Clifford the Big Red Dog in the Macy's Parade.

I took another shower and lay on the couch with cucumber slices over my eyes, praying for the puffiness to go away. I got dressed and went to the corner of 24th and Park. There I stood, on a corner, waiting for a man in a wheelchair, driving a specially built burgundy van to pick me up for a blind date. What a sad commentary on my life.

I saw the van approaching and the flight instinct tried to kick in. But the guilt would've killed me. I put on my best happy face and opened the door. I followed my natural instinct to shake his hand. I found that his arms were half the length of mine and only had three misshapen fingers on each hand. I quickly withdrew my hand, pretending I had been going for the seatbelt.

I observed myself having a conversation with him about what restaurant we should go to for dinner. We decided on a pub at Third and 19th and we managed to find a parking space less than two blocks away. I felt repulsed watching his deformed hands pressing the buttons for drive and reverse as he attempted to parallel park. I pinched the bone between my brows.

"Go ahead and get out, Rena," Vince said. "I have to back the wheelchair into the back of the van. That's where the lift is." I climbed out of the van and stood on Third Avenue waiting. After five or six minutes, he still hadn't emerged and I wrestled with whether I should call to him and offer help or whether he'd be offended. After another minute or two, the side doors swung open and I heard the grinding as the lift deposited him on the street next to me.

We walked, well I walked and he wheeled, down the street toward Molly's. I held the door open. As we made our way toward the back of the restaurant, I noticed several other men in wheelchairs. "Hey Bob," Vince smiled at the first one. Then it was hellos to Fred and Steve and Gary.

We sat, looking at the menus. "Gee," Vince said, "I really want the steak."

"Well, get it then," I said, thinking I was being helpful. "I'm going to have the shepherd's pie."

"That sounds good," he nodded. "I'll get that too."

"Get the steak if you want the steak," I insisted.

Vince looked down at his napkin. "I can't hold a knife and fork very well. I'd have to ask them to cut it up for me in the kitchen and I just hate doing that."

"Who's in trouble now?" Kali leered at Kuan Yin. "Compassion my Hindu ass."

Kuan Yin closed her eyes and placed her open palms on her knees. "Leave her alone," Inanna insisted. "At least she was motivated by something other than her own personal lust."

"So?" Kali laughed. "Where did it get KY? Or Rena for that matter?"

"Rena's trying," Kuan Yin opened her almond eyes and stared at Kali. Kali waited for her to get angry, but she didn't.

"Quit looking at me with those damned eyes!" Kali couldn't meet her gaze anymore. "It gives me the creeps."

The waitress brought our salads. Vince held the fork in the three fingers of his right hand. He stabbed at a cucumber, finally spearing it. He raised it to his mouth and took a bite. It fell off the fork into his lap. The fork found its way back to the bowl where it plucked a tomato from the bed of lettuce. Again, he raised it to his lips and took a bite. Pulp shot across the table and landed in the butter. I vigorously stirred the vinaigrette, trying to mix the oil into the rest of the dressing. Vince gave up on his salad.

"So, tell me about your job." I said.

"I work at a facility for homeless kids. The ones I work with have some type of physical challenge. They're either blind, or in a wheelchair or something."

"What do you teach them?"

"How to survive in a world made for people whose body parts all work the right way." He eyed his almost full bowl.

"Do you teach them English or Math or Science?"

"No. I just said I teach them how to survive. How to navigate around the city. How to read a bus map or make sure they get correct change after buying a Snickers. These kids come from no money. Most of them have lived in shelters their entire lives. Their parents are either drug addicts or alcoholics for the most part. They don't stand a chance without the help that St. Agnes' provides for them."

"That must be difficult for you."

"I'm used to it." The busboy asked if we were finished and then cleared our dishes. "I've been doing it for five years already."

"Where did you go to school?"

"I got my undergraduate degree from CUNY. Then I got my Master's in Education from NYU." I was pulling teeth. And dentist wasn't on my resume. The waitress brought our shepherd's pies. He had an easier time navigating that. A spoon tightly grasped in his hand, he dug in. I tried to be delicate. I was, after all, on a date. Halfway through his meal, Vince perked up.

"What is it you do again?" he asked.

"I work for the president of an advertising agency."

"That must be exciting."

"It would be if I was doing what I'm capable of. Unfortunately, she still uses my superhuman talents to pick up her dry cleaning."

"What is it you want to do?"

"She's let me do a few media buys. I like that. But she keeps feeding me excuses why she won't let me switch departments. I really need to get my shit together and send out resumes. I don't think she's ever going to let me work somewhere else in the company."

"You're articulate. I'm sure you could get another job." He grabbed a spoon and secured it between his fingers with his other hand.

"It's part of the game plan." I tried not to stare as he plunged the spoon into the casserole dish, like a two-year-old.

"Do you have any interest in seeing *The Ref* with Dennis Leary?"

"Sure! I love him."

"I know it's playing at the Sutton. The payphone's downstairs."

"I'll call." I cut him off. I grabbed my purse and hurried down the steps. There was a show in a half-hour. I went to the ladies' room and then returned to the table. He paid the check and we were off. We replayed, in reverse, the entire scene from earlier with him backing onto the lift and unlocking my door. Driving up Third Avenue, I thanked him for dinner. I tried not to watch him accelerate with his fingers. Knowing he was hitting the brakes for a red light with his thumb made me nervous.

As we were turning onto 57th Street, he suggested I jump out to see if the show was sold out before he tried to park. I obeyed and darted in between stopped cars until I was at the front door. "Is the eight o'clock show sold out?" I was slightly out of breath.

"No," the ticket taker blew a bubble with her gum. "Plenty of seats left." I dug in my pocket for a twenty to buy the tickets, when it occurred to me.

"Is the theater wheelchair accessible?"

"The eight o'clock show isn't because it's downstairs. But there's a nine o'clock show in the upstairs theater and you can get a wheelchair in there." She blew another bubble. It popped with a loud crack.

"Thanks," I smiled and shoved the bill back into my pocket. If I told him the truth, I was going to be more uncomfortable than I already was. If I lied and told him it was sold out, I'd feel like shit about lying. I scanned 57th Street for the burgundy van. I finally spotted him parked in front of an antique store. I jogged over and jumped in.

"Well?" He smiled.

"It's sold out." I slammed the door.

"Oh." He glanced out his window. "Well, we could wait around for the next show or go out for coffee or something."

"The next show isn't until ten." Lying gets easier the more you do it. "And I have a lot to do tomorrow morning."

"Do you want to go out for coffee or do you want to call it a night?"

"I think I'd rather call it a night if you don't mind."

"Sure." He put the van in drive and we headed toward Park Avenue. For the first time, I noticed a peculiar odor. I casually looked around, trying to locate its source. It smelled like sweat, but older, with a hint of mildew. I leaned toward the middle in between our seats, pretending to reach for my backpack. Behind his seat was a stack of chair pads that he used to cushion the leather seat of his wheelchair. The smell was definitely emanating from that part of the van. I tasted shepherd's pie.

We continued driving in silence. When we arrived on 24th Street, he double-parked on the corner. "I had a really nice time tonight, Rena."

"I did, too. Thanks for everything, Vince." He leaned over to kiss me. I turned my face and his lips grazed my cheek.

Pause

I was swiping at sugar crystals on the conference room table with a damp paper towel, my date with Vince a fuzzy memory, when Joni appeared in the doorway. "Your mother is on the phone."

"Thanks." I continued wiping.

"It sounds important." She placed a hand on her hip. "I wasn't going to answer it. It's after six. But it wouldn't stop ringing. I think you should talk to her."

I crumpled the blue paper towel in a pile of white sand and followed her out the door. "Mom?"

"Rena? I'm so glad I found you." Her voice was thin and tinny. "No one's been answering the phone there. I called you at home, but kept getting your machine. I've been trying for an hour, but it just kept ringing and ringing."

"Is something wrong?" My mother didn't ramble.

"It's your grandmother, Rena. She's in the hospital."

"What do you mean?"

"It's her heart. The doctors call it congestive heart failure."

"Is she … is she going to die?"

I heard a sniffle. My mother's mother had been dead since before I was born. My father's mother was the closest thing she had. "They're not sure. I think you should come home."

"I'll call the airlines."

"I hope you don't mind. I booked you a ticket for tomorrow morning at nine. You can pick it up at the USAir counter at LaGuardia."

"No. No, I don't mind, Mom. Thanks."

"I'll pick you up at the airport."

"OK." I rubbed my eyes, pushing the tears back in. "How long should I plan on staying?"

"It's not good, Rena. I don't know what to tell you."

"All right. I'll see you tomorrow." I hung up the phone and picked up the papers on my desk. She couldn't be dying. I walked to the filing cabinet in Joni's office. It was impossible. I opened the drawer and looked for the Speedy Lube file. She had plans to visit. A file sliced the tip of my index finger. I stuck the finger in my mouth. The taste of iron and salt washed over my gums and teeth.

"Is everything OK?" Joni sat in my chair, her legs crossed, spine erect.

I stared at the cabinet. "My grandmother is in the hospital." I shut the drawer and faced her. "They don't know if she's going to make it." Turning around, I opened another drawer and pretended to look for something.

"I'm sorry, Rena."

"It'll be fine."

"Are you going home?"

"Tomorrow morning. If that's OK?"

"Don't even think twice. Take as much time as you need." She got up and walked toward me. "Just call me and let me know what's going on." Her hand was on my shoulder, her bony fingers and huge diamonds.

"Thanks." I crossed in front of her to my desk. "All the correspondence is done. I'll print out your itinerary for the trip next week before I go." I handed her a pink message slip. "Frank needs to talk to you about some billing problem." Opening my drawer, I removed a small metal box. "I went to the bank today and petty cash is full, so you should be all right until I get back." Maybe rambling was hereditary.

"Rena, we'll figure it out. Don't worry." She flipped through my Rolodex. "What temp firm do you use?"

"Call Jeannie at Manhattan Temps in the morning. She'll have someone here by ten." She plucked the card out and tucked it in her jacket pocket.

"I think you should go. You have to pack." She smiled at me. "And find someone to take care of that cat of yours." As she was on her way back to her office, she asked, "Do you need any money? I mean for the cab to airport or anything?"

"No, I'm fine." I got my bag from the bottom drawer and took the bus home.

Thursday morning I got my ticket and sat in the lounge, smoking, waiting for my flight to be called. Sixty minutes later, I found my mother, hunched on a blue vinyl chair at the end of the jet way. She wore no makeup and was dressed in an aqua parachute sweat suit.

"She's asking for you, Rena." Faith's eyes were pink and the end of her nose was red and irritated. We picked up my suitcase and drove to the hospital, the air between us in the car cold and lifeless. I stared out the window, toying with snippets of dialogue in my head. "You don't look tired Granma, honest." "The only reason I came home was because I had to use up my vacation time." The sun played hide-and-seek with the clouds moving us back and forth between blinding brightness and dusk-like gloom.

"We're here," my mother announced as we pulled into the parking lot off the Boulevard of the Allies. An army of sterile chemicals marched into my nose as we entered the hospital. My grandmother was in intensive care, hooked up to machines that beeped and dripped and clicked. The plastic accordion of the ventilator sucked and gushed next to her head, which looked so tiny on the pillow. I didn't remember her being so thin. My father stood gazing at the parking lot out the window.

"Lillian?" My mother called. "Rena's here." My grandmother licked her lips and sucked her cheeks.

"Granma?" I touched her bruised hand, the age spots melted into the purples and blues left by the needles. She squeezed back but didn't open her eyes.

"Your grandfather went to get coffee." My father turned from his post. "He should be back in a minute." I hadn't seen my father in over a year. He had deep circles beneath his eyes and his stomach had grown. He wore khaki pants and a golf shirt, his casual retired look.

"Where's Rebecca?" His wife was the reason we hadn't spoken. To get the money to open her ballet school they had sold my grandparent's house and forced them into an apartment. My grandmother insisted it was all right with her, but I knew that it bothered her to get rid of so many mementos and antiques. I was appalled that my father was so blind. It was clear to me that Rebecca cared about no one but herself.

"She's with your grandfather." My father ran his fingers through his thick gray hair and stared at his feet. "You're not going to start anything, Rena, are you?"

"Yeah, sure Dad. I had nothing better to do with my life this week than to fly in from New York to pick a fight with your teenage ballerina wife whenever I needed a distraction from the death vigil around your mother's bed."

"Rena, don't talk to your father that way," my mother ordered.

"Are you serious?" I laughed. "He throws his parents out of the house they've lived in for thirty years so precious Rebecca can live her little dancer fantasy and you're telling me not to be sarcastic?"

"He's still your father."

"Thank you, Faith." My father cleared his throat. "But this is between Rena and me. We'll find a way to work it out, honey, won't we?" He tousled my hair.

"Don't touch me." I leapt up from the chair and my grandmother's eyes fluttered open.

"Rena, is that you?" she murmured.

I bent over and kissed her wrinkled cheek. "Yes, it's me."

"I must really be dying." She tried to laugh, but it came out dry and tired.

"Don't say that," I whispered harshly. "It's not true."

"Yes it is darling. It's OK." She pressed the button in her hand and the bed rose so she could sit. "It's my time."

"Jesus Christ, Ma!" My father yelled. "Why do you have to say shit like that?"

"Crap, Michael. Not shit. Shit is vulgar. Crap gets the point across without offending anyone." She rested her head on the flat hospital pillow and recovered from the exertion. Turning to me, she smiled. "I'm so glad you came so that we could say good-bye Rena. You're my only grandchild and you're very special to me."

My mother leaned against the doorway, pale and crying. "Look what you've done, Ma. You've made Faith cry," accused my father.

"There's nothing wrong with crying, Michael. Maybe if everyone in this family had cried a little more, you and Faith would still be married and your father wouldn't insist that everything is fine when anyone can see he's perfectly miserable." She reached out her hand to me. I took it. "And maybe, just maybe, Rena would be happy."

"What's this talk of me being miserable?" My grandfather held two cups of coffee in his meaty paws. Rebecca, in a leotard and leggings, carried two more.

"We figured you'd be here by now and might want some coffee." She offered my mother and me each a cup.

"But honey, that leaves none for you," my father said, taking the steaming Styrofoam from his father.

"The only decaf they had was Sanka." Rebecca scrunched her face. "So I got orange juice instead." She pulled a glass bottle from the waistband of her tights.

"You're always so considerate." He leaned over and kissed her cheek. "Thank you, honey."

"I think I'm going to be sick." I brushed past the two of them and into the hallway. My mother followed me out.

"Rena, I know this is a difficult time, but you don't need to make it harder than it already is." She had a firm grip on my elbow. "Come back in. And be nice this time."

"After everything he put you through?" I wrestled my elbow away. "After all the affairs? The bankruptcy? The divorce? The legal battles over alimony? And you're telling me to be nice?"

"This is about your grandmother, Rena, not you. And not me or your father. Lillian is dying. She probably won't leave this hospital alive. Don't be so selfish."

"Me? Selfish?" I stared at her. "That's a fucking hoot coming from you, Queen of 'Me First Land.'"

"Stop it Rena. I know you're upset, but this isn't the time or the place."

"Really? I think it's the perfect time and place. It's about time we got some of this filthy stinky laundry into the fresh air."

"Don't do this."

"Do what? Tell the truth? That's something that everyone in this family, except Granma, is allergic to."

"Your truth is your truth Rena, but it doesn't mean it's everyone else's."

"Oh no? Let's see, truth like maybe if you'd have paid a little more attention to Dad instead of worrying about your next tennis lesson or PTA board meeting or bridge tournament that maybe you'd still be married?" I sipped my watery coffee. "Or how about truth like if you'd have fucked him more than twice a year, maybe he wouldn't have been sleeping with every blond under thirty?" I caught Faith's hand before it landed on my cheek.

"You have no right," she hissed at me. "You have no idea what you're talking about."

"Don't I? I overheard the arguments. I listened under the dining room table when you and Granma had those conversations before you and Dad decided to divorce. I wasn't blind, Mother. And I wasn't deaf. You assumed that because I was a kid that I didn't understand what was happening, that it didn't affect me. You couldn't have been more wrong."

"I am sorry for any pain your father's and my relationship caused you, Rena. But you were not the reason for the divorce. Your father and I did the best that we could in our marriage and with you." She placed her cup on an empty chair. "And I will not stand here and listen to you talk to your father in that tone of voice, showing him no respect, while we stand around a hospital waiting for Lillian to die. I just won't." Her watery eyes locked with mine for a moment and then she disappeared back into the room.

"That was brilliant," Inanna slapped her hand over her forehead.

"What?" Kali asked innocently.

"You're a piece of work, sister." Kuan Yin shook her head.

"What the hell are you talking about?" Kali was confused.

"Losing Lillian is going to be tough," Kuan Yin admitted. "But this attack thing you're doing in the hopes that Rena won't hurt as much when she passes on is ludicrous."

"I'm only speaking the truth," Kali asserted.

"Whose truth?" questioned Kuan Yin.

"Rena's truth," said Erishkigal. "She saw what happened. She heard what went on. She was there."

"Yes," Kuan Yin agreed. "But as a child. Her truth about all of this is from a child's perspective, without the understanding that maturity brings. Now, as an adult, she doesn't really believe that her mother stopped making love to her father without a reason. She's looking to blame someone for what she can't comprehend."

"Kuan Yin is right," Inanna Yin nodded. "Rena couldn't possibly grasp what went on between her parents because emotionally she's stuck at eight, the age she was when they divorced. She views their entire relationship through the eyes of a child. It's her perception, not the truth."

"But her perception is her truth," argued Kali. "And to her that's all that matters."

"It's not logical to believe that truth is only what you see," Inanna shot back. "Rena is stuck in her little world about everything that happened. And I mean everything, even if she hasn't yet become aware of it."

"Lillian's going to leave her." Erishkigal was crying.

"If it's time for her to make the transition," acknowledged Kuan Yin, "it will be painful for Rena. Lillian is the only one who offered her unconditional love. But Lillian's passing will open the door for others to enter her life who will provide that kind of love."

"And you call me a piece of work!" Kali screamed. "Where do you come from? Where do you get these ideas?"

"She has no choice," insisted Inanna. *"It is not her decision. She can either continue to act like a spoiled selfish maniac, which is not very attractive."* She rubbed her heart-shaped lips with two slender fingers. *"Or she can be logical about this. Death is a part of life. There is no choice."*

I finished my coffee and followed my mother. Rebecca's arms were wrapped around my father's waist. My grandfather stood next to the heart monitor, the green dots bouncing off the lenses of his thick glasses. Faith sat next to my grandmother, holding her hand. "I'm sorry." I said. "I'm upset and I'm sorry if I took it out on anyone."

"It's all right, darling," my mother used her other hand to grab mine.

"It's a stressful time," Rebecca removed her arms from my father and walked toward me. I brushed past her and sat on the windowsill.

"Does anyone care what I have to say?" My grandmother asked.

"Of course we do, Mom." My father rested against my mother's back and massaged her shoulders.

"I'll tell you on one condition."

"What, Lillian?" My grandfather sounded annoyed.

"That no one interrupts me."

"Fine," we answered as one.

"You don't get to be my age without realizing a few things about life," she started. "And the realization I've had is that this family has been led around by the nose by fear." She coughed, slowly at first, then violently, her face turning red. The heart monitor blipped angrily. My mother wheeled the tray toward the bed and poured a glass of water. Lifting the cup to my grandmother's lips, Faith pointed the straw at her mouth and she sucked hungrily. The coughing subsided and the heart monitor returned to a calm steady rhythm. She breathed heavily for a minute and then continued.

"I love you all so much. And it's been painful to have watched all of you make decisions motivated by fear. Franklin," she turned her head toward my grandfather, "you have lived the last twenty years afraid of living. Things aren't always going to go your way in life. But instead of seeing them as a way of learning, you used them as an excuse to hide. You've believed for two decades that you are a failure. That having a business that failed meant that you failed." She sat up to sip her water and collapsed back onto the pillow.

My grandfather walked over to the chair in the corner and sat with a thud, his head face down in his hands.

"And that, Michael, was passed onto you. I know you had dreams of being an artist. And every year, I saw that dream fade a little more until there was nothing left. You were too afraid. So you forced yourself to get a business degree and scratched and clawed your way up the corporate ladder until you were successful in the eyes of everyone but yourself."

My father was motionless by the window, staring at the cars sliding in and out of the lined blacktop. "It's not too late, Michael. It's not too late until you're laying in a hospital bed, with saline and valium dripping into your veins so that you're hydrated and numb when you die."

A nurse intruded to take my grandmother's blood pressure and temperature. Faith moved out of the way while the nurse chattered needlessly, made a few notes on the chart and disappeared.

My grandmother smoothed the blanket, tucking it under her small frame. "Faith, I've loved you like a daughter for nearly thirty years. But getting married and having a family is not what you wanted. It's what your parents wanted. You are an incredibly gifted writer. You could've been published. But you chose to be afraid, to not stand up to people who told you to want things you didn't. And everyone has paid the price for that." The bed moaned as my grandmother raised it up a little more.

"Rena, learn from this. I'm begging you. Figure out what it is that will make you happy and do it. Don't run. Don't hide." She coughed again. "Not like I did. I saw what was going on all these years. But I chose not to say anything because I was afraid that they wouldn't love me if I spoke my mind. Always speak your mind. Be kind. But always speak your mind." Tears escaped from her eyes and began to roll down her wrinkled cheeks. "Don't lay on your death bed regretting not speaking your mind."

"All right, Mom, that's enough," my father insisted. "Everybody out for now. Give her a chance to rest."

"I want Rena to stay."

"Mom, you need to be quiet for a while."

"Don't argue with me, Michael."

"Fine, fine." He shuffled my grandfather and Rebecca out of the room. Faith stood behind me.

"Are you sure you don't want to be alone, Lillian?" She asked.

My grandmother touched her fingertips to my mother's arm. "I'm positive." Faith took her empty coffee cup and followed everyone else into the hall.

"I think you need to sleep," I said shutting the door behind my mother. An empty wood chair with a plastic seat cover stood alone next to her bed. It was the passenger seat. The seat that I would occupy, at my grandmother's request, to ride shotgun for the roadtrip of her death. Only I had no map, no flashlight, no pot.

"I just want you to sit with me."

"OK." She pulled her left hand from under the covers and reached for me. I held her hands, ice cold from lack of circulation, until she fell asleep. I stepped outside the room and found my parents. We sat in the hard plastic chairs outside my grandmother's room until the head nurse threw us out.

"I appreciate your coming home," my father touched my elbow. "I know how busy you are."

"I came home for Granma," I pried his hand off of me.

"Look, Rena," he guided me away from my mother, Rebecca and my grandfather. "I know I haven't been the best father to you."

"You could say that."

"Work with me here, Rena," I sensed the urgency in his voice. "I'm really trying."

"What do you want me to say, Dad? That it's OK? That it doesn't matter that you ran around on Mom? That it's all right that I had to work three jobs all through college to pay tuition and rent because you wouldn't send me money because you were using me to punish Mom?" I felt a stabbing pain at the back of my throat as I fought for control. "I can't do that right now, Dad."

"Please, Rena," I turned and looked at him, watery eyes, graying hair, protruding stomach. "I know the way I treated your Mother was wrong. And I can't explain why I did it." A sob escaped out of his puffy jowls. "I'm sorry. I wish you could forgive me, but I'm not going to stand here and beg you." He cleared his throat, sniffed mucous up his nose, and combed his fingers through his thinning hair. "I'll see you in the morning."

My mother and I stopped at Eat'n Park to get something to eat. Normally, my mother wouldn't be caught dead in an Eat'n Park, but it was the only thing open on Banksville Road at nine-thirty on a Tuesday night. We ordered sandwiches and tea and tap-danced around the conversation I'd had with my father.

"How's Raymond?"

"I haven't talked to him in over a month," she bit into her turkey club.

"Have you tried calling him?"

"I did at first," the dark circles under her eyes looked severe in the harsh neon light of the restaurant. "But he never called me back," she chirped a little laugh. "And then I got busy and just forgot." She wiped a drop of mayonnaise from the corner of her lip with a paper napkin. This was the longest amount of time I'd spent with Faith since that disaster in New York. The few times I'd been home since, for holidays, I'd stayed with my grandmother and massaged in a couple of visits with her and my father.

"What kind of odds are the doctors giving her?" I dunked my teabag in and out of the metal pitcher filled with hot water.

"It's not that simple, Rena."

"Yes it is. She's either going to die or she's not."

"You always want everything to be so cut and dry."

"Well?" I ripped the damp paper off the tiny plastic cup of cream and dumped it into my tea.

"The doctor told your father and me that it doesn't look good." She began to cry, the tears forming dark blue stains on the jacket of her fashionable sweat suit. "She probably won't make it through the night." I tossed my empty container of cream and watched it skitter across the table, ricocheting off the salt and peppershakers, finally coming to rest against the silver napkin holder.

"It's not fair."

"Not much in life is, Rena." We finished our meal and drove to her apartment in silence.

She placed fresh towels on the bottom of my bed and went to find an extra blanket. I sat down on the firm mattress and removed my shoes, praying to a God I wasn't sure I believed in. I stared at the print of *Sunday Afternoon on the Island of La Grande Jatte* that hung over the white wicker dresser. Soon, the figures blurred and the colors mutated into one strange shade of violet. I lay down for a minute, hoping to gather the energy to wash my face and brush my teeth. When I woke up the next morning, there was a fuzzy blanket on top of me and my socks and shoes sat orderly, toes pointed toward the dresser.

Early Friday, we drove back to Mercy Hospital after silently sharing coffee in her eat-in kitchen. It was a perky room, decorated with sunflower wallpaper, the towels and potholders in varying shades of yellow. We belted ourselves into her green Volvo and headed toward the darkness of the Liberty Tunnel. We emerged on the other side, the sunlight momentarily blinding us.

After scouring for a parking space, we waited, me not very patiently, with other visitors for the elevator. My father and grandfather and Rebecca stood outside my grandmother's room. I couldn't read the looks on their faces. "Michael?" My mother asked tentatively. "How is she?" My father turned toward us, Rebecca's arm snaked through his.

"I can't explain it." He had aged ten years overnight, "But she's better."

"What do you mean?" I interrupted.

"The doctor's don't understand it," Rebecca chimed in. "But her vitals are stabilized and she's breathing on her own. It's like a miracle or something." Her blond hair was gathered in a silver barrette. Wearing no make-up, she looked twelve. With her free hand, she played with the zipper on her pale pink leather jacket.

"Really?" I watched my grandfather sink, exhausted, into one of the plastic chairs against the wall. They had been married forty-five years. "She's going to make it?"

"It looks that way," my father detached himself from Rebecca and hugged me. I let him and soaked the front of his navy Polo shirt with my tears, the earpiece from his reading glasses pressing against my cheek. My mother rested her arm around my shoulders and the three of us stood in a rare moment of unity.

"When can I see her?"

"You can go in," my father answered. "We just spent fifteen minutes with her." I pushed the door open and saw a tall black woman drawing blood.

"I can come back." I didn't want to disturb them.

"Rena," Granma called. "Is that you? Come in, come in." The phlebotomist untied the rubber tourniquet and tossed the tube into a red plastic tray. I walked over to the bed and sat on the edge. Her forehead was cool and dry when I kissed it.

"I'm so glad to see you're feeling better."

"I guess it wasn't my time after all," she smiled, a rosy hint on her cheeks. "I'm glad. Now I can find out if Erica gets married again on *All My Children*." She pushed herself up against the pillows. "Rena, I need to ask you something."

"OK."

"Will you quit smoking?" She grabbed my hand.

"For how long?" I laughed

"It's not funny," she chastised, releasing my hand.

"If it's that important to you, I won't ever light up again." She smiled and dropped her head back to the pillow. "I'll let you rest, now. But I'm going to stay in town for a while." I folded the top of the blanket and tucked it around her.

"That'll be nice," she closed her eyes. "Thank you, dear." I joined my parents in the hall.

"How is she?" My mother asked, sipping her third cup of coffee that morning.

"I think she went to sleep, but her color is good and she doesn't have a fever." I fumbled in my purse for a tissue.

"Here," Rebecca handed me a Puff's from the miniature packet she pulled out of her jacket.

"Thanks," I wiped my eyes and blew my nose. I stayed in Pittsburgh for a week, spending long hours visiting my grandmother every day. I tried to reach Joni several times and finally left a message with the temp that I would be back the following Monday. By the time I left, my grandmother was only a couple of days from being discharged.

My grandfather insisted on driving me to the airport. My father objected, believing it was too great a distance for him to negotiate safely. But my grandfather won and as I transferred my bags from Faith's Volvo to his Valiant, I realized I hadn't spoken with him much in the time I'd been there. I hugged Faith and my father in the hospital parking lot. Rebecca laid her hand on my forearm and wished me a safe flight. I acknowledged the gesture by kissing the air next to her cheek.

We sped out of the lot and screeched to a stop at the light on Forbes Avenue. "Sorry," my grandfather said, lighting his pipe. He puffed while the flame from his Bic hovered over the bowl. We headed down Fifth Avenue. It would've been easier to have made a left at Grant Street, but I said nothing as the Valiant hurtled down Fifth, past Kaufmann's, and into Market Square. He dodged pedestrians, making an occasional clicking sound when his dentures clamped down on the stem of his pipe. He wore navy polyester pants and a pale blue sweater underneath his old winter coat.

"I really appreciate you coming all this way to see your grandmother," he finally spoke as we wove our way onto the bridge and into the tunnel. "I know how busy you are in New York."

"I wouldn't have had it any other way, Grandpa," I blew a bubble with my gum. "I'm just glad she's better." I sneaked a look at him. A ring of thick white hair peeked out from under the knit Steeler cap, framing his ruddy cheeks and dark, bushy eyebrows. The skin on his fingers looked plastic as he tightly gripped the steering wheel.

"She loves you, you know." His thick glasses were smeared with fingerprints and I wondered how well he could see.

"I know. I love her too."

"It's hard for me to say how I feel, Rena. A man didn't go around telling people how he felt in my day."

"Don't worry; they don't do it now either," I laughed.

"Your father's not good at it either."

"No kidding."

"Don't be too hard on us, Rena. You haven't lived our lives. You haven't been faced with some of the choices that were forced on us." We cruised passed Greentree. "You don't know everything about him. Or me." I sat there, quietly chewing my Trident.

"You're right," I agreed to pacify him. All I knew was that I wouldn't have hurt people the way either of them did. He nodded slightly for the rest of the drive, the hum of the engine the only noise in the car. I stared out the window wondering when they had built an Ikea the size of Three Rivers Stadium. I hadn't even noticed it on the way in. We pulled into an empty slot against the curb in the Departures area. He tottered back to the trunk to get my bags. I hailed a Skycap. I couldn't bear to watch him struggling to lift my bags. He planted a wet kiss on my cheek.

"Have a safe trip back, Rena."

"I will." I hugged him and felt his bones through his heavy wool coat. "I'll call to let you know I got in OK."

"Do that." A few wisps of snowy hair fluttered in the breeze. "Your grandmother will be worried." I walked into the terminal and watched him hoist himself in behind the steering wheel behind the enormous glass windows.

Pause

I was glad to be back at work when I arrived at eight-thirty Monday morning. My desk was in reasonable order, and the temp had left a file with my name on it full of messages and notes on the status of each current project. I had just bitten into my bagel when Joni breezed by and asked to see me in her office.

"How was the funeral?" She asked, sitting down.

"Good news," I plopped into the chair in front of her desk. "She pulled through. None of the doctors thought she was going to make it. But somehow she did." I sipped my coffee through the hole I'd ripped in the plastic lid. "She'll probably be discharged sometime this week." I watched the red work its way up Joni's neck.

"You mean you've been gone all this time and she didn't die?"

"Yeah, it's great. Right?" I was sensing she didn't think so.

"And you expect me to pay you for this little vacation?"

"It was hardly a vacation, Joni. I was at the hospital for six or seven hours every day."

"When you left here, Rena, you were certain she was going to pass away." She folded her hands on the blotter. "I assumed you were gone all this time because you were needed to help make arrangements for the viewing and the funeral."

"I tried to call you, plenty of times. I left my mother's number, but you never called me back."

"All I was told was that you were going to be back in the office today."

"Why would I lie?"

"I don't know." She counted the days I had been gone on her desk calendar with a perfect red nail. "You were gone seven working days. I'll pay you for three of them."

"What are you talking about? I'll take them as vacation days."

"Vacation time has to be approved two weeks ahead of time, Rena, you know that. Emergencies come out of personal time. You had three personal days left, so I'll pay you for them."

"I don't fucking believe this!"

"Excuse me?"

"My grandmother almost dies and you're worried about docking my pay?"

"I run a business, Rena. That temp cost me $120 a day. I wouldn't have had to get a temp if you were on vacation. We just would've rotated the other assistants in a day at a time. But we didn't have enough time to plan that."

"This sucks."

"I'm sorry you feel that way."

"First you jerk me around promising me a promotion and now you dock me pay because I went home to see my grandmother who I thought was dying. Instead of being happy for me that she didn't pass away, you're docking me four days pay. I don't need this shit."

"Try to understand where I'm coming from on this, Rena." She walked around the desk and put a hand on my shoulder. "If I paid you, I'd have to do it every time someone had an 'emergency.'" She quoted the word "emergency" with her fingers.

"Whatever."

"If you don't like it, Rena, you can always find another place to work. You're lucky I'm paying you for any of it." I jumped out of the chair and ran out of her office. I ravaged the rest of my bagel sitting at my desk going through the file the temp had left. Why hadn't she told Joni I called? I took a five from petty cash and rode the elevator down to the newsstand in the lobby. I stared longingly at a pack of Marlboro Lights. I grabbed five Snickers bars and handed the tiny Indian man the bill. I didn't wait for the change.

"It's not working your way anymore," Inanna faced Kali.

"Give me another chance," Kali tilted her chin up and stared at Inanna sideways. "I'll make it better."

"It's not a matter of getting another chance," Kuan Yin interrupted. "It's almost time for Rena to move on."

"Bullshit," Kali screamed, her face flushed with anger. "Joni is a real bitch. Rena deserves better."

"If Rena doesn't go back she's going to end up like Celia," Inanna said firmly. "She'll be stuck in some roach infested apartment, wasted every day and not knowing who's going to be in bed next to her when she wakes up."

"And Rena hasn't exactly been a delight to be around the last several months," added Kuan Yin. "We can't completely blame Joni."

"I say we give it another chance." Inanna stared at Kali spinning her sword. "What do you say, sister?" Kali felt her power diminishing. She might as well agree and at least make it look like she was still in control.

"OK," said Kali ignoring the fact that it had been Inanna's idea.

I went to work the next day determined to get back on Joni's good side. I marched into her office and told her we needed to talk. We agreed to meet after five. I spent hours that day reorganizing my files, cleaning out my desk, and doing all the things that had piled up on my desk for months because I didn't want to deal with them. I smiled at people instead of barking at them.

I approached Joni's office around five-thirty. "Come in, come in, Rena."
She smiled curiously. "What's all this about?"

"Joni," I began the speech I had written, "I know I've been a royal pain in
the ass for a while now. And I'm sorry. I went through a phase and I want to
assure you that it's over. And I want to express to you my gratitude for you
dealing with me while I was going through it." I paused to breathe, my
heart beating wildly.

"I also want to commit to you that I am here for the long haul. I'm
going to show you what this job means to me and what working here has
taught me." I rubbed my palms together, trying to distribute the puddle
of cold sweat that had formed in the hollow. "I want to be more in this
company than your assistant. And I'm willing to do whatever I need to
prove that."

She leaned back in her chair and crossed her legs, one pump dangling off
her foot as she rotated an ankle. "Impressive, Rena. What brought this on?"

"You've given me an opportunity and I want to show you what I'm capable of doing." I exhaled for the first time.

"You know you're still going to have to be my assistant."

"I know that. And when I've shown you that I can be the best assistant I
can be, I know you'll give me more responsibility."

"OK then." She leaned onto the desk. "I can't tell you how happy I am
that you reached this conclusion on your own, Rena. You haven't been easy
to be around. But I've always known that there was something in there
worth holding on to." She stood and held out her hand. "Let's start over.
Welcome to JC Communications."

"Thank you. I'm glad to be here," I smiled shaking her hand.

Over the next six months, I was in early and stayed late. I had no friends
left and the New York spring was rainy and cold, so it's not like I sacrificed
anything. I hadn't talked to Celia in quite some time. We never had a falling
out. It was a gradual division. She'd call. I'd wait a few days and call her at
home during the day. Then she'd do the same to me. After several weeks of
phone tag I thought, "What's the point?"

I cheerfully performed tasks that weren't in my job description, helping
out the creative or media departments with menial jobs to prove how dedicated I was. Once, I took the bus up to 125th Street to a production house
to pick up a tape of a commercial for a client. When I was told it wouldn't
be ready for another hour, I waited and returned to the agency triumphant
that we could get a print to the client on time.

I made copies, ran errands, and ordered breakfasts and lunches to help out on new business pitches. I cheerfully retyped version after version of copy for the creative department when their secretary was out on disability with a broken hip. I even bought and wrapped a birthday present for Joni's daughter Liz while Joni was tied up trying to acquire the Krispy's Chicken account.

Over the Christmas holiday, Joni was insane trying to get a set of media buys on the air for an important retail client. Her star media buyer had accepted a position at Foote Cone and Belding and bailed on her three days before the due date. She got a two-day extension from the client and I worked by her side for three nights doing whatever she needed me to do. I almost missed my flight home for the holidays, but we got everything booked.

When I returned from Pittsburgh after the break, I found a vase full of irises on my desk with a card. "Thank you for all of your help. I couldn't have done it without you. Joni." I carried the vase into her office.

"Thank you so much," I buried my nose in the center of a flower. "They're beautiful!"

"Have a seat, Rena." She looked radiant in a pale pink silk pantsuit. A single strand of pearls accented her delicate collarbone. I sat, placing the bouquet on the edge of her desk.

"What's up?"

"We got the Krispy's account!" She clapped her hands together, and held them to her lips. "I'm so thrilled I don't know what to do with myself. I couldn't have done it without your help."

"That's wonderful!" I was genuinely happy, knowing that I had participated in the win, even if it was only in a Gal Friday kind of way.

"I need to replace Kathryn," she twisted her pearls, the nails on her hand painted blush pink to match her suit. "I've been thinking that I would promote Jennifer from an assistant to a media buyer." The sunlight bounced the reflection of her watch crystal on the walls. "But that means I need an assistant in the media department." The edges of her mouth slowly curled upward. "Would you be interested?"

"Me? Really?" I leapt out of my chair, knocking the vase off the corner of the desk and into my disappearing lap. Drenched, I managed to catch the vase before it fell to the carpet and salvaged all but two of the flowers. I put the vase, dripping on the outside, on the coffee table next to the couch and ran over to give her a hug. "Thank you, Joni. Thank you so much," I gushed. "I won't let you down. I promise."

"We don't start doing the buying until second quarter. But Patricia is going to need your help with the set up." Joni gave me a quick hug, her breasts hard from the implants she'd gotten last year. "I know you'll do fine." Patricia Kendall, the media supervisor, had been working for JC for almost a year and a half. She had been employed by the billing department of Darcy Masius Benton and Bowles when she decided that being black wasn't going to prevent her from moving out of an underpaid and thankless job. In two years of delivering invoices for approval, she made an ally of the media director and eventually transferred over as an assistant, the first person in the company's history to make such a move.

It didn't take long before she was made a full-fledged buyer. When she discovered that she was earning a little more than half of everyone else in the department, she asked for a raise. After being refused, she aggressively pursued the position at JC. She had always treated me with courtesy and a friendly hello.

"Hey, girl," Patricia smiled on my first day in the department, "isn't this wild? You being an assistant now? We're going to have some fun!" I smiled back from the desk in my cube. The cube was a step up. Before I had been at a desk outside Joni's door.

"I'm looking forward to it." Clothes always draped Patricia's slender frame as if she were preparing to walk down the runway. Her long brown fingers were adorned with a small diamond engagement ring, a recent present from her long time boyfriend Marcus. I despised my pudgy hands with their squat fingers. And I had no ring. I had no boyfriend.

"We just got the specs for the second quarter Krispy's buys." She smiled, her pale green eyes sparkling under thick lashes. "Why don't you finish up here and meet me in my office?"

"Sure. I'll just be a few more minutes." I pulled my gaze from hers.

"Great. Stop by and get Jennifer on your way?"

"No problem." Jennifer Cohen, the other media buyer in the department, had started as an assistant six months ago. I had been in a drug and sex induced haze when the position opened. I had no desire to apply, preferring the comfort zone I had carefully built. Jennifer had long, frizzy hair and a bump in her nose. She wore thrift store clothes and didn't shave her legs, even in the summer.

"Hey, Jennifer," I called into her new office. Boxes sat on the floor surrounding her desk. I knew none of them contained Sweet'n Low or plastic silverware because the desk I now occupied had been hers and the drawers were full of pink packets and white forks. "Patricia wants to talk to us about the Krispy's second quarter specs."

"I really need to unpack," she whined nasally, her long hair pulled up in a ponytail reminiscent of Pebbles from *The Flintstones*. The dry ends were begging to be chopped off and I contemplated grabbing the scissors from her "Have you had your hug today?" mug sitting on the desk. A little boom box sitting alone on the bare windowsill pumped Simon and Garfunkle's "Cecilia" through its speakers.

"Can't we do it later?" She crawled onto the floor, opening boxes, digging through them, and moving onto the next, occasionally stopping to remove the long green sari skirt from under her knees. She looked up at me pleadingly, a puka bead necklace loosely clasped around her throat. "I've also got to finish the revisions on the United Motors buy in Hartford and I can't find the stupid file."

"I'll let Patricia know," I said, leaving her to rummage through the cartons. After explaining Jennifer's dilemma, Patricia and I spent a couple of hours going over the workload and what she expected of me. She patiently taught me how to estimate ratings, let me listen in on the negotiations she had with her station's sales reps, and showed me how to assemble radio and television buys. I basically handled the paperwork for her and Jennifer, but she assured me that I would become familiar with all the aspects of the department that way.

It wasn't too long before she was allowing me to do small radio buys on my own. She dutifully checked everything before it was ordered, but I got a real sense of accomplishment from completing the process on my own. After several months of radio experience, she allowed me to delve into television. It was a little more difficult but I enjoyed the challenge. I liked dealing with most of the reps. There were some constantly in my face, threatening to go to the client if I didn't give their station the share that they believed it deserved. There were others who never returned phone calls and some who tried to buy their way onto a schedule by sending me chocolates or flowers or offering to take me to lunch.

Patricia had warned me about reps trying to get on my good side for no reason other than to garner a good share. Because she was still checking all my work, the few times I got suckered, she made me redo the buys so that the client was being served and not the station. "Girl," Patricia said, stretching the word like it was saltwater taffy in the sun, "I hope they got you something extravagant. Their little piece of shit station would've been lucky to be on the buy, much less walk away with thirty percent of it." I threw out the thank you card that accompanied the spider plant sitting on the floor of my cube.

One afternoon in September, Jennifer stormed into Patricia's office as we were discussing our weekend plans, hair loose and frizzy, a scrunchy wrapped around her wrist. "I can't take this!" Her pale skinny arms were bent at the elbow, allowing her hands to rest on her bony hips. Several damp strands of hair were pasted to the underside of her arms. She wore Birkenstock sandals and a loud floral print skirt that extended to her ankles.

"There's no way I can get all of this crap done by the due date." She walked over and plopped into the chair next to me. The closer she got, it became clear that a razor wasn't the only thing she didn't use under her arms. She began to sob, her shoulders heaving up and down as the tears dripped from her chin.

"Good God, honey," Patricia's eyes were opened wide, "it's not that bad." She wadded a tissue into a ball and threw it at Jennifer. "Girl. Don't cry." I sat next to her, speechless. I had caved under pressure before, but I had never had a nervous breakdown like that, at least not in public. Jennifer walked out that night and never returned. Patricia heard from a friend of hers at another agency that she had gone home to Minnesota, abandoning her apartment and sticking her roommate for the rent. Bad for Jennifer. Good for me.

"See?" Inanna grinned smugly. "I told you a little attitude change would go along way."

"But where's the sex?" Kali grumbled. "She doesn't have fun anymore."

"Balance, sister," Kuan Yin whispered. "Rena had plenty of fun,' as you call it. Sometimes you have to go to the other end of the spectrum before you can find a happy medium."

"I don't like it," Kali objected. "It's dull and boring. But I guess that's to be expected."

"What's that supposed to mean?" Inanna asked defensively.

"Oh, nothing," mused Kali, innocently twirling one of the infant earrings between two of her fingers. *"Only that you are basically a dull and boring person, and so it would reason that you would make dull and boring decisions."*

"You're a hedonistic, selfish egomaniac who would cut off her own nose to spite her face." Inanna spat. *"I'll take boring any day."*

"Stop it!" Erishkigal squeezed her hands over her ears.

"Let go, Kali," Kuan Yin advised. *"Can't you see it's better this way for Rena?"*

"Oh, all right. For now," Kali sulked for a moment. *"But now it's my turn to watch you, Inanna."* She drew her sword from its sheath and gently pressed the tip of it against Inanna's forehead. *"Don't forget it."*

By the end of the summer, Joni had made me a full buyer and hired an assistant to replace me. Patricia took on most of the responsibility of training Lucinda. "Honey, sometimes I don't think that girl could find her way out of a paper bag with a flashlight," Patricia remarked to me one day after Lucinda had been working for us a couple of months.

"She seems efficient to me," I said. "She knows how to make copies, fax, and take phone messages."

"And that's about it," she laughed. "You spoiled me. I had you doing some of my work within a few weeks. I wouldn't trust her with any of it."

"I don't get the feeling the word 'ambition' is in her vocabulary," I agreed. "She's got a three-year old and a baby. Her husband works nights for Con Edison. I think she's in it strictly for the paycheck."

"Are you OK with that?" Patricia seemed concerned. "We've got a lot of work. Can you handle it without using an assistant to help you estimate?" I silently admired her silk wrap skirt with its hand-painted Chinese flowers, her flat stomach. I sucked mine in.

"Sure," I replied confidently, although I wasn't sure it was all going to be completed by the deadline. "I'd rather have someone I can trust to do a few things than worry about retraining someone at this point." Patricia combed her fingers through her pressed hair, smacked her glossed lips together, and nodded.

"All right. We'll give her a chance."

Lucinda proved to be a rock. Over the next few months, it became apparent she was perfectly content being a glorified secretary. But she knew how to politely blow reps off when Patricia and I didn't want to see them, keep the clients happy, and make a mean cup of coffee. For someone who couldn't have been more than twenty-four, she had an air about her that made you wary about messing with her. She reminded me of Celia.

One Friday in January, after a particularly long week, I agreed to join Patricia and Marcus and a couple of his friends for happy hour. I had declined the other times she'd offered to include me because I had been burned at a telemarketing job in Pittsburgh. I had become friends with a co-worker who blabbed about my taste for marijuana to our boss. She ended up with the promotion I deserved.

Patricia and I walked to Broadway and took the N train down to City Hall to meet Marcus who worked on Wall Street as an attorney for a brokerage firm. We navigated through the mad rush coming toward us as we walked up the steps, tightening the scarves around our necks. Above ground, we headed west to the pub where we were meeting everyone. "Can you believe that shit Joni's trying to shove down my throat?" she asked.

"I worked for her for two years. I can believe it." Joni had been promising to hire a third buyer for several months. Every time Patricia approached her, there was a different reason why it wasn't possible.

"I don't think I can take much more of it," she confessed. "Weiden and Kennedy has been giving me the full court press," she casually dropped a bomb at my feet. "They want me to be their media director. And I'm ready to say yes."

"But you can't." I struggled to keep up with her long-legged strides. "I don't want to work for anyone else. And besides, I'd miss you."

"Girl, don't play stupid." She threw me a look no white woman could replicate. "You know Joni will promote you when I go."

"I'm not ready for that." She looked at me thoughtfully in the glow from the streetlights on Chambers Street.

"No, you're probably not," she agreed. "But I know you could handle it. And Joni won't have to pay you what she pays me. That'll make her happy."

"You're not serious about this?"

"As a heart attack, honey." She put her hand on my arm. "That's why I'm glad you decided to come out with us tonight. I didn't want you finding out after I resigned." We walked in the bar, grateful to get out of the bone-chilling breeze coming off the Hudson. Marcus wasn't there yet.

"Are you Patricia?" The old bartender asked, his teeth yellowed from tobacco.

"Who wants to know?"

"Marcus called. Says he's stuck at the office. He'll meet you at home." He crumpled the message and tossed it over his shoulder into the trash.

"Well, girl. I guess it's you and me. What'll you have?" She laid a twenty on the bar and hopped up on a stool.

Inanna

The Fifth Goddess

Christmas time in the advertising media business was enough to suck the holiday spirit out of the cheeriest elf at the North Pole. All the annual media buys needed to be rated, negotiated, and placed before the end of the year. In addition, retail clients required immediate attention because they were advertising specific sales. The regular clients who were placing their money for first quarter also wanted their final spending totaled before December 31st.

As part of the deal I made with Joni when Patricia left, we hired two more buyers and another assistant. Jesse and I split the supervisory responsibilities. Sarah handled the medium-sized markets and Maria assisted all of us and bought tiny markets like Elmira, New York. For three weeks now Jesse, Sarah, Maria, and I had worked eleven-hour days, rarely even breaking for lunch.

Two weeks into the marathon, Butler's, our biggest retail account, decided to revamp their entire media strategy. Sales had been down since Thanksgiving, largely due to Macy's doubling their advertising budget and deciding to open the store Thanksgiving Day after the parade, a first in their history.

As supervisor on this account, I spent two days tallying all of their spending in radio, television, and newspaper for the month of December. I had orchestrated a complete breakout of all the media details, including reach and frequency statistics for television and radio; a cost per thousand analysis for each newspaper purchased; a summary of the television and radio stations used; and total ratings for their primary, secondary, and tertiary demographics. I designed the forms myself in Excel. And now, they wanted to change everything.

"Butler's marketing research shows that their shopper demographic is more Women 18–49, not Women 25–54 which is what we used to plan the goals." Joni explained. "So they want us to go back and re-do all the buys, using Women 18–49 as the primary demo and Women 25–54 as the secondary." She sighed. "The tertiary demo of Adults 25–54 stays the same."

"No fucking way." Jesse slammed her hand on the conference table. "Do you have any idea how much work that is? Do you have any idea how much work I have on my desk right now?" The red tips of her ears were visible under her short brown hair.

"Bitching isn't going to pay the rent." Joni silenced her. "Just do it."

"But, Joni, we have the annual deals for the North East United Motors Dealers to negotiate and place yet," argued Sarah. "And they want promotions and sports and all kinds of tickets to football games and stuff. That can't be accomplished overnight. And, the first quarter buys for Glasses Plus, Krispy's Chicken and the WPKL Bridal Fair are all due before Christmas."

"I am aware of your workload." Joni shot Sarah a look that frosted the can of Coke sitting in front of her. "What would you like me to do? Tell them no?"

"That would be a start," Sarah was disgusted. She tapped her pen on her notebook. "But how about hiring a freelancer or two to help out?"

"You know they never do as good a job," Joni slumped her shoulders and leaned back in the leather chair. "They're not as dedicated. I'm sorry, guys, I know this is rough."

"No, Joni, I really don't think you do." I stood up from the table and went to my office to retrieve a copy of the Butler media synopsis. I tossed it onto the conference table and watched it slide on the slick surface into Joni's hands. "That took me two days. Two days where I could do none of my regular work. Two days where I did nothing but eat, breath, sleep, and shit Butler's Department Store. And now it's useless." I reached behind me to the refrigerator, pulled out a Diet Sprite, snapped the metal pull-tab, and chugged, imagining it was fizzy lemon-flavored vodka.

"All right," I said resting the can in front of me. "Let's each take two minutes a piece to bitch and complain. Then we need to get down to business or we'll never finish." They all stared at the table. "I know it sucks. I know Butler's advertising department is a bunch of assholes who are desperately trying to prove to the bean counters that their jobs exist for a reason." I swigged the rest of the soda.

"I know they're grasping at straws, hoping against hope that if they change their target demo, a miracle will happen and in this shitty economy, their sales will go up from last year. But, they're our client and as their advertising agency, it is our duty—no, our privilege—to allow them their delusion." I paused and belched silently.

"So, let's do what they want and shove it down their throats when they're wrong. It's the only way we've got a prayer of them finally giving in and using our marketing and media planning departments instead of their own incompetent losers." I tossed the can in the trash. "And that's more money, which would mean raises for everyone—right Joni?"

The look on her face fell somewhere between hatred and respect. "You're right, Rena. And I'll give each of you girls a two-hundred-fifty dollar bonus if you get this done before the buys are scheduled to air."

"OK," Sarah, Maria, and Jesse responded in unison. "Food would be nice, too, if we're going to be here until ten o'clock at night," Sarah added.

"You guys are tough," a smile inched across Joni's face. "All right, order out any night you're here past eight and submit it on your expense report. Fair enough?"

"Not quite," answered Jesse, "but it'll do for now."

"All right, guys," I mustered my best head cheerleader voice, "let's get moving." Within a week, we had completely redone everything and presented the client with a synopsis. And somehow, we managed to get almost everything else done as well. We were still working on third and fourth quarter buys for the United Motors dealers because of the time involved in negotiating NFL packages. United Motors also expected the stations to throw in tickets, scoreboard announcements, and logos on the programs.

Gene Solomon, one of my sales reps, had gotten tickets to the Broadway show *Blood Brothers* with David and Shaun Cassidy as a thank you for the money I had put on the station he represented in Philadelphia. The station had no ratings and lousy programming. But, in exchange for getting on the fourth quarter Krispy's Chicken buy, they did a huge promotion, making Krispy's a sponsor of the Kite Fair they held in October at Fairmount Park.

Gene and I had driven down to Philly the Saturday of the Fair and were astonished at the organization displayed by a station that ran *Andy Griffith* four times a day. Krispy's booth, staffed by station employees, served samples of the new chicken nuggets and distributed coupons. There was also a king-sized kite with the Krispy's name and logo on it being flown in the contest by a world champion kite flier. I didn't even know kite flying was a competitive sport.

The station's sister radio station was on hand to broadcast live from the fair and plugged Krispy's every fifteen to twenty minutes. The promotion was a huge success and Krispy's had committed to the station for next year's fair. Gene got a bonus from his firm and a gift from the station. And Krispy's vice president of advertising sent me a two-hundred dollar American Express gift certificate and a note of thanks. Gratitude from a client was rare, so to celebrate Gene got tickets to a show we both had been dying to see. Thursday night couldn't come fast enough.

That morning, Joni wanted to know how much longer it was going to take me to complete the Philadelphia United Motors buy. I told her by Monday. That was still three days before the deadline. I worked on it all day, skipped lunch, and was touching up my make-up in the ladies room when Joni barged in, her hair madly standing on end, as if an invisible leprechaun held a magnet above her head. "What's up with you?" I asked trying not to giggle.

"Rena, you can't leave," she leaned against the wall. "I've been looking all over for you."

"Oh, no, Joni, you must have me mistaken for someone else who's going to work late tonight. I have tickets to *Blood Brothers* and I'm not missing it." I stared at the mascara smudged under her lower lashes. "For anyone or anything."

"I need you. Please, you've got to stay."

"What is going on?" I watched her in the mirror.

"Sarah's grandmother died. She left around lunch time." I was such a hermit all day, I didn't even know. "I've been trying to finish her United Motors annual in Hartford and I'm ready to rip my hair out."

"Yeah, that's a tough market. I sympathize." I clicked my compact shut and placed it in my purse. I opened my mouth and pouted in the mirror, outlining my lips in Deepest Plum.

"Don't be coy with me, Rena." Joni stamped her foot on the tile. "You know this has to be done by Monday and she's barely even started it. Her grandmother died in Kalamazoo or some god-forsaken place. I have no idea when she's coming back." I thought I heard her whimper. "What do I have to say to get you to stay?"

"You can say whatever you want. I'm not staying, Joni. I've had these tickets for two and a half months. I'm not missing this show. I'll help you tomorrow."

"Tomorrow's too late. Hartford is due the day before the rest of the markets because the dealer is such an anal-retentive yahoo. He wants to personally review the schedules. Having the dealer group sign off on it isn't good enough for him."

"I'm sorry, Joni."

"You walk out on me and, so help me Rena," her little hands curled into frustrated fists. "I'll fire you." I froze, the lip pencil resting on the middle of my bottom lip. She angrily pulled the bathroom door open and stomped out, her electrified hair traveling three seconds behind her. I kicked the gray marble wall, my eyes watering from the painful tingle. I forced the tears back down, finished applying my lipstick, put on my coat, and headed for her office. I walked in and slammed the door behind me.

"You have some nerve!" I dragged out each word. Joni, startled by the slam, peered at me over her half-glasses. When did she get old enough to need reading glasses?

"You heard what I said, Rena. It's your choice."

"You know what these are, Joni?" I stuck my hands, palms flat, an inch from her face. "These are my two hands. Yes, two. God only gave me two. And they've been working day and night for a boss who's extremely ungrateful," I pulled my hands back and crossed them over my chest. "So ungrateful, in fact, that she's forgotten that the only reason Sarah, Jesse, and Maria pitched in and helped with the whole Butlers' fiasco was because of what I said. So ungrateful that she's forgotten that I've been working sixty-hour weeks for the last month." I threw myself into a chair and crossed my legs.

"So fucking ungrateful, that it doesn't matter to her that I've done no Christmas shopping and will be lucky to get a flight home for the holiday because I haven't had time to call the fucking airlines and make a reservation." I uncrossed my legs and leaned onto the desk, hands folded and my index fingers pointing at her.

"And now, this extremely insensitive, ungrateful bitch of a boss just threatened to fire me if I don't cancel plans I've had for over two months." I paused, trying to sense her reaction. Then I realized it didn't matter. I had stepped way over the line. "How would you like to work for a boss like that?" I stood up, slung my purse over my shoulder, and turned to go.

"Well, I don't want to work for a boss like that anymore. So I guess firing me would be the best thing that could happen." I calmly opened the door and closed it behind me. As I waited for the elevator, I wondered aloud what the hell had come over me.

"Dammit, Kali!" screamed Inanna. "How could you have done that?"

"Simple. Joni was treating her like shit and I wasn't going to sit still for it. Not like the rest of you pussies." Kali's eyes were bloodshot and enraged.

"Rena was getting someplace here," Inanna argued. "She started out as an assistant, Kali. Washing coffee cups and running errands. She's worked

hard all this time. And now you and your big mouth have spoiled every-thing."

"Inanna, you are seriously delusional. Just because she has a title and makes more than minimum wage doesn't mean she's rocketing up the rungs of the corporate ladder. Wake up and smell the java." Her hands twisted the folds of her robe.

"Well, I think Joni was desperate," interjected Erishkigal. "Sarah's gone and she hasn't done this kind of work in a long time. It's intimidating."

"Tough shit," said Kali, filing an index fingernail on her third set of hands with her sword.

"That's not the point," hissed Inanna through clenched teeth. The skin at her hairline was bright red and a small blue vein thumped over her left eye. "You respect authority. You do what you're told. This is Rena's career we're talking about. What's more important? That or seeing Keith Partridge in some musical?"

"What's important," interrupted Kuan Yin, "is what makes Rena happy."

"Well, Miss Queen of Compassion, what makes Rena happy is being able to pay the bills. What makes Rena happy is having a job to get up and go to every day."

"She's not happy in this job, Inanna," Kuan Yin argued gently. "She hasn't been happy for quite some time. But, Kali, that doesn't excuse your behavior."

"Bug off, KY. I did what I had to do."

"Yeah, and you got her fired." Erishkigal retreated from her sisters and sat, head bowed.

"Don't worry, E.," Kali laughed evilly, "Joni can't live without her right now. Especially since Sarah's grandmother kicked the bucket. Trust me, Rena will be back at work tomorrow."

"How do you know for sure?" asked Erishkigal.

"Because it's not quite time for her to go yet," answered Kuan Yin. "She's almost ready to move on."

"I don't know about that, but I do know that if there isn't a message on Rena's machine from Joni tonight, you're in big trouble, Kali." Inanna wrapped her cloak around her slender frame and stared at Kali, the vein still throbbing.

Over dinner at Rachel's I told Gene what had happened with Joni. "I've known her a long time, Rena," he cut into his chicken. "She's not going to fire you over something that was so obviously heat of the moment. And besides, if she really did fire you, you can always come work for us." A few vodka tonics and a couple of hits off of the joint Gene brought with him helped me forget about it and the snow that was quickly covering Manhattan. God, I wanted a cigarette.

David and Shaun were amazing. I think I even detected a tear or two leaking from Gene's eyes when it was over. The light on my answering machine was blinking when I got home. I was afraid to listen. So I changed, washed my face, and circled around it a few times.

I finally pressed the play button. "Hi, Rena, it's Mom. Just checking in. Call me and let me know what time your flight arrives for Christmas." The next message beeped. "Rena," the voice was so hushed it was almost indistinguishable. "It's Joni. I'm calling because I want us to forget what happened earlier. I'll see you in the morning." I pressed delete.

Rest

By the end of January, we had gotten pretty busy again with the addition of two new clients, Pearsall Real Estate and Brooklyn Root Beer. I had assisted Joni in the acquisitions, developing sample media plans and budgets. We had all worked crazy hours and I was craving beach time.

"You can't take the time off now, Rena. It's too busy." Joni kissed herself in the compact mirror after applying her Chanel lipstick.

"You've been promising me I can take a week off for eight months now, Joni." I swallowed hard to keep my voice in check. "I need a vacation." I raised my hand, swirled my wrist, and snapped my fingers. "I want to lie on the beach and coo 'Oh, boy' to some tanned hard hunk wearing a thong. I can't deal with you putting me off anymore."

"Quit whining, Rena. You talk about wanting to get to the top rung of the ladder. You don't do that by taking vacations. You accomplish that by dedication and working long hours."

"I do work long—no insane hours." I refused to give in to the tears. "I am dedicated. I take work home with me on weekends. I order dinner in my office three nights a week. But I need some time off."

"I'm sorry. Not now." Joni replaced the earring on her phone ear and smoothed the jacket of her Dana Buchman suit as she stood up. "I'm late for an appointment across town, Rena. I believe we're done here." She threw her coach bag over her shoulder and breezed by me, leaving me damp in a mist of Givenchy's Amirage. I sneezed.

"Enough of Joni's slave driver bullshit," demanded Kali. "It's time for her to leave."

"Where will she go?" asked Erishkigal. "This is all she's ever known in New York. This is where all of her friends are. It's not that bad. What if she leaves and the place she goes to is worse?"

"It couldn't be worse," argued Kali. "And worse for more money isn't such a bad thing."

"How do you know she'll make more money?" Erishkigal questioned.

"You are such a pessimist. 'How do you know she'll make more money?'" mimicked Kali, squinting her eyes and tilting her head side to side. "Why would she leave unless she was going to make more money?"

"If you two could stop arguing for a minute, maybe we could figure out a plan," interrupted Inanna. "That sales rep of hers, what's his name? Gerald? Gene?"

"Gene Solomon?" offered Erishkigal.

"Yes, him. Hasn't he been trying to get Rena to interview at his company for a sales job?"

"He has," said Erishkigal, "but the problem is that she would have to take a pay cut." She glared at Kali. "So there, Miss Smarty Pants."

"Smarty Pants?" snickered Kali. "That's your witty retort?"

"Enough!" demanded Inanna. "The job at least has potential. Everyone in that business eventually makes more than Rena does now. It's something new."

"And there are men," smiled Kali. "That'll be a refreshing change. I say we look into it."

I waited for Gene at a table next to the fireplace at Café Centro, questioning whether I really wanted to sell commercial advertising. The chickens roasting on the spit crackled and popped as the juices dripped into the flames. I ordered a glass of blackberry iced tea and buttered a piece of french bread. The line at the hostess stand had grown and now extended out the door and into the Met Life Building. Glancing through the crowd waiting to be seated, I felt self-conscious in my clothes.

Many of the women in line carried the nondescript, but highly recognizable "Medium Brown Bag" from Bloomingdales or the white shopping bags with the bold red Lord & Taylor signature. Joni didn't pay me enough to shop at those department stores. And besides, I probably wouldn't fit into most of the clothes they carried. So there I sat in my black stretch skirt, big blouse, and 1X tights from The Avenue—Clothing for Women in Sizes 14–24.

"Hey, Rena." Gene smiled at me as I ripped another chunk of bread from the loaf. "Sorry I kept you waiting—you know how demanding those buyers can be!" He laughed and his teeth glistened against his tanned face. Gene reminded me of the guys that hang out at the Tiki bar at Club Hedonism, shirt unbuttoned to the navel, always ready to buy a beautiful woman a drink if he thinks he can get at least a blow job out of it.

"No, Gene, I have no idea." I played along, laughing.

"I'm so glad you decided to check into this. You're way too smart to be sitting on that side of the desk anymore." The waitress took his order for a Diet Coke with lemon and told us the specials. "I know you're concerned about the pay cut thing, but it's not as bad as it used to be. They'll probably expect you to sign a three-year contract, but with your experience I think you can get more than a straight trainee salary." He squeezed the lemon into the Coke.

"All I know is that I can't work for her anymore. This not letting me take a week off thing was the last straw. Tell me what I need to do." We ordered lunch and developed a strategy for me to get an interview at Silverman and Washburn. Gene's manager had recently resigned to take a job in Chicago, so his general manager was the one responsible for hiring. From what Gene said, he had a bit of a military mentality. I didn't want to be Private Benjamin marching around in the rain. But I was determined to make it work because I couldn't face working for Joni any longer. Gene told me he'd prep Lynn, his general manager and that I should call his assistant, Jackie, tomorrow to schedule an appointment. Sauntering back to the office, the most incredible crème caramel reverberating on my taste buds, I planned every detail of how I was going to tell Joni that I quit.

I called Jackie as soon as I got into the office the next morning. "Hi, Jackie, this is Rena Sutcliffe. Gene Solomon told me to call you to schedule an appointment with Mr. Yancy?"

"Oh, Rena. Honey, it's so nice to finally talk to you. I've heard your name around the office for such a long time."

"All good I hope?" I asked laughing, afraid to know the truth even though I knew she'd never admit it if it weren't.

"Of course, honey. Of course." Jackie laughed. I heard voices in the background. "Hold on, honey. People must be blind this morning. Either that or the phone became invisible after I picked it up." As I listened to Barry Manilow lament Lola's Copa Cabana tragedy I found myself chair dancing.

"Rena!" Joni stood in the doorway, one perfectly tweezed eyebrow raised higher than the other. "What in the world are you doing?"

"I, I, I'm on hold," I stuttered.

"With who? And what the hell are you listening to on Muzak?"

"With—ah, with a rep."

"Well, wrap it up. I need to see you and the other girls in my office now. I have a new client who needs to know what it's going to cost to implement their media plan. And they want an answer by close of business."

"Hello, Rena—hello?" Jackie yelled in my ear.

"Yes, just a minute." I put my hand over the receiver and looked at Joni.

"As soon as you're finished getting your exercise for the day, please join us." Joni abandoned the doorway, shaking her head.

"I'm sorry, Jackie, my boss came in while I was on hold."

"That's OK, honey. I was afraid I'd lost you." Jackie champed her breakfast in my ear. "Anyway, what can I do for you?"

"Gene suggested I call Mr. Yancy to schedule an appointment to talk to him about getting into sales."

"Oh. I wish Gene would've told me, but OK. Lynn's schedule is very tight this week. How's next Tuesday—say ten?"

"Is there any way I can make it before or after work? Or maybe at lunch? It's going to be next to impossible for me to sneak out of here during the day."

"Lunch is out. Lynn plays tennis at lunch every day." I heard her rustling through a calendar. "How about Wednesday, eight, OK?" I checked my Daytimer.

"Oh, Jackie, I'm sorry, I've got a client breakfast meeting that day."

"I'll tell you what, Rena, why don't you call me back when you know what time's going to work best for you." Her voice was clipped.

"Any other morning but Wednesday is fine, Jackie. I just can't reschedule that meeting."

"Tuesday morning—eight. OK?"

"That's great. Thank you so much." I felt like I'd just won a tug of war.

"You're welcome, honey. It's a good thing all the guys like you around here. You're a little difficult."

"I appreciate your help working around my schedule. I'll see you next Tuesday." I held out the receiver and stared at it. I grabbed my notepad and hurried into Joni's office.

I called Gene at lunch. "OK, is it me or is Jackie a complete whacko?" I heard the phone hit his desk and then muffled laughing in the background. After a minute or so, he picked up the phone.

"I'm sorry, Rena," he wheezed, trying to catch his breath. "No one's ever been quite that blunt before." I imagined him wiping his eyes with his shirtsleeve. "God, that was hilarious." Gene was always so buttoned up and I had completely unhinged him. "OK, OK, I think I can breathe now."

"I didn't mean to put you into orbit," I laughed, "but she was on some kind of major control binge this morning when I tried to make an appointment with Lynn. She even told me you hadn't said anything to her."

"That's bullshit. I told her you'd be calling. That's just her way of testing you. Don't worry about it."

"Are you sure this is a good idea? I've got enough aggravation here. I don't need to go from the frying pan into the fire."

"No, Rena, no. Calm down. Jackie can be crazy sometimes. And Lynn can be a bit of a control freak. But, the money, honey, the money. That's what it's about. You know that by the time you come off of contract, you'll be making close to $100,000. Where else are you going to make that?" That would bump me up to middle class in Manhattan.

Rest

I prepared over the weekend using Gene's advice. I had no one else to rely on because I wanted to keep it quiet. Advertising media was the kind of business where people knew what magazine you had in the bathroom in the morning and how many times you flushed. I didn't need Joni finding out about my interview at Silverman and Washburn.

I got off the elevator on the 38th floor and found the door to the offices locked. A numbered security pad blinked at me, daring me to break the code. I paced around the small foyer, talking to myself. No one had mentioned that the door would be locked. The hair on the nape of my neck dampened. It was 7:58. I was about to cry, when I noticed a phone next to the elevator. I retrieved Lynn Yancy's extension from my Daytimer and dialed.

"Lynn Yancy," a gruff voice answered.

"Mr. Yancy, this is Rena Sutcliffe. I have failed to decode the security system and seem to be stuck in the foyer near the elevator."

"Jackie didn't give you the code?"

"No, sir."

"I'll be right out." I quickly reapplied lipstick and fluffed my hair. I hated wearing business suits, but that's what they expected, so I had starved myself for five days and splurged at Lord and Taylor on a Jones New York pinstripe. It was a size sixteen, but it was a business suit nonetheless. I had stuffed a skirt and sweater in my bag because there was no way I was showing up at JC wearing a two-hundred-fifty dollar suit without arousing suspicion. I had just noticed a chip in my appropriately conservative mauve nail polish when the door next to the security pad flung open and I was face to face with Lynn Yancy.

His tie was already loose around his neck, but the rest of him was tailored—initialed cuff links, razor-sharp creases in his pants, thick brown hair slicked back off his forehead, a faint blush on his freshly shaven cheeks. Hazel eyes smiled at me as he extended his right hand. "Rena, sorry about the mix-up. Come in, come in. Can I get you a cup of coffee?" Remembering my pea-sized bladder, I graciously declined.

"This place is like a maze," he said as we wound our way through rows of empty cubicles. "We've been up here three years and I still don't know my way to the men's room and back." He attempted a laugh.

We arrived at his office in the corner of the floor. The view was of Central Park from one side and the Hudson River from the other. "How do you get any work done with this view?" I asked enthusiastically. Already sitting behind an enormous desk, he waved, dismissing the notion that anything could keep him from working. Gene had told me that Lynn and his wife had adopted his brother's two children after a fatal car accident five years ago and he was committed to making sure they had the best of everything.

"I don't even notice it." He picked up the resume I had faxed over and perched a pair of black rimmed reading glasses on his nose. "So, I see you work for my friend, Joni." His eyes swept from the page to my face. Friend?

"Yes, I've worked there for four years." I pushed through the panic. "I started as Joni's assistant and am now a supervisor on several of the media accounts."

"I see that." He looked up at me. "Besides money, why do you want to get into sales?" Gene had told me to say money. Money was the reason I wanted to get into sales. But Lynn didn't want to hear about how greedy I was.

"To be honest, after sharing the same litter box with four other felines, I need a change. I'm ready for some balance in the gender of my co-workers." I tried to gauge his reaction, but I knew then that he always won at poker. "I find the buying side has a tendency to be peppered with insecure women and, quite frankly, I'm sick of it."

"What makes you think this is any different?"

"First of all, I know you have men on this sales team. Secondly, it's the insecure people who want to be in total control in their jobs. And what a perfect way to think you have control—by being responsible for spending millions of dollars of someone else's money." I couldn't decide whether to shut up. Gene had said he liked people who could think on their feet.

"The reality is, that being a media buyer is like being the center on a football team. The quarterback, the equivalent of creative services, and the wide receivers and running backs, the account executives, get all of the glory, while you have your face in the mud and someone's hands constantly on your ass. I want some of the glory." A small laugh, disguised as a cough, escaped Lynn Yancy's throat.

"That's an interesting analogy, Rena. And quite accurate." His smile crinkled the skin around his eyes. "Gene was right about you. And I would love to hire you. But right now I have no positions open in the training program." I resisted slinking down in my chair. "I'll tell you what, though. If you'd be willing to relocate, I could probably hire you tomorrow."

"Relocate to where?"

"I'm not sure. Maybe LA—or Detroit." He smoothed a large hand over the light gray sprinkled above his ear. His hands were sexy; the skin callused; the knuckles defined with just a few sprigs of hair.

"When do you think you'll have an opening here?"

"It's hard to say. There are some things brewing right now that might pan out in the next month or so, but there's no way to be sure."

"I really don't want to leave New York, right now."

"Boyfriend?"

"Excuse me?"

"Is it because you have a boyfriend or family here?"

"No, I just don't want to leave."

"Well, I'm sorry we couldn't work anything out. When something opens up, I'll give you a call." He stood and came around the desk to show me out. "It certainly was a pleasure meeting you, Rena." I opened my briefcase, took put the pitch I had worked on over the weekend, and handed it to him as he rounded the desk.

"I prepared a sales piece about myself for you, Mr. Yancy. I'm not interviewing anywhere else because I really want to work here. I love the thought of selling indies. I'm not a CBS kind of girl, know what I mean?" I laughed, handing him the pitch.

"Call me Lynn," he took it from me, paged through it, and threw it on his chair. I had raced around to four stationary stores Saturday to find the perfect blue for the vinyl cover. "I really enjoyed our conversation. I'll be in touch." He placed a hand on the small of my back. Deflated, I stepped outside to find Jackie sitting outside his office.

"You must be Rena!" She shouted. Her wild red hair was swirled in a loose knot at the crown of her head. She wore bright red lipstick and liquid black eyeliner. Her petite frame was dressed in a pair of Donna Karan black stretch pants and a white cashmere sweater announced her ample breasts. A leather belt with a large brass buckle corseted her waist. "It's so nice to meet you, honey." She did a quick jog to Lynn's doorway and threw her arms around me. "Lynn, did you hire this girl?" She asked him, her slender arm making it halfway across my back.

"You know we have no openings in New York right now, Jackie. And Rena doesn't want to relocate."

"I don't blame her. Who the hell wants to move to Detroit? Ugh!" She removed her arm and returned to her desk and stabbed a piece of cantaloupe from a half-eaten bowl of fruit salad. "Don't you worry, honey. We'll get you a job here. Gene loves you. And I know Mikey's called on you, too. We'll figure it out."

"If you'll excuse me, I have some calls to return." Lynn quietly closed the door to his office.

"He can be such an old fuddy-duddy. But don't you pay attention to him, honey. He likes you. I can tell. But you need to show him what you've got. Make it irresistible for him to hire you. If you can figure out a way to do that, you're a shoe in."

There were no cabs when I got outside. I got to work a little late, but managed to sneak in without Joni catching me. On top of my mail, there was an invitation to Titanium, a new dance club in Times Square. "Who left this on my desk?" I asked waving the postcard in the hall.

"John, the guy from the mailroom, " answered Lucinda, my assistant. "His brother is managing the place. If you fill out the back, they'll print up invitations with your name so it looks like you're hosting a private party. Pretty cool, huh?"

"Who the hell would I invite?" I snapped, heading back to my desk. And who would actually come? Friends were a luxury I couldn't afford with this job. I tossed it in the garbage, turned on the computer, and dug into the huge stack of buys waiting patiently on my desk. At one-thirty I could no longer see straight from staring at the computer and ran out to get something to eat.

The receptionist buzzed me after lunch. "Gene Solomon is here to see you."

"Send him back." Gene danced into my office, in his Armani suite, holding his index finger and thumb an inch apart.

"You're this close," he smiled. "This close."

"Close to what?" I was confused. "There aren't any openings in New York. It would've been nice of you to tell me that before I wasted my time."

"Rule number one, never believe anything that Lynn tells you."

"What are you talking about? He said if he hired me, I'd have to relocate."

"Yeah, yeah, yeah. He says that to everyone. 'That Rena is full of piss and vinegar.'" Gene stood, paced and did his best Lynn Yancy voice. "She'll make a helluva salesman."

"Then why did he tell me I have to move?"

"He wanted to see what you're made of."

"I don't get it."

"He doesn't want someone who's going to cave and do what he says just to get the job. His thing is if you'll cave for him, you'll do it for a buyer. And that's not a good thing. Get it?"

"Kind of."

"Look, if you gave in and said you'd move, just to suck up and get the job, how does he know you're not going to give a buyer whatever the hell she wants, even if it doesn't make sense for the station. Capiche?"

"Oh – h – h," the cogs in the wheel of my brain finally clicked into place. "I get it. Now what?"

"You've got to do something radical. He needs to see how you interact with people."

"How the hell am I going to do that?" Gene drummed his fingers on top of his leather briefcase. Small clouds of his expensive cologne puffed toward me every time someone passed my door.

"You've got to get him out of the office."

"Yeah, right."

"No, I'm serious." The drumming continued. Then a smile crept from his mouth to his eyes like the Grinch. "You need to have a party."

"A party? In my three-hundred-fifty-square-foot apartment?"

"No," Gene gave me a face, "out somewhere."

"I can't afford that, Gene." I shook my head. "But I've got to get out of…." I jumped out of my seat and dove under the desk.

"What the hell are you doing?" He leaned over my desk as balls of paper, coffee cups, an empty orange juice carton, and the remains of my salad bar lunch flew out from under the desk.

"Ah-ha!" I crawled out holding John's invitation to Titanium. It was damp with juice and cold coffee.

"That's perfect!" Gene slammed his hand on my desk after I explained. "You'll need to suck up to Jackie to make sure he comes, but that's perfect."

I mailed invitations to everyone on Gene's sales team, including Lynn and Jackie. Mike Osborne had covered for Gene every time he went on vacation, so I at least knew him. I followed up with Jackie and she told me she and Lynn would come for a drink. I didn't even have to make idle chit-chat. I also invited a few other reps and some buyers I knew from different station functions. The following Wednesday, I was hosting a party at Titanium to show Lynn Yancy how I could work a room.

"This is a bad idea," stammered Erishkigal. "What if no one comes?"

"Oh, quit, for Buddah's sake," scolded Inanna. "This is just what she needs to do. We all want to leave JC, right?"

"Not all of us," whispered Erishkigal.

"Well, you're outvoted, sister." Kali danced around Erishkigal, waving all six arms to the sky. "We're having a party."

"We need to be organized." Inanna snatched a feather from Kuan Yin's headdress and dipped the quill in the blood from one of the severed hands on Kali's belt. "We must make a list," she scribbled on a piece of cloth. "1) Go to Titanium before next Wednesday to get the lay of the land. 2) Talk to John's brother and find out how many people are also having parties there that night. 3) Ask him how drinks are paid for—tickets, cash, etc." Inanna looked up. "Anything else?"

"New clothes," Kali winked. "That's a necessity."

I had six conversations with Gene on Wednesday. I wanted everything to be perfect. When I arrived at Titanium, I checked my coat downstairs and hit the ladies' room to examine my make-up one more time. I had starved myself for another two weeks with the help of Dexatrim and dropped ten pounds. The burgundy Carol Little dress I wore was a size fourteen, the first time I'd seen that number in a while. I'd also splurged at the Lord and Taylor salon on a great haircut and a manicure.

Silver tinsel glittered over the exposed water pipes hanging under the ceiling. There were five bars and an enormous iridescent dance floor surrounded by high tables and leather barstools. The DJ booth was on an elevated platform against the back wall. I hadn't been to a club like this since Richard and I had been at the Spectrum.

Gene and Mike were coming down the steps as I was going up. The bass from the house music vibrated the stair rail. "Ehh, Rena," smiled Mike, "how the hell are you?"

"Great!" I screamed back.

"You look real pretty." Mike gave me the once over, his arms open wide and his head rolling back and forth like one of those plastic dolls that sit on the dashboard of a '64 Chevy. I had never asked, but I would bet Mike was from Brooklyn. High, slicked back hair, nasal accent, always had a hundred women swarming around him. He could've been one of the guys on the street in Bensonhurst that night with Maristel. He leaned over and kissed me on the cheek.

"There's an alcove behind the bar in the back on the right." I held my lips an inch from Gene's ear and screamed over the bass. "The manager told me it doesn't get as crowded there. Why don't you guys head back there and I'll hang out up front until Lynn and Jackie get here." He gave me the thumbs up and I finished climbing the stairs.

As people I had invited wandered in, I sent them back to Gene and Mike. After twenty minutes, I was certain the guest of honor wasn't coming. I had turned to go share my panic with Gene when I heard, "Rena! Hey, honey, this is some club! How'd you get hooked up here?" I took a deep breath, plastered on a smile, and turned around.

"Connections, Jackie, connections!" I laughed as I gave her a quick hug and kissed her cheek. She wore a very short black skirt with sheer black hose and spike heels. She had stopped buttoning her blouse one button too early and the top of her cleavage winked hello from behind the ivory silk. Lynn stood behind her, not towering quite as much because of her high heels.

"I'm glad you could make it, Lynn," I extended my hand. His calluses scratched my palm and the cologne he wore made me tingle. "We're all in the back. Follow me." Jackie, walking in front of me, did a little cha-cha as we crossed the dance floor, skittering her high heels to the beat of "Turning the Beat Around" remix. I glanced over my shoulder and saw Lynn's stilted walk. He was looking down at the floor and tugging at his French cuffs.

"What can I get you guys to drink?" I yelled over the music.

"Gin and tonic, honey," yelled Jackie.

"What can I get you Lynn?" He reached into his pants pocket. "No—I've got it!"

"You don't have to do that, Rena," he undid his money clip.

"I insist. It's my pleasure." I had charged a dozen drink tickets earlier in the week. Somehow, it didn't feel like I was really paying when I used a credit card.

"I haven't had a pretty woman buy me a drink in a very long time," he smiled. "Scotch on the rocks."

When I turned around, Jackie was off talking to one of the other reps. I squeezed through the crowd and handed her the drink. She managed to say "Thank you, honey," before returning to her conversation. I maneuvered back to the bar, grabbed Lynn's drink and butted into the discussion he was having with Gene and Mike. They were complaining about the quarterly budgets for the stations on their team.

"They're all morons," Lynn shouted. "They spend no money on programming so they have no ratings and they still expect us to increase their shares by selling Little House on the Fucking Prairie. It's 1993 for Christ's sake!"

"The problem is they have a bunch of people who don't know sales running the station," Gene said. "Yeah," parroted Mike, "like Lynn said, they're all a bunch of fucking morons."

"So this is what I have to look forward to?" I laughed. "Here's to getting rid of the fucking morons." I raised my glass of seltzer. "L' Chaim!" They returned to their grousing and I excused myself to mingle with the rest of my guests.

I flitted in and out of conversations for the next half-hour or so. Lynn held court as the members of his sales team joined the conversation for a while and then moved on. I was applying powder at the mirror in the ladies' room when Jackie stumbled in. "Great party, honey." Her eyes were bloodshot and she wasn't as steady on those three-inch heels. "But I haven't seen you dance all night. Don't you boogie?" She shook her hips and her breasts jiggled.

"I love to boogie, Jackie," I tried not to sound defensive. "But I've been busy making sure everyone's having a good time."

"Well," she announced, "it's time for you to have some fun." She grabbed my elbow and shoved me out the door and toward the bar. "Lynn, this girl hasn't danced all night because she's too fucking worried about showing you how she can work a room." She fumbled in her purse, eventually holding up a cigarette as if it were a Golden Globe. Mike reached over and lit it for her. "Let her off the hook."

"I haven't had her on any kind of hook." Lynn sipped his drink. "She's been doing a fine job of paying attention to everyone."

"Then tell her she can lighten up," demanded Jackie. I stood there, invisible, as the two argued about me. She took a long drag on her cigarette leaving a bright red ring of wax on the filter. "You're such an old fuddy-duddy."

"Do you think maybe you've had enough to drink?" asked Lynn. Gene and Mike subtly turned their backs and faced the bar.

"I just want her to have a good time. She went to all this trouble to try to impress you. The least you can do is ask the girl to dance."

"Oh, no—that's OK." I objected. "I don't need to dance."

"Of course you do, honey!" She leaned an elbow on the bar and tried to form smoke rings as she exhaled. "Now get out there and dance."

"I don't think she's going to take 'No' for an answer," Lynn forced a smile. "It might be easier to appease her." He held his arm out and I snaked my hand through the crook of it. A remix of Natalie Cole's "Unforgettable" was playing. "I'm not very good at this, Rena. The waltz is more my speed."

"That's OK, we'll make the best of it." I felt the perspiration seeping out from my underarms. He placed his right arm around my waist and I leaned into him. His left hand found mine and the calluses rubbed up and down my palms. I had no idea the hands were such an erogenous zone. The music ended and we returned to the bar where Jackie was propped up on a stool, leaning on Gene.

"That a girl, Rena." Jackie was showing evidence of one too many gin and tonics. "Dirty dancing with the boss will get you ahead a lot quicker than a thank-you letter."

"Jackie," Lynn said sternly, "that's enough."

"You're right, Lynn," Jackie lolled her head toward him, licking her lips. "Nothing I say matters anyway." She slid off the barstool and bent over to get her purse, teetering on her heels. Gene grabbed her arm to prevent her from toppling. "Geney, honey, can you get me a cab?"

"What the hell is going on?" demanded Kali.

"Oh, who the hell knows," Inanna gathered the material from her dress and rapidly ran it through her thumb and index finger. "This is too weird. And I thought this was the perfect opportunity for her."

"I warned you." Erishkigal smugly raised one eyebrow.

"This doesn't help matters," said Inanna. "I don't know what to do now. Should she keep after him to hire her?"

"Look," argued Kali, "it can't be any worse than where she is now. Whatever problems Lynn and Jackie have, I'm sure they keep them out of the office. It wouldn't be professional. And besides, Rena wouldn't be working directly for Lynn after he hires a replacement for Gene's old manager."

"You're right," Inanna agreed still searching for an escape hatch. "I say we still pursue it, but don't put all of our eggs in one basket. Rena has reps at other companies who also could hire her. We'll look into that tomorrow."

"Done," smiled Kali.

I was very grateful the next morning that I had drunk nothing but seltzer. I placed three phone calls to other reps and lined up interviews over the next week. Two of the three wanted to pay me $17,000 a year to start as a trainee with no guarantee of when I would get a raise. I might have considered it except for the fact that both sales teams sold nothing but traditional affiliates.

How boring to sell nothing but network prime and eighteen hours of news a day. I wanted a chance to be creative—to do promotions and other fun things that affiliate sales didn't lend itself to. That was one of the reasons I wanted to work on Gene's team so badly. All they sold were independents and Fox affiliates. It was a little edgier, a tougher sell, a lot more fun.

The third interview I had was before work one morning with James Michaels, a small independent rep firm that sold mostly stations they owned. George Young, their Director of Sales, wasn't much older than me. He said they'd be willing to start me at $25,000 as a trainee and that I would get a raise within six months. The only hitch was that I may have to relocate to Dallas for a few months, but then he'd move me back to New York. I knew that if I wanted him to hire me, I needed to impress him and I wasn't up for another Titanium episode.

I wandered aimlessly around Fifth Avenue at lunch. Hordes of people milled around the main library, sitting on the steps in between the lions soaking up the late winter sun. A few brave tourists had separated chairs from the huge stack at the back of the patio and ate out of plastic salad bar containers, maneuvering their forks through gloved hands. I went into Weber's Closeouts, having no idea what I was going to concoct from the junk they sold. As I passed the flower seeds, an idea began to develop. I tore around the store like a maniac and raced back to my office to assemble my sales pitch "Thank You."

That evening on my way home, I delivered a silver gift bag to George Young. The note on top said, "If you're searching for a sales trainee candidate who ..." and underneath were five wrapped presents. The first was a packet of gardenia seeds with a Post-It that said, "is willing to grow with the company." The second was a pack of baseball cards, "is a team player." Next was a carton of nails with the note, "is tough."

Then I had a little plastic kid's toy with a metal ball that rolled around inside a bubble. When you moved it around, the ball raced over little hills and around obstacles. The note said, "is on the fast track." Finally, I wrapped a bright green Gumby doll, "is totally flexible." Under all of the presents was my resume.

George called the next day to tell me how impressed he was with the package and how much he enjoyed meeting me, but that the president of their company had a neighbor whose son had recently finished graduate school and wanted to break into the business. He was very sorry, but he was sure I would do well wherever I went.

"This is total bullshit!" Kali stomped her foot. "Is she going to be stuck there forever?"

"No," insisted Kuan Yin. "It is time for her to leave JC so she can move onto the next set of lessons. She needs to call Lynn back and see if anything has changed."

"No way," argued Inanna. "They're all a bunch of loons over there. She doesn't need that hassle."

"Trust me, they're exactly what she needs. Rena has a lot of learning to do. And that's where it needs to begin."

"So, she should call and beg?" sneered Kali.

"Not at all." Kuan Yin inhaled deeply and sat in full lotus in the center of her three sisters. "All she needs to do is call and touch base and let the Universe take care of the rest."

"She is miserable," Inanna admitted. "I guess one more try isn't going to hurt."

Rest

"Hey, Jackie, it's Rena Sutcliffe," I was a little too chipper.

"Hi, honey. How are you?"

"Great. I can't believe it's been two weeks since the party."

"Time does fly. What can I do for you?"

"I'm calling to touch base. See what might have changed since the last time I talked to Lynn."

"Honey, nothing and everything changes around here every day. Hold on, I'll let him know you're on the phone." I hummed along to "You're Having My Baby." What did ever happen to Paul Anka? And how old was that baby? "Rena, he's tied up right now, but he wants to know if you can meet with him after work tomorrow."

"Sure—has something opened up?"

"He didn't say, honey. Just be here by five-thirty."

I hung up and dialed Gene's number. His voice mail answered and I didn't leave a message. My intercom buzzed. Josephine, Joni's assistant told me Joni wanted to see me in her office right away. I had a lunch appointment, so I gathered my things and stopped in her office on my way out.

"Sit, Rena, sit." Joni waved to the empty chair in front of her desk. She buzzed Josephine and told her to hold any calls. Then she stood up, brushed by me to shut the door, and returned, positioning herself on the corner of her desk. "I heard an ugly rumor, Rena." Joni's eyes pierced mine. I squirmed a bit and pretended I was straightening my back along the chair.

"What kind of rumor, Joni?" I asked innocently.

"Don't play games with me, Rena." She slid off the desk and returned to her chair. "After everything I've done for you. How could you?"

"What are you talking about?" I wasn't going to admit anything.

"I heard about your little party at Titanium the other night. How could you throw a party and not invite me?"

"I didn't think you'd be interested. It was just a bunch of buyers and reps."

"And Lynn Yancy." I paused, trying to decide what approach to take. "Jackie told me when I called to see if he wanted to have lunch." Either Joni was lying or she wasn't that close to Lynn because if she were, she'd know he always played tennis at lunch.

"Gene, my rep brought him."

"That's funny, Jackie said you specifically sent both of them an invitation." Joni's gaze didn't budge. "Are you interviewing there, Rena?" I didn't respond. "You might as well tell me the truth. I'm going to find out anyway."

"They came after me for the training program." A small lie. "And yes, I talked to Lynn. But they have nothing available in New York, so it's a moot point." I threw my coat over my arm. "I have a lunch appointment. Is there anything else?"

"No." The smirk on her face implied victory. "Don't forget to be back here by two for the meeting with Pearsall."

"I won't." I stood at the elevator stabbing the button. As if that would get me out of there any quicker.

"Holy shit!" cried Inanna. "That was a close one."

"What's she going to do? Fire her?" laughed Kali.

"We don't need her knowing what's going on."

"More importantly," Kali said cracking the knuckles on all six hands, "what is up with this Jackie bitch?" She curled her hands into fists, dancing around an imaginary punching bag, and throwing jabs. "She needs to be reminded of right and wrong."

"It is a little confusing," admitted Inanna. "Maybe she wasn't thinking."

"Yeah, and I let Siva win that dance contest he challenged me to because I didn't want to appear unladylike."

"But you trampled him, Kali," Erishkigal reminded her sister. "In fact, you killed him, if I remember correctly."

"My point, exactly. Jackie knew precisely what she was doing."

"But why?" asked Erishkigal. "What could she hope to gain?"

"We don't have time to figure that out," said Inanna. "We need to concentrate on getting ready for the meeting with Lynn tonight."

"Are you joking?" asked Kali. "You're not going to let her go? Not after what Jackie pulled with Joni?"

"Look, she needs to get out of JC. Working with Gene is a good place to start."

"For the Goddess of Wisdom, that doesn't seem like a very wise decision," admonished Kali. "It seems loaded with problems before she even gets there."

"Rena can handle it," argued Inanna. "And besides," she looked at Kuan Yin, "Miss Compassion over there backs me up. Right?"

Kuan Yin smiled, pushed her palms together in prayer position, and bowed to Inanna.

I arrived a few minutes early and primped in the ladies' room at Silverman and Washburn. My period was due and I was retaining enough water to break the dam and drown the little Dutch boy. I tried to ignore the insistent twinges around my right ovary. Feeling a little leakage, I went into the stall and pulled down my hose and panties. There it was—a slick red reminder of my femininity, a monthly memento of my ability to procreate. I cursed as I wriggled my pantyhose up and dug a quarter out of my briefcase.

I scooped cold water in my hands after I washed them and washed down a couple of Motrin. I didn't want to pass out from menstrual cramps while trying to convince Lynn Yancy to hire me. Jackie was at her desk, phone attached to her ear. She continued talking after she saw me so I wandered into Gene's office. He was in the middle of what appeared to be a heated negotiation. I returned to Jackie's desk and smiled.

"Hold on, Dad. Someone is standing at my desk."

"I'm sorry to bother you, Jackie. Should I go back out to reception?"

"You're already here. Just a second." She rose, ran her hands over the back of her hips, down her tight rump, and sashayed into Lynn's office. Fingering her gold cross as she returned from his office, she smiled at me like I was about to be sent to the Russian Front. "He's on the phone right now. Why don't you go out to reception and have a seat. I'll call out for you." She picked up the receiver from the desk and continued her conversation.

I walked back out to reception and perused a copy of *Advertising Age*. Twenty minutes later I had read it cover to cover and started on *Broadcast and Cable News*. As the receptionist was getting her coat out of the closet, she turned and asked if I wanted her to call Jackie.

"No," I decided. "That's OK. They know I'm here, I don't want to annoy anyone."

"Leave it to me, honey." Hilda Zuppinger was a tall fleshy woman with beautiful blond hair plaited into one long braid that stretched to her lower back. "Jackie? Hilda. I'm getting ready to leave and Rena Sutcliffe is still waiting to see Lynn. I just wanted to remind you." She bounced her head in agreement with whatever Jackie was saying. "OK, I'll tell her." Turning to me as she hung up the phone, she said, "Jackie knows you're waiting. It shouldn't be too much longer." Her Nubuck Dr. Scholl shoes padded quietly out the door. She waved good-bye as she got into the elevator and I picked up another magazine.

"He's a very busy man," Inanna defended Lynn's behavior.

"Bullshit," retorted Kali. "No one's that fucking busy. She's been waiting almost an hour. I say we blow this Popsicle stand—now."

"Let's give it ten more minutes," countered Inanna. "Maybe there was an emergency or something."

"Yeah, like his tennis date for tomorrow cancelled and he's trying to find a replacement."

"She can't afford to be pissed off when she meets with him, Kali," Inanna shook an index finger at her. *"Keep it under control this time."*

"Or what?"

"Or you don't want to know what. You may be the Goddess of Destruction, but I have a few tricks, too. And I'm tired of you interfering with Rena furthering her career."

"I'm shaking in my boots," Kali rocked her head side to side two inches from Inanna's face, a snide grin on her face. "You're real scary." She pulled on her necklace of skulls, the hollow rattling echoing.

"Don't push me," Inanna said under her breath.

I heard voices coming around the corner. It was Gene and Jackie. "Are you still sitting out here, kid?" Gene asked.

"He's still on the phone with Philadelphia," Jackie offered. "Someone in the Dallas office got shut out on a five-million-dollar buy for Pepsi. Norm has been pitching a bitch for over an hour now." She rolled her eyes and smirked at Gene. "You know what a whiner Norm can be. Bet you're glad it's not your ass in that sling, huh Geney?" Her gaze returned to me sitting on the blue herculon love seat. "It shouldn't be too much longer, Rena. He knows you're out here."

"Thanks." I tried to be enthusiastic.

"Keep your chin up," Gene smiled. "Good luck." He and Jackie disappeared into a waiting elevator and I was alone again. I waded through another two issues of *Media Week* before Lynn showed up to fetch me, dripping apologies. I dutifully listened while he explained how it took him almost two hours to bring Norm Steiner, the general manager of their station in Philadelphia, in off the ledge.

"A tiny piece of that budget would have been a huge win, Rena," he ushered me into his office. "The rep in Dallas fucked up, plain and simple. But I can't tell the client that."

"So what did you tell him?"

"That the buyer is a dinosaur of an empress, hell bent on keeping her friends happy and not giving a shit whether or not she's doing the best job for the client."

"Did he buy it?"

"Not quite. It didn't help that the rep never called the buyer back to check the status of the business. He never submitted any kind of promotional package or talked to her about what kind of share he expected." He threw himself into the tall-backed leather chair, and pinched the bridge of his nose with his thumb and index finger. "Sit, sit. Let's talk about why you're here."

"I called to check in and Jackie said you wanted to see me." I slid back in my seat, believing myself an ally. "Has anything come up?"

"Well, as a matter of fact, yes." He leaned the chair back and thumped his feet on the garbage can next to the desk. "But I have to be honest, Rena, I have a few concerns."

"I don't understand."

"The last time you were here, you were so sure you only wanted to work here." He stretched his arms above his head, slid his fingers between one another forming a cradle, and brought them behind his neck. Elbows flopped out to the side, it occurred to me he had assumed the "suck my dick" position.

"That is what I said, Lynn. But when you gave me no hope of anything happening in the near future, I did start interviewing elsewhere."

"That's not exactly what I said, Rena. I said that things change all the time and that there were irons in the fire. Your lack of patience concerns me."

"I'm sorry that it does. But I feel I went above and beyond trying to show you how much I wanted to work here and I got no feedback in terms of when you thought that might happen. I don't want to be at JC any longer than I need to be." My composure was slipping away and retrieving it was like trying to win tug of war with oiled rope.

"I need someone who is committed to sticking it out to get the next position in the training program, Rena. I get a dozen phone calls a week from people who are willing to start at the bottom just to get their foot in the door." He removed his feet from the garbage can and spread his knees wide, ankles crossed. "I need to make sure I'm not getting sloppy seconds."

"Is this guy for fucking real?" screamed Kali. "I feel the need to do a jig."

"Calm down, calm down," hushed Inanna. "He's just trying to rile her. And if you were still in charge, he'd have succeeded." She smiled smugly. "But I know exactly what he's trying to do and I won't let him."

"He's a pig. That's sexual harassment. We could sue." Kali was stomping around. "And we'd win. I will not have her working for a slob like this."

"Quiet!" Inanna ordered. "And watch a master at work."

"Lynn," I scooped my voice. "I'm offended that you would even think I'd offer you sloppy seconds. Of course you deserve the cream of the crop." I stood, place my coat over my arm, and picked up my briefcase. "And when the chaff is separated from the wheat, I'm sitting on top with the rest of the grain. Someone will hire me. I wanted it to be you. But I won't sit here and be insulted so I can put Silverman and Washburn on my resume." I quietly turned and walked out of his office. It wasn't until I was in the cab heading downtown that I started to cry.

"Hah!" Inanna strutted around, nose in the air, smug in her victory. "I've still got it."

"Got what?" asked Erishkigal.

"That ability to say what she feels while maintaining composure and integrity," Kuan Yin smiled. "Nice job, Inanna."

"Thank you sister." Inanna bowed to Kuan Yin.

"I hate to interrupt this little mutual admiration society you two have going, but haven't any of you noticed that what just happened was WHACKED?!" Kali reached her hands to the stars. "Durga-Ma," Kali cried, invoking the power of the Goddess Mother, "Am I the only one who sees this guy for what he is?"

*"No, Kali," Kuan Yin whispered, "I see. But Rena needs everything that
will happen to her here to grow and move on from the patterns she's established. She needs to learn how to speak up for herself without letting her
temper taking center stage."*

*"I don't know about that," said Inanna. "All I know is I love a good
game of head chess. And Lynn Yancy is a worthy opponent."*

Two days later, Lynn Yancy called and offered me a job in the training
program. I grabbed a cab at lunch to meet with him and negotiate my salary
and benefits. With all the money I'd spent in taxis in the last couple of
months, I could've visited Negril and paid for several cocktails hand-deliv-
ered to my shaded lounge chair by my thonged hunk. Who knew when I'd
get some time off now?

I agreed to start in two weeks for $20,000 a year, a $15,000 cut from
what I was earning at JC. My father thought I was insane. "Rena," he
warned. "It sounds like indentured servitude to me." But I knew in a few
years I'd be earning more there than I ever would have with Joni. Or any
other agency for that matter.

Telling Joni was much more difficult than I anticipated. I'd devoted so
much time to my job there that my social life had come to a screeching halt,
forcing my co-workers into the starring role as my New York family. I ago-
nized all night about how I was going to approach her with it. The following morning, after our staff meeting, I asked to speak with her. "Shut the
door, Rena," she said quietly.

Taking a seat, I noticed the dark circles rimming her large brown eyes.
There were strands of gray in the french twist. Five years after the plastic
surgery, the skin on her neck had loosened and several liver spots dotted the
backs of her hands.

"Joni, I don't know how to say this," I coughed and took a swig of water
from the bottle in my hand. "So I'm just going to come out and say it. I'm
resigning. I feel that two weeks notice is fair, so I'll be here until February
28th. Unless of course, you want me gone before then. If not, I'm more
than happy to stay the two weeks."

"Rena, you're rambling." Joni was calm and unemotional. "I knew this was
coming. Don't think this is a huge surprise to me." She opened her desk drawer, removed a pen, and began scribbling notes on the desk blotter. "I'll place

an ad in *Media Week* for a buyer and I'll probably promote Sarah to your position." She drew circles and rectangles, going over the same shape repeatedly. "Two weeks is fine." Looking up, she nodded, "That's all. We'll get together to go over all of the work on your desk before you go. Have a good weekend."

"*What an ungrateful bitch,*" Inanna was furious. "*All of the years Rena has been here. Not a thank you. Not a sign of appreciation. Not a fuck off. Nothing.*"

"*She wasn't able to, Inanna,*" Kuan Yin said trying to comfort her.

"*What does that mean?*" Kali was skeptical. "*She could've said something if she wanted to.*"

"*Not necessarily,*" argued Kuan Yin gently. "*I don't think any of you realize what Rena means to her.*"

"*That's a load of crap,*" Kali wasn't buying it. "*She's a cold insensitive slave driver and I'm glad Rena is out of there.*"

"*Believe what you must,*" Kuan Yin was slightly irritated. "*You get so wrapped up in the whole world revolving around you that you never take into consideration what someone else may be going through.*" She lightly dragged a feather up and down her bare arm, watching intently as the goose flesh grew with each sweep.

"*Joni has a very difficult time expressing her feelings. And so does Rena,*" Kuan Yin nodded at Kali and then Inanna, "*thanks in large part to the two of you and your ego-driven motivations.*" She snapped out of her hypnotic revelry and looked at the two of them.

"*Joni is going to miss her. Granted, she is having a hard time expressing that but Rena isn't very open to hearing it. Rena is beginning to learn, though. This lesson will appear again to see if she's capable of changing her behavior.*" Kuan Yin finished.

"*Yeah, right!*" Kali and Inanna cackled simultaneously. "*It's not that complicated, KY,*" Kali flicked the tip of Kuan Yin's nose with an index finger. "*Joni is a hard-hearted bitch. Period.*"

My last two weeks at JC were tense. Joni wasn't saying much to me and I certainly wasn't initiating any conversations. Sarah, Jesse, Maria, and

Lucinda took me out to lunch to celebrate. We went to El Rio Grande and drank Blue Curacao margaritas until the manager cut us off because we kept flicking tortilla chips at the booth behind us.

Lucinda presented me with a Winnie the Pooh plaque and a card. "I've learned so much from you, Rena," she wrote. "You were always patient when I made mistakes. Good luck." She planted a kiss on my cheek and palmed a bag of M&M's into my hand. "Just in case," she smiled.

When I returned from lunch on my last day, there was a card on my desk. I recognized the flowery script and ripped open the envelope, anxious to read what Joni had written. It had a large white gardenia on a sky blue background. "To a special co-worker—you were appreciated and you'll be missed." It was signed, "Good luck, Joni."

Rest

Over the weekend, I consumed a large pepperoni pizza, a half-gallon of mint chocolate chip ice cream, a box of Rice Crispies, five bagels, a bag of Doritos, and enough chocolate to feed Botswana. The only time I moved was to go out to the deli or change from the couch to my bed. My back was so stiff from lying around for two days I could hardly stand up. I managed to throw myself into the shower Sunday night and I changed the sheets on my bed because they had orange smudges on them from the Doritos.

Grease-stained copies of the *Star*, *Soap Opera Weekly*, *Woman's World*, and *New Woman* were scattered on the floor in my bedroom. *Shape*, whose cover promised me tight abs and a firm ass in less than two weeks, lay untouched on my nightstand. I set the alarm for six and fell asleep watching a Victoria Principal movie-of-the-week thriller about a teacher who, after becoming impregnated by a sixteen-year-old student, is then stalked by him. I awoke wondering whether or not she survived.

I arrived at Silverman and Washburn at seven-thirty Monday morning. I had remembered to get the code from Jackie and punched in the numbers while fighting a carbohydrate hangover. To make my first day more interesting, I had woken up with cramps and my period. I needed eight-hundred milligrams of Motrin to even make a dent. I wove my way back through the aisles of cubes and found Lynn already in his office reading the *Wall Street Journal* and sipping coffee. A banana and cup of yogurt sat beside the section of the paper he wasn't reading.

"Good morning," I lightly tapped my knuckles on the door. He removed the reading glasses and smiled.

"Good morning, Rena. I didn't expect to see you so early."

"I wanted to get a jumpstart," I explained. "I figured the first few days were going to be hectic." He came out to Jackie's desk and dug around until he found a file folder with my name on it. Handing it to me, he suggested I sit at the desk next to the kitchen and complete the personnel paper work. When I finished, I returned to his office where he gave me a copy of the Silverman and Washburn Sales Trainee manual and suggested I peruse it and he would meet with me after lunch.

The first page outlined the S&W way of selling—be aggressive with the buyer and shove whatever deal you make with the buyer down the station's throat, promising them it was the only way to make budget. I read how to negotiate with a buyer by wearing them down so I could garner the highest share of their client's budget.

According to the S&W manual, all buyers were morons, sitting ducks waiting to be taken advantage of by the superior sales skills which I would possess once I completed the training program. It emphatically stated that I was to trust no one except the members of my sales team and management. No one was my friend, no matter how friendly they appeared—not any client, not any buyer. I waded through the rest of the manual, obviously written ten to fifteen years prior. *Three's Company* was listed as an example of premium prime programming.

After lunch, Lynn went over what he expected of me for the next few weeks. I was to be in before him and there after he left. The training entailed me being the starring player in the newest S&W role-play. Lynn, as the buyer, would assign me client specifications for a buy in a particular market and I would be responsible for selling the station I represented.

Stanley Klein, an S&W manager on another team would act as the national sales manager for the station. Kevin Burnside, another S&W manager, had been assigned to act as my manager, someone I could go to with problems and questions. Lynn then gave me a set of buy specs: demo, dayparts, cost per rating points, and a budget and sent me on my way to compile a list of programs, ratings, and rates.

I quickly learned Lynn's schedule so that I could get in a minute or two before he did and look fairly settled before he passed my tiny little trainee desk on the way to his enormous office. I smiled goodnight as he walked out for the evening, at which point, I counted to sixty to make sure he was on the elevator, then snatched my coat and made a beeline for the door. Over the next several weeks, I role-played with every manager in our division. I leaned heavily on Gene for advice and even started bugging Mike to help alleviate the pressure I was putting on Gene. I was supposed to meet with Lynn daily, but many times he would find me around seven-thirty or eight after everyone had left. He'd tell me he was going to be at least another hour and to go home. The first couple of times I offered to stay. After waiting more than an hour, I walked past his office to find him gone, having sneaked out a different way. From then on when he told me to go home, I did.

One time I showed up for a meeting with him in the role-play format without having a set of Nielsen overnight reports in my briefcase. He wanted to know how my station's new early afternoon lineup had been doing the last few nights. I tap danced around the subject, using what I could remember, but he busted me. "You don't have the overnights with you, do you?" he demanded.

"I, I thought I put them in here," I stuttered, rummaging through my case as though they would magically appear if I just kept digging.

"Get out."

"Excuse me?"

"Get out!" he stood behind the desk, hands on his hips. "Don't ever come back into this office without having at least three days' worth of overnights in that bag. Ever." His voice had intensified to a scream by this point. "Now get out!"

I hurriedly threw the papers I had scattered on his desk back into my briefcase and tried to snap it shut on my way out the door. I dropped everything on my desk and made it to the ladies' room in the nick of time. Locking the stall, I plopped on the toilet, fully dressed, choking back the tears.

"I don't remember this being in the brochure," Kali complained.

"He's just messing with her head," explained Inanna calmly. "He's trying to teach her the right way to do this job."

"Next thing you know he's going to demand she drop and give him fifty."

"Maybe," nodded Inanna. "He does seem to have a bit of a military thing going on. But Rena can be lazy. He's only trying to help."

"I think he's an asshole," insisted Kali. "But he is sexy." Her voice was husky. "I'd fuck him."

"He's not that bad," argued Inanna. "It's only been a few weeks. Give him a chance."

Four weeks later, Lynn called me into his office and shut the door. The expression on his face was guaranteed to win with a pair of twos. I picked at my cuticles. "Rena, I've been talking with Kevin and Stanley." He flipped through a folder. "And bottom line, they're very pleased with the progress you've made." I smelled a "but" coming. "We all actually feel that you're ready to hit the streets. But I have some bad news." He slapped the folder shut. "This is the worst part of this job."

"Spit it out, Lynn, I can take it." I was more nervous for him than I was for me.

"The problem is, we don't have any openings here in New York right now."

"OK."

"So, we can do things one of two ways. You can continue in training, even though you've proven you're ready to move on." He leaned back and put his feet on top of the garbage can. "Or, we can send you to our Las Vegas office for a few months to help out while they get up and running." I felt like someone had just told me I had to choose between boot camp or a Navy Med cruise. Either was going to be hell.

"There are no other options?"

"Not at the moment," he leaned up on the desk, staring at me intently. "But there are a few things that could pop any time now, Rena. And I want you to be ready. I think the Las Vegas thing would be best for you. I know you probably don't want to pick up and move for a few months, but it'll give you practical experience with buyers and stations without having to worry about your mistakes haunting you too much." An evil smile spread across his face.

"Plus, it's warm. You won't have to worry about slushing through a late winter snow storm when you go out on sales calls." Thoughts zapped around my brain like a metal orb in a pinball machine, the flippers involuntarily banking them off the walls of my cerebellum.

"I don't know, Lynn. Las Vegas is far." I had also gotten into a routine of walking before work, trying yet again to drop some weight. I didn't want to have to start again.

"But it's warm."

"When do I have to let you know?"

"As soon as possible, Rena. I have two trainees ready to go in the LA office, but to be candid, I think you're the most qualified. You've been a buyer and you seem to have taken to the sales thing like a duck to water." He stood and extended his hand. "I hope you make the right decision. Let me know."

"I've never been out west," Inanna was excited. "This will be cool."

"Are you joking?" Erishkigal's eyes were wide in horror. "She knows no one out there. How will she survive?" She squinched her face. "And in the desert—it's so hot. Rena's a sweater, you know."

"Cowboys!" exclaimed Kali. "Cool."

"That's not the reason," admonished Inanna. "It's the smartest way to further her career. It won't be forever."

Six days later I was on a United Airlines flight to Las Vegas, three over-stuffed suitcases safely stored below and my hanging bag crammed in the cabin's front closet. Two overnight cases were stowed securely in the overhead and my briefcase, seams bursting, was tucked underneath the seat in front of me. I squirmed in the seat to get the belt to buckle and sighed with relief when I heard the click. I splurged and spent the three dollars to see *Batman Returns.*

My grandparents had sent me five hundred dollars and told me not to use it for bills. I put half of it in my savings account, divvying up the rest over my six Visa's. "Use some of it on the slot machines, honey," my grandmother told me. "You only live once." My father and Rebecca had sent me a bouquet of daisies with a note that said "Congratulations! You're on your way!" Faith bubbled over with excitement about the possibility of visiting and seeing David Cassidy's musical extravaganza at the MGM. I told her I didn't know how busy I was going to be.

The line at Hertz was twelve people deep. After signing my life away, I got directions to the complex where S&W had rented me an apartment and handsomely tipped a SkyCap to hold my bags until I retrieved the car. The arid heat slapped my face when I stepped outside. It was still ninety-three degrees at six-thirty in the evening.

I headed down East Tropicana and turned north onto Las Vegas Boulevard. The traffic crawled at ten miles an hour as everyone gawked at the bright blinking lights of the country's largest playground for adults. I have to admit, even though I'm not a gambler and I would be OK going to my grave without ever seeing Siegfried and Roy, it was kind of, well, cool.

Everything was enormous, jumbo, and extra large. Each property had a gimmick. The Luxor hotel, shaped like an Egyptian pyramid, was the first property I saw. Then I noticed the multi-colored flags waving outside Excalibur, the Camelot-type structures dotting the walkway to the entrance. Next was New York, New York. The roller coaster rocketing around the outside of the hotel distinguished it from the other properties.

The Bellagio was exquisite. The reflection from hundreds of tiny lights sliced through the small geysers from the fountain out front. And the white marble pillars and statues of Caesar's Palace spread across its sweeping entrance, making its Forum Shops the most famous in the area.

Coming from New York, I tried not to act too much like a tourist. That was a capital offense to me. Once I passed The Desert Inn, with its private golf course and sweeping tinted glass entrance, the traffic thinned out a bit. I juggled my map and a cigarette, trying not to burn a hole in the seat of my rental. I squinted in the twilight, looking for Charleston Boulevard.

I arrived at Egrets on the Pond, "A Sophisticated Singles Community," a little after seven. The security guard had the key to my apartment and I followed him in his tiny golf cart as he led me to my new home. He was tall and thin and his left knee stuck out like a flagpole from the tiny vehicle. I tried to tip him for helping me schlep my luggage up the stairs, but he refused.

Desert colors of tan, pink, and periwinkle dominated the decor. The rented furniture was built for durability covered in Herculon and canvas. The walk-in closet in the bedroom was the size of my living room in New York. Off the dining room was a balcony big enough for a couple of chairs and a hibachi. I unpacked and collapsed on my itchy couch with the Yellow Pages in search of a pizza place that delivered to Egrets on the Pond.

Rest

The next morning, I frantically tore through the apartment searching for the keys to my rental car. I shook empty suitcases, dumped the clothes from the dresser drawers and rummaged through the overnight bags containing my toiletries. I found nothing but panic. I called for a taxi from a number I found on a sticker attached to the phone. Forty minutes. I had to be at the office on South Main Street by eight-thirty. It was seven-forty-five. My first day as a rep and I was going to be late.

I squeezed my ass into the director's chair near the television to wait for the cab. The more I thought, the more upset I became. Wiping the mascara that had leaked all over my face, I called Hertz. They said they could have someone at the apartment around twelve-thirty to make me an extra set of keys—for fifty dollars. I had no money but I made the appointment. Retouching my make-up, I heard an urgent honking. I peeked out the window from behind the plastic vertical blinds and was relieved to find a black Chevy with a taxi light on the roof.

I arrived at nine o'clock armed with a dozen lies and was surprised to find that I was the first one there. I stood outside the locked office door, remembering my first interview with Lynn. "You must be Rena." I turned to find a large man with a full head of white hair lumbering toward me.

"Tim?"

"Nice to meet you. I hope you haven't been waiting long." He placed a key in the lock and opened the door. The suite was small, three offices with a desk in front of each for an assistant. The fax and copy room doubled as the coffeebreak room. Tim's frame made every room he stepped into seem insignificant. He loped from his office to the one next door. "This is yours, Rena," he said with a large toothed smile. "The office on the end is Doreen's. She's the only one I've been able to talk into working for me."

Tim gave me a sad laugh. I knew he had been searching for a permanent salesperson for three months, but the dearth of talent had forced him to call Lynn for help. "I've been doing this a long time, Rena. I know it's hard doing a start-up office, but it's still frustrating. It's hard not to take it personally." I silently nodded, unsure if he expected me to reply.

Tim flipped on the light in my office with a meaty hand and asked if I had any questions. "I hate to bring this up on my first day," I began. "But my flight was late getting in last night and Hertz didn't have a car to give me, so I need to go back to the airport at lunchtime to pick up a car. Is that a problem?" It was the best I could come up with. I didn't want to tell him the truth that his new rep from New York had managed to lose the keys to her rental car.

He shook his head. "No problem, Rena. I've got to pick up my son from a physical therapy appointment near the airport. I'll be happy to drop you off."

"Oh, Tim. I couldn't. I've actually already scheduled a cab," I lied. "It's not a problem, really." This is what Lynn's going to look like in fifteen years, I thought.

"I insist, Rena. You've already had one bad experience in Las Vegas. We'll leave around noon." He removed his suit jacket, placed it over his arm, and loosened his tie. "I'm going to check my voicemail. Bridgett, the office manager should be in soon. She'll clue you in on all the administrative stuff. I think your assistant's name is Colleen. The assistants come in at nine-thirty because they're here until six. Look over the papers I've left on your desk and feel free to ask me any questions." I sat down as he moved slowly through the doorway.

The Las Vegas office of Silverman and Washburn was located on the third floor of an art deco building in an older section of town. I spun my chair around to see the view. Leaning toward the window, I realized I was looking down into someone's back yard, an old diner booth planted square-ly in the middle. A rusted swing set leaned against a weather-worn fence. A little boy played with a red plastic fire engine, running it across the gold-specked Formica surface on the booth.

I dug into the piles of programming sheets, agency lists, and research pro-paganda left on my desk. How was I going to get out of Tim taking me to the airport? I called the cab company and told the dispatcher I had to have a cab before noon. If the cab was there, I couldn't exactly blow the driver off, could I? She promised me the taxi would be at the office no later than eleven-forty-five.

"Hi, you must be Rena," chirped a voice from the desk outside my office. "I'm Doreen Christiansen." She clomped into my office, body parts swing-ing back and forth as if controlled by a giant puppeteer. She shook my hand for a full minute, pumping up and down as she chattered away about how much she was looking forward to working with me. Her short ash brown hair was sticking up in several directions from the crown of her head and she was pale for being a desert resident. She wore a sleeveless leopard print blouse, a short black wool skirt, no hose, and a thick gold belt with a zebra buckle. Large silver cat earrings dangled from the over-stretched slits on her lobes.

"So, how about lunch this afternoon?" She punched the word "lunch," bringing me back from my reverie about paying Hertz fifty dollars for another set of keys. I explained my predicament with the rental car and argued with her for a few minutes about not needing a ride to the airport. Finally accepting my decision, she exited, promising that we would have lunch together soon.

The cab caper came off without a hitch and·I was relieved to have a set of keys for the Buick. Fortunately, the locksmith took plastic. Doreen took me out on sales calls to meet some of the buyers that afternoon. She and Tim had been covering the whole city until my arrival. I settled in at the apartment that night with an Italian sub, a box of Chips Ahoy and a bag of chips from my old friend Frito Lay. This might not be so bad after all.

After four weeks in Las Vegas, I had been shut out, screamed at, told I was an idiot, and stood up for lunch. "You can't take it personally," Tim attempted to comfort me as we sat in my office. "A lot of these girls are doing this because they have to. Their husbands don't make enough money to support a family." He rubbed his eyes, producing more red veins. "They'd much rather be home with their kids and instead they're dealing with office politics, demanding clients, and pushy reps."

"That's their problem, Tim. They have no right to treat me that way, especially Debbi Hogle." Debbi, a senior media buyer at Thomson Sloan, tried to have me kicked off the shop by claiming to her supervisor that I was colluding with another rep that also sold a station in San Diego. She hated my National Sales Manager because he didn't invite her on a trip to LaJolla that took place a few years ago. Because she felt slighted, she had used every excuse not to buy the station, and now seemed bent on sullying my budding reputation.

I learned from Seth, my station person in San Diego, that he had invited the top three billers from Las Vegas and Debbi missed the mark by several hundred thousand dollars. He had explained to her time and again how his hands were tied by the billing run, but that didn't seem to faze her. The first day I showed up, she told me what an asshole she thought Seth was, how she heard that no one in Vegas wanted to work for S&W, why she was the buyer I needed to schmooze the most, and what kind of money her clients were planning on spending in San Diego over the next two quarters.

She told me when her birthday and anniversary were, in case I wanted to pick her up a little something. Then she shared with me the academic and athletic achievements of all three children, who I could only surmise must have been immaculate conceptions. She made some of the women I worked with in New York look like they were next on the list to be canonized.

"Debbi's not a bad egg," Tim insisted. "But she's ornery as hell and miserable to boot. You have to let it roll off your back." He leaned over, covering my hand with his large one. Puffy blue veins drew a map on the backs. "You'll get a thicker skin over time, Rena."

"You're right," I tried to assure him. "I'll be fine."

"And when you can't take it anymore, you come into my office, shut the door, and scream bloody murder. Venting is good." He patted my hand and rose, his knees cracking. "Remember, it's just a job." Smiling, he turned his back and left me to ponder the sanity of my decision to leave Joni.

After spending a colossal amount of time getting acclimated to places and personalities, I was finally slipping into a comfort zone. I had seriously neglected the domestic aspect of my life since I had arrived. When I first arrived, I was getting to the office before eight and rarely left until after the sun had set. I even brought work home to do on the weekends. After finding my underwear drawer empty one morning, I vowed to do laundry that night. I had already charged ten new pairs at K-mart. I could no longer avoid the tedious chore.

I shoved dirty clothes into one of my suitcases, bounced it down the steps and pulled it across the courtyard to the laundry room. As I got closer, I heard voices. I couldn't hear what they were saying but from the urgent tone, I knew they weren't debating the advantages of Tide over Cheer.

I abandoned the suitcase and walked softly over to the window. Clawing the window ledge I hoisted myself up, balancing on my toes. I peered through the fuzzy glass, curious and excited. Sitting on top of a washer was a woman in her twenties with long blond hair and thick eyeliner. Her skirt was wadded up around her waist. As she leaned back, her slender legs extended into a "V," allowing easier access for the bearded man standing in front of her with an erection poking out of his Levi's.

Her blouse was unbuttoned to her navel and her nipples strained over the top of her red lace bra. She pinched them, moaning as Bearded Man continued to stroke his penis. During the process, his other hand occasionally disappeared in between her legs. "Fuck me," she mouthed to him.

"Almost there, sugar." His voice was harsh and his knees quivered inside his jeans.

She scooted to the edge of the machine as he rolled on a condom. Throwing her arms around his neck and shoulders, she drew his T-shirt over his head. "You make me wet," she licked his ear and ran her hands over his hairy chest and back. With one arm, he reached behind and grabbed her ass as he guided himself into her with the other. My fingers were numb from clutching the window ledge, but I didn't want to move. For the next fifteen minutes they banged against each other, the washing machine slipping and sliding with each slam.

At one point he stood pressing her to him, his back resting against the machine as he held her. The blond's breasts were flat against his and her legs wound around his thighs, the tops of her feet snugly over his shins. Suddenly, he turned and flung her on top of the washer. He spread her legs and shoved himself into her, bucking like he was on mechanical bull. Her small cherry-capped breasts jiggled, stilled only when Bearded Man leaned over to suckle them. My toes were ready to burst from the pressure, but I couldn't stop watching.

He pulled out of her, stripped off the condom, and rapidly stroked himself, chin turned up, grimacing. She massaged and patted her clitoris, squirming on top of the white enamel. I wondered how much practice was necessary to rub such a sensitive place that vigorously with two-inch fingernails and not puncture something. I could feel my nipples harden and the moisture between my legs, but I could do nothing about relieving myself if I wanted to see their climax.

"In my mouth." The blond jumped off the machine and kneeled in front of him. She continued to touch herself as he squirted into her mouth, his entire body shuddering from the force. I slid down the wall. I retrieved the suitcase from the sidewalk and knocked laundry down a notch on the priority list, returning quickly to my apartment.

I didn't take time to pull off my pants, opting to squeeze my hand between fabric and flesh. I came in record time, waited a few minutes for the blood in my clit to subside. And then I did it again. I felt something cold against the small of my back. I reached behind me and extracted the original keys to the Buick from behind the couch cushion. Maybe I should do laundry more often.

My hard work had paid off and now being in Las Vegas wasn't so awful. I was happy to be getting home before dark. And I had become familiar with every Smith's and Albertson's within five square miles of the apartment. One morning, getting dressed, I caught a glimpse of myself in the mirror hanging on the door of the walk-in closet. The rolls were back. Flesh hung over my bra and the elastic around my underwear. The only reason things still fit was because I was forced to bring last summer's fat clothes since I didn't have the money to pay full price in March for new ones before I left New York.

I contemplated calling Overeater's Anonymous. In the land of the all-you-can-eat $3.95 lunch buffet, there were more than enough eligible candidates for membership. Instead, I drove to Dell Taco and ingested my allotment of corn products for the month. I was gassy and bloated, but I couldn't stop. The elastic waistbands of my fat clothes were stretched within an inch of their life. I just needed to make some friends.

Part of me wanted Doreen and Tim to include me in their lives. Most of me wanted to be left alone. Somehow, the part that wanted to be included was in charge the day Doreen asked me to go with her to the Las Vegas Advertising Association monthly mixer. "Lava," as they referred to themselves, was comprised of agency and sales people from the advertising community. Most of the time, they met just to drink and eat, but they also did a benefit twice a year for children with AIDS.

This year they had decided to put on a talent show. Doreen told me that there would be a brief meeting Thursday where jobs would be assigned and auditions scheduled. Then there would be an open bar and buffet. The tickets were twenty-five dollars but she'd be happy to pay. "Oh, come on. It'll get you out," she invited. I reluctantly accepted.

After work Thursday, Doreen popped into my office, a maroon pleather totebag slung on her shoulder. "Ready to go?"

"I have so much work to do, Doreen," I attempted to back out. "I'm not sure I can go."

"Oh, don't be a party pooper!" The way she pronounced "ar" in party pooper tipped me off that she wasn't born in Vegas. "You can finish it tomorrow."

"No, really, Doreen. I have six avails due tomorrow. Maybe I'll meet you there."

"Don't be ridiculous," I wasn't going to win. "Let me help. We can be out of here lickety-split." She grabbed the first few requests off my desk and disappeared. We finished in under an hour and I trailed her silver Nissan to the Rio for my virgin Lava encounter.

Valet parking was full and the next lot was overflowing. We could've used a shuttle bus to get us from the netherworld where we parked to the entrance. Winding our way up the path to the door, I got the Cliff's Notes version of Doreen's life. "I moved here from Buffalo because my fiancé got arrested for dealing cocaine three months before the wedding. They wanted to make an example of him so the trial was speedy," she chuckled sadly. "Then they sentenced him to twenty-five years because he refused to snitch on his buddies to get a reduced sentence."

"How long ago was this?"

"Six months. I was selling radio time at an adult contemporary station." We entered the Rio and were pelted with the clattering of coins entering and exiting the slot machines. She raised the volume of her voice. "I couldn't bear it. I sold everything from the apartment we shared, loaded my Sentra to the gills, and started driving." We wove our way through the casino. "And this is where I ended up." I tried not to gawk at the buzz around me.

Casino waitresses in skimpy black skirts and high heels rescued thirsty gamblers with free booze and uniformed attendants responded quickly with change when a patron signaled. The barstools in the lounge were occupied by video poker aficionados who happily coughed up ten dollars for a roll of quarters and a complimentary cocktail. It was a smoker's paradise, ashtrays displayed in the most obscure places.

The slot machines stretched for as far as the eye could see. Men and women dressed in everything from evening gowns to double knit polyester fed them nickels and quarters, hoping to match fruit and hear the magical sound of a big payout. Doreen walked quickly and I struggled to keep up with her. Lights blinked, bells rang, and patrons wandered around carrying large plastic cups emblazoned with the logo from the Rio.

We landed in a section of shops that sold everything from diamonds to lingerie. Doreen disappeared into an alcove as I attempted to rebalance myself from sensory overload. I spotted her safari print blouse and ducked into the dark hallway that led to the elevators going to the top floor. "The Voodoo Lounge is the highest outdoor vantage point in Vegas," Doreen commented. "You can see for thirty miles or so when it's a clear night."

My ears popped as we ascended the fifty-five floors. The doors opened and we stepped into a foyer lined with striped metallic wallpaper. We followed the checked carpet to the entrance of the lounge. The bar was crowded and it required skilled navigation to reach the door that opened onto the patio. The lights of Las Vegas formed the backdrop behind the throng of people milling about the terrace. Old-fashioned gas lanterns dotted the perimeter, casting halos around the heads of the people standing beneath them.

"It looks like we missed the meeting," Doreen said, waving to a man at the bar.

"I'm sorry."

"It's not a problem," she patted my arm. "I'll go speak with Jim and let him know I'm available if they need help selling ads for the talent show program." She walked toward a man sipping beer at the bar, leaving me to fend for myself. As I looked around, watching everyone engrossed in conversation, I realized I didn't have a nametag. I liked the idea of knowing everyone's name without having to reveal mine.

I made my way to the edge of the deck and leaned on the railing. I was impressed with the number of things I recognized as I looked out over the city. There was a slight breeze and I pulled my blazer around me, staring at the traffic below snaking in and out of the hotels on the strip. "Rena?" I turned to find Debbi Hogle coming in my direction. Other than jumping I only had one choice.

"Hi, Debbi," I forced my best happy, bouncy, perky voice.

"I didn't expect to see you here," Debbi smiled earnestly. I returned it warily.

"Doreen insisted I get out and try to recapture some of the social skills that have dissipated since I arrived," I joked. Turning back toward the railing, I waved my hand in the air. "This is beautiful. Do they have every mixer up here?"

"No," Debbi laughed. "They try to spread the wealth. We actually haven't been up here in almost a year. You're lucky. This is one of the more amenable locations." She sipped her drink. "Last month we were at some dive downtown near the Howard Johnson's. I was afraid to go to the ladies' room for fear something would bite me."

"You ought to see some of the sanitary, and I use that term loosely, facilities in New York," I rolled my eyes. "At least they're above ground here. In New York you have to go to the basement most of the time."

"I don't know how you live there," she shook her head. "It's dirty and expensive. Why do you stay when you could have a great job out here? And a huge apartment with a pool and Jacuzzi. Hell, on a rep's salary you could buy a gorgeous house and have enough left over to get a maid."

"I can't explain it," I admitted. "There's something about the city that's like a drug for me. I love living there."

"Do you have a boyfriend there?"

"Not for a year or so." I hesitated with my answer.

"I'm sorry, I didn't mean to get too personal," she placed her drink on a table and removed the clip from her hair, allowing it to fall to her shoulders. It took ten years off of her. She didn't look like a mother. "It's just that as buyers we always get to talk about ourselves and every once in a while I realize that I know nothing about the people who call on me."

"It's a crazy business." I felt like I had stepped into a parallel life. Three hours ago I would've paid for the chance to spit on her. And now I was standing on the patio of the Rio having a fairly pleasant conversation with her that revolved around something besides work.

"It sure is. My husband is a sweetheart and he works so hard. But with three kids, it's just not enough to make ends meet." She wore a pale yellow cotton sundress with gingham pockets. A blue sweater was held together with a gold chain clipped to the buttonhole. "Do you want to sit?" We dragged two chairs over to the table that held her drink. I noticed Doreen staring at me from across the floor. She lifted her cocktail in a silent toast.

"Do you like working at Thompson Sloan?" I avoided pregnant pauses at any cost.

"I used to," she crunched an ice cube. "But I've been trying to convince them to let me do a job share with Dolores Rains. We put together a proposal showing them how it would actually be more efficient. But they didn't even look at it." Debbi made slurping sounds through her straw as she hit the bottom of the glass. The sales rep in me took over.

"Can I get you a drink?"

"That'd be great. Bacardi and Diet Coke." I headed toward the bar. "With two limes," she called after me.

"So," Doreen laughed as I approached. "You and Debbi Hogle. There's one I never would've predicted."

"Me, neither." I ordered Debbi's drink and a seltzer for me. "But she seems human, talking about her husband and kids. I don't want to admit it, but I'm actually not hating her right now."

"Wait," she adjusted her belt. "Things will be back to normal before the night's over."

"Such the optimist," I chided, gathering the plastic cups and returning to the table. I arrived to find three people I didn't know sitting with Debbi.

"Rena, this is Jan, Brenda and Mary Anne. They work in accounting." She cocked her head to the side. "Do you think you could get them something to drink?" She directed a "do it if you know what's good for you" smile at me.

"Sure," I responded realizing Doreen was right. "What do you guys need?" I returned to the bar, drink orders memorized. I carried the three glasses to the table and discovered someone in my seat. "Here you go." I placed the beverages in front of Debbi's number crunchers. I stood at the table for a moment, listening to them gossip about the media director at their agency. Then I retrieved my bag from under the stranger's chair and walked away.

"Thanks for the drinks," Debbi's voice trailed off as I headed inside. Doreen had claimed a seat at the bar. I wasn't comfortable with the fact that she was my anchor.

"Why the face?" Her words weren't quite slurred, but the edges were dulled. I recounted what had happened with Debbi. "I don't want to say I told you so," she threw her arm around my shoulders and laughed, "but I told you so."

"You were right," I gently removed her arm and it flopped onto the padded leather of the bar. "I think I'm going to go."

"You can't," she yelled. "It's not even ten yet." She tried to focus on her watch, got frustrated, and gave up. Leaning toward the bartender, she called him over with a hooked index finger. "Get my friend a cocktail. I'm paying."

"No thanks, Doreen." I wasn't about to be swayed this time. "I have things to do at home." She sat up straight and looked at me seriously.

"Rena, you can't let this business affect you this way. Or else you'll end up like me, stopping for one beer on the way home and staying until the bar closes." She grabbed a pack of cigarettes from the man sitting next to her.

"I didn't know you smoked."

"I don't," she said striking a match. "You're smart enough to figure out that no one is your friend. Don't take anything anyone says or does personally. That's the golden rule for survival."

"Thanks for asking me tonight, Doreen. I had a nice time."

"Liar."

"No, really. I did. It was good for me to get out." I gave her an awkward hug. The crowd had thinned out and I had a straight shot to the elevator.

Tim came into my office a couple of weeks later, a big smile plastered in the middle of his ruddy jowls. "Good news, Rena."

"I can always use that," I smiled back from under a heap of paperwork.

"Steve Carn from our LA office has agreed to take a position here." He stretched his arms to the ceiling. "Halleluja!" He shouted. "Free at last. Thank God almighty, she's free at last!"

"I'm not sure I want to go," Erishkigal admitted rubbing her collarbone. "Rena's kind of become friends with Doreen. It'll be sad to leave."

"No fucking way are we staying in this sandy sun-baked gateway to hell!" Kali drew her sword and held it to Inanna's neck. "You're in charge. What's the call?"

Inanna batted away the sword. "I think we need to go back to New York. We could change our mind and I'm sure Tim would consider her for a permanent position." She grinned. "But I miss the stench of urine on the subway platform in the summer."

"That's disgusting," Erishkigal wrinkled her nose.

"Kidding," Inanna did her valley girl imitation. "You never did know how to take a joke."

"I'm very proud of Rena," Kuan Yin announced. "She is still using food to deal with her feelings, but she performed admirably here."

"Thank you," Inanna said sarcastically bowing deeply to Kuan Yin. "But I have things under control. Unlike Rena, I don't need anyone's approval."

"Enough of the self-admiration, Nanna. Let's get packed and hightail it back to the big apple." Kali dragged Inanna by the sleeve of her robe. "If we hurry, we can get back before it gets too hot."

"Thank you for everything, Rena. I couldn't have made it these last few months without you." Tim handed me a card. "Don't open it now. Wait until you're on the plane. I hate good-byes." I shook his hand.

"I appreciate everything you taught me, Tim. Steve's a lucky guy to be getting you for a boss."

"You're too kind," he clasped my hand. "If you need anything, Rena, you call me. I do know a trick or two. And don't let that Lynn Yancy bully you."

"I won't," I promised. Doreen bounced into my office and gave me a hug, her bony frame pressing against my mushy one, momentarily denying me my cushion of denial.

"I'm going to miss you," her eyes were watering. "I know you're going to do great in New York." She grabbed my hand and dragged me into the coffee room where there was an ice cream cake melting on the counter. We all grabbed a spoon and dug in, leaving the plates sitting next to the microwave. I felt a pang of melancholy. But it was June and I couldn't wait to sleep in my own bed.

Rest

"Rena, honey!" Jackie screamed from half way down the hall. "How was Vegas? Win any money? What'd you do with that five I gave you for the roulette table?"

"I played your numbers," I lied trying to forget the popcorn and Raisinettes I bought with it when I went to see *Jurassic Park*. "They just didn't come up."

"It's so good to see you," she kissed the air next to my cheek and put her hand on my arm. "Sonny's running a special at the gym, honey. You might want to think about it." She escorted me down the aisle and into Lynn's office. "Look who's here!"

"Nice to see you, Rena," he stood. "All reports were good. Did you enjoy yourself?"

"Except for the phenomenon that it's still eighty-five degrees at midnight and the fact that it's crawling with tourists, yeah, sure, I had a great time." I rolled my eyes and fell onto the loveseat against the wall. Jackie plopped down next to me.

"We've got a surprise for you," she winked. "Don't we Lynn?"

"That's something I need to discuss with Rena in private, Jackie. Do you mind?" He nodded toward the door. "And shut it on your way out. Thanks." She sauntered out in a huff.

"So, how's New York been?" I went to the window and stared at Central Park. "I've missed it."

"New York has been rainy and cold, Rena. Just like I told you it would be." He laughed a little and joined me at the window. "Sit down, I want to talk to you." He turned one of the chairs in front of his desk around and I returned to the couch. "I still don't have a permanent opening on this team, Rena." My face fell. "But Joanna had surgery on her hip and won't be back for six weeks." Grace, the other female rep had left to sell the New York Fox station while I was in Las Vegas, but Lynn explained that with her experience level, he couldn't pacify the stations by replacing her with me.

"What I'd like to do is have you cover for Joanna while she's on disability. This gives me a little more time to get things in order so we can get you a permanent position. Sound good?" I was suffering from jet lag, had put on at least twenty pounds, and came home to find that the super hadn't checked my apartment the way he'd promised and I had a family of roaches in residence.

"What choice do I have?"

"If you're not happy, Rena, then neither am I." Lynn tried to sound sympathetic. "What can we do?"

"I'm sorry. I'm tired and cranky." My eyes stung. "I know you're doing all you can. I'll be happy to cover for Joanna while she's out."

"That a girl!" He leaned over and lightly slapped my knee. "You can use her office. Jackie will get you straightened out with paper work." He returned to the chair behind his desk, the cologne he wore lingering around my head.

"What kind of salary are we talking about?"

"Well, technically, you'll be covering for someone, Rena, so it means you're still earning a trainee salary."

"Oh."

"And because it's not your agency list, you won't be eligible for commissions on anything you book."

"OK." I couldn't decide whether to blow a gasket or have a nervous breakdown.

"I'll tell you what, though. You did such a bang-up job for us in Vegas, let me see what I can do about getting you a bonus for the time you were out there."

"That would be great." I perked up.

"I'll let you know. Now go see Jackie and get started. Some of the fourth quarter clients are breaking early. It's actually kind of busy."

"This is complete bullshit!" Kali stomped her foot.

"He's making an effort, Kali," argued Inanna, "or haven't you noticed?"

"You're the one who's blind. He's throwing her a bone to keep her under control. That's all." Kali sat and leaned her elbows on her knees, imitating

Lynn's body position. In a gruff tone, she mimicked his speech, "Technically, Rena, you're still a trainee, so that means you get paid shit and are grateful for it." She let go a piercing shriek. "He's so arrogant."

"She has to pay her dues," contended Inanna. "She switched careers, Kali. She can't jump over everyone else to get to the top. She has to earn it."

"She is learning to be humble," agreed Kuan Yin. "That's a valuable trait."

"So is herding sheep, but I don't see much need for that either." Kali pummeled her fists against an imaginary enemy. "What's humble going to get her, but more broke? Maybe she could at least fuck him."

"It will teach her to be patient," said Kuan Yin, ignoring Kali's sexual reference. "Good things come to those who wait."

"If they don't die first."

"Don't be so damned dramatic, Kali," ordered Inanna. "She's on the right track. Leave it alone."

Lynn still hadn't hired a replacement for Dave Burnard, the former team manager who had relocated to Chicago to become the National Sales Manager at the Fox station. He claimed he was interviewing and was close, but I got the feeling that Lynn was enjoying having his fingers on the pulse of the daily goings on. It was evident he wasn't in a huge hurry.

Because I wasn't as experienced as the other sales people, Lynn did a temporary rearrangement of the agency lists. I ended up with the muck at the bottom of the barrel. Renee Woodson was my buyer at TVBS, and my first trip down to Sixth Avenue and 31st Street to visit her deluded me into believing we'd bonded. We bashed men for forty-five minutes as Renee regaled me with the details of her divorce four years prior and I shared a few pieces of Richard's demise.

I guessed she was about fifty or so, attractive and well put together. She didn't shop at Saks, but she wouldn't be caught dead at Wal-Mart either. She smoked like a fiend, lighting one cigarette with the butt of a new one before stubbing it out in an ashtray overflowing with pink stained filters. There were two cartons of Parliaments sitting on the stacks of dusty files on the windowsill behind her desk. The fan from the air vent ruffled the pages sticking out at odd angles. Several months worth of trade journals occupied the other side of the sill.

"We're going to work together fine, Miss Rena," she took what seemed like a three-minute drag on her cigarette and followed it with a wet cough. "As long as you get me what I need when I need it, we won't have any problems." She flicked the ash with the bright red of her manicured thumbnail. "Who was calling on me before?"

"I believe it was Mike Osborne."

"What's he look like?" The lipstick had dried in the cracks around the corners of her lips.

"He's a nice-looking man. Thirty-two or so. Dark hair. Looks like he could be Italian."

"Don't remember him." She was swathed in a halo of smoke. "Probably never brought his Dago ass this far downtown. Your stations do any numbers?"

"Depends on the market," I laughed. "Where do you place most of your business?" She spent the next half-hour educating me on her clients and what the TVBS way of doing business entailed. Then she gave me specs for buys in several markets, telling me she needed the rates by noon the next day.

I was at the office until nine and ran the avails down to her the next morning after my sales meeting. She refused to see me and I left the envelope with the receptionist. My biggest billing agency was Bluestone Advertising. They handled huge accounts like Proctor and Gamble, who I soon discovered, owned half of the products in every grocery store in America; Toyota; Paramount Studios and TGI Friday's.

The agency was so large that Gene, Mike and I split the markets and buyers into groups of four. Three of my buyers appeared like they were going to be easy to work with. The fourth, however, would not see me any time I was up there and had yet to return a phone call. I didn't have the strongest station in her market, but I couldn't figure out why she was ignoring me.

"Tania?" laughed Gene. "She's a horror and a half. I can't believe she's buying San Antonio. It used to be Jill Monovor. She was a peach." He threw his feet up on his desk and proceeded to educate me on the fine art of kissing ass. "I know she loves Aveda. What's your expense situation like?"

"Lynn didn't tell me."

"Then I would suggest going to him and telling him you need a hundred dollars to get a buyer to acknowledge you. He'll give it to you."

"Then go to Aveda and buy her what?"

"I would suggest a massage. That'll run about seventy dollars. And then a thirty-dollar gift certificate for her to do a little shopping afterward."

"Are you serious?" When I was a buyer, no one had to pay her way in to see me.

"That's how the game is played with some of these girls, Rena. You'd better get used to it."

I stopped at the Aveda on Madison Avenue on my way home that night and purchased the requisite gift certificate and massage. They wrapped them in their trademark tissue paper and gave me a gift bag and card. On the card, I wrote, "Sorry we haven't had a chance to meet. I know how crazy it is. Hopefully, this will help you relax." Then I enclosed a business card.

The next morning, while out on calls, I stopped at Bluestone on 53rd and Fifth. Again, an audience was refused. I left it with the receptionist. That afternoon, I was working at my desk when the phone rang.

"Hi," a voice gushed, "Rena, this is Tania Batrilli. That was so nice of you to get me the stuff from Aveda! Why don't you stop by tomorrow and we can finally meet. You call on my friend Lisa, too. Maybe we can all go out to lunch." A hundred dollars at Aveda wasn't enough? Now she wanted to go to lunch?

"I actually have a station lunch tomorrow, but I could stop by in the morning." It was a bold-faced lie, but I was damned if I was going to pay for her to eat tomorrow.

"Oh, OK," she said, obviously disappointed. "I have a meeting at ten. But after that would be good." We hung up and I ran into Gene's office, foaming at the mouth with the details of my first conversation with Tania.

"Get used to it," he laughed. "You can't let it get to you."

Reviewing my pending business, I realized that I hadn't heard from Renee in over a week. At our first meeting, she made it sound as if her client was champing at the bit to get on the air. I had left a message practically every day since I dropped off rates and she hadn't returned any of my calls. I left another message on her voicemail. The following morning I made my pilgrimage to Bluestone to meet Tania.

It was close to eleven AM by the time I arrived because Lynn loved to pontificate in our semi-weekly sales meetings. We started at eight and it was a miracle if we were out of there before ten. The receptionist, a handsome man in his twenties, and surely a resident of Chelsea if my gaydar was working, used the intercom to let Tania know I was there. "She says you'll have to wait," he smiled. "Have a seat." He returned to the magazine on his desk. Thirty minutes later, I was still waiting.

"Do you think you could try Tania and remind her that I'm out here?" I called out from the couch.

"She gets kind of testy when I do that," he hesitated. "But you have been waiting a long time." He dialed the number and asked how much longer it would be. I heard Tania's voice through the receiver, which the receptionist held several inches from his ear. "She says she knows you're here. She's in a meeting."

"Thanks," I apologized. "I didn't mean to put you through that."

"It's OK. They pay me such an exorbitant salary, it makes it all worthwhile." He smiled sarcastically. I crossed and uncrossed my legs, furious at being kept waiting and disturbed by the knowledge that I had no control. At five to twelve I went to the ladies' room and asked the receptionist to let Tania know I'd be right back if she called out. Unconvinced she was really in a meeting, I searched for her in the faces I passed. I had been by Tania's office so many times I could draw a portrait from memory.

Back in the lobby, I sat on the couch, my stomach rumbling. I heard laughing coming from the other side of the door which led to the buyers' offices. Giggling like schoolgirls, three buyers stumbled into the reception area, Guess backpacks swung over their shoulders and sunglasses strategically placed, sweeping the hair off their faces. Tania called to the receptionist as she repeatedly smacked the elevator button with the palm of her hand. "We're going to lunch, Tom. Do you want us to pick up anything for you?"

I gathered my things and caught the next elevator. I couldn't decide if I should be angry, humiliated or confused. I talked to myself on the walk back to the office, trying to imagine a rational reason for her behavior.

"There is no rational reason," Gene smiled. "So quit spending time trying to find one." He looked particularly dapper in a navy Hugo Boss suit accented by a burgundy and gold striped tie. He recently started wearing glasses and being Gene, had chosen a highly stylized pair of rectangular bronze wire rims. "The bottom line, Rena, is that you need to find a way to her inner sanctum. I know she's friends with Kristen Jablonski. Don't you call on her for Phoenix?"

"Yes."

"How's your relationship with her?"

"Fine, I guess. I haven't known her real long."

"Why don't you call Kristen and set up a lunch for the three of you. They're both princesses though, so don't take them to Friday's or something. Talk to Lynn about the expense thing."

"Do I have to?" I whined.

"Look, you've got to suck it up. Until you establish relationships with these people, you're going to have to kiss some serious bee-hind. It'll get better. I promise."

"Thanks," I kissed him on the cheek. "I don't know what I'd do without you."

"Someone has to keep your ass in line," he grinned.

I tried to reach Renee again. Voice mail. I documented the message I left on her file folder. I learned the importance of covering your ass as a buyer when I forgot to write down the date and time a rep lowered her station's rates. I gave her station a huge share of the budget only to have her call me later in the week and claim she never gave me the rates I used. The station refused to book the order without more money and I had a lot of explaining to do.

The next call was to Kristen. I set a lunch date with her and Tania for the following Tuesday and made a reservation at the Ocean Club after getting the OK from Lynn. Gene advised me to go to the agency and pick them up. "Next time meet them there," he said, "today, walk them there like they were five-year-olds crossing the street for the first time." Tuesday arrived much too quickly.

"I'm so sorry I forgot you were out here last week," Tania exclaimed, shaking my hand in the lobby. I thought I heard Tom snicker. "This is really nice of you to take us to the Ocean Club. And during Wine Week. This is awesome!"

"Wine Week?" I asked, hesitant to show my ignorance.

"Yeah," enthused Kristen, "it's a Prix Fixe lunch and you can try as many of the different wines they have as you want. We love wine, right T?" We headed toward 58th Street. It was a typical July day in New York, the humidity level comparable to the steam room at the Health and Racquet Club. We stopped at a red light on 55th Street and Sixth Avenue, next to a construction sight. The workers were lined up in front of the scaffolding, sitting on coolers eating their lunches.

"Hey baby, shake that booty for me," one called as we passed. "Hey, honey," hooted another, "can I get a kiss?" They all made smooching sounds and then collapsed into laughter.

"Can you believe those assholes?" Tania asked Kristen. "They have such nerve talking to the two of us that way. I wish we could get them arrested or sue them or something."

"They should all be muzzled," I agreed, suddenly embarrassed at the realization that they weren't talking to me. Kristen and Tania ignored me and talked about their plans for the coming weekend. It was warm, even in the shade of the scaffolding. Neither Tania nor Kristen exhibited any evidence of the heat, cool and dry in their skimpy sundresses and strappy sandals. Each had her long hair, Kristen's blond, and Tania's brunette, pulled into beaded scrunchies. I realized I weighed a little less than the two of them together.

I sweated profusely under my blue linen blazer. I refused to remove it because of how tight my skirt and tank top under it were. I continually swept the hair off of my forehead and pushed my sunglasses back up my nose. I was also wearing panty hose and sensible navy flats. How could I have thought, even for a split second, that those construction workers were including me in their remarks?

We arrived at the restaurant and I excused myself from the table to dry off in the ladies' room. I returned to find them flirting with the sommelier, a handsome olive-skinned man, who held two bottles of wine in silver carriers. "We've decided on the Merlot, Rena. What do you want?" asked Kristen.

"Thanks, but I really just want a Diet Coke."

"Oh, come on," taunted Kristen, "one glass isn't going to kill you. We won't tell anyone."

"We promise," agreed Tania, her large brown eyes staring at me over the candle in the middle of the table.

"I'll have the Merlot, as well," I acquiesced. "But could I also get a Diet Coke with lime?"

"I will inform your waiter, Madam." He gracefully poured the wine into our goblets while we perused the menu.

"I think I'm going to have the broiled salmon," Tania licked her lips.

"That's got a lot of fat in it," chastised Kristen. "Monkfish is much lower."

"You're right. I've been feeling so bloated lately," Tania pinched the skin under her arm, barely gathering enough to fit in between her thumb and index finger. "Look at this! Can you believe it? I guess that's what happens when you get older."

"How old are you, Tania?" I asked.

"God, I'm going to be twenty-four next month! Can you believe it?" She rolled her eyes. "And look at this, Kristen." Tania looked disgustedly at her stomach and repeated the pinching procedure. There was a tad more skin on her abdomen than under her arm. "I'll never get a man if I keep up at this rate. I'm going to be an old maid if I don't change my evil ways, right?" She smoothed her dress over her nonexistent belly.

"You need to do that Get Thin America diet. No carbs. Low fat. It's obnoxious, but at least they let you drink." She held up her wineglass, "Here's to getting skinny and drunk!" She and Tania clinked glasses. "You too, Rena. Here's to new friends." I tapped my glass against each of theirs. The waiter, his white jacket embroidered with "Claude," took our orders and instructed the busboy to bring us water and a basket of bread.

We spent a half-hour discussing other people in the business and the summerhouse in East Hampton that Kristen and Tania shared with fifteen other people every other weekend. Claude and his sidekick swept the table clean of dirty wineglasses and crumbs and placed our entrees in front of us with great fanfare.

Over coffee I discovered that Tania's family had been involved in the media business for three generations. She had wanted to go to law school, but her father got her a job at J. Walter Thompson the summer after college and she never made it to litigating. Kristen had attended the State University of New York at New Paltz for communications and had been hired into the business by the father of a classmate. We didn't talk about me at all.

Kristen and Tania split an order of fresh berries for dessert with the whipped cream on the side. I assuaged my wounded ego with the Ocean Club's famous chocolate basket. I tried to tempt them, placing it in the center of the table to make it more accessible. But they stuck with the strawberries and instead splurged on a shot of Bailey's for their skim milk cappuccinos.

I audibly gasped when the check arrived—$150 without the tip. I put my Amex inside the leather portfolio. The waiter passed several times and I finally flagged him down, waving it in the air.

"Madam," he said with a faint trace of a French accent. "There is a slot for your credit card here," he pointed. "This allows me to know that you have reviewed the check and wish to pay." He bowed slightly. "I will return in a moment."

We stepped into the afternoon heat. "This feels good," exclaimed Tania. "I was freezing in there. I should've brought a sweater."

"Neither of us was thinking," agreed Kristen. I felt the drips collecting in the small of my back. I walked them back to Bluestone, listened patiently while they thanked me profusely, and splurged on a cab back to the office. On my desk were four orders from Renee. The rates were now almost a month old and I knew there was no way they were going to hold in Phoenix and Philadelphia. There wasn't much of a chance of them clearing in Tampa or San Antonio either. But they totaled $450,000. Armed with documentation proving I was the sane one, I knocked on Lynn's door.

"Great job!" He smiled thumbing through the orders.

"There's just one problem." I sat and opened the file folder on his desk. "I've been trying to reach her for nearly four weeks and she never returned any of my messages."

"Are you telling me these rates are a month old?" I had never seen his brows furrow before. It was like watching clouds darken before a thunderstorm.

"Yes, but I've called her ten times, Lynn. It's not my fault she wouldn't call me back." His shoulders looked muscular in his sapphire blue shirt.

"Did you think about faxing her updated rates?" I tried to hide the fact that the thought hadn't occurred to me. "Rena, we don't have those sales meetings twice a week so we can eat breakfast together." He threw the orders on his desk and they fluttered around the photos of his wife and kids. He walked over to the window, staring at the traffic below.

"You've been listening for a month now about how tight these markets are. Every station specialist has reported that rates were being raised daily. In Phoenix sometimes hourly. How could you have made a mistake like this?"

"I, I don't know." I leaned back in the chair and pretended I had something in my eye.

"Don't even think about crying." He stood beside me and I felt the heat from his anger. "We've got to figure a way out of this mess." I sat while he called the general sales manager of each station and spun it so Renee was completely to blame.

"Of course Rena updated her rates, Tom," Lynn soothed our client in Arizona. "I'm telling you this Renee is a fucking nightmare." He threw his feet up on the desk, the soles worn slightly in the middle. "It's a buying service. She wanted to do the buys as cheaply as she could because she gets a commission on what she saves from the budget. You know she figured she

could ram the rates down our throats because we'd be hungry for business."
Seeing Lynn had things under control with our Phoenix station, I stood to
leave, but he motioned me harshly to stay seated.

"Let me fax you the order and see what you can clear. Whatever you can't,
I'll happily shove back down her throat and get a higher rate. But it is
$150,000, Tom." He retracted his legs and leaned his arms on the desk.
"Great. I'll put it on the fax right now." Lynn hung up the phone and hand-
ed me the order.

"Fax this to Tom Bradley right now. And then call him in an hour to see
what's not going to make it and how much it'll cost to change that. Then
call Renee and tell her she had no fucking business using rates that were a
month old and inform her she's lucky any of it's going to run." I almost
saluted. "Tell her how much money it's going to take to clear the entire
order and let it be her decision."

"I'm sorry, Lynn." He had already buried his nose in the stack of budgets
on his desk.

"Do it now, Rena." I retreated and sat in my office watching the clock
move slowly after I faxed to Tom. Because of Lynn's preparation, my
conversation with Tom was pleasant. I normally dealt with Josh, the
national sales manager, but he was on a vacation. I carefully wrote down
everything he stipulated and then called Renee. I got her voice mail and
transferred to the receptionist who informed me that Renee was in a
meeting. I left a message telling her none of her orders had cleared,
knowing that would get her to call me back. Five minutes later the
phone rang.

"What the fuck are you talking about, Rena?" Renee screamed in my ear.

"Hi, Renee. I'm fine today, how are you?"

"Don't be smart with me, Missy. What kind of idiot rep leaves a message
like that with a receptionist?"

"Renee, I've left almost a dozen messages for you. You haven't returned
one of them. I've been down to see you twice since our first meeting and
you refuse to see me. What choice did I have?"

"To clear the fucking orders I faxed you and be grateful for the money."

"I'm sorry. We can't. The markets are on fire this quarter."

"This is inexcusable. I want the Dago back."

"First of all, Mike is not Italian. Secondly, I'm the rep for your agency.
And third, you used rates that were a month old. You can't expect there to
have been no changes in that time."

"No, but I expect a rep to know what the fuck she's doing," she yelled. "My other reps faxed me changes in their rates. When I didn't hear from you, I assumed everything was status quo."

"Well, it's not," I broke the point on the pencil I was doodling with and threw it in the garbage. "I can tell you what cleared and what rates I need for the other time periods."

"Fuck that. Who's your manager?"

"I don't have one right now," I played with her purposely.

"That explains a lot. OK, who's your sales director?" I heard her exhaling smoke into the phone.

"Lynn Yancy."

"I want to speak to him now."

"I'm sorry, he's in a meeting." At least I wasn't stupid enough to transfer her to Lynn before I had a conversation with him.

"Well, you tell him that unless he calls me back within the hour I'll cancel all of those orders. We'll see how fast he moves for $450,000." She slammed the receiver in my ear. I sprinted into Lynn's office, my pulse racing and my hands trembling. I knocked rapidly three times and entered.

"This bitch is out of control," I hissed. His eyes rose above the half glasses balanced on his nose as he took in my rage.

"Who are we talking about, Rena?"

"Renee Woodson." How could he have forgotten?

"Do you want to tell me what happened or do you just want to stand there and seethe?" He removed the glasses and gestured for me to sit down. I recounted the conversation.

"What's her phone number?" He dialed as I read the numbers from the file. "Renee," his voice was smooth and comforting like hot chocolate, "this is Lynn Yancy, Rena Sutcliffe's director of sales. I understand there's been a little miscommunication." I heard her muffled screeching through the phone, but couldn't make out what she was saying.

"I know how frustrating it is to finish a buy and then be told that all your hard work needs to be redone," he mollified her, wrapping his silky tone around her and stroking her into submission. "But our stations seem to be very tight right now. If there was any way to clear all of your orders, Renee, we would." He nodded and leaned back in his chair. "No, Renee, that's a really good idea. Let me call the general sales managers and see what we can do. You sit tight. I'll call you back in a few." He replaced the phone in the cradle and looked at his watch.

"I don't get it," I said, confused.

"She needs to believe that I'm doing everything possible to clear her fucking schedules, Rena."

"But you've already talked to the GSM's." I glanced at his strong hands and imagined them wrapped around me in a hug.

"I know that and you know that, but she doesn't know that. It's much more effective to have her believe I'm doing it now than to tell her I already talked to them. Plus, she thinks it was her idea." He put his glasses back on. "We have a few minutes, why don't you get your pending list and let's review it together." I retrieved it from my office and we went over every piece of business I had on the table, Lynn making suggestions and asking questions. When we were finished, he hit redial.

"Renee," he smiled into the phone, "Lynn Yancy here." He hit the mute button. "Always smile when you're talking to a client, Rena. It comes through on the other end." He nodded listening to act two of Renee's ranting and retouched the mute. "I've spoken with Phoenix, Renee. And I gotta be honest, my GSM out there is a real fucking asshole." He laughed.

"You're right, the business is full of them." He hit the mute again. "Rena, did you give her any of the new rates or tell her specifically what didn't clear?" I shook my head and he reconnected the line.

"The bottom line is I got him to clear all but three of the time periods." He held the order in front of him. "I thought maybe we could shave some money off of the rates for the programs that did clear, but he's claiming he needs every dime." He chuckled, nodding his head in agreement.

"You're right, they're all greedy bastards. But let's see what we can come up with here." By the time he hung up, she had added money to the three areas that fell short, bringing the total order to $185,000. And I was no longer calling on TVBS. "Don't take it hard, Rena. We ended up getting the money and Renee Woodson's is one less ass you have to kiss right now."

I spent weeks beating myself up for not updating her rates. "You've got to quit," Gene scolded me one day after I had reiterated my mistake to him for the fifth time. "You did it, it's over. Let it go."

"But I can't."

"You don't want to. Or you would." He shook his head in frustration. "You've only been doing this for six months or so. Give yourself a break." I tried to listen to him, but the voice telling me I was an idiot was still louder. I had convinced myself the blunder with Renee was the reason Lynn had informed me earlier in the week that he had been unable to convince the powers that be to give me that bonus for my time in Vegas.

Rest

At our sales meeting one Tuesday, Lynn informed us that we were picking up a new station group. The owners, Renfort Broadcasting, were going to be in at the end of next week for a takeover meeting. "We all need to be prepared," Lynn stressed. "Do whatever you need to do in order to know these three stations like you've been selling them your entire career." Mike and Gene and I gathered in my office after the meeting.

"I wonder if he's going to hire a manager now," Mike wondered. "And he's going to have to hire at least one more salesperson." I had been placed permanently on the team almost a year ago. A station from one of the other divisions was moved to our team for political reasons. It was a weak independent in Birmingham, Alabama and Lynn vehemently argued that it didn't belong with us.

He acquiesced when he got budget approval to hire me. Twelve months later, Tania thought she was my best friend, I wasn't as affected by prima donnas like Renee Woodson and I had learned how to be humble when I encountered an unfamiliar situation.

"I heard a rumor," I smiled, "that Gene might be moving into the empty office next to Lynn's." I had started working out at the Manhattan Sports Club across the street from the office in an attempt to shed some pounds and Jackie let it slip one day when we were on neighboring treadmills.

"Where did you hear that?" He jumped down my throat.

"A little birdie told me," I winked at Mike.

"It's not official, yet," he shut my door. "You can't say anything to the others." The others included Monica, who had replaced Joanna when her hip proved too fragile for all the walking required for the job. She had two children and was always out the door by five-fifteen. And Darryl, who had been hired to replace Grace after she left to sell locally in New York. He was in his late forties and was an expert at looking like he was swamped when his phone hadn't rung in a week.

Gene, Mike, and I were the Three Musketeers. Now, according to Jackie, Gene was going to be my manager. Mike and I swore we would keep it to ourselves until Lynn made the announcement. The day before the Renfort meeting, Lynn told the team that Gene would be our new manager.

Jackie uncorked a bottle of champagne and we toasted Gene in Lynn's office. "I hope everyone will show their support of Gene by being prepared for the meeting tomorrow," he raised his glass. "Nothing has changed. These guys are probably assholes just like the rest of our clients, but they're worth some big money. So everyone on your toes." He guzzled the champagne and held it out for Jackie to refill.

The next morning, we were all in early, quizzing each other on the call letters for the Renfort stations and the names of the management teams. At eight-thirty we paraded into the conference room, yellow pads in tow. There were three men already at the table, oblivious to our territorial habit of always sitting in the same chair. We each introduced ourselves and shook hands with Michael Renfort, the president of the group, John Hodgkins, his director of sales, and Donald Menderling, who didn't include his job title with his name.

Lynn rushed in a few minutes later, all of us seated. The deal had been secured through upper management so Lynn was also meeting our new client for the first time. Michael Renfort looked to be in his mid-forties and wore a pompadour toupee. Lynn shook his hand and moved down the table to their director of sales. John Hodgkins appeared to be around forty-five and was impeccably dressed, his beard and mustache neatly trimmed.

Donald Menderling remained seated as Lynn rounded the table. "Lynn Yancy," he said shaking the man's hand.

"Donald Menderling," he replied, the tie around his neck was already loose and a blotch of coffee stained the tip of his collar. He was a bit over-weight and wore no belt.

"What is it you do for Renfort?" Lynn asked taking a seat.

"Let's just say I'm a gynecologist," he tried to hide his yellow teeth behind a smile. "I like to explore things." Lynn coughed.

"Donald is our marketing director," Michael Renfort jumped in.

"And I like to make sales calls," he made eye contact with all of us, his bushy gray eyebrows arched over black-rimmed glasses. "Sometimes you might go on a call and instead of it being just you and the national sales manager, you might have me, your manager, and John. And maybe even Michael." He picked a piece of bagel from under his thumbnail and flicked it onto the table. "That's the Renfort way, we like to gang-bang the buyers. Keeps them off guard."

For the next two hours we listened as the three Renfort executives listed their expectations for each station we now represented. I looked to Lynn for some sign that he found them as obnoxious as I did. He caught my glance once and rolled his eyes. As we stood around, shaking hands after the meeting, they casually mentioned that each of us would receive a quarterly report card for our performance.

Gene called us into his office after they left. "We need to be completely buttoned up with these assholes," he threw his pad on his desk. "They're going to be looking for us to fuck up. Lynn told me they wanted their stations to be on Ken Burnside's team and weren't happy when they were told they'd be with us after they signed the contract." He adjusted his glasses. "I need to know about any problems before they do. We can't afford to have something blow up. Got it?" We nodded our heads and filed back to our offices.

For the next six months Renfort occupied most of my attention, often at the expense of our other stations. Every other week, a different station manager was in town, requiring sales calls, lunches, and dinners. We also were expected to entertain in the evening, often returning to the office after cocktails with a national sales manager to finish work that had been abandoned for ass kissing and meaningless conversation.

"Gene," I complained, "this is ridiculous. How much money are these guys worth that they can command all of this attention?"

"Plenty, Rena, trust me." He and Lynn spent hours behind closed door every week talking on conference calls and orchestrating damage control strategies when Renfort wasn't happy with their share on a piece of business. The budgets Renfort had developed were totally unreasonable given the strength of their stations, but when they weren't achieved, it was S&W's fault.

Sid Hanlon was the national sales manager for the Renfort station in Tampa. He rarely returned a phone call, making it impossible to be competitive, particularly on business that required a quick turnaround, like retail or movie accounts. Lynn began to suspect that he had been ordered by John or Donald to keep us in the dark.

"I spent two hours on the phone with Michael Renfort last night," Lynn announced in a sales meeting. "He's very unhappy with our performance in Tampa."

"Maybe that's because his asshole NSM never returns a fucking phone call," I leaned back in my chair, crossing my legs. "We've been calling our own shots in that market for months because we can never get him on the phone."

"I'm aware of that, Rena." Lynn tapped his pencil on the table. "I told that to Michael. He informed me that Sid's been complaining that we never get back to him on time. That we make our own deals and then expect him to run spots at whatever rates we decide to quote."

"That's total bullshit!" I thought Gene was going to leap across the table. "You know that's not true." The rest of the team echoed his sentiments, words like "douchebag" and "prick" flying around the table.

"I know," sighed Lynn. "Rena, you do the most business in Tampa. And it's time to nail this son of a bitch."

"He's nothing more than a pawn," I pulled myself back to the table. "It's that dickbag Donald who's calling the shots."

"Even so, we can't let them win this one." Lynn sipped his coffee. "They need to know they can't fuck with us."

"What are you saying?" I asked.

"I'm saying we're going to document every phone call you make to this asshole. You're going to date and time everything. And if I have my way, Sid Hanlon will be history by the end of the quarter." He finished his coffee and threw the cup in the trash.

"But they'll just hire another lackey to take his place," I argued. "Wouldn't it be more effective to try to win him over? Convince him his pocket will be fuller if he does it our way? He seems like a nice enough guy, not the sharpest tool in the shed, but we can use that to our advantage."

"I'm sick of their bullshit," Lynn slammed a fist on the table. "I want him gone. And you're going to help me."

"God, he's sexy when he's angry," Kali smacked her lips and flicked her black tongue. "I want to throw him on the table and jump him."

"You're hopeless," Inanna's hair had come loose from the braids, strands covering her face and ears. "This is serious, Kali."

"Whatever," she played with her sword, using the tip to clean under her toenails.

"Dammit, I mean it," Inanna kicked the sword away from Kali's feet. "They want Rena to help get this guy fired."

"I don't think she should go along with it," Kuan Yin added her two cents. "It's not very spiritual."

"Lynn needs her help," said Erishkigal brushing her hair. "He's done so much for Rena. How can she refuse?"

"Where have we heard that before?" asked Kuan Yin.

"This could be kind of fun," Kali twirled her sword around. "There hasn't been any bloodshed for a while."

"I don't know," Inanna squashed the uneasy feeling in her stomach. "But if she's going to keep moving up here, I guess she doesn't have a choice."

I faithfully kept a log of every attempt to reach Sid Hanlon during the Toyota negotiation. Allison Raritan was my buyer at Bluestone and was one of the few pleasures of my job. She was the only buyer I'd taken out to lunch without an NSM since Tania. We'd talk for hours when I made calls at the agency, discussing how she was handling single motherhood since her husband left to marry his secretary. I'd been invited to her house in Tarrytown a few times, but had declined, Lynn's warning "No buyer is your friend," echoing in my head.

"I promise I'll have you revised rates by tomorrow, Allison. My NSM has been in a meeting at the station the whole day." I crossed my fingers.

"You know the only reason I'm letting this slide, Rena, is because it's you. I could put this buy together tonight without you, no problem." I heard her cracking gum over the phone.

"I know, Allison, and I really appreciate it."

"You're sure you'll have something tomorrow?" I pictured her sitting in her office, crayon pictures from her kids hanging on the wall.

"I'm positive." I hung up and went to Gene's office. "I've documented everything," I laid the log in front of him. "There's $500,000 on the table. They want added value stuff too, like concert tickets and passes to the Buccaneers' games."

"He hasn't left one message?"

"He called me back at lunchtime yesterday," I pointed to the note. "Other than that, no."

"And he knows Allison's deadline?" I nodded. "And how much money it is?"

"A half a million."

"Let me call his GSM. I'll let you know."

"I've got to have something to her by tomorrow. And it's five-thirty already." He picked up the phone and hit Tampa's speed dial. I was packing my briefcase to take work home when the phone rang.

"Rena?" The southern voice drawled. "Sid Hanlon. Sorry we keep missing each other." We spent an hour and a half working out rates and he promised me six tickets to Bucs' football games that fall. I warned him that the rates were high compared to the competition and I couldn't guarantee the fifteen percent he was looking for. He assured me he had given me his lowest rates and I stayed at the office until nine, massaging the numbers and putting together a proposal for Allison.

"I'm sorry Rena, it was the best I could do," Allison apologized, handing me the order. "The other stations were more efficient. I probably shouldn't have given you as much as I did, but I know what you're up against there." Six percent. I wasn't looking forward to telling Gene.

"This is it?" Gene scanned the few lines of the order. "Sid's gonna have a heart attack."

"We wouldn't have to worry about getting rid of him then," I joked. We sat for an hour reviewing every number, trying to see if I could've done anything differently. "You covered everything, Rena," he said, dropping his pencil and rubbing his fingers. Sid and Renfort Broadcasting weren't happy, but Lynn just smiled and slid copies of my notes into a file folder.

The tightrope I walked, trying to please everyone, the buyers, the stations, and Gene, seemed to be getting smaller and I wondered if there'd be a net if I fell. Even the buyers who allowed their human side to show were forced to make unreasonable demands because their agencies didn't know how to say no to their clients. The Renfort stations occupied much of my time and I began to be grateful to Lynn for inadvertently teaching me the finer points of head chess.

Four agencies were added to my list since Gene's replacement had yet to be hired. "We haven't seen anyone we like," Gene insisted. "It won't be forever." But I was tired of working sixty-hour weeks. When I had been given a permanent position on the team, my salary finally came back to where it was at JC, but I had used my credit cards to live on for a year and still dodged phone calls because I didn't have the money to meet the minimum payments.

"Gene, can I talk to you?" I approached his office tentatively.

"Sure, what's up?" I closed the door and sat down across from him.

"I think I've been doing a pretty good job," I began. I could scrap like a pit bull to get a station a higher rate, but I didn't know how to get more money for myself. "And I haven't had a raise since I was placed on the team. That was a year-and-a-half ago." He sat back in his chair and listened, his silk tie knotted perfectly in between the flaps of his button-down collar.

"I ran some figures, Gene, and I account for thirty-two percent of the billing for this team. And I'm pretty sure I'm not getting the same percentage of the salary budget." He crossed his legs and folded his hands in his lap. "I know I'm the only one on the team still under contract and you have to take care of the people who can actually leave to go somewhere else. But I'm working for slave wages and it's not fair."

"Rena," his voice was silky and slick, like a used car salesman's. "You knew when you took this job that the money wasn't going to be there until you were off contract."

"I know that, Gene. But thirty-six a year? When I bill almost five million? Come on." I wrapped my foot around the bottom of the chair to keep my leg from shaking. "No one, not even you, expected this kind of a performance from me."

"You're right," he uncrossed his legs and leaned onto the desk. "The problem is that to get all of the Renfort stations, we negotiated a much lower commission rate than normal. We're billing a ton of money for their stations, but S&W isn't making a whole lot." He crossed his wrists and pointed his index fingers to the ceiling. "My hands are tied right now, Rena. The big boys upstairs won't give me any more money for salaries."

"Then I'll have to get a part-time job, Gene," I heard myself say. "And I won't be able to put in sixty-hour weeks anymore. I've got to pay my bills. I'm tired of living paycheck to paycheck." I felt the tears forming. "And I'm really tired of playing Russian roulette when I pick up the phone, not knowing if it's going to be someone looking for money I owe them." He looked at me through his designer glasses as if I was a child who hadn't been invited to her best friend's birthday party.

"You know you're the best salesperson on this team, Rena. I don't know what I'd do if I lost you." He paused for effect. "You can outsell half the people in this town and you deserve to be making more money."

"You know what, Gene?" I leaned toward him and put my elbows on his desk. "Don't bother stroking me if you're not going to make me come." He stared at me, his mouth open and his eyebrows knitted in surprise.

"OK, OK. Let me see what I can do." He scribbled himself a note. "I'll talk to Lynn tonight."

"Thanks, Gene." I patted his hand as I stood up to leave. The phone was ringing when I returned to my office.

"Rena? Allison." She sounded panicked.

"Hey, what's up?"

"You know those tickets that you promised Sid would mail to Toyota a few weeks ago?"

"Yeah."

"They still don't have them. Their advertising VP called my media director who called my supervisor; well, you know the drill," she stopped for a breath.

"Where the hell are they?" I swore under my breath and clenched my teeth.

"I'll call him right now, Allison. I'm really sorry."

"You don't know the heat I took from my supervisor for even putting you on that buy as expensive as you were. The whole reason I convinced her to leave you on was because of those tickets," she was disgusted. "And now I've got to explain why the client doesn't have them. Like I need this aggravation, Rena."

"I know, I know," I tried to soothe her. "I'll get them there tomorrow. I promise." I hung up and immediately tried Sid, who, of course, was in a meeting.

Sid Hanlon came into town a couple of months after the Toyota ticket fiasco and wanted to take the team out for drinks. Forced socializing was at the bottom of the list of things that made me want to tap dance, but Lynn was adamant that we all go. We headed over to Ye Triple Inn on 55th and Eighth after work, Lynn promising to join us after his conference call. It was a Tuesday night and the place was deserted, dark except for the Christmas lights blinking under the tinsel.

It was June, but the decorations were a part of the décor year round. Darryl, Mike, and I grabbed a table and ordered beers, waiting for Sid who had gone back to the hotel to change. Gene was on vacation and Monica, my only female compatriot had bailed, claiming one of her kids was sick.

"Have you had any calls with this guy?" Mike asked as the waitress set down the bottles. "He's a fucking moron!"

"I have lunch with Allison at Bluestone tomorrow," I swallowed some Amstel. It was cold and bubbly.

"He actually told a buyer of mine that their inventory is wide open. Can you believe that?" Mike laughed and fiddled with the empty ashtray. "She's got $150,000 up right now for Burger King and he tells her our inventory is wide open. What kind of idiot shares that information with a buyer?" Mike took a swig from his Amstel Light. "Why don't we just let her make up her own rates? What an asshole." He slammed the bottle on the table.

"That's OK," Darryl chimed in. "He told Beverly Russo at Bozell that he had to fire his assistant because she made so many mistakes." Fleshy jowls hung over his jaw and the bags under his eyes needed handles. "I've been lying to her for two months now, telling her the reason her spots keep getting bumped is because Home Depot opened two new stores and put a fortune into the market." He sipped his Coors. "And Mr. To Tell the Truth spills the beans."

Sid waved from the door and headed to the table. "Hey y'all!" He was dressed in khakis and a golf shirt. His thick black hair was swept off of his forehead. "Great bar." He slid his windbreaker over the back of the chair and ordered a beer. "Here's to making budget with my kick-ass sales team," he toasted, his green eyes twinkling under the Christmas lights. "Up and attem boys!" He looked at me sheepishly. "And girl." He clinked his bottle with each of ours, the smiles pasted on our faces plastic and tired.

Lynn wandered in a half-hour later and rescued us from the conversation that had revolved solely around Sid's twelve-year-old son and his foray into little league baseball. We called it a night around nine. Sid paid the tab and we put him in a cab back to the hotel. "Nice guy," said Darryl. "Too bad he doesn't have the foggiest idea what he's doing."

I picked up Allison at twelve the next day and we headed to Meltemi on Second Avenue. We ordered iced teas and sampled the garlic spread and Greek bread while we waited for Sid. He arrived a few minutes late, perspiring slightly and out of breath. "I am so sorry, ladies," he wiped his brow with the linen napkin. "I couldn't get a cab and had to walk from 47th and Third." He shook the napkin and placed it in his lap. "The only walking I do in Tampa is on the golf course."

We ordered, and over appetizers Sid apologized profusely to Allison for the ticket mix-up. "I'd arranged for them to be mailed," his southern accent charmed her and the anger she'd shown to me was nowhere in sight. "But my assistant was having marital problems and was out for a few days," he smiled at Allison, his teeth appearing whiter against his Florida tan. "I take full responsibility, though," he bit into a puff pastry. "I sure do appreciate you putting us on the buy, Allison. I know you got some flak from your higher-ups." He opened his nylon briefcase, removed an envelope, and handed it to her.

"What's this?" She ripped it open. "Oh my god! You didn't have to do this!" She held up a gift certificate to Bloomingdale's for a hundred dollars. "Thank you so much!" She leaned across the table and kissed his cheek.

"You're gonna make me blush," his index finger lingered over the pink frost from her lipstick. "It's the least I could do." Over lunch, Allison and Sid exchanged photos of their children and swapped stories of parenthood, laughing like they'd known each other forever. During dessert, Allison shared the story of her husband's departure.

"My wife passed three years ago," Sid said returning the pictures to his wallet. "I know it's not easy doing it alone." When he looked up, his eyes were wet. "She was only forty-one. Breast cancer."

"I'm so sorry," Allison touched his hand. He smiled and returned his attention to the plate in front of him. Pushing the apple tart around with his fork, he was quiet. He looked up and grinned, "Hey, if you ever want to take the kids on vacation to Busch Gardens, let me know! I can get you tickets. And I promise there won't be a problem this time," he laughed. "Maybe me and my rugrats'll join y'all."

"He's so sweet!" Allison gushed on the walk back to the agency. "But that's so sad about his wife. No wonder he's been tough to get in touch with." We headed upstairs. I needed to see Tania. "I'll let my supervisor know what the situation was," she ran a comb through her short red hair as we stood at neighboring sinks in the ladies' room. "Maybe the client will get off our backs about the tickets being so late."

"See?" Erishkigal was indignant. "I knew there had to be a reason he was being so difficult to work with." She sympathized with Sid and his situation.

"I'm sorry he lost his wife," agreed Inanna, "but Rena can't deviate from the plan now. Lynn's counting on her."

"But he's so nice," whined Erishkigal. "How can you even think of letting her go through with it?"

"I concur," Kuan Yin nodded her head, lashes closed over her elongated eyes. "It's not good karma."

"Karma, schmarma," Kali made a face. "She's come this far, she can't stop now." She adjusted her belt. "And besides, losing your wife doesn't excuse you for being a yahoo."

"I wouldn't go quite that far," Inanna straightened her spine, her head a full six inches above Kali's. "But she's worked too hard to go soft now. Everything that Sid does needs to be reported to Gene or Lynn. If they see she's cooperating, maybe she'll get that raise."

"Lynn wants to see you," Gene called as I passed his office. I threw my bag and coat in my office and stood in Gene's doorway.

"About?" I raised my eyebrows.

"A couple of things from what I gather," he looked tired, hunched over a stack of spreadsheets on the desk. "I spoke with him about the money thing. And he also wants a report on lunch with Sid."

"Are you OK?" I watched him punching numbers on the adding machine.

"Yeah, yeah. Fine." He forced a smile. "Budget time, that's all. It'll all be done by the end of next week. And then I can get back to a semi-normal life." I left Gene to his number crunching and walked over to Lynn's office. Jackie sat at her desk, a half-eaten gyro on her desk.

"Street meat?" I laughed. "That's hardly part of your usual repertoire."

"These fucking budgets are going to kill me," she slurped her diet soda through the blue straw sticking out of a flowered paper cup. The red of her hair was a bit brighter than I remembered and I noticed the crow's feet around her eyes had deepened. "Lynn needs to talk to you." She waved toward the door with her hand, still holding the cup. I walked over and knocked before entering.

"Come in, come in." His hair looked like he'd been sitting in front of a fan, and Jackie's glasses were balanced on his nose. "I can't find my damned glasses," he explained removing them and throwing them onto the blotter. "How was lunch?"

"Pretty good, actually," I sat and tried to cross my legs, pulling my skirt over my knees. "He smoothed things over with Allison. Even bought her a gift certificate to Bloomie's. I didn't know his wife died a few years ago."

"Yeah, I remember hearing something about that," he stared at me. "You're not going soft on me, Rena? I've almost got enough evidence to go to Mike Renfort so we can get this asshole out of the way." He wore a maroon-striped shirt, the lines from his T-shirt visible because of his enormous arms.

"Renfort held our balls to the fire negotiating our commissions, Rena. And we're not anywhere near making budget here, so we're not going to see the bonus that was agreed on for achieving it. And there's only one reason. Sid Hanlon." He pushed his chair back and put his feet on the desk. "I don't care how nice a guy he is. He's the reason I can't pay you the money you deserve." I sat quietly.

"I can't emphasize that enough, Rena," he smoothed his hair into place. "This guy is an obstacle. He's got to go. Capiche?"

"But he's got two kids," I picked the cuticle on my thumb. "Can't you just talk to him?"

"I've tried," he stared at the ceiling. "If you're going to succeed in this business, Rena, you can't look at it like that. We're all losing money because of this guy." I shifted in the chair. "If we had an aggressive NSM at this station, we'd be kicking ass. And because of the things he's claiming we fucked up on, Renfort thinks it's our fault."

"Like what?"

"He told Mike Renfort that you never asked him for those tickets. He also told him that you never gave him any competitive information, which is why he was so high on the rates for the Toyota deal." Jackie wandered in and placed a stack of files on Lynn's desk, the miniskirt she wore revealing plenty of leg. "He's covering his ass, Rena, at our expense. And then I end up with Mike's foot in my privates, bitching about having a rookie like you handling such an important account."

"That's not fair," I pounded my fist on the arm of the chair.

"Exactly," Lynn nodded while he sifted through the files. "Look, Gene talked to me about getting you a raise and it wasn't easy, but I managed to find a few thousand dollars. I know it's not enough for all the money you've brought in, but at least it's something." He looked up at me. "Let's start with that and I'll see what I can do about squeezing some more out of the budget after we remove the roadblock in Tampa."

"When is it effective?" I squirmed.

"The fifteenth," he returned the glasses to their perch. "I know you're doing a deal right now with Allison for TGI Friday's. I want to know what's going on every step of the way. OK?" I nodded and stood up.

"Thanks for the raise, Lynn," I turned to go.

"There will be more where that came from, Rena. Just keep doing what you're doing." I returned to my office wondering why I wasn't as happy as I should be.

I hadn't been faithful about going to the gym in the last few months. But lately I needed to sweat to alleviate the stress. I picked up the new class schedule at the front desk on my way out Monday. There was a blurb at the bottom about a new yoga class. "De-stress and unwind!" It invited. "Stretch your body and soul. Join us for Darla Stevens' new yoga classes—Thursday nights at six-thirty." I threw it in my gym bag and headed to Burke and Burke to get something to eat.

Later that week, I bumped into Mike Renfort in the elevator coming back from calls. The ride was quiet, neither of us having much to say. I escorted him to Lynn's office and Jackie showed him in and fetched him a cup of coffee. Word was that Lynn was presenting his CIA file on Sid Hanlon. I retreated to my office and made some calls. At 6:00 that night his door was still shut.

I knew I was having lunch with Allison the next day, so I wouldn't be working out. Wanting to wash my dirty gym clothes over the weekend, I dug through my bag and found the class schedule buried under a sweaty T-shirt. I looked at the clock on my desk. At first I made excuses. I was too tired. I didn't want to miss *Friends*. Then I pulled a fresh pair of tights from my bottom desk drawer and headed to the gym.

A tall woman with an olive complexion stood near the stereo in the aerobics room on the 3rd floor. Her feet were bare and she wore a black unitard. Curly black hair cascaded down her back, unruly and free. Six mats were lined up on the floor, four of them filled with women in tights stretching.

"Hi," she smiled at me, her brown eyes welcoming me. "I'm Darla." Her slim arms held a cassette case.

"Rena," I said stiffly.

"Have you ever taken yoga before?" I shook my head. "That's fine," she waved me over to a mat. "Sit down and make yourself comfortable. I'll be starting in a few minutes." I glanced at the clock. Great, I might not make it home in time for *Friends*. Birds chirped through the speakers and soon I heard rain falling. Darla turned out the lights and sat on a mat in the front of the room.

"Welcome," her voice was husky and soft. "I'm Darla Stevens. And I'm so glad you all are here." She curled her legs underneath her. "I know that some of you haven't practiced yoga before, so we'll start slowly. Is anyone having problems with a particular area of the body tonight?"

"My lower back," the young woman next to me called out.

"Me too," agreed the blond at the end.

"OK. We'll do some hip work." Darla noticed the confused look on my face. "Many times, lower back pain is a sign of tight hips. If we open the pelvic area, the back pain disappears." She stood up. "We'll start with some sun salutations." She slowly performed a series of movements, explaining the meaning of each as she did it.

"Let's all try," she smiled. "We'll go slowly. And remember, this is not a competition. It's not about how fast you can learn it. It's not about how quickly you can complete the movements," she stood with her hands in front of her heart, palms pressed together. "It's about honoring your body. If you feel tightness anywhere, breathe into it. And remember to inhale and exhale through your nose."

An hour and a half later, after the guided deep relaxation, I felt like Gumby. "Thank you," I went up to her after class.

"*Namaste,*" she pushed her palms together and pointed her fingers at me. "That means that the divinity in me acknowledges and appreciates the divinity in you." Her cheekbones rode high on her face and a few freckles danced in their hollows.

"Oh," I stuttered. "*Namaste.*" I mimicked her hand gesture. Too tired for public transportation, I hailed a cab and collapsed in the back seat.

I struggled to stay awake during our sales meeting the next morning. Sipping my orange juice, I began to wish I had gotten coffee. Lynn marched in, Gene behind him, with a Cheshire grin on his weary face. They sat at the head of the table, eyes dancing.

"Well," Lynn started. "I'm happy to say that Mike Renfort was receptive to the information I shared with him last night." He coughed. "And we will no longer be dealing with Sid Hanlon in Tampa." The team applauded. I sat there silent and numb.

"What's the matter, Rena?" Gene asked. "I thought you'd be thrilled. You do more business in that market than anyone does. This'll make your life a whole lot easier."

"I know," I said quietly. "What happened to him?"

"Mike is going to move him into the local sales department," Lynn answered. "The best news is that Mike is looking hard at the candidate I gave him for Sid's replacement."

"Who is it, chief?" Darryl asked.

"Bob Murray, an old friend of the house who's working in Orlando." Lynn surveyed the room. "This is a huge win. And I'd like to thank each of you for being so diligent with your record keeping." He glanced at me. "Especially you, Rena. We never would've been able to pull this off without you."

"Way to go, Rena!" Mike Osborn rubbed my head. "Ding, dong, the wicked witch is dead!" The rest of the team, including the research analysts, hooted their approval. "Maybe now we can all make some money!"

"Let's hope so," agreed Lynn. "It's been a long week. How about we all have lunch at the Carnegie Deli today. How's twelve?"

"I can't," I answered. "I have a lunch with Allison Raritan."

"Cancel it," ordered Lynn. "Make up something. It's been a long haul getting rid of this moron. You deserve to be there to celebrate." We filed out of the conference room and back to our offices. I didn't want to go to lunch. I wanted to go home and go to bed, pull my goose down comforter over my head, and sleep through the weekend.

"Rena?" Lynn followed me into my office. "I have news for you."

"Oh?" I sat on the windowsill.

"I talked to the powers that be and told them how much you helped with the Sid Hanlon situation. Effective next month, your salary will be $50,000."

"Really?!" I leapt across the room and threw my arms around his neck, the stubble from his beard grazing my cheek. "Thank you."

"No, thank you," he hugged me back. "You deserve it."

"She did it!" Inanna shouted. "Now maybe she can make a decent salary."

"Nice job," Kali danced a jig around Inanna. "I didn't think you could pull it off."

"She did," acknowledged Kuan Yin. "But at what cost?"

"That poor man," Erishkigal curled into a ball, tears running down the smooth skin of her pretty face. "What about his kids?"

"It's not like he got fired," argued Inanna, "They're not going to starve."

"It was calculated," Kuan Yin ran her bracelets up and down her arm. "This was a step backwards for her." She looked softly at Inanna. "And you know it."

"Bull," Inanna defended herself.

"Nanna—you're naked," Kali squealed.

"What is this, a conspiracy?" Inanna shouted, crossing her arms over her breasts, her hands stretching to cover the blond thatch under her belly button. "Where's my robe?"

Rest

The bus on Sunday morning was a bonsai sample of New York City life. A young black woman, colorful in an island caftan, sat on the back bench reading to a little white boy. I smiled and thought of Celia. That part of my life was cloudy and unfamiliar. It still gave me a chill to think of how close I had come to sliding into that abyss. After practicing yoga for almost a year, I recently started going to a private class with Darla in SoHo. I was suffocating behind the mask of super saleswoman. The duplicity required for my job left me empty. Yoga provided balance.

In the seat opposite me was an older man. The bright red bumps on his nose revealed his fondness for liquor and disclosed the way he chose to deal with his humanness. We all have our red bumps, I thought; some people just hide them better. I couldn't hide mine anymore than the man across from me because my choice was still food. I worked out several times a week but still ate whatever I wanted as a reward for tolerating the game playing in my job.

The bus sped down Broadway, past Madison Square Park, through Union Square, and into the Village. The city was deserted. Everyone slept late on Sunday. I got off on Prince Street and walked the four blocks to the Ravi Center. I saw Darla bouncing toward me. I stubbornly refused to believe that someday my hipbones would be seen pressing to escape a tight black leotard the way Darla's did. I waited for her to recognize me. "Rena!" Darla's breathy voice echoed on the empty street.

Upstairs, a half-dozen people removed their socks and shoes in silence, gathered pillows, and filed into the tiny room where Azan sat in full lotus under the large casement window. A tinkling of chimes filled the room as the wind breezed through the windows.

The old wool rug scratched my feet. Everyone sat on pillows, legs tucked underneath, open palms resting on their knees. As if on cue, Azan began to chant, "*Om nima shivaya.*" The group echoed her, creating an electric energy. Azan guided the start of the mediation.

"We are grateful for this beautiful fall day," she began softly. "The sun is shining; the temperature is cool and invigorating. The leaves have succumbed to autumn's command and are now brilliant shades of gold, red and orange. Through the change of the seasons, we see God's work." My foot fell asleep at this point every week and my nose itched. It was easier to ignore now that I'd been coming for a month.

"But the rejoicing will soon end when the leaves turn brown and fall to the ground. This makes us sad." Azan's voice was gentle and melodious. "But the truth is that it is necessary for the leaves to rest on the ground. They decompose and become fertilizer, allowing the tree to survive the long, cold winter. They provide the nourishment needed so that new leaves can bloom in the spring."

Azan paused for a minute and the tinkling of the chimes seemed deafening. "What needs to fall off the tree of your life," she asked, "so it can decompose into the experiences of your past and make you the person you were meant to be tomorrow?" Azan paused, allowing the group to absorb the question. "So that we can all see the wonder of God in ourselves."

"Isn't this wonderful?" asked Kuan Yin. "She's finally starting to see."

"See what?" Kali questioned. "That the two top skills on her resume have become lying and manipulating? That's real peaceful."

"No, Kali. That she is growing. That is what she is beginning to see." Kuan Yin shook her head.

"But people won't like her at work if she stops doing those things," voiced Erishkigal.

"Who cares who likes us?" said Kali wrapping her six arms around herself in a bear hug. "I say we do whatever feels good and screw what anyone else thinks."

"That's not practical," Inanna sighed at Kali's selfishness. "We have to care to some degree. It's the only way to get ahead."

"That's not true," argued Kuan Yin. "Rena has to come first. She has to decide what she wants and needs out of her life and not be so concerned with what everyone else thinks and needs. It's the only path to peace. Don't you see?"

I was shaking. No one else in the room appeared affected. I was afraid to sniffle, not wanting to make a sound. "Meditate upon this, my friends." Azan finished. I felt a seed of hope for the first time. Cynicism still got the best of me most of the time, but now there was at least a seed. The hour closed with the *slokas*, or prayers, developed by Ravi.

Azan prayed for peace and truth to be the norm in the world. I was skeptical that praying for it would make it so. Even though I didn't fully believe, the hour made me feel better. It gave me a sense of belonging and purpose. I had grown dependent on this group of seven New Yorkers with not much in common except the time they spent together. It provided me with a way to spend time that wasn't destructive. That was something I had been searching for my whole life. I placed my pillow with the others and went to collect my things.

"Henry's going to join us for lunch," Darla whispered in my ear. No one was allowed to talk in anything but a whisper in the studio. Her Patchouli, reminiscent of the sixties, tickled my nose. "You don't mind, do you?"

"No, of course not." I lied. My time with Darla on Sunday was special. I didn't want Henry or anyone else intruding.

"He wants to grab something to eat with us, but he has to be at work before eleven, so we'll have time to talk after breakfast." It was as if Darla had read my mind.

"OK," I smiled, admiring her long lashes and inky gray eyes. Darla's kinky black hair was gathered in a yellow bandana. I knew she was thirty-five, but her slim arms gave her a sense of youthfulness. "Where are we going?"

"Lucky's is open." Darla licked her lips. "I have a craving for carrot-grapefruit juice."

"Sounds yummy."

"I have to talk to Azan about the class she wants me to teach. I'll meet you guys downstairs." Darla glided to the front of the room and folded her body into a perfect lotus at Azan's feet.

"Hey, Rena. Ready to go?" Henry's loud voice shattered the silence.

"Shh," I scolded him, putting an index finger across my lips. "We can talk outside."

Henry blushed and I felt guilty for criticizing him. But rules were rules. We rode down the elevator in silence. Outside, I inhaled the fall air deep into my lungs and sighed. "What a magnificent day."

"Yeah, it's OK." Henry rummaged through his backpack.

"How can you say that?" I defended. "There's not a cloud in the sky, the temperature is perfect. What could possibly be wrong?"

"I have to work today. OK? I have to freakin' work today!" His voice cracked.

"I'm sorry, Henry. But you could enjoy the time you have now." Strands of his long hair escaped the rubber band wrapped around his ponytail.

"How am I supposed to do that when I know what I'm going to find when I get there?" He rolled his eyes in exasperation.

"How can you assume that?"

"Because I know, OK? It's the same every damn day."

"Then why do you stay there?"

"Where else am I going to go?" I was afraid he might deck me, but I didn't stop.

"If you believe you have no options, you'll stay stuck there." I crossed my arms.

"You sound just like Darla. So I guess that means you're full of crap too."

"I'm just trying to help."

"Who asked you to?" He glared angrily.

"Well, you're standing there complaining. What am I supposed to do?" I defended myself.

"Nothing, OK? Not a Goddamned thing."

"You don't have to curse."

"No? How about fuck you? Is that cursing?" Henry was shouting.

"What is your problem?"

"You. I don't need this crap. I'm out of here." He grabbed his backpack and stormed down the street. I watched him go, feeling sorry for him that he was so miserable. I had been trying to help. How could he be so ungrateful? How dare he take away the glow I had created in that meditation? What was I going to tell Darla?

"That was smooth," Kuan Yin chided, trying hard to remember that she was the goddess of mercy. "Henry needed compassion, not a lecture."

"First of all, he thinks for some reason he's immune to all of the rules," Inanna explained. *"Secondly, who wants to stand around and have a pity party for him? If he's not happy, let him change his job. No one's keeping him there."*

"Like Rena's not stuck where she is? How can you be so judgmental?"

"She's not stuck! She's making close to six figures now that she's off contract. She's paid off all of her bills and even started a savings account."

"I know she is enjoying the money, Inanna. I am merely trying to get you to see that staying stuck is part of the process of change." Kuan Yin's need to educate her sisters was a priority.

"Rena's been stuck plenty, even with our help. And the longer she remains critical of other people's processes, the longer it's going to take her to complete the change she's initiated. Don't you see? Rena chastising Henry is, in essence, condemning herself."

"That's the most asinine thing I've ever heard," laughed Kali, the cobra around her shoulders flicking his tongue. "Where do you come up with this crap? He was whining, she tried to help and he freaked out. Case closed."

"You'll see, I'm right." Kuan Yin prayed.

Darla placed her hand on my shoulder. "Where's Henry?"

"He had to go." I rationalized that I really wasn't lying since he had taken off so suddenly.

"Is everything OK?"

I felt Darla's invisible force pulling the truth out of me. "Not really. We kind of had an argument."

"About what?" The tone was neutral.

"He was complaining about his job and he was really bringing me down," I stared at my feet, then looked up at her. "So I told him as long as he felt he had no options, he was going to stay stuck there. He told me I was full of crap, like you." I stole a glance at Darla, hoping that dragging her into it would unite the two of us against him.

"Henry isn't in a place to hear a lot of stuff like that, Rena. I know you were just trying to help." She touched my arm.

"That's what I told him."

"And I understand that. But Henry is new to this." Her head was tilted, like an antique doll. "Think about how you were when you first started practicing yoga and meditating. You certainly didn't want anyone telling you how to live your life, much less pointing out what you were doing wrong. We all need to discover that on our own." She paused for a breath. "Know what I mean?"

"I really thought I could help him."

"And that's great that you wanted to. But everyone needs and accepts help a little differently. Henry is pretty miserable right now." She stretched her arms overhead. "He hates his job, his girlfriend dumped him a month ago and his mother is getting remarried at Thanksgiving. He's got a lot on his plate right now."

"He's not handling it real well."

"Who's to say? He's handling it the best he can." We crossed Broadway and headed to Houston.

"I don't think he's trying hard enough." I refused to give in.

"Or do you think you're not trying hard enough?"

"What the hell is that supposed to mean?"

"Rena, most of the time, when we feel so strongly about something—in this case, Henry and the way he's dealing with his life right now—it's really about how we're feeling about a part of ourselves."

"Can we drop this?" I adjusted my backpack. "I don't agree with you and I really don't want to argue. Let's get breakfast. OK?"

"Sure, I can taste that carrot-grapefruit juice." She smiled. "And they make the best banana bran muffins." Darla took my arm and we turned left on Houston Street. I was proud of myself for avoiding an argument. I was making progress.

Lucky's was crowded with NYU students and statuesque models wearing black, a fresh juice fix the only thing on their minds. Darla threw her bag on an empty table and got in line. Blenders whirred and the aroma of fresh fruit misted the air. "Darla?" The woman at the next table jumped up and followed Darla to the counter.

"Angelina!" Darla threw her arms around the tall brunette. "How are you?" Angelina looked like a model, thin, her hair short and stylish. She wore no make-up and her large blue eyes were framed by the arch of her thick eyebrows. Darla escorted her to our table.

"Rena, this is my friend, Angelina," they had their arms around each other. "We spent a year together at the Kripalu Ashram in Massachusetts."

"Nice to meet you," Angelina held out her hand. It was soft; her nails short and well manicured.

"Why don't you join us?" Darla asked. "What a wonderful surprise!"

"I'll get breakfast," I offered heading to the counter. "Do you want anything Angelina?" She declined, retrieving her glass and bag from her table. I ordered our juices and returned, balancing two muffins in between the cups.

"I thought you were through with Manhattan," Darla sipped her juice.

"David and I bought a horse farm near Red Bank," she was excited. "We closed last week. This is my last Sunday in New York."

"Where do you live now?" I asked, breaking off a piece of muffin.

"We have an apartment in Battery Park." She wore sweat pants and a blue crewneck sweater. Tiny gold hoops hung from her ears. "It was such a beautiful day, I went out for a walk and this is where I ended up." She squeezed Darla's hand.

"A horse farm?" Darla looked surprised.

"It's been my dream for the last year or so. We spent months looking for something. One of David's clients helped us buy the horses." She looked like a five-year-old talking about her first day of school. "Two of them arrive this week."

"I love horses," her excitement was contagious and I wasn't immune. "How many are you going to have?"

"Five or six eventually," she circled her straw around the bottom of the glass, sucking up the last of the grapefruit. "Once we get organized, we'll probably board horses as well."

"Big change." Darla's voice was reserved. "I guess things are OK with you and David?"

"I wasn't sure we were going to make it there for a while," Angelina admitted. "But he's going to keep his job on Wall Street and I'm going to run the farm." She glanced at her watch. "I'm sorry, Darla, I've really got to run. David's home packing and he's going to wonder where I am." She threw on her jacket and pushed back the stool.

"Call me with your new phone number?" Darla got up to hug her.

"Of course. You'll have to come down to visit. We'll go for a ride." She kissed Darla's cheek. "You're welcome to come with her Rena," she leaned over and kissed me too. She smelled like lemons. "It was nice meeting you." Darla and I sat in silence.

"Wow," Darla broke the stillness. "That was so weird running into her."

"Why?" I let a piece of banana from the muffin melt on my tongue.

"The last time I spoke with her, she and David were talking about getting divorced. Now she's moving to Jersey. And a horse farm?" She shook her head. "Whatever. As long as she's happy." She stirred her juice. "So, what are you doing the rest of the day?"

"Absolutely nothing," I laughed. "And I'm looking forward to it. It's going to be a long week at work." Darla and I finished breakfast and I walked home, looking forward to being a couch potato for the rest of the day.

Clients from three stations were in on Monday. Between calls, the sales meetings they each wanted, lunches with buyers, entertaining at night, and trying to squeeze in regular business, I was wiped out by Wednesday. I missed yoga class Thursday night because I had to take out Tania with my San Antonio manager.

At Tania's request, we dined downtown at Pó, a tiny Italian restaurant on Cornelia Street. Tania was a big fan of the owner, who had his own cooking show on the TV Food Network. They only did two seatings a night and I had made a reservation a month ago when I found out that my station manager was coming into town. The food was delicious, but after four straight days of ass kissing and listening to people who weren't my friends ramble about their lives, I was ready for Friday.

At the sales meeting Friday morning, I looked around the room and realized that Mike and I were the only two people left from my original team. Monica had left to be a full-time mother. Gene had realized that Darryl was proficient at appearing to be busy when he was doing nothing and had fired him six months ago. Since Mike had four years experience and I had over three, Lynn had replaced both of them with trainees, two young guys right out of research.

I tried to be available when they had questions or problems, but didn't have time for the most part. And when I had the time, I didn't have the energy. I appreciated now what Gene and Mike did for me when I was new like I couldn't then. The contents of the meeting were status quo: bitching about the stupid things the stations did; bitching about how nasty some of the buyers were; bitching about how the agency's clients all wanted something for nothing; and bitching about the computer system, which in the last twelve months had really proven to be antiquated. I needed a break from bitching.

I bought the *Times* with my lunch at the deli. The clients were all gone and I wanted to eat my tuna and read the paper in peace. Well, as much peace as one could get in a midtown deli at high noon. I treated myself to a bag of chips and a chocolate chip cookie and flipped through the pages of Friday's travel section. "Continental Airlines announces their new route to Lisbon, Portugal," caught my eye. I hadn't had a real vacation in a few years. I made the kind of money now that should afford me luxuries like this. But I didn't want to go alone.

I called Darla when I got back to office. "Are you sitting down?" I almost jumped through the phone. "Continental just started flying to Portugal. It's only $350 round trip. How about it?" Silence.

"I would love to Rena, but I don't think I can afford it right now."

"How much can you afford?" I asked impulsively. I heard the wheels spinning.

"Maybe three or four hundred all together, why?"

"I'll take care of the rest."

"I couldn't let you do that," she argued.

"Why not? Aren't you always the one telling me to just say thank you and accept a gift when it gets dropped in your lap? Just say thank you."

"Thank you," she replied. We picked a date. I cleared it with Gene and called the airline to purchase the tickets. I was grateful I kept my passport up-to-date, even though I hadn't used it since I did a tour of Europe in high school with my choir. I looked at the piles on my desk. There was plenty to do. But it could wait until Monday. I yelled to Gene that I was going on calls and headed to 55th and Lexington to get a manicure and a pedicure.

Darla offered to spend a day at Barnes and Noble, researching hotels and places we should visit while we were there. We made a reservation for the first night and decided to wing it the rest of the trip. Two weeks later, at the beginning of June, we were in a limousine to Newark Airport for a seven o'clock flight. We woke up as the sun was rising over Lisbon.

I had stashed two joints in my suitcase and tried not to panic as we headed through customs. The guards were busy talking to each other and didn't stop anyone from our flight. I promised myself if we didn't smoke it, I would get rid of it before we went back. The day was gray and cloudy, more than a drop of moisture in the air. We waited in line for the bus to downtown Lisboa. According to the tour books, cabs from the airport were outrageously expensive. And we liked the idea of a free bus tour on the drive in.

The area around the airport was crowded with highways and overpasses. Darla and I sat across from each other so we could both have a window. I practiced Portuguese out loud, reciting from my dictionary as Darla hovered over her seat, staring out at the traffic. The bus dropped us in the center of town at the Rossio, a cobblestone area covering about four New York City blocks. We headed over to Rua Augusta, a pedestrian mall lined with shops and restaurants.

We walked through the Triumphal Arch and into the Praca do Commercio. A statue of Portugal's King José, who ruled in the eighteenth century, was the focal point. We later learned that the statue was built on the site of the king's ruined palace, which was destroyed by an earthquake in

1755. We each had one suitcase and dragged them behind us, searching for a place to get something to drink. We sat outside at a Casa de Cha, a Portuguese teahouse, and managed to order from the waiter who spoke no English.

We sipped our *cha com limao,* the lemons fragrant and juicy. Our hotel reservation for the night was in Cascais and we studied the map, trying to locate the Praca Rossio where we would catch the train for the half-hour ride. "I know we still have our luggage with us," I started. "But we're right here," I pointed to the enormous cast-iron elevator behind the row of shops. "It's called the Santa Justa Elevator." I thumbed through the guide-book. "It goes to the top of the Bario Alto and it was designed by Gustave Eiffel."

"Sure, we're here," Darla finished her tea and left a 500 escudos bill, around five dollars, on the table. A wrinkled little man in a booth with a brass gate sold us roundtrip tickets for a little less than a dollar. Twenty of us squeezed into the huge car and the conductor threw the switch, the cables grinding and moaning as we climbed to the top of the hill.

We really couldn't see much with the clouds and our movement was limited by the renovation that was ongoing from the fires that destroyed much of the area in the late eighties. Ready to dump our suitcases, we rode down and headed to the train station to stow our bags in a locker. We wanted to do some sightseeing in Lisbon before heading to Cascais since it was still early. We walked down the narrow sidewalk toward the river, amazed at how heavily trafficked the streets were. Autos were small in Portugal, partly because gas was so expensive and partly because trying to find a parking space was an arduous task.

After finding a locker at the train station, we took a cab to the top of a huge hill to visit the Castelo de Sao Jorge, which was surrounded by the crumbling remains of its eighth-century towers. Darla jumped out of the cab and ran to the perimeter, her wild hair flying behind her. "Look at this, Rena!" She hung over the stone wall, looking down on the Rio Tejo and the entire eastern section of Lisbon. To the left were the hills of Alfama, buildings squeezed together like Lego's.

We stood near an ancient tree with delicate pink blooms and asked another tourist to take our picture. As we climbed the steps to get into the garden, Darla turned around and held a finger to her lips, pointing to what looked like a white peacock. It stared at us for a moment, fanned its feathers, and skittered away.

The hills of Alfama weren't difficult to navigate going down. We stopped at a flea market and Darla leapt across the language barrier, negotiating for a beaded bag from an old woman wearing a white apron over her black dress and sandals. Antique stores lined one of the side streets and we wandered in and out, proudly displaying our finds to each other.

Finding a passageway to the street below, we skipped down crumbling steps, the houses surrounding them cracked and in need of paint. Laundry flapped in the breeze, the lines strung above us in the area once occupied by the Portuguese elite who abandoned their homes during the earthquake in 1755. Lisbon's poor, who at the time lived closer to the river, ran into the hills, squatting in the empty houses that had survived because of the mountain's granite base. The area was still inhabited by the economically challenged.

We arrived in time to catch a four o'clock train to Cascais. We bought our tickets at the station since the guidebook warned of extravagant surcharges for purchasing a ticket on the train. We sped past northern Lisboa and out toward Estoril. The train was a local and the seats were subway-like, plastic and hard. We arrived in Cascais a half-hour later and walked to the bed and breakfast where we had our reservation.

We pulled our suitcases down Avenue Valbom to the Casa de Pergola. "Oh my God!" Darla stopped in her tracks when we arrived. A quaint garden fronted a house that had slipped out of a fairy tale. Ivy crept up the front of the structure, the royal blue shutters and red trim accenting its stone white finish. Statues of angels hid under trees in the yard and a covered patio held several white iron tables and chairs. It was quiet except for the squeals of three girls jumping rope down the street.

Senhora de Gama showed us to our room and informed us that breakfast was served from seven until nine-thirty. Two twin beds in antique mahogany frames rested in the center of the room. Six-foot windows, overlooking the roof of the terrace, were protected with slatted wood shutters. In the bathroom was a bear claw tub and stand-alone sink. "It's gorgeous," I said, flopping on the bed. "You done good. I really needed a vacation."

"I knew I was right about her taking this trip," Inanna smiled smugly.
"You can't run efficiently on an empty tank. And Rena's tank was on empty."

"It is peaceful here," agreed Kuan Yin.

"Where are the men?" Kali asked shaking her hips. "Enough of the sight-seeing!"

"What if she gets caught with that marijuana?" Erishkigal questioned. "I shudder to think of what jail would be like here?"

"Rena hasn't touched that marijuana," Kuan Yin remarked. "And I doubt she will."

"Quit worrying!" commanded Inanna. "Rena's been going non-stop for years. She needs fun and rest."

"And it's the first time Rena's idea of fun isn't self-destructive." Kuan Yin glanced at Kali. "She's making progress."

"Indeed, sister. Indeed." Inanna placed her hand on Kuan Yin's shoulder.

Darla and I walked to the center of town when we were done unpacking. We gorged on roast chicken with hot sauce and fries at a little café called Jardim dos Frangos. The tiny restaurant was devoid of atmosphere, but the food was mouthwatering and we feasted like kings for less than ten dollars. The next day we strolled the narrow streets of Cascais, shopping and relaxing. Later that afternoon, we sneaked into the Hotel Baia, sunning ourselves at the rooftop pool, the Atlantic still too chilly for a dip.

We ate our way through three days in the tiny resort town, supping on fresh sea bass, robalo, and red mullet. Although I had been pretty faithful about going to the gym, I hadn't managed to take off any significant weight, so I saw no reason to count calories here. The concept of dried cod, a Portuguese staple, didn't thrill either of us, but we piggishly sopped up the cream sauce in the *bacalhau lisbonese* with fragrant *pao de millo*, the native corn bread. Eventually we grew bored, having sunned and shopped to excess, and decided to rent a car and drive to the hills of Sintra.

The car was a standard and I rode shotgun because I never learned how to drive a stick. The ride only took a little over a half-hour since we mapped out a route before we left Cascais. As we climbed into the mountains, the scent of eucalyptus trees enveloped us. Darla had called ahead and made a reservation at Tivoli Sintra, a moderately priced hotel near the center of town. The bedrooms were enormous; each had a sitting room and a balcony with views of the lush forest and the gardens of the local houses.

I stood outside, admiring the bright red flowers on the bougainvillea vine that wrapped around our trellis. Closing my eyes, I let the net of my nasal passages capture the scent of gardenias and camellias as it drifted into our room. We changed into shorts and shopped on the cobblestone streets, which were crowded from the buses that dumped hundreds of tourists into the tiny village every day.

I loved listening to the natives speak. The language sounded like a mixture of Spanish and French, with a pinch of Italian. Darla struggled to remember her high school French, since that seemed to be the second language of choice. We stopped in a tiny linen store built into the side of the mountain. "What do you think of this bedspread?" Darla held up the lace trimmed antique white cover.

"It's beautiful," I said. "How much?" she asked the owner in French.

"About seventy dollars." Fingering the cotton, she said something to the woman, the nasal tones rolling naturally off her tongue. The storekeeper, an older woman in her sixties, nodded vigorously. "She said she'd let me have it for fifty because I remind her of her daughter in Chartres." Darla dug in her bag. "Wasn't that sweet?" She paid the woman and we continued up the hill to the next store, a large plastic bag hanging over Darla's back like a Santa sack.

We had dinner at a tiny restaurant called Alcobaca, hidden in an alley off the main street. Our second night in Portugal, we had discovered that most places charged a *couvert,* or cover charge. Our bill had included an extra six dollars for the bread, olives, and tiny cheeses that the busboy served while we waited for our dinners. Since then, we asked what was free.

Almost everyone at the other tables at Alcobaca was eating something out of a wok-like dish that smelled heavenly. The waiter spoke no English and no French, so we pointed until he understood what we wanted. Our covered silver dish appeared a few minutes later, overflowing with a flavorful stew of clams, sausage, and bacon. We washed it down with a carafe of Redondo, a local wine known for its high alcohol content. After paying the bill, we stumbled out of the restaurant, grateful for the cool night air on our flushed cheeks. We rounded the corner and heard music coming from a local bar. "Shall we?" Darla giggled.

"Why not? We're on vacation," I pulled the door open. It was warm and smelled like roasted pork inside with a top note of cigar and cigarette smoke. A black-and-white television sat on a shelf behind the bar, a soccer game fuzzy on its screen. A three-piece band performed El Fado, the native folk music, in the back. It sounded more South American than Spanish, the driving beat of Flamenco absent.

"What do you want?" Darla shimmied her way through the crowd to the bar. "Let's stick with wine," I shouted over the guitar and saxophone. We shuffled to the back of the narrow bar, the red wine sloshing against the short glasses, and found a table near the band. The music was melodic and the sound of the words soft and rounded, not harsh like American English. I knew the handsome singer was crooning a love song, even though I didn't understand a word, from the way he purred into the microphone. We were silent, allowing the music to transport us to a place far from our thoughts and lives.

The next morning, we drove to Palacio Real, a jumble of a castle containing architecture from several centuries. We parked our car for a nominal fee and hiked a half-hour up the mountainside, which was exuberant with chirping birds. We paid the few dollars for the guided tour and traipsed through the enormous structure, our mouths agape at the antiques and opulence. The blue, green, and white Mudejar tiles, called *azulejos,* in the kitchen and guestroom were from the sixteenth century and had been impeccably preserved, only a few chinks noticeable on their shiny surfaces.

When the tour was finished, we climbed into the turrets and stood breathless at the top of the stairs, looking out over the eucalyptus-covered mountains and the lush valley of Sintra. We continued our feeding frenzy, venturing into more local dishes like *pasteis de bacalhau*, spiced codfish cakes, and *caldo verde*, a potato and sausage soup with kale. My clothes had gotten a bit tight, but I promised myself I'd put some extra time in at the gym when I got home.

"I don't want to go home," Darla whined as we took a final walk around Sintra the night before our flight. A group of three young boys sang a cappella, an old, beat-up purse at their feet collecting escudo coins.

"I could live here," I sighed, breathing in the clear clean air. "Lord Byron had the right idea." We grabbed a bite to eat at a tiny restaurant in the maze of shops built into the hill above the Praca da Republica and stopped at a *pastelaria* for rice pudding and café. The coffee was strong, but without the bitterness of espresso.

Before driving to the airport the next morning, we ordered room service and enjoyed a basket of Portuguese rolls and jam on the balcony. We loaded the car and headed out of town, slipping through the village of Sao Pedro as it woke for the day. While Darla sped toward Lisboa, I foraged in my suitcase for the two joints I'd packed. I hid them in the pocket of my jeans and flushed them down the toilet in the airport after we returned the rental car. We landed in Newark around three and, exhausted, took a cab back to the city.

Rest

My desk was covered with file folders and pink message slips. I sorted through everything, eating a bagel and wishing I was on the balcony in Sintra. Gene appeared in the doorway, his pants loose around his slender waist. "How was the trip?"

"Wonderful!" I smiled. "How are you?"

"It's been a little hectic," he came in and sat down. "Mike is on vacation this week, so I hate to do this, but I need you to cover Darcy for him."

"Sure," I agreed, laughing sarcastically, surveying the stacks on my desk. "I have nothing else to do."

"I know, I know," his long fingers straightened the creases in his pant legs. "But P&G is re-rating their annual buys since the May Nielsen book came out. I don't trust anyone else to do it." Portugal was fast becoming a distant memory. I spent the day returning calls and familiarizing myself with the pending business at my agencies. Around three I slipped out to drop off revised rates to Mike's buyers at Darcy. The walk back was the first time I'd breathed all day.

There was a message taped to my door when I returned. My father had called. I dialed his number wondering why he was calling me at work. "Dad?" I dropped a stack of files on the floor.

"Rena, I'm so glad you called," his voice was different, no edge, no drive. "What's wrong?"

"Your grandmother passed away last night." The words hung in the air, unwanted and distasteful, like an unexpected sip of sour milk.

"How?" I felt the familiar tingle in my nose paving the way for tears.

"She died in her sleep, Rena. It was peaceful."

"How's Granpa?" My hands began to shake.

"As well as can be expected. The doctor gave him some Valium." The three hundred miles between us seemed endless. "The viewing is scheduled for tomorrow and the funeral for Wednesday."

"Can someone pick me up at the airport or should I rent a car?" I silently ran through my workload, giving my teammates assignments while I flipped through my Rolodex for USAir's number.

"It might be best for you to rent one, unless your mother can get you." I felt rejected. "I'm sorry, but I really have my hands full between the funeral arrangements and checking on your grandfather."

"That's OK, Dad," I lied. "I'll call Mom." I walked in a daze to Gene's office.

"You look like you've seen a ghost," he stood up and guided me to a chair. "What's wrong?" I swallowed my sadness, not wanting to cry in front of him.

"My grandmother died last night."

"Great!" He threw himself into the chair and slammed his elbows on the desk, his head cradled between his hands. He looked up at me. "God, I'm so sorry, Rena. That was a completely selfish reaction." Loosening his tie, he picked up a tablet and a pen. "I know you're upset right now, but can we go over what you have pending so I can make sure your list is covered?"

"It figures," whined Erishkigal. "She finally does something fun and comes home to this."

"It's awful," Inanna agreed. "Who did this?"

"No one did this," Kuan Yin soothed. "Death is a part of life. It is sad, but Rena can grow from this experience."

"This is too fucking weird." Kali separated a plait of hair and rapidly ran the strands, from root to tip, through the thumb and index fingers of both hands. "Why now?"

"It was time for Lillian to make the transition," explained Kuan Yin.

"I get that. I'm not an idiot," Kali hissed. "But why do I feel this way?" She continued pulling her hair through her fingers.

"Doesn't that hurt?" asked Inanna, making a face.

"What?" Kali barked.

"Yanking on your hair like that."

"I think Kali is using that pain as a distraction so she can deny that Lillian's death is causing her pain." Kuan Yin gently pulled Kali's hands from her hair.

"You and your fucking insight," Kali snapped, resuming the tug of war with her hair. She appeared to be getting smaller. "You think you're so smart, but you have no idea what you're talking about."

"You never allow yourself to experience pain or sadness, Kali. You're all about feeling good or being angry." Kuan Yin turned from her and wrapped her feet under her as she sat.

"When Siva died, you acted like it was the happiest day of your life. You danced over his body. The world was yours to rule—alone. But I know you loved him." Kali turned away. "You've never understood that it takes more strength to mourn and grieve than it does to pretend that nothing is wrong."

Kali's hair was coming out in clumps. Tears danced around the corners of her third eye. "Why are you doing this to me, Kuan Yin? What the fuck did I ever do to you?" A nest of black hair collected at her feet and she stared at it, as if she didn't understand how it got there.

"Let it out Kali. We're not going to judge you or laugh at you. You've been carrying around centuries of pain. It's time to begin to tear the walls down. They don't protect you anyway." Kuan Yin's face was tranquil, but her eyes were sad.

Kali stopped tugging her hair. The moisture in her eye evaporated like ice in a desert. She bent over, gathering the loose hairs in cupped hands. Puckering her lips, she exhaled powerfully, disintegrating them as she blew them into the air. Standing erect and still, she looked at Kuan Yin. "Thanks for your advice, sister, but I know what's best."

Kali closed her eyes, drew a deep breath, and raised her hands to the heavens. When she was done mumbling a prayer, her eyes flew open and she was the old Kali, strong and protected.

I sat on a DC-9, travelling to Pittsburgh for the first time since Christmas. The last time I spoke with my grandmother, she was excited about having won the Volunteer of the Year award at St. Clair Memorial Hospital. "I wasn't sure I could go back," she had confessed to me. "I thought it would give me bad memories from being in the hospital. But I realized it was important because now I really know how scared these people are."

I hadn't accepted my mother's offer to pick me up, opting instead for the freedom a rental car would provide. I flew down the Parkway, calculating my time frame. The viewing was at the Milton Hamel Funeral Home in Bethel Park. It started at two, which gave me enough time to shower and change and make the twenty-minute drive from my mother's apartment.

"Mom?" I used my key to let myself in.

"In here!" I dragged my overnight bag behind me, into the guest bedroom. I followed the trail of cigarette smoke into my mother's bathroom. She'd put on some weight since Christmas; the black gabardine dress she wore was a little snug over her backside. I leaned in from behind her and kissed the side of her head. A half-stubbed out butt smoked in the crystal ashtray.

"You look pretty." I sat on the toilet seat. A pile of dirty clothes was cornered near the tub.

"Don't say anything nice and don't say anything mean," she ordered. "It took me twenty minutes to put on my mascara. It kept running all over my face because I couldn't quit crying." She puckered her lips over a tissue. "So let's talk about the weather. OK?"

"Fine by me." I walked out. "I need to get a shower." I tugged on the navy silk granny dress I'd brought. I was the only appropriate thing in my closet that fit. I'd have to wear it to the funeral as well since I had no time to go shopping before my flight. I prayed my mascara was really waterproof. My mother was now in the living room, smoking a cigarette, wearing a wide-brimmed black straw hat. Her hair was pulled up underneath and a pair of diamond studs sparkled from her ears.

We had trouble finding a parking space at the funeral home and ended up across the street. The room was crowded. Some nurses from the hospital whispered quietly, sitting in a row of chairs near the window. Heavy gold curtains were secured at the window frames with brocade ties. Friends of my grandmother's from St. Louise's bingo night, their blue hair stylishly coifed, huddled in a corner clutching their pocketbooks tightly against their bodies.

Green carpet covered the floor and a metal track held the wood-finished plastic wall, now crunched like an accordion, that sometimes separated the room into two. Three chandeliers hung from the ceiling, their crystal drops dusty. A couple of nuns stood praying at the casket. I noticed my grandfather leaning on a table at the front of the room. His shirt and pants draped him like a scarecrow. Rebecca and my father stood next to him, talking to a priest.

"Hey," I lightly touched my father's arm. "How are you?" I kissed his cheek and gave Rebecca a hug. "Granpa?" I put my arms around him and touched his soft cheek with my lips. "How are you holding up?"

"Rena? I'm so glad you came." His eyes were glazed and he leaned heavily on the table behind him.

"He's had a few Valium today," my father whispered in my ear. "I was afraid he wouldn't make it through the day without it." I smelled scotch on his breath. I stared at the casket and saw my grandmother's hands peeking out from the satin-lined interior. My father headed to the front of the room.

"May I have your attention?" He coughed and grabbed a handkerchief from his pants pocket. "I know there are some people who'd like to say a few words." He waved his arm at a man in a white coat. "Jim, would you like to start?" It startled me that I knew so few of the people in the room. How many friends did my grandmother have? An elderly man with a patch of white hair swooped across his scalp approached the casket and cleared his throat.

"I'm Jim Adler, the Director of Volunteer Services at St. Clair Memorial Hospital." He trembled removing a wrinkled sheet of white paper from his jacket. "We're all going to miss Lillian Sutcliffe." He fumbled with his reading glasses. "She was one of our best-loved volunteers. Her ability to make the patients laugh, even when they were in pain, was a gift few of us possess." I noticed heads bobbing in agreement.

"She was never too tired or too busy to help." He stopped reading from his scribbles. "And even after she'd been in the hospital herself, she faced her fears and returned to help us out, keeping patients company while they waited to be taken to X-ray." He paused, blowing his nose in a pink tissue.

"One time an old gent got a little, uh, cantankerous when Lillian told him she didn't know how much longer he'd have to wait. He swiped a stack of papers off her desk and onto the floor." Jim's hands were shaking, and he shoved one of them in his pocket. "He was angry because he had been waiting for a CAT scan for over an hour. He was cold and hungry and frustrated." He slipped into a slight southern accent.

"Lily took her time picking up those papers and piled them neatly while the old man sat in his wheelchair, glaring at her like she was the daughter of the devil himself. When she was through, she wheeled him behind the desk and sat down next to him. She took his hands in hers and leaned into him, his crotchety old face all knitted up in anger."

"'Mr. Morris,' she said to him in a real low voice, 'Do you know why a cow wears a bell?' Well, he looked at her like an alien spaceship had just beamed her down from Mars. After a minute or two he shook his head. She stared at him, all solemn-like and whispered, 'Because their horns don't work.'" A few people giggled, their eyes darting around the room, seeking permission. Then a few more chuckled; and it snowballed, the room filled with laughter and snorts and tears.

"That old man sat in his wheelchair, bald and wrinkled, a toothless grin stretched from ear to ear." He wiped the tears from his face. "I'm going to miss her." He turned around to face the casket. "Who's going to make me laugh now, Lily?" He crossed himself and returned to his seat. I heard my mother sniffling and tears spilled down my face, oblivious to my attempts to suck them back in.

My grandparent's former neighbor, Bethany, was standing at the casket. "I lived next to Lillian and Matthew," she nodded at my grandfather, "for ten years before they moved into their apartment." She wore a short-sleeved black dress and black lace gloves. On top of her short brown hair rested a black satin pillbox hat. She needed a trip to Saks with my mother.

"My daughter, Emily, spent a lot of time with Lillian. She would come home and tell me how Lillian let her arrange pictures in a photo album or what fun they had baking brownies," she took a small breath. "Or how Lillian let her watch *The Little Mermaid* two times in a row." She accepted a tissue from one of the nuns in the front row.

"I didn't want Emily coming today. I thought it would be too hard for her. But she insisted. 'Mommy, I want to say good-bye before she goes to live with God,' she told me." Bethany smiled and a little girl, about eight or nine, stood up and went to hug her. Her strawberry hair was gathered in a silver barrette and she had on a pink taffeta dress with a silk ribbon around the waist.

"This is Emily," she put her arm around the little girl. "And we loved Lillian very much." They returned to their seats, Bethany hunched over, her face in her hands. Emily stood next to her chair, stroking her mother's back and assured her, "It's OK Mommy, Aunt Lily's in heaven now." I bolted out of the room and pushed the front door open, the exhaust fumes and noise from the traffic drowning my sadness.

That night we all went to the Olive Garden for dinner. My mother wanted to go to Poli's in Squirrel Hill, but was outvoted. "Faith, I'm not dragging my father, half-stoned on Valium, all the way out there," my father scolded. "It's a thirty-minute drive. We're going to the Olive Garden in Bethel Park." So, there we sat, my family—and Rebecca, sipping wine and picking at the all-you-can-eat salad and breadsticks.

"How's work?" my father asked. I picked the onion out of my salad.

"Fine."

"Looks like I was wrong about you quitting," he swirled the ice cubes in the scotch he ordered after tasting his wine. "You're rolling in the dough now. Right?"

"I can pay my bills." I speared a tomato and plopped it back in the big bowl.

"Rebecca finally made a profit last month," he squeezed her hand. My mother looked at her watch. "Didn't you honey?" he asked. Rebecca nodded, reminding me of a puppy whose master just rewarded her with a biscuit.

"I have four full classes," she sipped lemon water, her blond hair pulled into pigtails and wrapped in blue ribbon. "All my girls love ballet as much as I do."

"That's wonderful," I smiled and returned my attention to the salad. My grandfather sat, comatose, his hands resting on the arms of the chair.

"Granpa?" I shouted. "Are you going to eat something?"

"Leave him alone, Rena," my mother ordered. "If he's hungry, he'll eat."

"Rena's right," my father intervened. "Dad?" My grandfather stared straight ahead, his glasses smudged with fingerprints. "You really should eat something."

"He just lost his wife," my mother whispered harshly to my father. "He's probably not hungry, Michael."

"He's my father, Faith. I can handle it," he hissed at my mother. Faith threw her napkin on top of a bread stick.

"Fine." She pushed back the chair and left the table. Rebecca continued chewing an olive. The waiter served our dinners and we ate in silence, grateful for the distraction of steel knives grating against chicken bones and the clanking of forks on the china plates. When my mother hadn't returned after ten minutes, I got up to find her. In the ladies' room I checked shoes under each stall door, looking for my mother's pumps. Two pairs of sneakers and a pair of Easy Spirits my mother wouldn't be caught dead in. I headed outside to the benches where the overflow crowd waited to be seated.

I perused the parking lot, trying to remember where we had left the car. I saw it lit harshly under a lamppost. My mother was inside. I approached the car rehearsing my speech. "It's a tough time for all of us. Dad didn't mean it." But I knew he did. He was tolerating my mother's presence for my sake. And she knew it. I knocked on the window.

"Mom? Are you OK?" She rolled down the window, black streams running through her blush.

"I'm fine," she nodded. I walked around the other side and motioned for her to unlock the door. I sat in the motionless car, the only sound our breathing.

"I know you're upset, Mom. But so is Dad. Tempers can get out of control in a situation like this."

"Your father doesn't want me here, Rena." Her hands rested on her lap under the steering wheel. "He feels it was his mother, so he's the only one entitled to grieve." She stared ahead at the restaurant. "It's not fair. She was my mother too—for a lot of years." My mother's parents had both died right after she and my father got married. "I think I should go. Your father can drop you off when you're through." I ran the silk of my dress through my fingers, quickly, skimming its softness.

"I'll be right back," I opened the door. "Don't leave without me." I hurried inside and found my father with his arm around Rebecca, most of the dishes cleared away. I grabbed my purse from under my chair. "I'm going home with Mom," I announced. He pulled his arm back and slammed his fist on the table. Water from the glasses sloshed onto the white tablecloth.

"Your grandfather needs you, Rena." His attempt to control the level of his voice caused spit to fly into the air.

"He doesn't know who's here and who's not right now, Dad. And you have Rebecca." I crossed my arms and held my bag against my chest. "Mom's upset, too. Granma was like a mother to her." He picked up his cocktail and took a sip.

"Fine. Go." I leaned over and kissed his cheek. It had wrinkles I didn't remember.

"I'll see you tomorrow at the funeral." I walked around the table and kissed my grandfather on the forehead. "Good night, Granpa." He nodded slightly and pressed something into my hand and squeezed it. I went to open it but he clamped it shut and pulled me down to whisper in my ear.

"Your grandmother wanted you to have this. Don't tell your father." I pretended I was receiving a kiss on my cheek, playing along." His tie had come loose at the neck and there was a large gap between the collar and his skin.

"Try to get some sleep." I stood up clenching my fist. "I'll see you tomorrow, Rebecca," I tried to smile. She looked at me, her large blue eyes knowing more than I wanted her to. I stopped in the bathroom on the way out and locked the stall, finally opening my hand. My grandmother's diamond engagement ring gleamed back at me from my palm. I sat on the toilet and unrolled enough toilet paper to wrap it carefully before slipping it into the pocket of my dress.

Faith and I drove home listening to jazz, the art of conversation escaping both of us. That night, as I lay in the bed of my mother's guest room, I hugged a pillow to my belly and wished I was Emily. Sometime during the night, in a dream, I saw my grandmother, rested and serene, sitting in her prized Louis XIV chair. She had it recovered in a blue-and-green-striped velvet to match the carpet when they moved into the apartment after their house was sold.

"Rena," there was an slight echo to her voice and the tone was calm. "I only want you to be happy. Are you happy, honey?" I sat, a small child in Winnie the Pooh pajamas, at her feet.

"Yes, Granma, I'm happy." I hugged her calf. She ran her fingers through my hair and straightened the collar on my pajama top.

"You can't depend on your parents for happiness," she folded her hands. "They don't know how to be happy themselves. You need to find your own happiness." She removed a pale yellow crocheted throw from the back of the chair and wrapped it around her shoulders. "You only get one chance in this lifetime."

"But Granma," I argued. Now I was an adult. "I am happy. Remember that tiny apartment you stayed in when you visited me?" I knelt at her side, my hands resting on her knees. "I moved. I have a beautiful two bedroom apartment in Grammercy Park," I stood and paced in front of her. "With a fireplace. And I just got back from Portugal. Portugal, Granma." The carpet began to wear away from my foot steps.

"But are you doing what you want to do?" She stared straight ahead. When I turned to see what she was looking at I saw nothing but clouds.

"OK," I admitted. "Maybe I'm not totally happy with my job. But I can use the money I'm making to do things that make me happy. Isn't that good enough?" She pulled the shawl tighter.

"Is it?" The tighter she pulled the throw around her, the smaller she became.

"But I don't know what it is that will make me happy," I cried. "Can't you tell me?" She was a shadow now, wispy and surreal, a faint image projected on the screen of the chair. "No!" I screamed. "Don't go until you tell me. You can't leave!"

"You do know, Rena. But you never allow yourself enough quiet time to hear the answer." I tried to get to the chair, but my feet were caught in the fibers of the carpet that had melted from my pacing. I held out my arms toward her, crying.

"How can you get quiet with that job you have?" Her voice surrounded me. "The phone always ringing. People always needing something. Lying. Manipulating." The shawl collapsed onto the seat of the empty chair. "You'll never know as long as you're not true to yourself." I fell to my knees and banged my head on the floor, my feet still stuck, sobbing.

The next morning I awoke exhausted, my eyes burning and red. I let the hot water pelt me into consciousness as I stood in the shower. I got dressed and found my mother staring at the *Today Show,* Matt Lauer's face serious as he interviewed Kato Kailen about the fiasco that was the O.J. Simpson trial. I plopped onto the couch next to her. "You look like hell," she said glancing at me and returning her attention to the screen.

"Thanks," I laughed. "You look lovely too." The funeral went smoothly, the weather cooperating and my parents keeping their distance. There was a sizeable turnout and the priest from St. Louise's gave a beautiful eulogy. Father Shaughnessy had offered and my father accepted, figuring his mother adored the tiny priest. He also didn't want to offend anyone and figured that having a priest do it would eliminate that possibility. My father had a cookout at his house after the burial. "A good barbecued burger was one of your grandmother's favorite things," he said to me, drinking a beer at the grill.

He had come up to my mother at the cemetery and apologized for snapping at her at the Olive Garden. "I'd love for you to join us," he said extending his hand. "Lillian would've wanted it that way." My mother agreed and for a funeral party, it was kind of fun. We both had a nice time, reminiscing with my grandmother's friends while Rebecca waited on us, bringing us wine and clearing our dirty plates.

I had no dreams that Thursday night. I was alone in my sleep. I woke to the hot sun beating through the ivory sheers of the bedroom window. Gene knew I wouldn't be back at work until Monday and I was planning a peaceful three-day weekend since my flight landed at LaGuardia ten-thirty Friday morning. Maybe I'd be able to find some of that quiet time my grandmother had talked about in my dream.

Rest

Over the summer it became increasingly difficult to deal with the lying and scheming that were required for the job. I was a fanatic about getting to Darla's Thursday night yoga classes, not caring what client was in town or what work was left on my desk when I walked out. And every week it took me until Tuesday afternoon to really get motivated to look at any of it.

I began meditating in the morning before I left for the office, praying for an answer about what it was that would make me happy. On Fridays, I found myself sneaking out at lunch time to catch a four-dollar movie at the World Wide Plaza Cinema, sometimes returning to the office with barely enough time to organize my desk before I left for the weekend.

Every Saturday, Darla and I took the F train out to Brighton Beach and schlepped our lounge chairs and beach bags to the ocean. We arrived by ten and shared a breakfast of fruit and granola bars, watching the sand fill up with families and teenagers, anxious to soak up the sun's rays and splash in the waves. "How did you find out about this?" I asked her while she lay in her bikini on a bright orange chair. I hadn't had a bathing suit without a skirt since I was fifteen.

"One of my students lives out here and told me that it never gets as crowded as Coney Island," she twisted the stem off an apple. "And it's a lot closer than Jones Beach or Fire Island." If it wasn't too hot, we'd do sun salutations at the water's edge, our feet digging into the wet sand as we stretched and warmed our bodies. We could sit in silence for hours, reading or listening to music, lost in our own thoughts.

We'd often walk the two miles on the beach to Coney Island, dodging the kids running back and forth with pails full of water. After stuffing fanny packs with our valuables, Darla would ask whoever was sitting next to us to guard the chairs while we were gone. If it was cloudy, we'd get a snow cone on the boardwalk and meander through the flea markets on Ocean Avenue. In one, there was a tiny booth where a shriveled Russian woman sat, reading tarot cards.

"Come on," Darla teased one day. "You know you want to." I reluctantly coughed up the five dollars and sat across from the tiny woman. Her white hair was piled in a knot on top of her head and she wore black from head to toe. She drew the death card for the third position. I shivered at the skull and cross bones.

"Ees goot," Madam Anna insisted. "Death card ees change," she tapped the deck. "You have much change coming." Darla nodded in agreement. I fidgeted during the rest of the reading. "You have beeg loss. Are very sad," she studied a card. "But you weel not be crying in your sour milk much longer." I giggled. "Ees not funny!" She clenched her teeth. "You must prepare. Ees coming fast." I thanked her when she was through and Darla and I continued our shopping expedition.

"Do you really believe in that stuff?" I asked her while we sifted through stacks of old records.

"Madam Anna may not be the most reputable reader I've ever seen," Darla acknowledged. The old woman had pretty much scared us into each giving her five dollars for the prayer candle she had burning behind her chair, claiming that a dark visitor would follow us if we didn't. "But I've had a lot of the things predicted at a reading come true." She pulled "The Divine Miss M" out of the sleeve and examined the vinyl.

"Don't you kind of think it's really a self-fulfilling prophecy?" I argued. "If someone puts that information in your head, can't you help create the situation?"

"Maybe." Darla flipped the record over to inspect the other side. "So if you're uncomfortable with it, put it out of your head." I nodded and moved to the next booth, searching for a vase for my apartment.

By September, I had seriously neglected my housecleaning obligations and one Saturday, dressed in old shorts and a T-shirt, I scoured the bathroom and kitchen. Months of grease and grime got wrung into a bucket filled with Mr. Clean. I attacked my closet, determined to get rid of whatever clothes didn't fit. In the back, tucked behind winter blazers and skirts, I found the dress I'd worn to my grandmother's funeral. I held it up to me looking in the mirror, debating whether or not to keep it.

As I was rolling it in a ball for the Salvation Army, I felt a bump in the pocket. I removed a wad of toilet paper and was ready to throw it in the garbage when I remembered. I unraveled it and held the diamond ring up to examine it. It sparkled in the sun, the refracted light causing a rainbow to bounce on the wall. I gave silent thanks that I hadn't sent the dress to the thrift store with the ring stuffed inside the pocket. I curled up on my bed and slipped the ring onto my finger. The warm September sun lulled me into a sound sleep and again, I dreamt about my grandmother.

She was sitting in the same antique chair she occupied in my last dream. Her feet were bare and she wore a white robe, held together with a satin sash. I couldn't see myself, but she talked to me as if I were in the room. "It's time, Rena." Her face was still wrinkled, but her hands were smooth and free of dark spots.

"For what?" I heard myself say.

"You've prayed for an answer and I'm going to give you the next step in the process." She was still, not even her lips moved when she spoke.

"What are you talking about?" I strained in the dream to see myself.

"The ring," the words hung in the air, echoing.

"What about the ring?" She leaned toward the edge of the chair smiling.

"Sell it."

"Why?" I asked. "It's all I have of you. Why would I want to do that?"

"I'm always with you Rena. You can't hold my spirit in a piece of jewelry."

"But Grandpa gave that to you the first year he made a profit," I argued.

"He'd hate me." She stretched her back and rested against the velvet.

"No he won't. He won't even know."

"What will I do with the money?"

"Give yourself the chance to decide what you want to do without worrying about how to pay the bills." I saw my hand stretching toward her.

"I can't."

"You must," she whispered. "You have the chance to discover your dream. I was too afraid. You cannot be."

"Why?" Wisps of smoke swept into the room, hiding her from my vision.

"Because I will haunt you if you don't," she laughed and the smoke swallowed her. I watched it swirl around my feet and then it went black.

I stretched awake, squinting against the sun and curling my toes. I couldn't believe I had fallen asleep in the middle of the day. I had to finish gathering my clothes if I wanted to drop them off before the thrift store closed. I hopped out of bed and went to the bathroom to rinse the oil off my face.

With the first splash, the dream jumped into my consciousness, landing loudly, the bang snapping my head out of the sink. I closed my eyes and squeezed hard, trying to remember the details. I stared at the ring on my finger. Shaking my head, I removed it and placed it in my jewelry box. I loaded two plastic bags full of clothes into my granny cart and headed to the Salvation Army on 23rd Street.

I picked up a *Village Voice* on my way home and read the classifieds while I ate a tuna sandwich. I saw the heading "Jewelry." It couldn't hurt to find out how much the ring was worth, I reasoned. I left a message for a woman named Marjory who had an ad listed in that section and flicked on the television as I flopped onto the couch.

"Darling, this is Marjory Horowitz," I heard when I answered the phone. I explained what I wanted to do. "You know, I don't return every call I get," her voice was sweet, like a kindergarten teacher. "I only call people back when I get a good energy from their message. And you, my dear, have a great voice."

"Thank you," I hit the mute button on the TV. "I've never done anything like this," I admitted.

"That's OK, let's talk." I spent the next fifteen minutes telling her about my last dream. "Fabulous, darling!" She sounded excited. "Let's meet." Her office was on 24th Street, four blocks from my apartment. We set a time for the following week. I hid the ring in the freezer. I wanted to make sure it was there when I went to see her.

Marjory's office was in her apartment, a huge loft in an old building. We huddled in her bedroom where she kept her jeweler's glass and tools. She was about forty, but looked much younger, the skin around her eyes soft and clear. Her petite frame wore her black slacks and sweater comfortably. A beaded headband held her shoulder-length light brown hair off her face. She examined the diamond, tiny sounds of approval escaping her heart-shaped lips.

"I can get you seven or eight thousand," she handed me the ring.

"Dollars?" I gasped.

"Darling, this is a two carat, I-class diamond," she smiled. "Trust me, it's worth that. Do you want me to sell it?" I sat across from her, picking my cuticle. I heard my grandmother's voice. "You can't be afraid."

"Do it," I told her. Three days later I opened a money market account for seventy-five hundred dollars. Marjory took half her usual commission, insisting she knew I was special and that I would repay her somehow. I called Darla and invited her out to dinner.

"Sounds wonderful," her enthusiasm carried across the line. "Would you mind if Angelina came? She had an appointment with her attorney this afternoon and decided to stay instead of taking the train back to Jersey." Nothing could spoil my good mood.

"Sure, bring her along." We agreed to meet at Il Cantanori on 10th Street. Angelina and Darla were already at the bar when I arrived, both dressed in black stretch pants and sweaters, their slender legs showcased by the material. I wore a big blouse over my black stretch pants. "Hey!" I called to them. "I'm starving." The maitre d' showed us to a quiet table in the window. As we sat down, I noticed Angelina had been crying. "Is everything OK?" I asked after ordering a glass of wine. Her smoky eyes watered. "I'm sorry, I shouldn't have said anything," I apologized.

"No," she smiled, her teeth perfectly straight. "It's all right. David and I have decided to divorce."

"Oh God!" I said munching on my foot. "I'm so sorry." Darla buttered a piece of bread.

"I'll be fine," Angelina ran her hand through her short brown hair. "It's been a long time coming. I thought buying this horse farm would solve things," she smiled. "You know, we'd both be able to have what we needed to make us happy. But we started fighting worse than ever." She shivered. "It's for the best." Darla rubbed Angelina's knee.

"It's hard at first," she said with her mouth full. "But you know that this is the worst part of it."

"Yeah," agreed Angelina. "And now I have a horse farm to run by myself. I don't know how I'm going to do it alone." Her chin dropped onto her chest and she began to cry quietly.

"You know you can hire someone. You needed to do that anyway," Darla tried to be practical.

"I don't trust myself to make a decision like that right now, Darla," she lifted her head and dabbed her eyes with the napkin. "I've got horses worth hundreds of thousands of dollars to take care of."

"You love horses," Darla looked at me. "Too bad you couldn't help her out." The waiter came and we put the conversation on hold to review the menu. When he returned a few minutes later we all ordered pasta.

"What exactly would this person have to do?" I asked. "On the farm." Angelina sipped her wine.

"I really wanted someone to live in the cottage that's near the barn. But I don't want to hire a stranger to live on my farm with me living there alone." She spun the wine around the top of the goblet. "I need someone who can help me clean the stalls and take care of the horses"

"Do you need someone who has a lot of experience?" I felt Darla staring at me, her eyes blazing holes in my face.

"I'd prefer someone who'd worked around horses before. But I'm not in a position to be real picky." I cut into my portobello mushroom, the garlic from the butter sauce pungent and warm.

"What would you say if I told you I was interested in talking about it?" Darla kicked me under the table.

"How could you do that?" she asked. "Don't tease her." I filled them in on the dreams with my grandmother.

"That's why I sold the ring. I need to figure out what I want to do with my life. I know it's not being in this job for the rest of my life." I took another bite of my appetizer. Angelina picked through her salad and Darla stuck to the bread. "I think about doing this when I'm fifty and I shudder. What would you be willing to pay?"

"When David and I did the budget, we calculated three hundred dollars a week, plus the cottage. So you wouldn't have to pay for rent." She smiled for the first time since I'd walked in. "Are you serious?" The busboy removed our dishes and served our pasta. I wouldn't be able to afford to eat in places like this for a while. And I probably wouldn't be getting a whole lot of manicures on that salary. But the thought of being around horses, and not having to deal with the lies and duplicity of corporate America sounded pretty appealing.

"I'm serious if you are," I nodded. Angelina jumped out of her seat to hug me, the water glasses tipping over and cascading over the edge of the table.

"I don't believe this," Darla sat, stunned. "This is amazing!" She called over the waiter and ordered another bottle of wine. Giddy and drunk, we stumbled out of the restaurant two hours later.

"I'm not happy about this, Kuan Yin," Inanna stood nose to nose with her sister. "I worked very hard to get her to the point where she's making this kind of money and finally enjoying life a little bit."

"But how much is she really enjoying Inanna?" Kuan Yin fanned herself with the willow branches. "She hates the duplicity."

"She wouldn't have even known about it if it weren't for that damned yoga," Kali jumped between them. "It's Darla's fault."

"It's no one's fault," Kuan Yin stepped back. "And besides, Inanna, at least you're not naked anymore." Inanna looked down and realized she was wearing her cloak. She smiled at Kuan Yin, running her hands up and down the blue silk.

I stood in the doorway watching Gene negotiate a deal. He waved me in and I sat. "What's up, Rena?" He asked hanging up the phone.

"I need to tell you something," I swallowed hard, my eyes moist.

"No!" He jumped up and closed the door. "What are they offering you? How much? I'll match it."

"You can't," I smiled. He sat motionless while I explained.

"You lucky stiff," he finally moved, nodding his head. "And there's nothing I can do to change your mind?" I shook my head. "Let's go tell Lynn." We walked to the corner office, the intimidation it once held now gone. Jackie smiled and waved us in. Gene shut the door.

"Lynn, I'm afraid I have some bad news," Gene sat on the windowsill. Lynn removed his glasses and tossed them onto the desk. "Rena has decided to leave us to pursue a career as a horse farmer."

"What?" Lynn laughed. "You gotta be kidding me!" He turned from Gene to me. "Is this true?" I nodded. "A horse farmer?" I nodded again. He loosened his tie. "Well, I've got to admit. I didn't see this one coming. Did you Gene?" Gene shook his head. I crossed my legs and relaxed in the chair. "You're serious?" Lynn laughed again.

"I am." I picked a piece of lint from my skirt. "I'm ready to wear jeans and clean stalls and ride horses. For a while, anyway." My legs were uncomfortable, so I uncrossed them and rested my feet side by side. "This job eats my soul. I can't do it anymore. And it's best for me to get out before I'm so miserable that I make everyone around me miserable."

"And you're ready to leave New York?"

"Uh-huh. It's not like I'm moving to North Dakota. I'm only going to New Jersey." Gene's chin rested in his palm.

"How long are you going to stick around?" Gene asked.

"I figured three weeks or so. That'll give you a little time to try to replace me." Lynn nodded.

"Get on it, Gene." He turned cold. "Make sure you stay on top of whatever she's got pending." It was like I wasn't in the room. "Good luck, Rena." He dismissed me. Gene stayed and shut the door behind me. I retreated to my office, feeling exhilarated and terrified all at once.

I found myself working late until the day I left. I'd come in early and sometimes stay until eight. I missed Darla's class two weeks in a row. The team took me out for lunch and gave me a huge going away card with a cartoon of a horse on it. "Try not to get into too much shit!" Mike signed. "I'll miss you." Gene gave me a print of Secretariat, signed by the photographer. "For your new house," he grinned.

My last day, everyone stopped into my office to wish me good luck. Jackie kissed me on the cheek. "I got you this," she handed me an envelope. It was a gift certificate for a manicure at the Saks salon. That night, I carried a carton of plants, knickknacks, and personalized memo pads out of the building and hailed a cab. Four years of my life and all I had to show was an overstuffed Hammermill paper box.

Kuan Yin

The Fifth Goddess

I stood on the landing of my apartment like Scarlett surveying her fields. I had learned a lot living in this apartment and I was grateful. For all of it. The memories were worth remembering, if only to ensure that nothing remotely similar occurred again. I loaded my bags in the rented Grand Am.

I had managed to sell almost everything by taping "Apartment Sale" signs to every phone pole and bus stop in a twenty-block radius. All that remained were a couple of framed posters and two beat-up resin chairs. My entire life's possessions had been worth six hundred twelve dollars and seventeen cents, one-sixth of which had gone to the Hertz on 24th Street for the privilege of having a car to drive to New Jersey.

I locked the door and slid the key into the super's mailbox. I stepped outside, the day a perfect October temperature, and slid into the car. I rolled down the window with Z-100 blasting and headed west on 23rd Street. I sped down Seventh Avenue, passed the gay coffeehouses of Chelsea, and into the West Village. I hit a red light on Greenwich Street next to St. Vincent's and sat for a minute watching people scurrying on their Saturday morning errands. The line for the diner on Greenwich was out the door, people willing to wait however long they had to for their blueberry pancakes.

There was no traffic going into the Holland Tunnel and I cruised through in record time, emerging in the land of gas stations in Jersey City. Every fuel company in the country was represented on the quarter-mile strip either leading into or coming out of the tunnel. I followed the signs for the turnpike and within forty minutes was at the Garden State Parkway, a much simpler life beckoning from the hills of Tinton Falls, New Jersey.

I had visited Angelina several times in the month it took me to tie up all the loose ends, and my anxiety eased as I recognized the sign for the Garden State Arts Center, which announced that 10,000 Maniacs was playing that night. I paid the exiting fee of twenty-five cents in Red Bank and took Route 520 east. The traffic got a little heavier as we approached a soccer game taking place on the field of Brookdale College. I turned right on Route 50 and headed south toward Tinton Falls Road.

It had gotten warm inside the car and as I rolled the window down, I got a whiff of fresh-cut grass. I drove past the famous horse farms that lined the road, some established as early as the 1600s. They had names like "Due Process Stables" and "Synergy." Thoroughbreds wandered around the fenced-in pastures, some wearing green blankets buckled across the tops of their legs.

Many of the houses were set so far back you couldn't see them without stopping. All were protected by huge gates and long winding driveways. But one enormous white farmhouse, columns supporting the front porch, was close enough to see. I noticed an old swing and several gliders on the veranda and there was a pond covered with Canadian geese.

I turned left on Hockhockson Road and made my way toward Angelina's farm. I saw the little pink cottage I'd be living in as I crested a hill. It sat to the right of four large patches of grass, each surrounded by a wooden fence. The driveway to the main house meandered past the cottage and barn. I crossed a sturdy wooden bridge that traversed a skinny creek and pulled my car in behind Angelina's Jeep. The sliding glass doors of the patio were open and I heard the hum of a vacuum cleaner under the tones of Joni Mitchell's "For Free." I left everything in the car and peeked in through the screen door.

"Hey! Come on in." Angelina greeted me wearing a towel on her head; her translucent skin still blushed from her shower. "Sorry," she said, realizing she was naked. "I guess I should put some clothes on. I'm so used to being alone, I don't even think about it anymore." She disappeared into a bedroom.

I was drawn to the bamboo etagere laden with pictures and knickknacks. I held a pewter frame containing her wedding picture when she emerged wearing jeans and a Bob Fosse T-shirt, her short brown hair tousled from a quick rub with the towel. I quickly returned it to the shelf, hoping she wouldn't be offended at my invasion of her privacy.

"It's OK." She slid her hands into the pockets of her Levis. "I haven't been able to take it down, yet." She padded barefoot over to the etagere and removed the frame. Kneeling next to the tapestry-covered sofa, she shoved the picture underneath. "There," she announced triumphantly. "I should have done this long ago." She stood and brushed imaginary dirt from her thighs. "Can I get you something to drink? I have a pot of coffee that's not too old."

We sat at the butcher block table in the colossal kitchen. The chairs were large and inviting with their thick padded cushions. She poured coffee into our mugs as if she was performing a ballet, graceful and controlled. "I haven't eaten yet, have you?" She asked pulling yogurt and fruit from the industrial-sized refrigerator. Grabbing a box of cereal from the antique pantry, she joined me at the table. "I forgot bowls," she said to herself. "And spoons. I'd forget my head if it wasn't attached."

We ate strawberry yogurt with apples and cinnamon granola. "I'm so glad you decided to come down and help me, Rena," she mumbled through her breakfast. "I had no idea how much work this would be." Staring out the window at the maples blazing red and orange, she sipped the coffee, blowing occasionally to cool it.

"I'm glad you offered," I let the tang from the strawberry rouse my taste buds and mashed a piece of banana between my teeth with my tongue. "I had no idea what I was going to do after I quit. I've always wanted to work around horses. I think they're such magnificent creatures." I scraped the last of my breakfast from the bowl and placed it in the sink.

"Well, as far as I'm concerned you're a godsend. We bought five horses, six if you include the foal that Peacock had three days ago. And I can't take care of them alone. Feeding them and mucking the stalls alone is almost full-time work." I rested against the range and surveyed room. A wrought iron rack containing a set of copper pots and pans hung in the center of the ceiling over a natural wood work station.

The cabinets were pine and the simple brass hardware allowed the beauty of the intricate carpentry to show. The floor was marble tile with what looked like hand-painted flowers, not the linoleum I was used to. The peach-and-green color scheme ran through the seat-cushions, dishtowels, and china. And the walls were painted ivory with a pansy wallpaper border around the top.

"I'm grateful to be out of New York," I reiterated. "This is a magnificent house, Angelina."

"Thanks. It was our dream house."

"I'm sorry."

"Don't be. Why don't we get you settled and then I'll introduce you to everyone." After she put on boots and a jacket we drove my car to the cottage. "Now that someone will be living here, I'll have it painted for you Rena," she said peeling some paint from the wood with her index finger. "It's been empty since we moved in." She inserted the key into the front door. "And if you'd like another color, my feelings won't be hurt." Her blue eyes smiled at me over her shoulder.

We stepped into a small living room, the hardwood floors buffed to a sheen. The kitchen was off to the right and down the hall to the left were two bedrooms and the bathroom. A green-and-white striped couch sat under the picture window in the living room and an empty entertainment center rested against the opposite wall. We retrieved my two suitcases from the trunk. "Is this all you have?" Angelina asked, her slender arms belying her strength as they bulged at the biceps as she lifted one.

"I sold everything except what's in these bags," I patted the luggage. "I wanted a fresh start."

"Sometimes I wish I could do that." We threw the bags on the twin bed in the one bedroom and headed for the barn. "I have an extra television in the basement you can use. We can get the cable guy out here to hook it up." She kicked a stone with the pointed tip of her boot. "I think I have a boom box down there too. It was Dave's. You're more than welcome to it."

"Thanks. I didn't think about how I'd listen to my CD's without a stereo." We entered the barn, the sweet hay and sour manure fraternizing in a heady marriage. There were four stalls on each side of the barn.

"Morning, Bogota," Angelina walked up to the first stall making a loud kissing noise until a large chestnut-colored head appeared over the wooden gate. The horse snuffled his lips, hoping for a carrot or apple. "I fed you this morning, you rascal." She planted a kiss on the end of his long nose. He reached behind her neck and nuzzled her ear. "This horse thinks he's a Labrador Retriever," she giggled while his large pink tongue snaked around her ear. She patted his neck and scratched his ears. "Come say hello." I walked over to him.

"He's huge," I tentatively patted his head and rubbed the patch of white hair between his eyes.

"About sixteen hands," she answered standing at the next stall. "But he's a baby. Not like Helga." I saw her petting the horse next to Bogota. "She nipped me last week. Didn't you, Fraulein Bitch? She's German. Ja wohl, right, Helga?" Angelina continued running her hand up and down the horse's head. "She's a brood mare. In the next month or so she'll be heading down to West Palm Beach. She comes from a long line of champion race horses. She raced herself until her shin splints got too bad."

We made our way around the barn, ending with a double stall on the other side where Peacock and her foal, Jezebel, were. "You're going to have to be careful with her," Angelina warned. "Peacock's still not feeling well."

She leaned over the gate and held out her hand. "You can tell if a horse doesn't want to be messed with if her ears are back. That basically means leave me the fuck alone." The foal struggled to walk with its huge body and skinny stick legs. She ambled over to Peacock and stuck her head under the mare's belly to nurse.

"I should've turned them out already. It's almost eleven and they don't stay out past three. Do you want to help me?"

"Sure," I was excited and scared. "Just tell me what to do."

"Have you ever put a harness on a horse before?"

"No," I admitted. "I rode when I was a kid. My parents would take me to this family camp for vacation and I spent the whole time at the horse barn. But I really haven't been around horses much in a long time." Part of the reason was because the last time I'd tried to ride, the stable owner told me he only had one horse who was strong enough to accommodate a big girl like me, but he was out with a trail group. I sat on the fence while my college friends headed out on an hour-long ride.

"That's OK. We'll take it slow." I watched Angelina put the leather harness on Helga, her long fingers running over the horse's body, massaging away any twitches while she gently cooed in her ear. "You try it on Bogota," she instructed. I followed her lead, talking to him and gently tried to pull his head toward the harness."

"Gentle is good, but you need to be firm," she instructed. "He needs to know who is in charge. Especially since he doesn't know you." I straightened my back and commanded him to turn his head. He obeyed and I slid the harness over his head and attached the lead rope. "Helga and Bogota actually get along pretty well, so I put them in the same corral."

"You always put the two of them together?"

"Well, they're like people, you know? They have personalities. Helga and Peacock hate each other. I could never put them together. Bogota gets along with everyone." Angelina talked to me over her shoulder, walking ahead of me with Helga. We took them to the farthest pasture and watched them trot off looking for grass to nibble. She rested one foot on the rung of the fence and turned her face up toward the sun.

I watched the horses frolic, communicating in their own language, butting up against one another and whinnying. I noticed tears on her cheeks when I turned to ask her if we should get the other horses. "Are you OK?" I wanted to hug her, but she seemed so fragile, I was afraid I'd crush her. She brushed the drops away.

"Fine. Yeah, I'm fine." She sniffed, the tip of her nose still damp. "Let's go get the others." We returned to the barn to get Alabaster, the Palomino, and Seuss, another thoroughbred. We freed them in the pasture closest to the barn and for the next few hours, while the horses frolicked in the sun, Angelina taught me the fine art of mucking a stall.

I watched while she used a pitchfork to sift out the obvious clumps of manure and then turned over every wood shaving in the stall, making mountains against the walls so that the lumps rolled to the cement floor where they could be easily removed. "It's really important to make sure you get every wet spot," she said scraping damp shavings from the concrete, "the ammonia in their urine can cause all kinds of problems if they stand in it for prolonged periods of time."

For each stall we took at least two wheelbarrows full of manure and shavings out to the dumping ground. "I keep the stalls really deep," she admitted. "Dave thought I was nuts, but I think it's important for them to have a big enough cushion against the cement."

"Is it true horses never lay down?" I asked, sifting for manure like I was in a giant litter box.

"No, they lay down," she answered from another stall.

"In their own shit? Ick!"

"They're not picky," she laughed. "And they only sleep a few hours a night." I stopped to catch my breath and watched her through the slats, her thin arms wielding the pitchfork like she could bench press four hundred pounds. She stopped for a second and I pretended to shovel. I couldn't resist watching her and when I sneaked another glance, she was removing her windbreaker. Maybe she weighed a hundred and ten pounds in a thunderstorm. When she grabbed a bottle of water from the ledge of the stall and stood sideways drinking, I couldn't help noticing that her breasts, the size of large Georgia peaches, held up her shirt without the support of a bra.

We sat on the floor in the tack room enjoying a Diet Coke. "I need to get more organized here." She shook her head looking around the small room. "It's taken all the energy I've had to take care of the horses." She patted my thigh, "But now that you're here, I can focus on some other things. Like building the riding academy I've always wanted." She raised the can to her mouth and drained it. We finished sweeping the fronts of the stalls and brought in the horses. After we put fresh water in their pails and gave them a few flakes of hay, she locked the barn door.

"I guess you probably just want to get a shower and crash," she assumed, her smoky blue eyes grazing my face.

"You're right about the shower," I raised my arm and pretended to take a whiff of what was underneath. "I'm not fit for human company. But it's only four or five. What's there to do around here?"

"We could go into Red Bank and go to dinner if you want. My treat. Kind of a welcome to Tartan Farm."

"That sounds great," I answered. "Let me get washed up and …."

"Why don't you drive up to the house when you're finished? Take your time. I need to get a shower too." Angelina started up the driveway toward the house.

I let the hot water pelt my back and arms. I was going to be sore in the morning. I reviewed the contents of my closet. I had purchased some casual clothes to replace the skirts and jackets I donated to the Salvation Army before I left. The jeans were a couple of sizes bigger than the last time I'd bought them, but I was trying to get better at keeping the bats and chains in the closet. Beating myself up about my weight hadn't ever gotten me anything but fatter. After throwing on a pair of fresh jeans and a sweater, I grabbed my leather jacket and headed to Angelina's.

We drove to Highlands instead of Red Bank and feasted on fresh fish and shrimp at Bahr's. "I make a mean espresso," she taunted as my car approached her house after dinner.

"Have any Grand Marnier?"

"Is there any other way to drink espresso?" We sat on the plush sofa, the burgundy and mauve flowers on its tapestry slipcovers bunched under our feet. She lit the jarred candles that sat in a cluster against the sliding glass door, the flames' reflection bobbing on the moss green walls. Vanilla and plumeria joined forces, creating an interesting aroma as I absorbed the energy in the room. A deep green Berber area rug sat underneath the bamboo and glass coffee table that held our tiny espresso cups and crystal snifters of Grand Marnier. A row of masks hung on the wall going up the steps to the second floor.

"These are great masks." I walked over to the banister. "Where did you get them?"

"From all over." She joined me and removed a wooden one with a delicately carved face from the wall. "This one is from the trip Dave and I took to Greece three years ago." She touched it lightly and then rehung it. "And this," she grabbed a colorful round coconut shell with cornstalk braids hanging from each side, "came from Caracas. Dave got it for me while we were dating when he was in Venezuela on a business trip." I returned to the couch, not wanting to mix sad memories with the liquor we were consuming.

"It's OK, Rena," she flopped onto overstuffed gold pillows strewn on the floor and crossed her legs. "I'm still sad about us not being together anymore, but it's part of the process. I'm trying to honor that as much as possible."

"But doesn't it hurt?"

"Of course," she laughed, "I love him. I don't know that I won't ever not love him. But I affirm every day that Divine Order is in place and that I am where I need to be."

"Wouldn't it be easier to just kill him?" I leaned over and took my snifter from the table.

"No, because then I'd have to deal with it in the next life."

"You're serious?"

"Of course I am. David and I have a connection that goes back centuries."

"How do you know that?"

"I'd always sensed it, but I've had a few past life regressions done to help me clarify it."

"Past life regression?" I sipped my coffee. "What the hell is that?"

"You've never had one?" I let the liqueur warm my throat and belly. "I guess I assumed you had experimented with this kind of stuff since you and Darla are so tight."

"You mean Darla's done it too?"

"Once that I know of." She sat up and placed the edge of the cushion under her tailbone. "You ought to consider it; it's a fascinating experience."

"I don't know. Reincarnation? Past lives? Seems a little out there to me." I watched her sip espresso from a china cup, her tiny waist accentuated by the cropped pink sweater and tight black corduroys.

"It's OK, I'm not going to force you," her white, straight teeth gleamed at me in the candlelight. "But if you ever change your mind, let me know."

It had been a long day. I was too tired to discuss the afterlife. I took my dishes to the kitchen and slipped onto the patio. Angelina stood barefoot in the doorway, her delicate ankles barely noticeable under the heavy cuffs of her pants.

"Thanks, I really had a good time." I leaned over to kiss her cheek but she turned her head and my lips touched hers, shocking every nerve ending in my body.

"So did I." Her hand played with one of my curls. "I'll meet you at the barn around eight?" I drove to my new home, tingling and exhausted.

"Well, well, well," chuckled Kali. *"Life with you might not be so dull after all, Kuan Yin. I've always wondered what it would be like to have a relationship with a woman."*

"That's disgusting," groaned Erishkigal. *"Women are meant to be with men, not other women."*

"All I know is that Rena spent all that time struggling to reach the top in her career and now she's going to be shoveling horse manure," Inanna was disgusted. *"Where's the justice in that?"*

"You all are missing the point." Kuan Yin pulled the pearl pin from her straight brown locks and allowed her hair to cascade over her shoulders. *"This is part of Rena's evolution. You're so attached to your perspectives, which force you to pronounce it good or bad. Try not to judge it. Just let it exist."*

Later in the week, while I was mucking stalls, I heard a truck rumbling outside the barn. Angelina had gone to the bank and she hadn't said anything about company. I saw a big red flatbed truck backing up to the entrance. "Can I help you?" I called over the din from the hole in the muffler. The driver's door opened and a young man jumped down. He had dark wavy hair and a thick mustache.

"I'm Jack, ma'am." He gave me a half wave. Ma'am? Was he kidding? He wasn't much younger than I was. "I'm from Bud's Feed." He addressed the puzzled look on my face. "I've got the hay and wood shavings you ordered."

"Oh, Angelina didn't tell me you'd be coming." I noticed the dwindling bales against the wall of the barn.

"I was supposed to be here yesterday, but our shipment didn't arrive until last night," his jeans hugged his slender hips and round ass. He wore a flannel shirt over a thermal T-shirt and suede hiking boots. Jumping up on the flatbed, he began to throw the paper bags of wood shavings onto the barn floor. "You new here?"

"Yes," I walked toward the truck and held my hand up to him. "I'm Rena."

"Jack." He continued throwing bags and when he was finished, he jumped down and began stacking them on the wood platform that already where a few bags remained. "When did you start?" He had hazel eyes that twinkled when he smiled.

"The beginning of the week."

"How do you know Angelina?"

"She's friends with a friend of mine in New York," I silently debated how much to tell him.

"Do you like it?" His breathing was slightly labored from hoisting the heavy bags.

"I love it," I grabbed a broom and swept the fronts of the stalls I'd already mucked instead of moving on to the next stall. When he was finished, he jumped back onto the truck. "You can put the hay over there," I pointed.

"Actually," he said, running his hands over one of the bales, "this is straw."

"What's the difference?" I asked ignorantly. He let out a loud laugh.

"You really are a novice, aren't you?"

"What's so funny?"

"Horses eat hay. They sleep on straw." He set aside two bales and tossed the remaining ones to the ground. "Didn't Angelina just have a foal?"

"Peacock did."

"The straw's probably for her stall." Two fine trickles of sweat originated at the tips of his sideburns. "The babies shouldn't sleep in wood shavings. It's not good for their lungs to inhale the tiny particles. Are they over here?" He pointed around the corner to Peacock's stall.

"Yep," I followed him, dragging a bale of straw.

"That's OK, I'll get it," he gently took it from me and swung it onto the empty platform outside the stall. "Your pretty little hands have enough work to do cleaning out those stalls." I tried to be offended, but he was so charming, I couldn't muster it. I did another stall while he finished stacking the hay and the straw. I was wiping my brow, leaning on the pitchfork when he appeared in the doorway.

"Hard work, huh?" He had a slight gap in between two of his top teeth.

"I can handle it."

"Never said you couldn't," he pulled a piece of paper out of his shirt pocket. "Can you sign for the delivery since Angelina's not here?"

"I'm sorry," I leaned the pitchfork against the wall and stepped outside the stall. "You just caught me off guard, that's all."

"I'd hate to see what you're like with your guard on," he laughed. I walked to the tack room to find a pen.

"Thanks," I said, "for the hay and everything."

"Keep up the good work," he saluted me. "It keeps the roses in your cheeks." He headed back to the truck. "See you next week." He turned over the engine, and I watched from the doorway as the truck ambled up the driveway.

Breathe

Angelina patiently taught me how to brush and groom the horses and gradually I became more comfortable. She taught me how to pick their shoes to remove pebbles and dirt without hurting them. How to treat a cut. How to pay attention and make astute observations. I assisted the vet when he came to care for Peacock, flushing out her uterus and stitching where she had ripped while giving birth to Jezebel.

She went into a foaling heat a week after the birth, causing her milk to be rich with extra hormones. Jezebel had diarrhea for a few days. Angelina and I took turns taking the foal's temperature every few hours to make sure she didn't have an infection. It was physical and exhausting, but I looked forward to getting out of bed every morning. Even if it was raining or snowing.

When I originally accepted Angelina's offer, I planned to go into the city a couple of days a week just to get a fix. But I enjoyed what I did and had no desire to deal with the crowds and dirt. After I got a system in place, I started looking for a car. I found a '91 Jetta for less than what I had budgeted and Angelina helped me, having her mechanic check it over and driving me to the DMV to get the registration. On my one day off I haunted consignment stores and thrift shops, congratulating myself when I discovered a find. A week at a time, I made a home by purchasing an antique dresser or a bookcase.

Angelina's library was eclectic and I spent hours reading books like the Bhagavad-Gita, *The Power of One* by Bryce Courtenay and Francis Scovill Shinn's *The Game of Life*. The common message was that I had been created to honor my truth. I still wasn't sure what that meant, but I started to believe that perhaps I could be happy. Following the advice in books like Louise Haye's *You Can Heal Your Life*, I began to write affirmations, repeating them out loud every morning after I prayed and meditated. I didn't have the kind of money that I did when I worked at Silverman and Washburn and I hadn't had a manicure in God knows when, but an unfamiliar feeling had settled over me. I think it was peace.

The first time Angelina offered to let me ride, I blurted out what had happened in college. "I wouldn't do anything to hurt you or the animals." She had held my hand. "I think you'd be comfortable on Bogota." My heart raced as we saddled up and headed for the trail, but it didn't take long for me to settle into a trot behind Angelina and Seuss. The muscles around my knees stretched like rubber bands over Bogota's broad back, and my knees buckled under me when I jumped off back at the barn. That was the first night Angelina and I did yoga.

Now, a few times a week, Angelina and I would practice yoga together in the basement, which she had made into a studio filled with pillows and incense. I had limited experience with partner yoga, but she serenely repeated the technique of each *asana* until I absorbed it.

I especially enjoyed Friday nights where we would practice positions for an hour or two and then make dinner. We took turns cooking, most of Angelina's choices consisting of vegetarian dishes while mine deviated with a steak or something fried. "Moderation, honey, that's the key," she insisted when she saw my selection for that evening. "But this is sure gonna taste good!" She leaned her nose into the chicken cordon bleu that I was rolling.

"I bought asparagus," I argued, "doesn't that counteract the ham and cheese?"

"I don't think so," she laughed, pulling off her shirt and heading for the bedroom. "I'll meet you downstairs in five." I finished preparing the cutlets and put the cookie sheet in the fridge.

I grabbed my towel from the kitchen table. I lit the candles in the studio and placed fresh incense in the burner. I placed the pillows in a circle and lined up a few blocks against the wall. I needed a good stretch through my chest and arms. The moon series was just the sequence of *asanas* I needed, and the blocks helped me get the full stretch when I couldn't touch the floor.

"It smells delicious down here." Angelina trotted down the steps wearing a pale blue leotard. Her firm legs displayed no hint of cellulite and her ass was the shape of a pearl onion. I didn't understand how she could look that way at thirty-seven. She rarely wore make-up and had been mistaken for a boy in junior high school on more than one occasion. "Is that the new musk we got at Earth Spirit?" I nodded, proud that the scent had been my selection at our favorite book store in Red Bank.

"It's amazing, right?" We sat in lotus, her in full, me in half. I still couldn't manage to get my right foot on top of my left thigh. We recited a Sanskrit prayer for peace, love, and truth and then reinforced our faith by silently expressing gratitude for everything we had. I opened my eyes before Angelina and was momentarily envious of the angelic serenity she possessed.

I didn't understand how it was possible when she was obviously still in so much pain over David. She never ate too much. She never drank too much. And she wouldn't know cocaine if someone handed it to her on a gold spoon. I didn't get it. She caught me staring at her and I blushed. "What do you want to work on tonight?" She rose from the floor in one fluid motion.

"I'd love to do the moon series," I pointed to the blocks.

"Great idea." We spaced ourselves on the wall and began, inhaling and exhaling only through our noses. I struggled, trying to get a perfect 'C' curve with my upper body.

"Here," she said touching my waist, "try this." She pulled my torso up through my rib cage and gently twisted my body over to the side. Her one hand remained on my hip as she stretched my arms toward the steps. I could no longer smell the musk incense. It had been blocked out by the Fleur de Weil she wore, a gift to herself the last time she visited Paris.

When we were finished, we agreed to stretch together for a few minutes before starting dinner. We sat across from each other on the floor, legs opened wide and the soles of our feet touching. She extended her hands into the middle of the diamond and I met her half-way. We held each other above the wrist bone and began moving clockwise in the "Witch's Cauldron," making slow circles, stretching our hips and hamstrings.

After a half dozen rotations, we reversed the direction. When we were finished, I lay on my stomach and extended my arms behind me for Angelina to hold. She clasped her hands around my wrists and gently lifted my trunk off the floor, stretching the muscles across my chest and in my arms. "Breathe," she commanded. I inhaled deeply to push oxygen into the tight areas and alleviate the discomfort.

As I rested on the floor, my face turned to the side, Angelina requested that I spot her for a headstand. I took my time getting up, not wanting to get a head rush. She positioned her arms at the correct angle and placed her head in between, legs extended out behind her. I knelt next to her left hand, ready to guide her legs to the upright position.

She walked on her toes toward her head and her legs naturally took flight, reaching for the ceiling. I steadied her, one hand resting on her stomach, the other on her lower back. My hand moved with her breath and I felt her warm exhalations on my right foot, which rested near her chin. After a couple of minutes, her feet returned to the ground and she rested in child's pose, forehead on the floor and butt touching her heels.

I ran my hand up and down her spine, massaging the muscles that had allowed her to remain inverted. "Hmm, that feels so good," she murmured. "Don't stop." I continued rubbing, working my way up to her shoulders and neck. "You could do this professionally." I felt her smile. I enjoyed bringing her pleasure. She sat up slowly. "Why don't you get in child's pose, and I'll sit on your back and see if we can't get your bum closer to your heels."

I obeyed, reclining into the *asana*. She put her weight on my lower back, stretching it toward my feet. My muscles rebelled, preferring to remain tight and knotted. Her weight cajoled them into cautiously releasing, allowing me to get a much better stretch than I could on my own. I was sweating from breathing so heavily. "Uncle," I joked.

"Seriously?" She seemed surprised. "It hasn't even been two minutes yet."

"Really?" I gasped into the carpet.

"Pussy."

"Excuse me?" I pushed up on my arms rising like a crocodile out of a swamp. She tumbled off and lay on her back.

"Oh my God! Are you OK?" I crawled quickly to her side on my knees forgetting I was in bike shorts until I felt the burn. She was still, her eyes closed. I leaned over, placing my hand in front of her mouth to make sure she was breathing. I felt the moisture, but before I could pull my hand away, she bit my pinky finger. "Ow!" I sucked my finger. "What the hell was that?"

"Payback," she lifted herself and cocked her head at me. "That wasn't very nice."

"Neither was this," I wagged my pinky near her face. "Oh, that's right." I snatched it back. "I don't want to give you the chance to bite me again." I playfully slapped her thigh.

"What if I can't resist?"

"Excuse me?" She held my gaze for a few seconds.

"Nothing." She stood and walked toward the candles. "Do you want to do a relaxation or are you hungry?"

"Hungry."

"Me too," she bent over and blew out the candles, her ass pointed in my direction.

"I'll throw the chicken in the oven," I said walking up the steps. She sneaked up on me while I cleaned lettuce under the running faucet. I jumped when she placed her hand on the small of my back.

"How's it feel?" She rubbed it in circles. I felt my nipples stiffen and was grateful the sound of the water drowned out my gasp.

"Better," I cleared my throat. She removed her hand and placed both of them on each side of me on the edge of the sink. They were large and masculine, the nails short and unpolished. She sniffed behind my ear.

"Dinner smells great." She pulled away and started setting the table. "Excuse me," she grazed my abdomen opening the drawer under the sink. "I need to get napkins."

"Sure, no problem," I sprung back like her hand was a branding iron. When she'd finished putting the dishes and silverware out, she pulled a bottle of Zinfandel from the wine rack and uncorked it.

"Wine?" She filled two goblets while I checked the asparagus that was simmering on the stove.

"How about some music?" I needed a distraction from the deafening silence. She padded into the living room and I soon heard the strains of "Passion Play" from Joni Mitchell. Angelina's favorite record in the world was *Misses*. "They're the most passionate songs she ever wrote," she insisted. "The emotion in 'A Case of You' could make Hitler weep."

I pulled the chicken from the oven, golden and smelling of garlic and lemon. We sat and ate quietly, savoring the moistness of the ham and melted cheese. The asparagus was fresh and crisp. "Do you like the sunflower seeds on the salad?" I asked, straining to make conversation.

"Everything is delicious." Her chair was pushed back a couple of feet from the table. She sat with her knees up near her chin, bare feet clutching the edge. Leaning in, she stabbed a piece of chicken, brought it to her lips, and blew on it. I squirmed on the flowered cushion and took a sip of wine. When we were finished, we wrapped the leftovers and loaded the dishwasher.

"I guess I should be going," I said drying my hands on a dish towel. "I have to be up early tomorrow." I had no plans, but the flight instinct had me in its grip.

"Can't you stay for coffee?" She removed the can of espresso from the freezer. "It'll go great with the fresh strawberries I picked up earlier."

"I don't know, Angelina." I stood frozen and terrified, like a child who's been caught slipping a candy bar into her pocket at the 7-11.

"It'll just take a minute to brew," she said as if that answered all the questions rattling around my brain. "We could play cards or something."

"Double solitaire?"

"Sure," she laughed. "Let's live dangerously."

"What the hell is going on?" demanded Erishkigal.

"Rena's about to do it with a woman—and she's sober!" The grin on Kali's face was lopsided. "Well, mostly anyway. A little wine doesn't count."

"I want it on the record that I'm not pleased with this." Erishkigal paced back and forth. "No, not pleased at all."

"Duly noted." Kali smacked her on her back.

"This is not a joke, Kali," Kuan Yin scolded.

"It certainly isn't," Inanna's lips were pursed. "I see nothing humorous in it at all."

"It's about being open," Kuan Yin attempted to explain. "Rena has been terrified about admitting that she wants to love someone. That she wants someone to love her. She's bonded with Angelina. And she feels vulnerable right now. But this experience will open her up to many things."

"Yeah," laughed Kali, "like being eligible for membership in the GLAAD."

"Make fun if you must," Kuan Yin turned her back on her sisters.

"You're only doing it because you're afraid." Kali raced around to face Kuan Yin. Sticking her chest out, she waved three index fingers under Kuan Yin's nose.

"I am not afraid."

"Me thinks thou dost protest too much," Kuan Yin laughed. She took Kali's hands. "It's OK to have trepidation about a new experience, Kali. This is where trust and faith come into play."

"Trust in who?" Inanna refused to face Kuan Yin.

"God. Goddess. A higher power. Herself." Kuan Yin turned to look at Inanna. "Isn't this what she's been working toward?"

"I guess I see your point," admitted Kali. "But I still think it's cool that she wants to be with a woman." She rubbed her hands together gleefully,

then held them in the air, searching for a high five from Kuan Yin,
"Woman power!" She slapped Kuan Yin's palms. "I guess this is what
Gloria Steinem and Erica Jong were talking about. Next thing you know,
Rena will be burning her bras and getting a tattoo!"

We each chose an end of the sofa and curled up facing each other, shuffling our decks of cards. Angelina finished first and spread them in front of her for the game. She grabbed a strawberry from the bowl on the coffee table and I pretended not to watch as she bit into it and sucked the juice from the tip. The lamp next to the couch was on the lowest setting, giving off barely enough light to differentiate between a king and queen.

In double solitaire, you play the way you would alone, except that you use your opponent's cards as well. The game moved along swiftly as we drank espresso and munched on the strawberries. "They're as sweet as sugar, aren't they?" Angelina asked, a dribble of red running down her chin. She tilted a leg toward her hand and placed a card in between her toes. Stretching it across the sofa, she deposited the card on one of my piles and placed her foot on my calf.

"You're cold," I rubbed her heel and instep in between my hands. "Do you want a pair of socks?"

"That'd be great," she retracted her leg like a cat curling up for a nap. "They're in my dresser upstairs." I got up carefully, trying not to disturb the piles of cards. I skirted the coffee table and walked up the steps, suddenly feeling naked in my bike shorts as I felt her eyes on me. Her bedroom was my favorite room in the house. The centerpiece was a queen-sized antique four-poster bed topped with a pink silk cap. The mauve carpet was plush and heavily padded.

In between the two windows that looked out on the barn was a copy of Degas' *Dancers, Pink and Green.* Over the 1940s cherry dresser hung Monet's *Woman with a Parasol.* My favorite, Seurat's *Sunday Afternoon on the Island of La Grand Jatte,* was in a gilded frame next to the walk-in closet. All had been gifts from David while they were dating. Angelina had studied psychology in grad school, but her first four years had been devoted to art history.

She and David married before she finished her thesis and the unfinished research sat in a box in the back of the garage. David's take of the financial portfolios he managed was more than enough to keep them in the style to which they had grown accustomed. Even though he was gone now, the alimony arrived every month, preventing Angelina from experiencing the financial worries of the average Joe.

I slid open the top drawer of the dresser in search of the socks, but found only silky bras and underwear. I ran their softness through my fingers, wondering if she ever really wore a bra. I felt something behind me and before I could turn around, her mouth was on the back of my neck, soft and nuzzling. "I wanted to make sure you didn't get lost up here." Her hands rested firmly on my hips, not allowing for much movement.

"I was admiring the paintings," I closed my eyes, held my breath.

"And I was admiring you from the doorway." She buried her nose in my hair and circled her hands around my waist.

"I don't know if I can do this, Angelina," I rolled a pair of her blue satin panties into a ball and threw them back in the drawer.

"You're not going to know if you don't try, Rena." Her lips found my ear, tongue snaking around the lobe. "I'm not asking for any commitment here. Let's just see what happens." She took my hand and led me to the bed, pulling me down next to her. She caressed my stomach and gently pushed me back, climbing on top of me, hands beside my ears. Her sweet boyish face hung above me for a second and then she lowered herself and our lips touched, soft and dry.

I held her face as she explored my mouth with her tongue, searching for a response. She sat her behind between my hipbones and slid her hands under my shirt, pulling it and then my sports bra over my head. Her long fingers cupped my breasts and squeezed each one like it was the prize fruit at a county fair. When she pinched my nipples, a bolt shot through me and, despite my resistance, caused a tender wetness, like weeping, between my legs. I thought briefly about strategically choosing a position that would not emphasize my rolls and handles. I decided it wasn't necessary.

She lay on top of me, the material of her leotard pressing against my nakedness. Our breathing became synchronized, and for a moment we lay still, listening to each other's quiet exhalations. "Do you want me to stop?" she whispered.

"No," I murmured. I felt her hands on the elastic band of my shorts, seeking permission to enter. I sucked in my stomach and she pulled them down past my bellybutton to the top of my triangle. She raised her head and kissed me again, harder this time and wetter. Her fingers danced around my pubic hair and without warning plunged into the slick unknown.

"Oh, God!" slipped from my mouth.

"You ain't seen nothing yet," she smiled, removing her fingers so she could undress. Her naked body rested beside me, not a stretch mark in sight. She played with the curls on my head while the other hand rested on my belly. "How are you?"

"Fine," I lied. I felt like a piece of rope in a tug of war. I couldn't even admit I was attracted to her, yet here I was, nipples at attention, her fingers stroking my ribcage. And I knew I wasn't going anywhere. She licked my neck and surprised me with another kiss, harder and wetter than the last. I responded, reaching for her breasts and hoping I would know what to do once I found them.

"Gently," she placed her hands on top of mine and forced them to relax. I caressed her back and shoulders, hoping to delude myself into believing that this could fall into the category of a special massage. She climbed on top of me again and slid my shorts over my ankles, leaving me as naked as she was. Starting at my forehead, she kissed her way down my body, chin, collarbone, and the hollow between my breasts.

When her mouth reached the base of my abdomen, she stopped and her fingers crawled up the satin duvet cover toward my breasts. After quickly tweaking my nipples, she pulled her hands back, using them to open my legs, allowing her access to kiss inside my thighs and behind my knees. Her tongue was warm and moist on my legs and I couldn't lay still. Hands pushed my hips against the mattress in attempt to stop me from squirming.

She buried her face between my legs and when her tongue darted around my lips, the canopy above me melted, dripping pink satin onto my body like hot wax. I tried to steel myself from feeling anymore, but my body wouldn't cooperate. The more she moved her tongue around, the more I whimpered and moaned. She sucked my button and grazed it with her teeth, causing bright silver stars to collide with the melting wax in the Tim Leary acid trip that was my first real lesbian experience.

I screamed and sat up abruptly as if I had been yanked into that position by a giant crane. Just as suddenly, I fell back and Angelina slid her body up mine until we were face to face. She held her fingers under my nose. "Sweet like sugar," she licked them one by one. I lay panting, unsure of how to return the favor. Sensing this, she guided my hands and placed my timid fingers inside of her.

I massaged them around, not knowing what kind of response it was going to elicit. She moaned a little and rolled off of me onto her back. Grabbing my arm, she moved my hand up to her breasts and directed my fingers to her nipples. I duplicated what she had done to me and was pleased when she smiled and gasped. I sat on her belly, my moisture dampening her skin, and reached behind me to play with her pubic hair. But there wasn't much there.

Curious, I scooted down the bed and spread her legs open. She had a thin strip of hair at the crest of her pubic bone. Everything else was bare. And soft, like a well-worn baby blanket. I opened her lips with my fingers and tentatively leaned into her. I felt her squeeze the muscles in her butt. "You don't have to do this if you're not comfortable." Her left hand fingered with my curls. I looked up and caught her crystal blue eyes. She smiled at me and I returned to my position between her legs. My tongue instinctually knew how to flicker and suckle her, the way a baby bird knows how to return to its nest, and soon she was sliding up and down, forcing herself into my mouth.

After she came, we lay, our limbs entwined, on top of the down comforter, her slender arms and legs wrapped around my heavier ones. As I felt a tiny drop of sweat trickle down my back, I realized that sex with women wasn't the primal banging and humping that I had experienced with men. Making love with Angelina wasn't anything like watching the horses couple, forceful and almost angry. It was erotic. And sensual. And powerful in that it provided strength instead of an attempt to determine who had more leverage. There was no quest for domination. Only a desire for mutual pleasure.

We fell asleep, our bodies spooned against each other. My eyes fluttered open around dawn and I gently crawled out of bed and dressed. I kissed her forehead as she lay sleeping and tiptoed out of the room. The sun was being summoned over the horizon by chirping robins and blue birds. The air was crisp and tasted earthy, frost sparkling on the tips of the grass. I looked forward to spring. I rolled my hands up in the bottom of my shirt and went inside to shower.

Breathe

That morning I was wiped out and it took forever to finish the stalls but I was awake enough to realize that for several days Bogota's was missing the usual number of piles. I mentioned it to Angelina and she told me to keep an eye on him. When he snapped at me and nipped my index finger while I was placing the harness on him, we knew something was wrong.

The vet told her it sounded like colic. If walking him didn't work, he would come out and examine him. "Horses," she explained stroking his neck, "cannot vomit or belch because their alimentary canal is one way." She patiently walked him around the barn while the snow piled up outside, hoping to dislodge the gas that made him so uncomfortable and irritable. "The bubbles get trapped in there and can expand, eventually killing them if they're not passed."

I polished saddles in the tack room, staying out of the way while she tried to coax Bogota to fart. As I swirled wax over the leather of Angelina's saddle, I heard the first rumblings of the gas being released. The sound was wet and forceful, and it wasn't long before I was soaked in a damp pungent odor that overpowered the sweetness of the wax.

"Good boy!" Angelina continued circling the barn, loose turds dripping from behind Bogota. I wished he had one of those attachable poop holders like they made the carriage horses in Central Park wear because I knew I was going to be the one to clean it up.

After an hour of walking, he had passed all of the gas and was hungrily devouring a flake of hay in his stall. "I didn't realize how much work horses are," I commented.

"It's a ton of work, Rena," she leaned against the wall and slid down until her bottom rested against the barn floor. "But I don't know what I'd have done if I'd lost him."

"But you didn't," I said quickly, uncomfortable more with my fear about comforting her than with her show of emotion. "He's fine now, right?" The pale skin on her face had blotches of red from the cold. She removed her heavy suede gloves and slid back up the wall, her parka making scratching noises against the rough surface.

"We should talk about last night."

"What's there to talk about?" I joked. "The fact that I could've used a How to be a Lesbian instructional video?"

"Serious, Rena. Be serious." Her voice was hard, her lips taut.

"I can't." My head was spinning. "I don't know what it means. I don't know how I feel. It's taking everything I have to hold it together right now. OK?"

"You don't need to yell at me." She turned away from me and I watched her shoulders move up and down as she began to cry. I put my hand on her shoulder.

"I'm sorry. I don't know how to deal with this." I shoved my hands into the pockets of my anorak. "Does this mean I'm gay? How do I talk to you now? Was it a one-time thing? Do I want it to be?"

"This isn't just about you Rena," she faced me, her eyes red and watery. "This is why David left. He found me with another woman." I gasped. "And I loved him. I still do. How do you think I feel?"

"I'm sorry," I hugged her. "I was being totally selfish. That's something I'm really good at." I thought I heard a laugh mixed in with the sobs. "Was that a laugh?" I held her at arm's length. "We'll figure this out Angelina. I'm not sure how I love you, but I know that I do. And we'll deal with it."

"Aren't you the philosophical one?"

"Who's the one who taught me about Divine Order?" I dropped my arms and gripped her eyes with mine. "Who's the one who has helped me move on with my life? I don't know what I'd have done after I quit if you hadn't offered me this job. I've learned so much from you."

"Sometimes I think I'm nothing but a fraud, Rena. I preach about being responsible as a co-creator with God. I lecture about letting go and releasing. I encourage people to evolve spiritually. And where am I? Mired in the same bullshit that got me divorced from the man I love." The tears started flowing again, raging and hot.

"Do you think that what happened between us last night was bullshit?" I was pissed. "You opened me up, Angelina. I never experienced anything like that before. With anyone. I never even dreamt it was possible. And it was because I trusted you. I haven't trusted anyone in," I counted on my fingers, "well, forever."

"I'm sorry. I didn't mean that what happened between us was bullshit." She wiped the snot from her nose with the sleeve of her parka. "I don't know what the fuck I mean anymore."

"What would you tell me if I were in your shoes?" She stood silently. "You'd tell me that I have all the answers, right? That all I have to do is be open to receiving them. That meditation is the only way to get in touch with that still, small voice that is the truth? Right?" I gently shook her, hoping it would evoke a response.

"I appreciate what you're trying to do here Rena, but it's not going to work." I didn't relent.

"Aren't you the one who told me that a relationship is about learning how to love, not needing someone to love you? I think what happened between us last night had more to do with needing someone to love us than it did with wanting to learn how to love. And both of us need to look at that." I stood back from her and shook off her fragility. "I'm willing. Are you?"

"How did you get to be so fucking smart?" She slapped my arm.

"If you want to be with David, you need to figure out what split you apart. The fact that he caught you with a woman is only the manifestation, not the reason."

"When did you learn all this?" She zipped her jacket up to her neck, the cold air and lack of motion causing her to shiver.

"I've listened. To Darla. To you. I've read most of the metaphysical books you have. And I'm trying to learn. I want to get better. I want to be better. I want to be happy."

"OK, OK. I heard you."

"Good." I turned her shoulders and pushed her toward the door. "Now go home and make some tea before you freeze to death. Bogota's fine. I'll keep an eye on him and call you if anything changes." She walked slowly up the driveway and I watched her for a little while before I returned to polishing the saddles. It took me a few hours to finish my chores and I returned to my cottage, anxious to draw a steamy bath and get a good night's sleep. It was only four, but it was February so the daylight was already beginning to fade. I struggled to stay awake after my bath, knowing that I'd have a tough time sleeping through the night if I napped.

I settled back onto the pillows of my couch and tried to keep my eyes open. Every time I closed them, images I didn't recognize were trying to force their way into my consciousness. In an attempt to prevent them from entering, I concentrated on Oprah's guest who was discussing the pros and cons of the latest exercise equipment. I went over in my head the tasks I had completed at the barn. I stared at the ceiling. But every time I closed my eyes, there they were. Nothing was working.

A small voice told me to ride it out. See what it was about. I argued with myself. I didn't want to know. But the pictures kept coming. "All right," I said to no one. "Buckle up, it's going to be a bumpy ride." Inhaling deeply, I started nadi sudi, an ancient Indian practice that cleanses the body of toxins. Breathing into one nostril while pinching the other, I moved my thumb and pinky finger from the closed nostril and exhaled. After several minutes, I was calm, the oxygen in my blood re-balanced.

Closing my eyes, I allowed the images to come. I saw a woman running through a field. She was dressed in a corset, prairie skirt, high-necked blouse, and boots. Her blond hair was piled on top of her head, two pearl hairpins securing it at the crown. I felt myself watching, as a child, from behind tall reeds as the woman, crying, continued running. The woman kept looking back, fearful of the person who was chasing her, her face twisted in pain.

My conscious and subconscious existed simultaneously, placing me in two places at the same time. It was like I was watching a movie and couldn't stop it. A man wearing a top hat and a cape appeared on a horse, closing in on the woman. As he got closer, he leapt off the horse, grabbing the woman around the neck and dragged her to the ground. She kicked and struggled and screamed.

I was too far away, safely hidden in the reeds, to hear the conversation. The man stood over the woman, his leather boot on her stomach. He ripped his cape off and knelt beside her, roughly pulling up her skirt. He ripped off her bloomers, his legs on each side of hers, trapping her. Unable to move, the woman looked at him in horror as he unbuckled his belt and mounted her. She screamed and pummeled his back with her fists, but he kept pumping.

"Why isn't anyone helping her?" I screamed in my head. "Why is this happening to her?" A large black woman appeared next to me in my hiding place. She wore a white turban and apron, worn work boots on her feet. "Hush, child," she chided. "You can't do anything to stop this. It's how it's supposed to be."

"Why?" I pleaded.

"It just is." And she was gone.

I looked back to the field. The man had collapsed on top of the woman and lay there, motionless, his need sated. The woman was sobbing, her hair undone and the white petticoat trapped under the man's left hand, resting near her shoulder on the grass. The man rolled off and lay on his back, his nakedness limp. The woman turned on her side, away from him, curling herself into a ball.

I didn't want to watch anymore. I kept trying to open my eyes, but it was as if they were glued shut. The Rena in the reeds was crying, devastated by what she witnessed. I wanted to kill the man. I wanted to run to the woman and comfort her.

The woman noticed the man's belt with its holster laying in the grass near her leg. Silently, barely moving, she slid the revolver out of the holster. She stood up and the man wrapped his hand around her ankle, almost knocking her off balance. She spun around, cocked the gun, and fired a shot into his chest. He gasped loudly and tried to sit up. She kept cocking and firing the revolver. Six shots. Until he lay still on the grass.

The woman screamed and threw the gun far into the field. She waved her hands in the air, yelling and sobbing. Then she grabbed her bloomers from beside the dead man, pulled them on, and climbed onto the horse. Her hair flying behind her, she rode off.

The movie was over. I had been detached consciously as I had watched, but now fear and pain and sadness grabbed hold of me. The emotional trio tap-danced in my belly and the tears finally came. I opened my eyes, afraid the dead man would be laying next to my bed. Sitting up, I realized this woman would be exiled for the rest of her life. Rape wasn't considered a crime then. She would be running until she died. How would she find any peace? How could she ever have a relationship, happiness, a family, knowing that at any moment she could be caught for murdering this man? A man who had raped her.

I sobbed for her, for what she had endured, for what she was going to endure. In the stillness, after the crying, a small voice spoke to me from my soul. "You are her."

"What?" I answered out loud.

"You are she. That is who you were the last time you were here."

"You're crazy," I said to myself.

"That is your soul from another lifetime," the voice continued. "You need to resolve this with who that man is today."

"This is insane!" I threw the covers off and stumbled into the bathroom, trying to escape the voice, the feeling, the knowing. I ran the water until it was very cold and splashed it on my face. There was no escape. The unwanted knowledge permeated every cell. The realization that something that violent had occurred trapped me in an invisible padded cell. I couldn't do any damage to myself trying to get out, yet the imprisonment still isolated me.

Freaking out about it wasn't going to solve anything, I told myself. Maybe if I meditated, things would become clearer.

"*This was too much for her.*" *Inanna was concerned.*

"*Hell, it was too much for me—and I'm a goddess,*" *Kali was in shock.*

"*The time was right,*" *insisted Kuan Yin.* "*It was time for her to know of her history.*"

"*But modern day humans really don't believe in past lives, Kuan Yin,*" *Kali argued.* "*She doesn't need to feel like a freak.*"

"*There are plenty of people who know the truth,*" *Kuan Yin argued.* "*This will enable her to find more truth seekers. If she chooses to talk about it.*"

"*This is terrible,*" *frowned Erishkigal, twisting her long hair around a finger.* "*Her whole life she's felt left out, not included. If she tells people about this, they're going to think she's crazy.*"

"*She needs to learn that not everyone is meant to hear everything,*" *instructed Kuan Yin.*

"*But we've already done the descent-to-the-Underworld thing,*" *Inanna shook her head.* "*It's not fair.*"

"*You're right,*" *Kuan Yin conceded.* "*But this is part of the ascent. Trust me.*"

"*Hey, look,*" *shouted Inanna.* "*There's my belt.*"

I sat in full lotus, months of stretching allowing my legs to finally get into the *asana*. A stick of jasmine incense burned in an ashtray. I breathed deeply, instructing myself to allow my mind to fall into the place between thoughts. My mind was not cooperating. Random images and thoughts ricocheted in my head. It was as though there were four distinct voices arguing silently inside my skull. One who thought I had gone off the deep end, one who wanted to ignore the entire episode, one who said it was from too much liquor last night and one who insisted it was the truth.

Unable to concentrate, I unfolded my legs and put a tape of chants in the stereo. The sitar whined and the calming words *Ishq Allah, Ma'bud Allah* filled the room.

Caught between my current reality and the one I experienced an hour ago, I began to cry. There was no energy left in my body to protect me. I was naked. But the only place to go was forward. I sat back down on the pillow, crossed my legs, and sang with the tape. Soon I was lulled by the music into a place I had never been before.

From deep in my belly came a voice, "Do not be afraid."

"But I'm terrified," I responded silently.

"Feel it."

"I don't want to."

"But you must. It's the only way through." The voice was strong. Tears rolled down my cheeks and I started shaking.

"Tell me."

"What you saw was a memory from another lifetime." I struggled not to think. "The woman you observed was you, a hundred and fifty years ago; the man, someone in your life today. What he did to you then caused you pain. But you responded with violence, with the same kind of hatred that he displayed toward you."

"He raped me," I defended myself silently. "How was I supposed to respond?"

"With forgiveness."

"No." I screamed out loud.

"It's the only way to move on. The sole reason you're in this world, on this plane, is to forgive."

"But he hurt me."

"You cannot be hurt. Your soul is incapable of it. You may experience the appearance of being hurt. And as long you allow yourself that perception, you're going to be trapped in this cycle until you find a way to forgive him."

"I don't want to."

"It's the only way out. It's the only way to prevent you two from hurting each other in the next life."

"He's a son of a bitch. He should have never done what he did."

"Who are you to say that? Your perspective, your understanding is so limited. The facts are not always the truth."

"Whose truth?"

"The only truth is love and forgiveness." I stilled the voice and tried to absorb what I'd been told. It was true, I had been caught in the net of resentment and anger and self-righteousness for a long time. But how could I be expected to forgive this man, whoever he was now, for what he did? Would it really free me?

"Yes," answered the voice.

"Who are you?"

"I am Shakti, *devi* of all female energy. Since the beginning of time I have known that love is the only answer."

"I don't believe you."

"Why do you think you have such a difficult time with your menstrual cycle? The cramps, the backaches, the heavy bleeding. Your female center is off balance. Your sexuality has been an issue for you for hundreds of years. Work on forgiving and see what happens."

"That's really the reason?"

"Every emotion you hold onto manifests itself in your body. You've studied enough to know that to be the truth. You never wanted to look at it before."

"Why now?"

"You have been studying, searching for the truth. You've read, you've discussed, and you've questioned. You asked for the truth and it's being given to you."

"But you haven't told me who that man was."

"It's not time yet."

"That's not fair."

"Trust that all information necessary to the fulfillment of your Divine Plan will be released to your consciousness when it is time."

"What do I do in the meantime?"

"Continue to grow. Look at every experience as an opportunity to learn."

The tape player clicked; the music over. I sat very still, afraid to move. I wiped the tears away from my cheeks and unfolded my legs. My foot was asleep.

"What a terrible thing to do to her!" Erishkigal was crying.

"I can't believe I'm going to agree with the great and powerful simperer, but that was awful," agreed Kali.

"It was neither good nor bad," Kuan Yin insisted. "It simply was."

"I've always known you were out there, KY, but how can it not be good or bad?" Kali demanded.

"Try to let go of your judgments, Kali," she turned to her other sisters. "You as well. You all are looking at her experiences from your limited

understanding, which is based solely on your own experiences. But you heard Shakti, a fact is not necessarily the truth."

"What the hell are you talking about?" Inanna's logical brain was in a tizzy.

"The fact is that Rena left a job where she was making over $100,000 a year to move to New Jersey to clean stalls and groom horses. Some," she nodded at the three goddesses, "think she's insane. The truth is that she's happier doing this than she has been with anything else in her life."

"What about Angelina? Is Rena a lesbian?" Erishkigal shivered.

"It's up to Rena to determine what she wants from life," Kuan Yin twirled her pearl hairpin. "But can't you see that she is opening up to new experiences? That fear is not the number one factor controlling her life?"

"She wasn't afraid when I was in control," Kali argued.

"Oh, yes she was," Kuan Yin was firm. "She was terrified of dealing with the pain that ending her relationship with Richard caused, so she drank and snorted and fucked her way through it instead." Kali hung her head and skulked away.

"I only wanted what was best for her. She wasn't scared when I was guiding her." Inanna leaned righteously into Kuan Yin's face.

"No?" Kuan Yin smiled at her as if she were a child. "Rena completely obeyed what she deemed to be authority out of fear of the consequences."

"But," Inanna started. Kuan Yin held up her hand.

"Remember the time that some of the stations on her team were broadcasting the comeback fight for Mike Tyson? And Rena told Lynn she refused to sell commercials in it?"

"He would've fired her if she'd stood her ground," insisted Inanna.

"Are you sure about that? It could've been an empty threat. But she was too scared to stand firm in her convictions and find out." Inanna joined Kali scrunched in the corner. Erishkigal and Kuan Yin were quiet, their gazes locked.

"It's time for her to be open, to not be motivated by fear. Who knows what glorious things can happen?" Kuan Yin beamed and extended her hands. "Rejoice with me, sisters. Rena has opened the door." Inanna stood and walked toward Kuan Yin.

"Look!" cried Kali pointing at Inanna's feet. "There are your sandals!"

For weeks, I searched for the man in my vision in the face of everyone that I encountered. At the grocery store. The library. Dunkin Donuts. I'd get as close as I could, hoping for a flicker of recognition. Shakti's words of faith about me knowing only when it was time echoed, but I couldn't stop hunting. I wondered if it was Richard. We'd certainly had enough issues. It took me a few days to work up the nerve, but I finally called directory assistance and got his number. Even if it wasn't him, I owed him an apology for treating him the way I did.

"Richard?" I thought about hanging up.

"Yes." He sounded tired.

"It's Rena." Silence. "I'm calling to apologize."

"For what?"

"The shitty way I treated you the last time we were together." I paused. "I was in a lot of pain, Richard. I was angry and hurt at the way our relationship ended. I could've found a more productive way to express that."

"Yeah, you could have."

"I wasn't capable of it then. I'm sorry."

"You're not the only one to blame here, Rena. I was a complete ass for a lot of the time we were together."

"No argument here." I laughed. He joined me. "How are you?"

"Pretty good. I'm actually being transferred to San Francisco next month."

"You're leaving New York?"

"I know. I never thought I would. But I've got an opportunity to open their new West Coast office. I couldn't pass it up." He cleared his throat. "What are you doing?"

"I stopped trolling the East Village not long after that night, buckled down at work, and really got the promotion I told you I already had."

"Oh," he said like he'd discovered the Theory of Relativity. "That's why you were so testy about the money I was making."

"Yeah." I winced. I filled him in on the next few years with Joni and then Silverman and Washburn. A half-hour later, I finished by telling him about Tartan Farm and Angelina. Well, not our extracurricular activities, but I explained what it was like taking care of the horses and told him a little about Angelina and David.

"You sound really happy, Rena."

"I am." I realized. "Leaving that corporate grind was the best decision I've ever made." The conversation came to a natural close, both of us having spoken our peace.

"I'm glad you called. Thank you for apologizing. And I hope you know I'm sorry, too."

"I do. Good luck in San Francisco."

"Thanks. If you ever get out that way, call me."

"I'll do that." I hung up, curled my feet under the cushion of the sofa, and closed my eyes, knowing he wasn't the man I saw in my vision. It felt good to take responsibility for my actions. He certainly hadn't been perfect, but I couldn't control his behavior, only mine.

Breathe

The summer started hot and humid. That morning, Angelina had told me that after several weeks of talking on the phone, she and David were planning a date for the weekend. We never had another physical encounter after that night, even though we continued to share dinner once a week and worked side by side in the barn most days. I wasn't interested in her as a partner, yet I was experiencing the sting of the green-eyed monster. I hurried through cleaning the stalls and in my rush to be alone, almost ran into the delivery truck from Bud's.

Angelina had taken Bogota out for a ride, so I turned around and waited while Jack unloaded the supplies. I sat on a bale of hay, watching his tanned muscles ripple under his T-shirt. Sweat poured off his face. "It sure is hot for so early in the morning," he commented, tossing bags of wood shavings from the flatbed. I heard him from a distance, my head still swirling from Angelina's disclosure. "Has the sun fried your brain already?" He snapped his fingers in front of me.

"Huh?" I held my hand above my eyes to block out the sun.

"Are you OK?"

"Yeah, fine, why?"

"'Cause you're sitting there looking like someone just sentenced you to thirty years in the county jail." He pulled a bandana from his back pocket and wiped his face.

"No, no," I shook my head. "I just have a lot on my mind, that's all."

"Sometimes, it helps to talk."

"No, really, I'm OK. But you look like you're going to expire. Can I get you a drink of water?"

"That'd be wonderful," he smiled broadly, the gap in his front teeth yawning at me. I went into the bathroom and ran the faucet until the water was ice cold. I filled a cup and brought it to him.

"Thanks, Rena." He took a sip and then poured the rest of it over his head.

"Would you like a towel?" I laughed, water dripping from his nose and chin.

"Do you have one?" he asked hopefully. I returned to the bathroom and threw the towel at him from the doorway.

"How do you stay so cool?" he asked.

"It's an illusion. I am Queen of the Sweat People." I held my arms out, sweeping into an exaggerated bow. "The only reason I appear cool is because I've already mucked the stalls and had a cold shower." As I walked toward him I noticed his neck was sunburned.

"Get enough beach time in?" I joked, pointing to his neck.

"I lifeguard on the weekends at the beach in Poplar's Cape." He rubbed the towel over his wet hair and dried his face.

"That explains the tan," I nodded, admiring his hard body as much as the color.

"You ought to come down some weekend," he smiled and winked. "Lots of gorgeous men, Rena."

"So you're not asking me on a date?" I fanned myself like a Southern belle.

"I wish I could." I cocked my head and questioned him with my eyes. "You're not my type," he said.

"Oh, you go for the blond model type?"

"Yeah, the kind with a dick." He blinked and then held my gaze, gold flecks twinkling in the sunlight.

"So I don't have to take it personally then?" I asked, relieved.

"I know plenty of those straight boys who'd make a play for you," he pinched my cheek with his callused fingers. "I work ten to two Saturday and Sunday. Beach area two." He kissed my cheek, climbed into the truck and turned over the engine. I followed him out of the driveway, anxious to dive into a cocoon of solitude.

I drove down 537 on my way to Freehold, the air conditioning and Z-100 cranked. I loved going out for random drives. Every couple of weeks, I would get in the car and purposely turn onto a street I wasn't familiar with to see how long it would take me to recognize something. I had found some great antique stores and cafes this way. And I was the queen of shortcuts. It was also very therapeutic.

I drove past the new developments being built in Colt's Neck and into Freehold. The Freehold Grill Diner still wore the original edifice from the 1950s and had the best coffee around. I grabbed a newspaper from the stack on the counter and plopped into a booth. "What can I get you, honey?"

Doris' robotic voice came from a device in her throat that was placed there after part of her esophagus was removed. Two packs of Newports a day for forty years had singed it beyond repair.

"Coffee, Do'. Decaf. And cream, not milk." I noticed the apron on her pink uniform was clean today. It was usually peppered with clam chowder broth and grease from the fryer. She scribbled on her order pad and pulled several tiny plastic cups of half-and-half from her pocket. I flipped through the paper to see what was going on in the world. A chipped china mug clattered on the Formica table as Doris dropped it in front of me. She poured the hot liquid into it, the steam from the nectar rising into my nose.

"How've you been Rena?" She asked, holding the button on her throat.

"Good, Do'. You?" I stirred a Sweet 'n Low into the coffee.

"Same old, same old." She rested the glass pot on the table. "How's Angelina?" I had brought her here for breakfast a couple of times.

"She's fine. She and her ex-husband have a date this weekend."

"Do you think they'll get back together?" The hairnet holding in her thick gray bun was torn and a few stray hairs peeked out.

"I don't know," I answered. "I don't know if they should."

"Sounds to me like that's not for you to decide." My spoon clanked against the china cup.

"You're right. I don't know why it matters."

"You care about her, that's all." She picked up the pot. "Get you anything else?" I ordered a toasted bagel with cream cheese. She brought it out to me a few minutes later and I bit into it, the crunchy seeds mixing nicely with the smooth texture of the cream cheese. I tried to take my time, but devoured it in only a few bites. As I paid the check, I knew I had to go home and talk to Angelina.

I left a two-dollar tip and said good-bye to Doris. "You take care, Rena," she commanded in the stilted voice emanating from her throat.

"I will, Doris. You, too." The soggy air made my skin damp. Clouds had rolled in and it looked like rain. I hurried back to the farm in case Angelina wanted to bring in the horses. As I pulled down the driveway, I saw an unfamiliar car parked near the barn. I left my Volkswagen near the cottage and walked to the barn. Inside I found Angelina talking to a tall, well-built man with blond hair.

"Hey," I let them know I was there. "I came back. It looks like rain. I didn't know if you'd want to bring the horses in." I continued walking toward them. "Hi, I'm Rena," I held out my hand and he took it.

"David Hennerton."

"What are you doing here?" I blurted and they both stared at me. "What I meant was, I know you work in the city, that's all. And we're in Jersey." I realized I was stammering so I grabbed a couple of lead ropes from the wall to hide my burning cheeks. "I'll go get started." I turned around to leave.

"I was visiting a client in Rumson," David offered. "I thought I'd stop by and say hello." He smiled at me, his teeth white and perfectly aligned.

"It was nice meeting you," I forced a smile and headed outside.

"Rena, I'll be out to help you in a minute." Angelina called. A little while later, I heard David's Jag and noticed Angelina sprinting toward me as I walked Bogota and Seuss back to the barn. She stopped a few feet from me.

"What the hell is going on, Rena?"

"What are you talking about?" I tap-danced in my head, trying to quickly fabricate a story that would explain my behavior.

"The way you acted with David. The way you acted this morning when I told you we'd been talking." She took Bogota's lead rope from me. "We need to have a conversation." We returned the rest of the horses to the barn in silence.

"Why don't you get changed and come up to the house," she offered. I took a shower. Then I changed my sheets. Then I made a list for the grocery store. At four I couldn't think of anything else to do, so I walked in the rain to Angelina's, actually Angelina and David's house. The aroma of coffee greeted me when I opened the sliding glass door.

I sat sullenly on the couch, waiting for her to bring in the coffee. "I'm glad you were paying attention to the weather," she said. "It would've been a real pain in the ass trying to get them all back in during this storm." She filled our mugs and leaned back on the cushion, carefully folding her legs up under her. Blowing on the coffee, I noticed the tension lines that had marked her forehead for as long as I had known her were gone.

"I'm sorry," I put my cup on the table. "I don't know what the hell is wrong with me."

"It's OK. Let's try to figure it out." She was dressed in turquoise terry-cloth shorts and a pink-and-yellow halter top, the fullness of her breasts visible around the edges. "Everything was fine until this morning when I told you about David."

"I've gone over this in my head a million times," I confessed. "I'm OK with the fact that we're not together. I like men. I don't want to be in a serious relationship with a woman." I didn't want to insult her. "I love you,

Angelina, but not in that way." I sighed. "That's why I'm so frustrated, trying to figure out why I feel jealous."

"It's taken me months to accept my role in David's decision to leave," she stirred more sweetener into her coffee. "I was never satisfied with anything. That's why he compulsively bought me things. The paintings. Jewelry. This farm." Her arm swept around her toward the door overlooking the barn. "He felt like he could never please me. And he got tired of trying, Rena. And I had the perfect excuse to fulfill my own prophecy that no one was ever going to be able to give me what I needed or wanted."

"Or deserved," I added.

"You're kind," she patted my leg. "Despite all the work I'd done on myself, the yoga, the meditating, the reading, I wasn't happy with me. Realizing that a couple of months ago made me very sad. I felt like I've worked so hard. Shouldn't I be further along the path than that?"

"You're always the one telling me what a process it is," I interjected.

"I understand that, but it didn't make it any easier to deal with in the moment." Her eyes watered and she rubbed them, whisking away the tears. "My whole life I've searched outside for validation, acceptance. I never permitted myself to look for it inside. And for someone who considers herself to have been on a spiritual path for the last ten years, trust me, that hurt." We sat in silence for a minute, her words hanging in the cool air while the rain pelted the concrete patio and the wind brushed the branches of the trees against the windows upstairs.

"I've been seeing a therapist the last few months, Rena." Her confession stunned me. She had adamantly been against Darla trying therapy a year ago, claiming that all the answers were inside. It was as if she read my mind. "I know what I told Darla. I was wrong." She scratched a mosquito bite on her ankle. It was angry and red.

"What I didn't realize is that the more aware you become, the more clever your demons get. They don't want to be banished, so they learn how to be resourceful and, without even realizing it, they weave their fears into your thoughts and actions. It's insidious." I wasn't sure I fully understood what she meant, but it seemed to make sense to her.

"What I realized is that David and I are soul mates."

"Soul mates or wound mates?" I said, parroting from a book I read by Carolyn Myss.

"That's not fair, Rena." She rose and went to the kitchen. I was about to follow her when she returned with an ice cube wrapped in a paper towel.

"All I know is that trying to work things out with David is what I have to do right now. And I'm sorry that I sprung it on you this morning. You had no idea of most of this process I've been going through. It probably wasn't fair."

"As long as it makes you happy." I still wasn't sure it was right for her, but I did my best to appear sincere.

"So why do you think you were so affected?" She rubbed the ice on her ankle and the red dissipated.

"I don't know. I guess I need to work on that."

"Do you mind an amateur interpretation?"

"Of course not," I hugged my knees, shielding myself from whatever she might say that I didn't want to hear.

"From what you've told me, you didn't feel very loved as a kid. You attracted all kinds of people and situations to you that were a reflection of that. Richard wasn't in a place to really love you. Neither was Celia." She wrung the wet towel into her empty coffee cup. "Maristel was the only one you've ever mentioned who offered you pretty much unconditional love, but you weren't ready to accept it. Am I on target so far?"

"Yes," I whispered, rocking back and forth.

"Joni never really gave you the recognition you needed or deserved. And that sales job ate a piece of your soul every day you were there. Then you came here. And not only did I accept you for who you were, but you were also ready to accept at least part of that." I felt a tingling in my nose and knew that tears weren't far behind.

"Then we ended up making love that night, both of us motivated by wanting to be loved instead of the real reason to be involved in a relationship, to learn how to love. I think that on some level you're afraid that if David and I get back together, I won't love you anymore. And also that if I don't offer you that kind of unconditional love, no one else will." She scooted down the couch and wrapped her arm around my shoulders. "And that's not true, Rena." She wiped my tears with the damp paper towel and the coolness soothed my burning cheeks. "You've made the commitment to unfold, to discover who you are. I know that includes sharing your life with someone. Be patient." I couldn't speak.

I sat there sobbing while she comforted me and handed me tissues. Eventually, my breakdown ran its course and petered out. I wiped my eyes and drank the glass of water she had left on the table. "You've been so good to me. I don't want to lose that," I admitted.

"That's not going to happen," she promised. "No matter what happens between David and me." I took a deep breath and told her about my vision.

"That is so cool," she was excited. "I've had to pay two hundred dollars to have a regression done and you managed to do it on your own. For free."

"Do you really think that's what it was?"

"Definitely," she nodded her head, her blue eyes huge and focused. "You'll just have to wait and see who it is now."

"But I want to know."

"You can't rush stuff like this," she lectured. "When it's time, you'll know. And there won't be any stopping it."

Breathe

The next time Jack made a delivery, he convinced me to go dancing with him in New York Thursday night. I hadn't been out since I'd moved to the farm, and, according to Jack, I needed to get my ass out of Jersey and mingle. My bedroom was strewn with the outfits I had tried on and vetoed for numerous reasons. Working on the farm had magically melted some of my excess weight, but I still wasn't happy. I wasn't sure I ever would be.

The gray skirt made my stomach look huge. My butt appeared to double in size when I put on the black stretch pants. And the lavender sweater made me look like a linebacker. I finally settled on a long black tank dress with an oversized peach shirt. "You look fabulous, darling," he kissed each cheek and presented me with a bouquet of wild flowers.

"You didn't have to do that," I insisted while digging for a vase.

"I know I didn't. I wanted to."

"Well, it was very sweet of you." I placed them in the vase I'd bought with Darla in Coney Island and watched him flick around the channels, intently watching the screen. "I'm ready whenever you are." He snapped back to reality and we headed toward the city, a six pack of Budweiser in a lunch cooler between us in his Chevy Nova.

The traffic at the Lincoln Tunnel was backed up around the curve past Union City. We crawled for twenty minutes before hitting the tollbooth. Then it was another twenty to get through the tunnel. "Where are we going?" I had neglected to ask him that question before I got in the car.

"The Men's Room is having a party tonight. I thought we'd start there first."

"The Men's Room?"

"Yeah," he looked over at me and winked. "It's a theme kind of thing." He scratched his head. "Basically, there are a bunch of theme parties and they rotate around different locations. They have the Ladies' Room, which is for dykes. Then there's the S&M room." The way he smiled revealed a side of him I wasn't aware of and wasn't sure I wanted to know. "Anyway, you get the idea."

"So, the Men's Room, I'm guessing is for gay men?"

"That's what I love about you. You're so quick."

"So basically what you're telling me is that I got all dolled up to hit the dance floor with a bunch of homosexuals?" I flopped my hand in the air.

"Rena, you haven't been out in so long," he patted my knee. "I figured it might be easier for you to let your hair down if there wasn't a chance that somebody was going to try and pick you up."

"That's lovely, Jack. So you have the opportunity to get lucky, and I get to drool over all the gorgeous men who have absolutely no interest in me or my voluptuous breasts." I stuck my out chest and tilted my chin in the air.

"We don't have to stay there the entire time," he offered. "The Limelight's not too far away."

"We can play it by ear," I joked. "But this is the last time I go anywhere with you without getting a complete itinerary first." We parked in the lot on Sixth Avenue where the Flea Market takes place during the weekend days and walked toward Broadway.

"This is it." He held open a steel door that appeared to guard the entrance to a sweatshop. The building had graffiti spray painted on the facade, and there was no sign indicating the name of the club.

"Are you sure," I hesitated, peering inside the doorway. All I saw was a dimly lit staircase with a metal railing. Then I noticed a flyer, hung with masking tape, above the steps. "Men's Room—Hosted by the Sweat Factory. Party all night long with DJ Pepper Rivera. Half-price well drinks 'til 11pm. Private meeting rooms available. Come hang if you're hung." A faded photocopied image of two ripped guys dancing in boxer shorts was in the middle of the copy.

"Oaky, dokey, pokey!" I made a face and entered the vestibule wondering what I had gotten myself into this time.

"This seems more like my turf, Kuan Yin," Kali chuckled. "Aren't you a little out of your league here?"

"It's all part of the unfoldment, Kali," Kuan Yin assured her.

"It could be a little dicey in there. Do you want me to go first?" Kali swept her sword from its holder and stood in warrior pose.

"No thank you," Erishkigal, Inanna and Kuan Yin replied in unison.

"Good God," sighed Erishkigal, "with some of the places you dragged us to, I'm sure this will be a walk in the park."

"Don't count on it," warned Kuan Yin.

The dance floor was empty and a handful of men circled around the bars set up at each end. Jack looked at his watch. "We're a bit early, I guess. Things don't really get moving until midnight or so."

"What time is it?"

"Ten forty-five." He smoothed his palms over his black jeans. The white T-shirt he wore showed off his tan and a thin leather belt encircled his slender waist. "What do you want to drink?"

"Vodka and tonic, please. Two limes."

"Women." He rolled his eyes.

I noticed the other men in the club as he sauntered to the bar. I observed them as if I was on an African Safari. Their energy was predatory and focused, zooming in on whatever part of Jack's body pleased them the most. He returned with a bottle of beer and a plastic cup.

"Jesus!" I said accepting mine. "Could those guys have been any more obvious about the fact that they wanted to rip your clothes off?"

"I didn't even notice," he replied wrapping his mouth around the neck of his Bud.

"Why don't we sit down? It'll start to get crowded in the next half-hour or so." We claimed two stools at the closest bar and I squeezed the limes into my drink. Multi-colored lights flashed over the dance floor and I noticed a few small cocktail tables and chairs scattered near the bars. The ceilings were thirty feet high and exposed pipes wove a maze over our heads.

"So, handsome, come here often?" I threw my arm around him.

"You better watch it," he laughed. "You don't need them thinking you're a drag queen."

"Thanks a lot." I recoiled my arm and got a cigarette from my purse. I only smoked when I went out drinking. And that wasn't too often.

"That didn't come out right," he apologized. "You don't look like one." His eyes swept me from head to toe. "At all. It's just that sometimes people see what they want to see and I don't want you to, never mind. I'm sorry."

"Were you being protective of me?" I fanned myself with my hand.

"You're not exactly used to moving in these circles." He put his empty bottle on the bar and ordered another. "It can be surreal." We sat it silence for a few minutes, listening to the house music and watching a black and white episode of *My Favorite Martian* on the enormous screen on the far side of the bar. The same video was playing on the three smaller screens surrounding the dance floor.

"How long have you lived in Jersey?" I asked, wanting to close the gap between us.

"Since I was seventeen, so that's, what, seven years."

"Where were you before?" I sucked on an ice cube, wanting to pace myself with the alcohol.

"Allentown." He let out a small sigh. "That's in Pennsylvania."

"I know where it is. I'm from Pittsburgh."

"Really? My one sister lives there now."

"What brought you to Jersey? It certainly wasn't the lure of easy driving," I joked referring to my constant whining about the jughandles.

"I came to live with my Aunt Jo in Keyport. She's my mother's sister."

"So," I recapped, "you finished high school and came to Keyport to live with your mom's sister because …." He poured the rest of his beer down his throat. I felt the burn.

"My mom died from MS when I was ten. I don't remember her ever being healthy. I guess I kind of flipped out my senior year in high school because I was ready to drop out of school and join the army. I had to get out of there." He laid a ten-dollar bill on the bar and signaled for another beer.

"My dad called my Aunt Jo and asked if I could stay with her for a while. She has a son my age and my dad thought he might be a good influence." He laughed. "Only problem was, Jake is a coke addict." He sipped his Bud. "Funny thing is, he actually was a good influence because he made me realize I never wanted to fuck around with drugs like that." I wasn't sure what to say next.

"You don't have to say anything," he read my thoughts. "I wasn't dealt the best hand in the world. But you do with it what you can, that's all." He turned around to face the dance floor, his back against the bar. "So, Miss Rena, what about you? What's your sad story?"

"I moved to New York eight years ago for kind of the same reason. I had to get out of Pittsburgh. My parents had finally gotten divorced after twenty some years of bickering and cheating." I swung around to join him. "I graduated from college and couldn't find a job. My father had an old friend who worked in advertising and he got me an interview with this company called JC Communications." We looked out over the club, watching as it began to fill.

"Then I got into sales and after a few years finally admitted to myself that I was miserable. My yoga teacher is friends with Angelina, and the rest, as they say, is history."

"Well, I'm glad your yoga teacher is friends with Angelina," he tipped his beer bottle and I tapped it with my plastic glass. "Do you know what my dad is doing right now?" He peeled the label from the bottle. "He and his girlfriend, Dolores, are driving to the Grand Canyon in a Winnebago." He laughed. "Can you believe that?"

"I think it's kind of sweet," I sucked on a strand of lime through my teeth. "A bit clichéd perhaps, but sweet."

"It's pathetic." He swallowed his beer and his Adam's apple shifted up and down. "My mother's been gone seventeen years. He never dated while I was growing up. He worked and slept. That's it. And now, he's trapped in a two-ton hunk of steel with this crazy seventy-year-old woman who's the widow of one of his masonry buddies. And they're driving, probably more like crawling, all the way to Arizona."

"Where do you want to go on vacation?"

"I've never had a vacation in my life. But I can sure as hell tell you the first time I take one, it won't be in a fucking Winnebago." The music had grown louder and we were shouting to be heard. Men poured in from the doorway. Some wore jeans. Others were dressed for an evening out in satin shirts and silk pants. A tall brunette sashayed by in a red miniskirt and halter-top, his make-up more up-to-date than mine.

"See what I mean?" Jack tapped my arm.

"I don't think I fulfill the height requirement," I laughed. "I'd need six-inch heels." I glanced up at the video screen and gasped. In full color spectravision was a man squeezing what, Jack later told me, was a cock ring over his huge erection.

"It lets you stay hard for hours," Jack informed me. "And without having an orgasm. It's an amazing little device." I looked away but didn't want to seem like a prude. I casually looked up and saw a tanned blond man with ripped abs receiving fellatio from a mustached man on his knees. Whoever shot the film wanted to make sure we saw exactly how it was done. No one else in the room seemed to notice the sex act occurring on a six-foot screen.

I excused myself, needing to pee. Only there was no ladies' room. I was in a gay male club. What use did they have for a women's bathroom? I strutted into the one bathroom, past the two men standing at the urinals and headed for a stall. I tried the first one and the door opened easily when I pulled. Inside, bent over the toilet was a naked man, his ass shining toward me and his hands gripping the silver plumbing above the commode. Standing behind him and directly in front of me, was an older man, pants still on, just unzipped, humping away.

I quickly shut the door and gratefully collapsed in the neighboring stall and attempted to block out the groaning and gasping from my bathroom buddies. I ran out without washing my hands, getting back to Jack the only thing on my mind. When I returned to our seats at the bar, he was gone. I scanned the dance floor. Everyone was gyrating to Madonna's "Vogue." But Jack was nowhere in sight.

I slid onto my stool and squeezed in between two muscular Latino men. I was beginning to believe that twenty-inch biceps were a requirement for homosexuality. I ordered a cocktail and tried to drink it slowly. I gnawed the plastic stirrer and had a dozen conversations in my head imagining what I was going to say to Jack when he returned. Four vodka tonics later, I was bleary eyed and pissed, tapping my foot on the rung of my seat.

I turned around to watch the dancers and saw that a table had been dragged into the middle of the floor and a young Latino man in boxer shorts and hiking boots was dancing on top of it. He pumped his pelvis back and forth to the beat and several men circled around the table cheering him on. He didn't even look old enough to have a fake ID. I pushed myself back to face the bar and ordered another drink. The bartender placed the glass on a napkin in front of me. I was stirring it absently when I felt a hand on my shoulder.

"Hey," Jack shouted in my ear, "having a good time?" I spun around and glared at him.

"Sure, Jack, great time." I slurred my words. "Sitting here in a room full of faggots, drowning my sorrows in generic vodka and wondering what could've possibly distracted the friend who dragged me here." I shot spittle onto his cheek when I said "possibly."

"I'm sorry, Rena. I met someone." I noticed a tall black man in cutoff jeans standing behind him. He came up behind him wrapped his hands around Jack's middle and nuzzled his neck.

"So what were you doing for an hour that you needed to be alone with him?" I answered my own question, images of the two men in the bathroom and the words "private meeting rooms" meeting in my mind.

"You know how it is." He turned his head and kissed his short shorts friend.

"No, Jack, I don't. Why don't you tell me." He stood there, silent while his friend caressed his nipples through his T-shirt. "Were you just going to die if you didn't get your dick sucked tonight? Going out with me wasn't enough excitement for you? You had to find some stranger to fuck anonymously? Is that it?"

"You're drunk."

"And you're a typical fag, not giving a shit about anything besides getting off." He squinted like I'd hit him with a right hook. "I want to go home." I hopped off the stool and slung my bag over my shoulder.

"Come one, Rena. It's only one."

"You've already had it your way once tonight," I snapped. I waited at the doorway, watching him kiss the man who, for an hour, had not been a stranger. We walked to the parking lot in silence.

The drive home took forever. I sneaked looks at him while he sped down the Parkway, trying to see if the sex made him look different. It had been so long since I'd had sex I struggled to remember how it felt to be touched. His brows were furrowed and the muscles in his forearms kept twitching as he gripped the steering wheel. I wanted to ask him what made him do it. But my mouth was sour from the alcohol and I was afraid if I spoke, I would throw up. He spun into my driveway and I got out, not saying a word. I gently shut the door and he sped off, tires squealing.

The room was spinning as I lay in bed. I bargained with God, promising not to drink ever again if only I could get off the merry-go-round. I eventually passed out and was woken by someone pounding on my door. Holding my head at the temples, I threw a robe around my naked body and shuffled into the living room. "Who is it?" I whispered through the door.

"It's Angelina. Are you OK?" I opened the door a crack, a sliver of sunlight blinding me.

"What time is it?"

"Ten-thirty. I came down to the barn and all the horses were still in their stalls. No food. No water. What's going on?" She came in and while I downed a handful of aspirin, I told her what had happened with Jack.

"I'm really sorry, Angelina. Let me throw myself in the shower and I'll be down in fifteen minutes." I met her in the barn, the day already sweltering and moist. Together, we took care of the horses and got them outside. My arms and legs felt like rubber and my stomach was a volcano waiting to erupt.

"You look a little green," she giggled. "Why don't we go up to the house and get some iced tea?"

"Are you mad at me?" I asked sheepishly.

"No, concerned maybe, but not mad. The horses are out. They've been fed and the stalls are clean. No harm done." The air conditioning was a welcome change from the steamy outdoors. She put ice in two glasses and set a pitcher on the table. The tea was absorbed immediately into the cotton that someone had stuffed in my mouth and I quickly drank two glasses.

"You better be careful," she warned. "You don't need it coming right back up. I know you're dehydrated, but small sips are going to work a whole lot better. Trust me." I obeyed, reducing the size of my gulps. The throbbing in my head began to subside. "Do you want to lay down?" I nodded. She guided me to the sofa in the living room and placed a cool wet rag on my forehead.

I woke up an hour later feeling much better. Angelina was watching me from the overstuffed chair in the corner. "Well, Princess, bet you won't be doing that again anytime soon." I slowly nodded, testing the ratio of movement to pain. I pushed myself up against the cushion. "How about some soup?"

"That sounds really good," I licked my lips. "And water. With lots of ice." She left and came back carrying a tray of chicken soup, saltines, and ice water. I dug in hungrily but then remembering her advice about the iced tea, downshifted from inhale to devour. When I was finished, I laid back and pulled the blanket she had covered me with up to my neck.

"So, what really happened?" She sat in the chair, one leg dangling over the arm.

"I told you." I reached for the glass of water.

"You told me Jack abandoned you for an hour and that you got nice and drunk on cheap vodka. Something tells me there's more to the story." I sighed, knowing that I would tell her the truth. When I was finished, she pulled her leg under her and placed the other one on top.

"So, why were you really mad?"

"He wandered off to get a blow job from some stranger and left me at the bar alone, isn't that reason enough?"

"Of course it is. If you don't want to find out what it was really about."

"What are you talking about?" I wasn't up for an esoteric exploration of the roots of my feelings.

"Nothing is ever that one-sided, Rena. It would be very easy to blame him for the entire thing. And on the surface, that's totally legitimate." She leaned her elbows on her knees and propped her face in her hands. "But you and I both know that what he did pushed a button."

"No buttons, here," I laughed. "Just someone who I thought was a friend ditching me for anonymous sex." She wouldn't stop staring at me.

"What?" I snapped. "What?"

"May I?"

"Me and what army are going to stop you?"

"If you don't want me to say anything, I won't." I didn't want to hear what she wanted to tell me.

"Go ahead." I closed my eyes and tossed the rag, which was now room temperature, over my eyes.

"You used to be just like that." I ripped the towel off my face, scrunched it into a ball and threw it at her. "It's true. From what you told me, you and Celia have stories that could rival Jack's from last night."

"That was different." She cocked an eyebrow. "It was," I defended. "You and I discussed this how many times? I was attracting people like that to me because I didn't believe I could get unconditional love. But I was only self-destructive. I didn't hurt anyone else." That damned eyebrow of hers was relentless.

"What about blowing off Maristel? What about what you did to Richard?" I hugged my shins.

"You just had to say it, didn't you?" I knocked my forehead against my knees.

"I asked permission." She came over and sat next to me on the couch. I punched the pillow and let out a scream.

"You mean he's in as much pain as I was then?" The sting in my eyes made them water. She nodded.

"He needs your compassion and understanding, Rena. Not your judgment."

"But he left me alone."

"You could have struck up a conversation with whoever was around you. You didn't have to sit there and sulk. And you certainly didn't have to get drunk."

"So now what?"

"You need to talk to him."

"He's furious with me. He didn't say a word the whole way home." I winced, remembering him racing off.

"Appreciate where he is, Rena. You've come a long way in a few years. You've already started to blossom like a tree in the spring. Jack's still naked and leafless. But just because you can't see the blooms doesn't mean they're not already there."

We headed outside to bring the horses in. I walked Bogota back to the barn while Angelina led Peacock and Jezebel. The foal had grown into her head and legs in the last few months and walked more gracefully. We collected Alabaster and Seuss and returned them to their stalls. Helga's breeding trip had been successful and she was pregnant, but the vet didn't want her traveling because her blood pressure was high. He preferred that she have the baby in West Palm Beach.

I got a second shower and put on my satin pajamas, loving the soft feeling against my skin. I lit a few candles and put on an Etta James CD. I started the conversation with Jack out loud, wanting to rehearse enough to give myself a comfort zone. Finally, I said a quick prayer and picked up the phone to dial his number. He picked up after three rings.

"Hey," My heart was racing. "How are you?"

"Fine." I shivered from the tone.

"I'm calling to apologize."

"You should."

"You're not going to make this easy, are you?"

"Nope." I thought I heard him smile.

"So, what do I need to do? Wash your work clothes for a week? Unload the truck for you the next time you make a delivery?"

"That's a start."

"Are you going to let me off the hook?"

"I'll think about it." Silence. "OK, I've thought about it."

"And?"

"You buy me dinner tonight and we'll call it even." I told him I'd pick him up at seven. I beeped my horn outside the tiny house in Belford where

Jack rented the 3rd floor and waited. He climbed into the car, the fresh scent of soap trailing him. He leaned over and kissed my cheek.

"How's Mexican sound?" I asked.

"Fine, as long as it doesn't involve tequila," he laughed. We drove to Mi Amigos and ordered enchiladas and iced tea. I crunched a tortilla chip and watched him stir sugar into his tea.

"You know there's a reason I acted the way I did last night," I offered. He continued to stir his tea, the ice cubes tinkling against the glass and harmonizing with the music from the Mariachi band flowing out of the speaker next to our table. "I was pretty wild at one point when I lived in the city." I told him about Celia and how I met her.

"One time, we went to Brooklyn to hang out with her cousin," I broke a corner off of a chip and dipped in salsa. "We went to a bar called The Cellar. I met this guy at the bar and flirted with him while Celia and Rosa were shooting pool. I wasn't in a very good place and ate up all the attention he gave me." The waiter brought our food. We ordered more tea and I continued.

"One thing led to another and I had been drinking and getting high and the next thing I knew, he had his hands down my skirt and was fingering me right at the bar. Part of me was loving it, the danger and excitement. Another part of me was disgusted."

"Didn't anyone notice?" He asked, his mouth full of cheese and sour cream.

"I stood facing him, so it just looked like we were standing really close. He had me ready to come right there when he pulled out his hand and suggested we go to his car."

"Did you?"

"Not only did I go with him, I blew him in the front seat."

"No way! You?"

"There's a lot about me you don't know," I picked at my rice and beans. "Anyway, when I was finished, he said 'thank you,' handed me a twenty and told me to go back inside and freshen up our drinks." I put my fork down and stared at him. "He never came back." Jack chewed silently, watching as I sat there naked. "I don't think I've ever felt more like shit than I did at that moment."

"I'm really sorry, Rena, but what does that have to do with me?"

"When I realized what you'd done last night, it pushed a button, Jack," I blinked and sighed. "Actually a few. First, I was probably a little jealous because it's been so long since I've had sex. Second, I know the kind of pain it took for me to allow myself to act that way with that guy. And seeing you last night brought back all those memories." My food cooled in front of me.

"I also recognized that pain in you," I reached across the table and put my hand on his. "And I care about you, Jack. It hurt me to realize that you were doing the same thing I did." I saw a flicker of recognition in his eyes and then the gate slammed, permitting denial to cushion the reality.

"That must have been really horrible for you, but I don't see how it's related to me." He shoveled forkfuls of rice into his mouth. I wanted to push him, break him, get him to see that it was. But I had tried that with Henry from Azan's yoga class a year ago and the results hadn't been too successful. Then I remembered Henry. I realized Jack wasn't in a place to understand and I needed to honor the fact that he needed to unfold in his time, not mine.

"All I'm saying is that I'm your friend. And if you ever want to talk, I'm here." I picked up a pair of plastic castanets from the table and clicked them in time to the music in the air around his face. "I feel like fried ice cream, how about you?" We ordered dessert and I forced myself to drop the subject.

"Can I ask you a personal question?" I cracked the shell of my ice cream with a spoon.

"You can ask, doesn't mean I'm going to answer it," he poured chocolate syrup over his bowl.

"When did you know you were gay?" He smiled.

"I always knew. I just didn't know what to call it."

"How did you find out?" His tongue caressed the spoon, licking the melted vanilla.

"I had a crush on my shop teacher when I was a freshman in high school, Mr. Donotti. He was six feet tall with blond hair, a mustache, and incredible blue eyes. And the strongest hands I've ever seen." He continued sucking ice cream from the spoon. "I was making a bird feeder for my dad for Father's Day. My dad loves birds. Anyway, I was having trouble with it and Mr. Donotti told me that if I wanted some help after school, he'd stay."

"A teacher?" I asked trying not show my disapproval.

"Yep. It was him and me in the shop room. He guided my hands using the saw and the sander. When he touched me, it was like I had been zapped by an electric fence. While I was standing at the sander, he stood behind me and I felt his erection in my back."

"Weren't you scared?"

"Terrified. But incredibly excited too." He took a sip of coffee. "I won't bore you," he smiled, "or titillate you as the case may be, but we both ended up quite satisfied in the little office off the classroom."

"Did it ever happen again?"

"For the rest of freshman year."

"Then what happened?" I took a drink of water to replace the moisture that had evaporated from my mouth.

"The year was over and I moved into tenth grade. But he taught me a lot, and not just about how to make a bird feeder."

"Didn't you feel like he was taking advantage of you?" I bit my tongue to keep the judgment from rushing out.

"Not at all. In fact, I'm grateful to him for helping me to realize exactly what I'd suspected for a long time." The waiter put the check on the table and I slipped my credit card in the holder. We were quiet as we walked to the car, the honesty we shared stifling, like the humid July night.

Breathe

"David and I are planning a picnic at the beach Saturday. Why don't you join us?" Angelina glowed. "I'd love for you to get to know him better." I was still fighting some envy since she told me he was moving back in, but I knew it was important to her.

"I'd love to."

"Good. I'm going to make barbecued chicken and potato salad."

"Why don't you let me make cookies or something for dessert," I offered.

"That'd be great." She stretched out her arms and hugged me. "I appreciate you making an effort, Rena."

"Would you mind if we went to Poplar's Cape? Jack works Saturday until two. Maybe he could join us when he's through."

"That'd be great! I'll call David and let him know." She left me in the barn and ran to the house. I grabbed a saddle and walked to the far pasture to get Bogota. I was in the mood for a ride. I tied him to the fence with his lead rope and secured the saddle. We walked to the other side of the pasture and I opened the gate that led to the trails. Climbing on, I smacked him lightly with the leather strap and he began to trot.

Cantering through the woods, I welcomed the sweetness of the wild flowers and the musty scent of the moss that grew on the trees lacing the bank of the creek. It wasn't long before he reached a full gallop and I bounced in the saddle, leaning toward his head, becoming part of him. We raced along the path, Bogota occasionally leaping over a broken branch or rock he found in his way. Both of us covered in sweat, we slowed down and rested near the edge of the lake where the creek's mouth formed.

I jumped off and guided him to the water. He bent down and drank hungrily, thirsty from the ride. We walked around the lake conversing, me in words, him in snorts and snuffles. I petted his long nose and scratched his ears as we strolled the perimeter. When I had walked off the burn in my legs and my knees felt stable, I decided to go back. "Ready, boy?" I asked, climbing on. We cantered most of the way, beams of sunlight breaking through the shade of the leaves. I rode him all the way to the stable and bathed and groomed him, taking care to remove all pebbles trapped in his shoes.

I was almost finished when Angelina showed up to help me bring the other horses in. Her eyes beamed and she wore an enormous grin. "Tomorrow at twelve work for you?"

"Sure, that's great." Her smile was contagious. "But who's going to take care of the horses?"

"David's brother is home from college. Somehow he bribed him into spending the weekend here and helping out tomorrow." I was exhilarated from the ride and after returning Bogota to the barn, I fed him and threw hay in the other stalls. Then Angelina and I retrieved the other horses and locked the barn.

The next morning, I helped David's brother, Alex, take out the horses and muck the stalls. After I showered, I walked with my beach bag up to the house. David sat on the couch in the living room reading the paper.

"Hey, Rena," he got up and slid open the screen. "We're almost ready. Angelina's in the kitchen packing the cooler."

"Thanks," I said heading to the kitchen.

"Rena," he called after me. "Can I talk to you for a minute?"

"Sure," I answered tentatively and returned to the living room. He gestured for me to sit and I chose the chair facing the sofa.

"You mean a lot to Angelina," he began. "And I know you two have a special relationship." I opted to not ask him what he meant by that. "What I mean is, it's important to her that we get along. I know you were around her as she was trying to deal with us divorcing. I know you saw how hurt and sad she was and, to be honest, if I were in your shoes, I'd probably hate me." His elbows rested on his bare knees earnestly and his hands were clasped in between his legs. He wore bright plaid walking shorts and a green golf shirt.

"I don't hate you David," I picked the cuticle on my right thumb. "I just want what's best for her. And if you're it, that's wonderful."

"Please don't placate me, Rena. If you and I are going to have any kind of a relationship, we've got to be honest."

"You want honesty? OK." I waved my hands at him and sat back smugly in the chair. "I was the one who handed her tissues when she cried and hugged her when she was paralyzed with sadness about losing you. I witnessed her struggle. I don't want to see her slide backwards, that's all." I was getting a nosebleed from being so high up on my self-righteous soapbox.

"On the other hand, Angelina seems to have gotten to the root of her part in the break up and is working on changing." I stood up and held out my hand. "So if you two can find a way to work through your shit and find happiness with each other again, I think it's wonderful."

"Really?"

"Really." Taking my hand, he drew me toward him and put his arms around me in a big bear hug. He was a large man, muscular and over six feet. I felt a wetness on my cheek and realized it was his tear.

"I love her, Rena. You've got to know that." He pulled back and rubbed his eyes, uncomfortable with the exposure.

"I understand why. You're a lucky man."

"I know." We stood in awkward silence for a moment.

"Let me go see what's keeping her." As I headed toward the kitchen, I heard footsteps scampering across the tile. When I stepped inside, her back was to me and she was chopping vegetables near the sink.

"Nice try," I joked. "But I know you heard everything."

"What are you talking about?" She turned around, looking fresh and innocent, her blue eyes watery.

"Nothing," I shook my head. "Must have been my imagination. Are you almost ready?"

We drove to the beach in David's convertible Mercedes, a Grateful Dead CD blaring from the rear speakers. We found a parking space and schlepped the cooler, chairs, and boom box down to the water line. Jack's lifeguard stand was a few feet away, and I waved as Angelina and I fought the wind to secure the blanket.

It was a clear, dry, hot day and the ocean was layered in deep blues and greens. Sailboats crisscrossed the water in the distance and a few wind surfers braved the cresting waves off the shore. A group of children diligently filled pails with salt water and dumped them in the moat around the sand-castle their father was building.

Two teams batted a volleyball back and forth over the net that had been erected near the boardwalk, yelling and whooping when a point was scored or a dig missed. And the music filling the air ranged from Salsa to Pop to Rock and Roll. Poplar's Cove was mostly a young beach, but there were a few older folks walking leisurely along the coast, searching for shells and shiny pebbles.

David had ditched his shorts and jumped headfirst into a wave as soon as we arrived. When Angelina and I were finished arranging the blanket and chairs, I walked over to say hello to Jack, the hot sand burning the soles of my feet. "Hey, Mr. Lifeguard," I called approaching the chair.

"Hey!" He smiled down on me with that gap-toothed grin, his nose white with Bullfrog. "How's it going with the ex?"

"Good!" I climbed up the wooden rungs to his seat. "We had a talk this morning." I put the word "talk" in quotes with my fingers and leaned over to hug him. He wore a red windbreaker and pants made from the same material.

"And?"

"He really loves her," I admitted. "We'll see." I sat next to him, surprised at how far I could see from that height. I pushed my sunglasses into my hair like a headband and squinted in the sunlight. "You're off at two, right?"

"No, actually, someone called in sick and they asked me to pull a double."

"So you're working 'til six?" I was disappointed.

"Yeah. I'm going to be a lobster by the time I get out of here." He blew his whistle at two boys who were dangerously close to a buoy near the jetty and waved them back. "What are you doing tonight?"

"Nothing. What do you feel like?"

"I was kind of hoping you would have dinner with Paul and me." I cocked my head and raised my eyebrows. "He's this guy I met a few weeks ago. I haven't said anything before this because I didn't know where it was going. But he hasn't left yet, so that's a good sign."

"Sure," I felt the familiar pull of dichotomized feelings. On the one hand, I was thrilled he'd met someone and would stop trolling. On the other, if he found someone, that left me odd man out. "What time?"

"Why don't you meet me here at six-thirty. I brought clothes to change into and I'll take a shower in the locker room."

"Six-thirty it is," I agreed going backwards down the steps. "I'll come visit before we leave." I danced on the hot sand and collapsed in one of the chairs on our blanket. David was stretched out like Goliath, saltwater dripping onto his towel. And Angelina sat nestled under the umbrella, a huge sombrero and dark sunglasses protecting her pale face from the sun.

"So," I announced. "Jack's met someone."

"Really?" Angelina looked up from her magazine. "That's wonderful for him."

"And not so wonderful for me," I complained. She tapped her glasses down her nose and peered at me from under her hat. "I know, I know. I'm happy for him. But if this thing works out ...." She kept staring until the conversation we'd had about her and David fluttered through my head. "OK, OK. Point taken." David sat up, the skin on his hairy chest white as bread dough.

"First trip to the beach this year?" I joked nodding at his ashy complexion.

"We can't all have your golden glow, Rena," he shot back.

"Don't hate me 'cause I'm beautiful," I laughed, still secretly hating the dimples on my thighs and ass.

"How about getting in on that volleyball game?" He nodded at me and then toward the net.

"Seriously?"

"Yeah. I haven't played beach volleyball in years. I used to be a pretty good server."

"He's telling the truth," Angelina piped in from her shaded hut, never looking up from the article she was reading.

"All right," I agreed. "I'll give it a shot." We put on our shorts and shoes and headed up toward the court.

"Need a couple of pros?" David called to a man coaching from the side.

"Sure, we can always use help," he answered and rotated David. I followed quickly because David slammed the other team's serve right back over the net. We were older than anyone else on the team, but David was a helluva player. He slid across the sand on his belly to make a dig more than once and won his serve six points in a row.

After forty-five minutes or so, we had played a couple of games and were sopping wet. "Race you to the water!" He called sprinting away from me. I ran as hard as I could but my inseam was miniscule compared to his and he beat me easily. I stopped at the blanket to remove my shorts and sandals. I followed David's path, like Hansel and Gretel's trail of breadcrumbs. First a sock, then a shoe, another sock, another shoe, and then his plaid shorts, leading right into the tide. I dove into a wave and immersed my overheated skin in the cool, invigorating water. I swam out to where David lounged, face up, bobbing on the waves.

"What took you so long?"

"Some of us prefer to undress properly instead of subjecting the crowd to an ugly strip tease!" I playfully splashed him.

"It was the best show they've had all day," he splashed me back. I flipped onto my back and closed my eyes, allowing the sea to gently move me with its rhythm. "It feels so good to escape work today," he sighed.

"Do you usually work weekends?"

"Trust me, you make the kind of money I do and they expect you to work twenty-four hours a day, seven days a week."

"My job wasn't quite that bad, but it was close enough," I opened my eyes and craned my neck to see how far we'd drifted.

"When you're dealing with people's personal money, they want you at their beck and call."

"Angelina said you were a stock broker?"

"Portfolio manager. It's even worse." He lay still with his eyes shut, the waves bouncing his large frame. "But it's what let me buy the horse farm and I've been investing a lot of it so I won't have to wait until I'm sixty-five to retire. I want to be able to enjoy what I've earned."

"Delaying gratification."

"Excuse me?" He looked at me with one eye.

"You're delaying your gratification," I explained. "You're working hard and not really enjoying much now, but you're doing it so you can retire early."

"That's what Angelina says," he closed his eye. "I prefer to think of it as being smart." We let the water continue to move us until I sat up and realized we weren't too far from the jetty that Jack had warned those boys about.

"Hey!" I tapped David's arm. "We've really drifted." We swam across the current until we washed up on shore. When we got back to the blanket, Angelina had lunch spread out on a towel. We feasted on chicken and potato salad and reclined, like beached whales, into the chairs munching the oatmeal raisin cookies I had made. Skin tight from the sun and our energy levels completely depleted, David and I begged Angelina to leave around four.

We packed up the bags and cooler and folded the blanket. I waved to Jack and held up six and a half fingers. He gave me the thumbs up and we trudged back to the car, warm and sandy and tired. David's neck turned bright red on the drive home, a result of his stubbornly refusing sun block. "You're going to be in pain tonight," I teased sitting behind him and watching it darken. "You won't have the St. Tropez tan," I spoke in my best French accent, waving my arm in between him and Angelina. "That, Monsieur, can only be provided by Bain de Soleil."

"You know, you're a real pain in the ass," he brushed away my arm.

"But I have a mean volleyball serve!" I flicked his shoulder. Angelina protected herself from the wind by holding the sombrero in place with her left hand, but I saw her smiling. They dropped me off at the cottage and I smacked the sand from my tennis shoes, shook out my towel, and headed for the shower.

By six o'clock I was washed, moisturized, and ready to go in a pale pink sundress and strappy sandals. I grabbed a sweater to ward off the chill I knew I'd get that night from being in the sun all day and headed back to Poplar's Cape. I double-parked in front of the lifeguard station and called into the locker room. When I got no answer, I headed around the side and walked up the ramp to look out onto the beach. There were only a few people left, either too tired to move or too dedicated to leave before the sun set. But I didn't see Jack anywhere.

I returned to the locker room and called for him again. No answer. I went back to the car and got a cigarette from my purse. I hadn't been able to put them down completely since that night at The Men's Room. Maybe Paul had picked him up early and they had run to get beer or something. I paced the sidewalk, puffing and exhaling. Some of the stragglers finally having given up and calling it a day walked past me, chairs and umbrellas in tow. Down to the filter, I finally threw the butt on the concrete and stubbed it out with my shoe. I went back up the ramp and looked out onto the beach again.

Confused, I walked into the locker room to see if Jack had left his beach bag. The space was empty, a stray sandal hiding under one of the benches. I called Jack's name and wandered over to the bathroom. I thought I heard water trickling. "Hello? Is anybody here?" I followed the sound of the drips to the showers. When I rounded the corner, I saw Jack's bag lying outside one of the stalls. "Jack? Are you here?"

As I got closer, I saw a pair of bare feet on the other side of the bag. I peeked around the wall and found Jack naked on the floor of the shower, curled in the fetal position, his hands and knees pulled into his stomach. "Are you OK?" I bent down and touched his legs. He didn't move. As I stood up, I noticed the word 'Faggot' written in red on the white tile. I began to shake. Jack's right eye was swollen shut, angry and purple, the tissue around it tight and shiny.

I moved the bag out of the way and my eye caught a reflection below his waist. It was the neck of a beer bottle and it was protruding from his rectum. I screamed and ran out of the locker room searching for a phone. I found one on the wall of the building and dialed 911.

"Poplar Falls emergency, may I help you?" A woman answered.

"My friend," I panted, "he's been beaten, help me please. He needs help. He needs an ambulance."

"OK, Ma'am. Where are you?" I was crying hysterically, trying to secure my dress against the breeze.

"The lifeguard station at Beach Area Two." I stuck my head into space next to the phone, the wind kept blowing sand in my eyes. "He's not moving. There's blood everywhere. Help me please."

"Beach Area Two?"

"Yes!" I screamed. "Do something—now!"

"On Coastline Road?" Her voice was even and methodical.

"Yes! How many fucking times do I need to tell you?"

"Please calm down, Ma'am. I want to make sure I send the ambulance to the right place."

"Yes. Coastline Road. Hurry. I'm afraid he's going to die."

"Is he conscious?"

"No."

"Is he breathing?"

"I don't know."

"I'll dispatch an ambulance, Ma'am, but I need you to put the phone down and go find out if he's breathing and see if he has a pulse. It will help prepare the paramedics."

I dropped the phone and ran back to the locker room. I kicked the bag out of the way and knelt beside him, feeling for a pulse on his neck. I saw two cuts right below his ear. There was a faint throbbing under my fingers. I held my hand in front of his mouth. I felt only the slightest puff. Getting up, I slipped on the pink water covering the floor and grabbed for the shower knob. It was slippery and when I removed my hand it was covered in Jack's blood.

Running outside, I held my hand away from me like it was diseased. The phone was dangling from the wall and I reported to the operator that Jack was barely breathing.

"What the fuck is going on here?" demanded Inanna.

"It's the next step." Kuan Yin was serene. "It is all necessary, trust me."

"And you say I got her into some whacked out situations," snickered Kali. "I don't ever want to hear any of you bitch about me again." Erishkigal cried, rocking back and forth, her knees pulled into her chest.

"This is hateful. Who would do this?"

"Someone who doesn't understand that hate hurts them as much as it hurts the person they act it out on," Kuan Yin sat in lotus and began chanting.

"This is a fine time to tune out, KY," Inanna scolded. "Rena is standing there, dripping blood, her best friend laying on a cold tile floor with a beer bottle shoved up his ass. I repeat, what the fuck is going on?"

"Patience," Kuan Yin whispered. "She is about to learn true compassion."

"Compassion my Hindu ass," Kali sneered. "How is this any better than her escapades in the East Village?"

"Quiet!" pleaded Kuan Yin. "Be still. And you will know."

I smoked four cigarettes and tried calling Angelina twice while I waited for the ambulance. The answering machine was on, so I hung up. I kept running back and forth between the parking lot and the shower to check on Jack. I was rubbing his leg, trying to warm him, when I heard the sirens. I bolted out the door, my dress smeared with the blood from Jack's eye and waved the ambulance over.

They jumped out of the truck and rushed toward me. "What seems to be the problem, Miss?"

"We were supposed to have dinner," I rambled, "I couldn't find him and then I heard water and, and," I started to cry again. "I found him in the shower." The one charged inside with a medical bag while the other went back to the truck to call the police. I followed him inside, pointing to where Jack lay on the floor.

"What happened here?" He was in his forties, gray hair at the temples and his biceps straining the fabric of his uniform. He bent over Jack, pulling on a pair of latex gloves. I told him I had no idea who might have done this or why. "I need you to step back, Ma'am." He checked Jack's airway to make sure it wasn't obstructed and then tested the pulse on his neck, wrist, and behind one knee.

Opening the bag, he grabbed a pen flashlight and forced Jack's swollen eye open to inspect his pupils and then wrapped a cuff around Jack's arm to take his blood pressure. "I need a bag of lactated ringers," he yelled to his partner.

"What the hell is that?" I asked shivering, my arms blanketed in goose bumps.

"If you can't stay out of the way, Ma'am, I'm going to have to ask you to leave." The other paramedic, younger and out of breath, came running in with an I.V. bag. "Open wide," he instructed, removing the cuff. He inserted a needle into the back of Jack's hand. The one who was in charge called the hospital from his radio. "I have a Caucasian male, approximately twenty-five years old. Unresponsive. BP 80 over 50, hypovolemic, pupils reactive. It looks like someone beat him up pretty bad. Suspected orbital fracture, two lateral cuts under his right ear, minor." The radio hissed and crackled.

"Here's the thing, doc," the paramedic turned from me and spoke softly. "Someone inserted a beer bottle into his rectum. All that's showing is the neck. He's curled up in the fetal position. Do you want us to remove it or board him like this?"

"Kind of gives a whole new meaning to 'bottoms up.'" The doctor on the other end laughed. "No, bring him in that way. We don't know if the bottle is fractured and I don't want him bleeding out on the way."

They secured a cervical collar around his neck and slid a spinal board under him. One fastened the belts around Jack's naked ankles and waist while the other retrieved a gurney from the truck. "Ma'am please, we need room," the senior medic barked, covering him with a blanket, and I stepped backwards into the locker room. They wheeled him past me and except for the black eye and the bruises, he looked like a sleeping child, still and small.

"What hospital are you taking him to? Can I follow you?"

"We're signed out of St. Luke's tonight, Ma'am, but I think you ought to wait for the police to get here. You might be able to help." They rolled him out and slipped the gurney into the ambulance. Sirens were wailing and lights flashing as the ambulance sped off. A police car passed them, heading toward the lifeguard station. The two officers asked me to wait outside. A few minutes later, one of them found me, smoking another cigarette, pacing near the ramp.

"Ma'am?" He startled me and I jumped. "I didn't mean to scare you. I was hoping I could ask you a few questions."

"Sure," I picked up the bottom of my dress and wiped my eyes, leaving black smudges on the hem.

"You knew the victim?"

"He's still alive, Officer." I flicked the cigarette into the parking lot and searched my purse for a piece of gum. I told him Jack's name and that I didn't know his next of kin. His aunt was his mother's sister and I had no idea what her married name was.

"Any idea who might have done this?" The officer was young, maybe twenty-five, and he seemed nervous, shaken from what he'd just seen. His red hair was clipped short and freckles dotted his cheeks and nose.

"None," I shook my head. "What do you think happened?"

"As near as we can tell from talking to the paramedics and inspecting the shower, it appears he was held at knifepoint and beaten. It's pretty obvious it was a bias crime."

"Bias crime?" I laughed. "More like I fucking hate all gay people." I chewed hard on my gum, hoping to alleviate my anger. "I'm sorry," I apologized. "I'm a little upset." He put his hand on my arm.

"I'm sorry, Miss."

"What's the chance you'll find them?" He flipped his notepad closed and stared over my head.

"Honestly? I'm not sure. We'll talk to whoever is left on the beach tonight and come back tomorrow to canvas. And we'll speak to his co-workers and his boss. I promise, we'll do our best. The detectives are on their way now."

"Can I leave to go to the hospital?"

"Sure. Just give me your name and phone number in case we need to get in touch." He walked me to my car and I told him where he could reach me. I made it to the entrance of the parking lot before the tears blurred my vision and I had to pull over. I blew my nose in a Starbuck's napkin and fumbled in the glove compartment for my cassette of chants.

The sitar and melodic repetition of the words *Ishq Allah, Ma'bud Allah* lulled me into coherence and I accelerated, anxious to get to St. Luke's. As I turned into the emergency room parking lot, calm for the first time in an hour, I felt Shakti's presence deep inside me. I knew what she was going to say and I didn't want to hear it, so I turned off the tape and raised the volume on the radio, singing along with the woman crooning the jingle for Weight Watchers. But I couldn't stop it. "It's him," the silent voice reverberated in my head.

"It can't be," I argued out loud.

"And this is your chance to do it differently," she insisted.

"But he's done nothing to me," I assured her, "you must be mistaken." Again, the silent voice, quiet and firm.

"It's him. Jack is the man from your vision. This is your opportunity to break the cycle."

"I can't," I announced to the steering wheel. "If he's the man who raped me in that vision, how can I even care if he lives or dies?"

"Because love is the only answer," Shakti's voice permeated my being, ringing in my head, making the hairs on my arms and neck stand on end. I shut off the engine and debated whether or not to go inside.

"You must," I heard. I made no effort to get out of the car, but somehow found myself walking toward the emergency room entrance.

"Is Jack Crandall here?" I asked the clerk at the desk. "I'm a friend of his." She looked down at the clipboard on her desk and repeated his name.

"Yes, yes, he's here," she looked up at me. "He's in with the doctor right now. Why don't you wait in chairs and a nurse will come get you as soon as we know anything."

"But I want to know now," I yelled.

"I understand you're upset, Miss, but screaming at me isn't going to help your friend." She pointed to the waiting room. "Please have a seat and we'll let you know as soon as he's done being treated." I retreated to the tiny room with the vending machines and threw myself in one of the hard plastic chairs fastened to the floor. I noticed a pay phone and decided to try Angelina again.

"Hello?"

"Angelina?" I whimpered.

"Rena? Are you OK? You sound horrible. What's wrong?"

"Jack's been beaten. The police don't know who did it. They did it because he's gay," I was surprised there were any tears left. "I'm at St. Luke's. Can you come?"

"Oh my God!" I heard her telling David what happened. "We'll be right there. Don't move." The phone went dead in my hand. I dug some change out from the bottom of my bag and bought a soda. People coming into the waiting area avoided me and nobody would sit next to me. A young mother grabbed her child's arm when he started to move toward me. I didn't care.

I emptied the can and went to the restroom to pee. On my way to the stall, I passed a woman next to the sink who appeared to have been in an accident. Her hair was wild and loose, her pretty sundress stained. She'd obviously been crying because her face was puffy and red. When I washed my hands, she stared back at me from the mirror. I splashed cold water on my face and tied my sweater around my waist, hoping to hide some of the blood. When I returned to the lobby, Angelina and David were standing at the desk, talking to the clerk.

"Rena," Angelina called, noticing me. "Are you OK?" I filled her in on the details as she walked me to a chair.

"I need to talk to you," I glanced at David, "no offense."

"None taken," he smiled. "Why don't I go get some coffee? The real deal, not the cat piss they have in this machine." He patted my leg and strolled to the elevator.

"What's wrong?" Angelina wiped my face with a tissue. "I'm so sorry you had to deal with this by yourself." I pushed her hand away and dropped my head into my lap, sobbing. "Rena, I know it's upsetting, but he's going to be OK, you know?"

"You don't get it," snot mingled with saliva and I sat up, grabbing the tissue from her. She looked at me, confused and curious. "It's him," I blew my nose, grateful she had another tissue ready to catch the overflow. "Jack's the man from that stupid vision I had a few months ago." I pulled at my hair from the roots.

"Jesus!" She stared straight ahead, silent. After a couple of minutes, she turned to me. "Are you sure?" I gave her a look.

"Like I'd want it to be true."

"I'm sorry. I don't know what to say." She removed her feet from the floor and tucked them under her, the position always giving her strength. She inhaled deeply and exhaled slowly. "One thing at a time. Let's find out how he is first, and then we'll deal with that." She put her arm around me and drew me to her, stroking my hair and trying to soothe me. I let her. "It's going to be all right."

David returned with three steaming cups of coffee. I blew on it before sipping, grateful for the hot moisture on my face. "Crandall? Anyone here for Jack Crandall?" I looked up to find a nurse at the edge of the waiting room.

"Me!" I jumped up, almost spilling the coffee on my lap.

"Are you a relative?" She asked tersely.

"No, a really good friend."

"I'm afraid we can't disclose any information to anyone besides a relative," she insisted. "It's hospital policy." Angelina stood beside me, ready to take over.

"I understand the policy, Ma'am," she smiled and spoke softly. "But Jack's only relative in this area isn't available right now. Rena's the one who found him at the beach. She's been waiting a long time and is very concerned." Angelina pushed me toward David. "I'm sure you can understand," she whispered. "It's been a very difficult day for her." The nurse tapped her clipboard with a pen.

"Let me talk to the doctor. I'll see what I can do."

"Thank you," Angelina gently touched her arm. "Thank you very much." Turning around to face us, she winked at me and whispered, "Be patient." The nurse returned a few minutes later and offered to escort me to Jack's room.

He was on his stomach, his head turned so that the battered eye faced me. "Is he awake?" I asked her.

"He's conscious, but I don't know how alert he is." She closed the curtain around the bed. I softly stroked his fingers, not wanting to frighten him.

"Hey," I whispered. "How are you feeling?"

"Rena," the sound was garbled. "Is that you?"

"Yeah, buddy, it's me."

"I feel like someone shoved a space ship up my ass." I bit my lip, hoping the pain would distract me. "What's up with you?" He was covered in a white blanket up to his neck and an I.V. dripped into the tube attached to his hand. A heart monitor beeped rhythmically, almost synchronized with the twitching of his eye. I heard the sliding of rings on the metal track and a man in scrubs approached the bed.

"I'm Doctor Jannaro," he smiled. "I'm the surgeon on call. You're Jack's friend?"

"Yes," I said, shaking his hand. "Rena Sutcliffe." He guided me into the hallway.

"We don't normally discuss a patient's condition with someone who isn't a relative, but my nurse explained the situation." He flipped open a chart. "Jack was beaten pretty severely. We've taken X-rays and done a head CAT because of the damage to the eye. Fortunately, he has no internal bleeding, but he does have a few bruised ribs. The cuts under his ear are minor and didn't require stitches." He took my hand and accompanied me to a chair. He gently pushed me down and sat next to me.

"We do, however, need to do surgery to reconstruct the orbital process." I tightened the knot in the sweater around my waist.

"What does that mean?"

"It means the bone of the cavity surrounding the eye has been fractured. Apparently, he hit it on something." I flashed to the bloody shower knob. "He has a serious gash above his right eyebrow." I began to cry. He sat patiently for a moment.

"Any time someone has surgery, it's a risk," he spoke cautiously, "but this is a fairly routine procedure. We need to clean out any bone fragments and make sure there was no damage to the eye organ."

"I don't believe this," I repeated the phrase two or three times.

"Dr. Mihalski is our orthopedic surgeon on call. He's excellent. He doesn't think there's any reason to believe Jack's sight will be impaired. But we need to operate as soon as possible to reduce the risk of the bone fragments lodging anywhere."

"Does he know?"

"Kind of. He's been in and out of consciousness since they brought him in. We've been trying to get the name of his nearest relative, but he hasn't stayed awake long enough." I chewed the inside of my mouth and slid the strings of skin through my teeth.

"What about the bottle?"

"We were able to remove that without any breakage. There are some tears in the rectal area, but no damage was done to the colon."

"He'll be OK?" I paused. "Down there?"

"The colon wasn't punctured, so that's good news, but we don't want him to evacuate anything through his rectum. It's standard procedure to insert an NG tube during this kind of surgery. This will drain the waste that the stomach produces even when you don't eat. It'll be removed before he's discharged."

"When will that be?" He shook his head.

"I'd like for him to be here for five or six days. Unfortunately, insurance companies won't pay for anything more than four days for this type of case. But I'll find a way to keep him for that extra day." He stood up and looked down on me, my hips not quite fitting into the seat.

"Jack's going to be OK," he assured me. "Do you have any questions?"

"You can do the surgery without him signing a release?"

"It's considered an emergency, Rena. We've got to remove those bone fragments from the fracture as soon as possible." He held out his hand to help me up. "We'll be taking him up soon. If you want to see him before surgery, you'd better go now. But don't stay too long." He cautioned, turning to go. "The nurse will let you know where to go to wait."

"Thank you doctor," I headed toward Jack's room. "How long?" I called after him before rounded the corner. "How long will the surgery take?"

"About two hours. Give or take." He disappeared, the movement of his body stirring up the layers of disinfectant hanging in the sterile air. I peeked around the curtain in Jack's room, hoping he was awake. I walked over to the bed and stood next to the steel railing and clenched my fingers over it tightly.

"Rena?" He sounded like his mouth was full of marbles.

"Yes," I brushed his hair. "I'm here."

"When can I get out of here?" I sucked in a mouthful of air and held it. I moved my hand to his back and made small circles on the blanket.

"You need to have surgery, Jack. For your eye." I continued rubbing. "The doctor says it's a routine procedure, but they've got to check for bone fragments." I squeezed his hand under the covers. "Can you hear me?" Nothing. "Jack?" A nurse breezed into the room and opened the curtain.

"I'm sorry, we need to prep him for the surgery. You can wait on the 4th floor." She moved quickly around the bed, pulling down the blanket. "Someone will come get you when he's been moved to recovery." I stepped into the hallway and rested my back against the wall. I slowly banged my head against it, hoping to shake loose any information that would help me understand why this had happened.

I found Angelina and David in the waiting room and filled them in on the elevator ride to the 4th floor. "Will he be blind in that eye?" David asked.

"The doctor says they don't think so," I answered, pushing the button. "They'll know for sure after the operation." The waiting area there was more comfortable than the emergency room, the chairs actually padded and the reception on the television clear. By ten o'clock, I had become anxious and paced in the corridor outside the waiting room.

"How can she be the same with him after finding out that he raped her in another lifetime?" Kali demanded. "He's lucky the surgeons didn't have to reattach his penis."

"Anger perpetuates anger, Kali," Kuan Yin's patience was worn. "The truth is that nothing can hurt Rena's soul. The appearance of harm may be present in the physical plane, but the soul is pure and eternal. No one holds the power to destroy it."

"But you were there," Kali insisted. "You saw what he did to her, how much pain she was in. How can you deny that?"

"Sometimes humans need to experience pain in order to learn." Kuan Yin wrapped her robes around her and stood in front of Kali. "Why does a child have to burn her hand on a stove before she knows not to touch? Why does a child have to break a bone before she understands that jumping out of a tree isn't a good idea?" She touched Kali's hair, brushing it off her face.

"Rena's soul is learning. And because the ego is so resistant, sometimes pain is the result." She pulled her hands back and slipped them under the silk of her garment. "Rena is a very intelligent person. Her intellect has been in charge for a long time. That makes it more difficult for the soul to evolve because the intellect is ego driven." Kali shook her head.

"I don't know KY. I don't know."

"It's logical," Inanna nodded. "Ego is diametrically opposed to spirit. It's selfish and immature. And Rena's ego," she glanced at Kali, "is pretty strong."

"Ego cannot believe that love is the answer to everything. Because what then would be its purpose for existing? There would be no need for ego." Kuan Yin smiled. "And ego will not be reduced or removed without a fight. That is the struggle that Rena is experiencing right now. Her perception of right and wrong is prohibiting her from understanding. Her evolution, her unfolding has already begun. The ego can retard it for a while, but the more she resists, the more pain she will cause herself."

"So," acknowledged Inanna, "the best thing for her to do is to let go."

"Ah, wise sister," Kuan Yin looked at her approvingly, "that is the secret."

"I can't take much more of this," I flopped on the couch next to David where he patiently sat reading an old *Newsweek*. Angelina and I had tried talking about the meaning of my vision, but I couldn't focus.

"It shouldn't be too much longer," Angelina yawned. A brother and a sister waiting for their mother's appendix to be removed were the only other people in the room. We all stared at the screen as CNN reported on the dangers of not wearing enough sunscreen.

"Rena? Rena Sutcliffe?" An Asian nurse in maroon scrubs stood in the doorway. I leapt from the couch.

"Yes?"

"Your friend is out of surgery. Everything is fine," her almond-shaped eyes disappeared when she smiled. "The doctor will be out to talk to you in a minute."

"Thank you," I pumped her arm. "Thank you very much." I felt my shoulders slump, as if the bricks of worry I'd been carrying suddenly disintegrated. I hugged Angelina and David, grateful for the company and their ability to know whether I needed conversation or silence. I saw the doctor coming down the hall and went to meet him.

"I'm Doctor Mihalski." He didn't smile. He had thick forearms, the freckles almost hidden by a downy blanket of gold hair. "The surgery was successful. No damage to the organ. His vision will be blurry for a few days, but he'll recover full sight." He fingered the surgical mask in his left hand. "I'll be in to check on him tomorrow. Dr. Jannaro will be along shortly to fill you in on the rest." I paced the floor, waiting for him. I was about to ask Angelina for company when I saw him shuffling toward me, his shoes covered in surgical slippers.

"How are you holding up?" He looked concerned.

"Fine," I lied. "How is he?"

"I'm guessing Dr. Mihalski already spoke to you?" I nodded.

"The NG tube is in. It'll be in for a few days. As I told you, the colon wasn't punctured, so that's good news." He slid the blue cap off of his head. His hair was damp, strands of it making a band along the top of his forehead.

"He's in recovery now. He'll be there until he wakes up and then he'll be moved to a room."

"Will he be able to eat?"

"He'll be NPO, that's no food or water, until we hear bowel sounds. Then we'll put him on a strict liquid diet for a few days and see how he tolerates that. He probably won't be on full liquids until he's discharged."

"What does that mean?" I inquired.

"Pudding, oatmeal, foods like that. We'll take it a step at a time and see what he can handle."

"OK."

"I want to warn you, he's going to be in some pain." He scratched his neck and I noticed the dark stains under his arm. "Not so much from the eye surgery, but from the bruised ribs and the rectal issue. I've ordered a PCA pump so he can administer the Dilaudid to himself according to his pain level. He'll still have an I.V. in when you see him in the morning."

"At least he's going to be OK." I caught a tear with my thumb before it dropped to the floor.

"Why don't you go home and get some rest? You can't do anything for him tonight. He won't even know you're here."

"I think that's an excellent idea," Angelina snuck up behind me, slipping her arm through mine.

"I'll be in to check on him around eleven. If you have any other questions, I can answer them then." Dark circles were beginning to form under his eyes. "Good night."

The air was dry and a crisp breeze snapped the American flag hanging outside the emergency room entrance. We left my car in the parking lot, Angelina promising to bring me back the following morning. David slipped a Billy Joel CD into the stereo and I lay down in the back seat with my eyes closed, leaking tears, listening to the "The Stranger."

Breathe

I asked the nurse if Jack was awake. "He had a rough night," she walked out from around the desk. "But he ate some broth and apple juice earlier."

"Can I go in?"

"Sure," she hesitated. "But he looks pretty bad. The police were here this morning to ask him some questions. I don't know what kind of mood he's in." She toyed with her stethoscope. "He's in room 816." I walked slowly toward the door, holding my breath. I exhaled loudly and forced a smile before I pushed it open.

"Hey!" I tried to keep the reins on the cheer. "How's it going?" He turned his head toward the window. "Are you awake?"

"Unfortunately."

"Can I get you anything?"

"Yeah, a gun." I sat on the chair next to his bed. The other bed in the room was empty.

"Don't even joke about something like that." His right eye was covered with gauze, but the bruise had spread to his cheek, staining it in several shades of purple. A thin tube protruded from the blanket emptying into a small bag. The I.V. stand was at the top of the bed, and his hands clenched the cotton covering him.

"Who's joking?" I sat quietly, everything I had planned to say now suddenly seeming trite or tired.

"Have you called your aunt?"

"No!" He whispered harshly. "And I don't want you to either. I don't want her knowing about this."

"What about your father?"

"Were you listening? I don't want anyone to find out about this." I kept my opinions to myself, not wanting to upset him more.

"Do you want to talk?" He turned toward me and I pinched my thigh to avoid gasping at the swelling that disfigured the side of his face.

"About what, Rena?" His voice was angry, like jagged glass. "About the fact that some homophobic teens didn't appreciate Paul kissing me before he went home to get a shower? About how they stalked me and followed me into the locker room?" Drool glistened on his bottom lip and slowly leaked onto his chin, clear and wet. "Let's talk about how one held a Swiss Army knife to my neck, calling me a fudge packer and a faggot while the other one punched my stomach like he was trying out for the Olympic boxing team." I sniffed and bent down, pretending to need something in my purse, not wanting him to see me cry.

"I'm sorry. We don't have to talk. I can just sit here," I leaned over the bed and grabbed the remote control. "Maybe we can watch television." He pushed a button and the bed groaned, raising him slightly.

"No, no, you brought it up," he refused to drop it. "Let's talk about the one without the knife pulling my bathing suit down over my knees. Then we can discuss how he and his friend made fun of my dick, joking about how I must be a bottom because my tiny pecker wouldn't be enough to satisfy a real homo."

"Stop, Jack," the tears weren't in my control any longer. "Please."

"Then I can mention how they forced me to bend over, leaning me against the wall because the one rocket scientist wondered if a beer bottle would fit backwards up a homo's ass." He was shaking and there was a wet spot on his pillow. "I didn't want to stick around to find out, so I tried to get away. He slammed my head against the tile, but I was struggling and my eye hit the knob." I flicked around the channels, *Talk Soup,* CNN, Sheryl Crow's latest video.

"I screamed. And screamed; the blood was everywhere. But nobody came." He turned his head back to the window. "And then everything went black. I guess they left." A wistful laugh escaped. "No sport in fucking with a faggot who's unconscious." I squeezed his hand.

"I am so sorry, Jack."

"Yeah, well, that's life." He pushed the button to administer some Dilaudid.

"What did the police say?"

"They're going to ask around the beach today, see if they can find anything out." He pulled the blanket up closer to his neck. "But I don't give a shit. It's not going to change what happened."

"But those kids need to be punished," I insisted. "Or they could do it to somebody else."

"Tough shit." He closed his left eye. I stood up and kissed his forehead. "I'll let you sleep. I'll come back later." He nodded slightly and I made it to the hallway before the last thread of my composure unraveled. I escaped to the bathroom, grateful for the solitude and tissues. I drove straight to Angelina's, hoping she was home. Alex, David's brother, answered the door wearing loud Hawaiian shorts and a T-shirt. His long blond hair was pulled back in a ponytail and he was munching an apple.

"She's down at the barn, man." His surfer dude accent had been perfected with years of practice. I raced down to the barn and found her saddling up Alabaster.

"David asked Alex to stay for a while because I didn't want you worrying about the horses while all of this was going on," she said when I told her Alex had answered the door. She tightened the strap around the Palomino's belly. "How's Jack? I didn't expect you back this soon." I gave her a condensed version of our conversation. "I'm so sorry, Rena. He's angry. It's bound to leak out on the people he feels the closest to." She unclipped the lead rope from the wall. "Do you feel like going for a ride?"

I ran to the cottage and put on my chaps and boots. The chaps were a bit tight and I struggled to get them all the way up. I hadn't been paying attention lately to what I was eating and the pounds crept on so easily. I shoved it to the back of my mind, not capable of dealing with one more issue.

Angelina had already saddled Bogota and we walked through the one corral to the trails. Alabaster and Bogota walked side by side, the path still a bit damp from the rain a couple of days ago.

It was a warm day, a bit muggy and thick. "What do I do?" I asked Angelina. "I feel bad for him. But if he really was the man in that vision, I'm furious." She leaned forward and rubbed Alabaster's silky golden fur.

"First of all, feeling bad for him isn't going to help Jack. Pity doesn't solve anything. You need to focus on visualizing him whole and well, not spend your energy feeling sorry for him." I nodded in agreement.

"You're right. That I can do. What about the other thing?"

"What makes you doubt that it's true?"

"Because it seems insane."

"By whose standards?" She brushed a branch out of the way. "Trusting yourself is the only way to get through life. You can't listen to the voices of your parents, or other friends or me. You have to trust you. The problem is you don't want to because then you'd have to deal with it. It's much easier to expend the energy doubting than it is dealing with it." I felt rage bubbling in my stomach like a cauldron of liquid steel. Birds chirped in the trees above my head.

"I'm afraid that if I let myself get angry about it, I'll never stop being pissed off."

"But that's the secret," she laughed. "If you honor the feeling you have, allow yourself to feel it as fully as you possibly can, you take away its power. By suppressing it, you're giving it control and you spend all your energy fighting it, pushing it back down." We continued to walk along the trail, the horses occasionally shaking their heads or whinnying to each other.

"I have an idea," she started to trot. "Follow me." We sped to a canter and then galloped all the way to the lake. It was deserted and pristine, the water clear and inviting. We tied the horses to a tree, leaving them enough room to wander over for a drink. Angelina grabbed my hand and pulled me toward a large rock. "Sit down," she commanded. "Close your eyes."

I let the sun wash over my face, warming it and I saw bright red behind my eyes. "Now I'm going to repeat what you told me was in that vision," she began. Several minutes later I felt myself flushed and angry, violated. "He raped you, Rena. He would've left you for dead if you hadn't killed him. Now, how do you feel?" I couldn't speak. "Answer me Rena. How do you feel?"

"I'm furious," I screamed, throat burning and eyes bulging. "I hate him for doing that to me. He had no right."

"Good," she egged me on, "what else?"

"He's a motherfucking cowardly prick!" I continued to yell, startling the horses nuzzling water from the lake's edge. "How dare he think he can take whatever he wants without permission?"

"Do you want to hit something?" I stood up and walked over to a tree, my hands balled in fists. I lifted my leg and kicked, digging my heel into its trunk. Then I did it with the other leg. After several rounds of tree karate, I collapsed on the soft grass, punching and slapping the ground with both hands. Primal screams rose from my toes, piercing the air around me. The horses pointed their ears and turned in my direction. I screamed and sobbed, battering the clover and dandelions. Finally, I lay on my back, the sun drying the tears.

"How do you feel?" I had forgotten she was there.

"Exhausted."

"But not angry?"

"No." My voice was hoarse. My mouth dry.

"You need to do a final cleanse," she instructed. "Let's go for a dip." She got up from the ground and removed her shirt and jeans. I did the same and together in our bras and underwear we allowed the mud to slide between our toes as we entered the lake. The water was brisk and exhilarating. I no longer felt tired. We swam to the middle and treaded water.

"That was amazing," I swirled my arms under the surface. "How did you think of that?"

"My therapist had me do something similar." Water dripped from her nose and chin as her legs moved rapidly under her. "I'm glad it helped."

"I've never felt anger like that before."

"It's scary, right?" She flipped onto her back and floated in the sun. "But doesn't it feel good to release it?" We swam back to shore and lay on top of the grass, letting the hot afternoon rays dry us. I shut my eyes and fell asleep.

"Siva might still be alive if you'd have done that Kali." Erishkigal's eyes were opened wide, her long lashes almost touching her eyebrows.

"Yeah, and maybe Enki's trolls wouldn't have had to rescue Inanna from your rage and resentment," countered Kali.

"Sisters," Kuan Yin clucked her tongue. "We all experience anger. But it need not exert total control. Erishkigal, you were so angry about being trapped in the Underworld that you tried to destroy your sister. But the gods resurrected her and she forgave you. That is the lesson. Not the degree of destruction."

"But Rena was so angry." Inanna shivered. "I was afraid she might explode."

"Acknowledging anger is the only way for her to move forward. Her parents weren't the best role models in teaching her how to love," Kuan Yin admitted. "But she chose to be born to them to learn. If she continues to believe they are at fault for the things that don't go right in her life, she will never progress." She folded her hands and held them at her stomach.

"By allowing herself to feel that anger, she has taken the first step in accepting responsibility for where she is. They have been her choices that have brought her to where she is." Kuan Yin stood silently for a moment; her hands now pressed together in prayer position. "No blame, only acceptance. This is how change begins."

"Now what?" Kali asked.

"Now she must finish the cycle with Jack."

"How?"

"By caring for him when he leaves the hospital," Kuan Yin answered.

"No way!" Kali argued. "He's a big blob of rage. She doesn't need to be fighting with him all the time."

"Jack's lessons are just that. His lessons," admonished Kuan Yin. "This is about what Rena needs to learn. And the only way to learn compassion for herself is to practice on others. It is the law."

"Well, I'm not happy about this," Inanna was not convinced.

"No offense, sister. But I didn't ask for your permission." Kuan Yin smiled, and with a corner of her robe polished the bronze now covering Inanna's chest. "Nice breastplate."

Jack was released from the hospital five days later. He still refused to let me call his aunt or try to reach his father or sisters. And Paul had disappeared. The bandage over his eye had been removed and the skin was a palette of purples and yellows, making him appear slightly jaundiced. He was only allowed clear liquids; culinary delights like oatmeal and pudding were at least another three days away.

I insisted he come home with me. "No way, Rena," he argued. "I can handle it."

"It's not a question of whether or not you can handle it by yourself," I replied. "You don't have to." I picked him up the day he was discharged. He was as ornery and angry as the day after surgery. A volunteer wheeled him to the elevator.

"I'd really rather go home." He had lost weight and his pants puckered at the small of his back. "I'll be fine."

"Mr. Crandall," the older volunteer offered. "It'll be nice to have someone to make you soup and fetch your prescriptions."

"Did I ask you?" he barked.

"Jack!" I lightly flicked his shoulder. "Stop it!" He shifted in the wheelchair, shaking his left foot against the steel rest. The trembling spread and soon his entire leg bounced uncontrollably. The volunteer was unaffected by his outburst and continued to wheel him toward the exit.

"Let me pull the car up. I'll be right back." The electric doors opened and I stepped into the sunlight. When I returned, Jack was struggling to get out of the chair, one arm wrapped around his stomach, his breathing labored.

"I can do it," he hissed to the candy-stripe-clad woman, her white hair tucked neatly underneath a pink cap. I reached out and lent him my arm for support. He grimaced walking to the sidewalk. "Jesus, it's hot," he complained as I opened the car door. The atmosphere around him had been cool and dry for almost a week, no extremes of heat or rain. I placed the inflated donut on the seat before he got in.

"We're actually having a cold spell," I joked. "It's only eighty-two today. It was in the nineties last week and really humid. I'm finally having a good hair day." I fluffed my hair and posed. He didn't laugh. I pulled out of the entrance, careful not to make any sudden moves. The last thing Jack needed was the seat belt locking around his bruised ribs. We pulled into Tartan Farm's driveway and I slipped around the side of the cottage.

"We're here!" I wanted to sound cheery, but not syrupy. From the look on Jack's face, I don't think I succeeded. We got inside and he collapsed on the couch, on his side, panting. "I'll get you settled and then go get your prescriptions," I said getting a pillow and blanket from the closet. I retrieved the donut pillow they'd given us at the hospital from the car and re-inflated it.

"I don't have any money on me," Jack hoisted himself off the couch.

"Sit down," I ordered, throwing the puffy plastic ring on a cushion. "Don't worry about it right now. We can square up later." He dropped back down.

"Why are you doing this?" His face was squeezed in pain.

"Doing what?"

"Being so nice to me? We haven't even known each other that long." I laughed. "What's so funny?" He adjusted the donut under his bottom.

"Nothing." I tucked a pillow behind his head and unfolded the blanket. "I'm demonstrating compassion. Can't you just say thank you?"

"I don't need to be your charity case." He bounced his leg and his shoeless foot thumped softly against the hardwood floors.

"And I don't need you fighting with me." I covered him. "Look, you need some help. I'm willing to offer mine. Let's just leave it at that. OK?" I picked up my bag and car keys from the table. "Now, can I get you anything before I run to the drugstore?" He shook his head and I opened the door.

"Wait." I turned around. His swollen face made it look as if he'd been in make-up for an hour prepping for a horror movie, the steri-strips glowing white over his eyebrow. There were a couple of scabs on his cheeks from the hospital razor and a tiny piece of tissue clung to a red spot on his chin from this morning's shave. "Where's the remote?" I tossed it to him from the top of the television, followed by the *TV Guide*.

"Anything else?" I cocked my head. He flipped on the television and the room was filled with the strains of Sheryl Crow's "All I Wanna Do."

"Maybe some Bubble Yum," his eyes were glued to the screen. "And a bag of Doritos. I'm starving."

"Very funny," I smiled. "I'll see what I can do about the gum." I drove to Rite-Aid to pick up the suppositories, eye drops, and pain pills the doctor had prescribed. I scanned the magazines while I waited, debating whether or not to pick up a copy of *Surfer*. I settled on *Entertainment Weekly* and *The Star*. All innocuous. I tossed in a pack of Bubble Yum and box of Mike and Ike's for me. A hundred and fifty dollars later, I headed to the grocery store. He wasn't allowed anything but two ounces of clear liquids every two hours, basically juice or broth. By Sunday night, one week after I'd discovered him in the shower, he'd be allowed to try pureed fruit and vegetables.

Over the weekend Jack and I played gin, Monopoly, and backgammon. He didn't need much of the Demerol, using it only at bedtime. Before Jack was released, David and Alex hauled down the extra bed from their guestroom and set it up in my empty second bedroom. I dumped the contents of my nightstand into a carton and put it beside the bed to hold Jack's medication. I finally convinced him to give me the key to his apartment and drove over to retrieve some clothes and toiletries.

By Sunday night he wasn't quite as cantankerous. I boiled apples on the stove, preparing for his first solid meal while he watched the Yankee game. "Oh my God!" I heard him yell. "NO!" I ran into the living room.

"What's wrong?" He pointed to the screen, tears rolling out of his good eye. An anchor sat at a news desk, a picture of Princess Diana behind him, labeled with the dates 1961–1997. "What the hell happened?" I sat down next to him, listening to the report. A car accident. Chased by photographers. Driver of her limo possibly drunk. The words swirled around in my head, none of them penetrating.

Jack sat silently as clips of the Princess danced across the television. Diana at a fundraiser for the homeless. Diana comforting a grieving mother in Sarajevo. Diana on a roller coaster with Princes William and Harry. The darkness of Paris, lit only by flashing bulbs as Diana and Dodi Fayed escaped from the paparazzi into the limousine that would crash in a tiny French tunnel, forever changing the world she had finally begun to enjoy.

"Why?" Jack asked me. "Why did this happen to her?" I put my arms around him and pulled him to me, my chin resting on his head. "It's not fair." The sobs started silent and slow, gaining momentum from their own sadness. He shook and shivered and I held him, afraid he might disintegrate if I let go. I cried with him. For her. For him. For me. The Yankees were up five to three over the White Sox and Jack was finally silent, his head pressed against my chest. My shirt was wet with the proof of his pain.

Alex had gone home and Angelina and I had to take care of the horses alone. For a week, I got up at five, made enough pudding, Jell-O, and oatmeal for the day and worked in the barn, periodically checking on Jack. He started to visit us a couple of times a day and gradually his walks stretched up to the pastures near the road where Bogota and Seuss spent the day. When I had returned the last horse to the barn, I ran errands or did laundry.

Twelve days after the surgery, Jack and I sat down to a dinner of mashed potatoes, gravy, and peas. He was only using the donut on hard surfaces and the bruising on his face had ebbed, the shades more muted. The cuts under his ear were almost completely healed and he had stopped using the suppositories. He washed the dishes and I dried. "Let's go for a walk," I suggested. "Why don't we drive to the beach at Sea Bright?"

"The beach?" He flicked the soapy water off his hands and grabbed a towel from over the sink. "I don't think so."

"Jack, you've got to talk about it at some point," I put the plates back in the cupboard. "I'm not pretending to understand what you've been through. And maybe I'm not the person you want to discuss it with. That's fine." He leaned into the corner near the back door. "But you've got to talk about it." He snaked his arms around his stomach until they touched his back, circling himself in a hug. His knees bent slightly and he dropped his chin to his chest.

"I can't." I walked over and stood next to him, wanting to touch him but afraid he might crumple if I did.

"Yes, you can." He shook his head and whimpered like a puppy whose been left behind. He brought his hands up and covered his face.

"You're stronger than me, Rena. I can't do it."

"I'll help you." I touched his hair. "You can't push all this back down, Jack. It'll kill you eventually."

"I'd rather die." I debated how much farther to push him. Maybe it wasn't time yet. Maybe I wanted him to cleanse himself because I hadn't found a way to do it for myself. Maybe if he dealt with his pain, it would give me the courage to deal with mine. Maybe I just needed to be a friend who'd listen when necessary, advise when asked, and love unconditionally. I hugged him, wrapping him in my softness.

"I love you. If you ever need to talk, I'm here." He slid down the wall and I followed, the two of us huddled in a corner of my kitchen while Joni Mitchell warbled "Free Man in Paris" in the living room.

I dropped Jack off at his apartment in Belford a few days later. I had gone over and cleaned it thoroughly, trying to scrub away two weeks of horror and pain and sadness. "This place looks great, Rena," he hugged me. "Thank you."

"No problem," I stepped into the kitchen and opened the refrigerator door. "I loaded you up." It was full of juice and cooked oatmeal and chocolate pudding. The doctor had told him at his check-up that he could start eating solid foods but advised him to do it slowly.

"I don't know how I can ever repay you," he unpacked his shaving case.

"No need," I insisted. "Just promise me that you'll call me if you need me." He smiled. It was the first time I'd seen the gap in his teeth in over two weeks.

"I will. Bud said I could start back part-time in the store until I feel up to delivering."

"That was nice of him," I jangled the car keys in my hand. "OK, well I'll let you be in peace." I pushed the lever on the screen door.

"You saved my life, Rena." I felt his hands massaging my shoulders. He kissed my neck. "I owe you."

"No," I smiled, turning around and kissing his forehead. "We're even."

When I got home there was a message on my answering machine from Angelina. "David and I want you to come for dinner. I'm stuffing Cornish game hens as I speak. Call me."

We sat at the kitchen table, David in sweat pants and Angelina in leggings. A vase of fresh daisies rested in the middle and the only light came from a candelabra, the flames flickering with our breath. We ate slowly listening to Mozart. "How's Jack?" David asked.

"He's feeling a lot better physically," I answered. "But he won't talk about what happened."

"Maybe he's not ready," Angelina thoughtfully chewed a broccoli floret. "You can't control that, Rena."

"I know," I folded the napkin in my lap. "It's hard though."

"Guess what." David grinned. "Angelina and I have a proposition for you." I eyed him suspiciously. "It's a good one, really." His eyes pleaded with his wife for help.

"David and I were talking," she patted his hand. "We know you've been through an awful lot lately."

"I'm fine," I insisted. "There's no reason to worry."

"We're not worried," she soothed. "I know you can handle whatever is thrown at you."

"Face it, Rena, the last few weeks have been tough," David interjected. "We just thought it might be nice for you to get away for a while."

"What do you mean?" My stomach rumbled.

"What David is trying to say is that if you'd like to take a break from here, it's OK."

"But I love being here," I said, trying to convince myself. I didn't know where I wanted to be.

"We know that," David grabbed a roll from the basket. "And we're not trying to get rid of you because I know that's what's tripping through your head right now. We just thought a little time alone after everything might be good for you." I sat quietly.

"I have some money, maybe I could take a trip," I thought out loud.

"How would you like to spend some time in Manhattan?" he offered.

"I can't afford a hotel there," I argued.

"David still has the condo in Battery Park," Angelina smiled.

"I'm going to sell it," he said with his mouth full, "eventually. But when Angelina said she thought some time away might do you good, we agreed it could wait for a while."

"Really?" I felt excitement for the first time in a long time. "But what about the horses?"

"Alex decided to take a semester off from school," David laughed. "He doesn't know what he wants to do with his life."

"He enjoyed helping out while you were tied up. He's agreed to stay here and give me a hand," Angelina added. "So you wouldn't have to feel like you were abandoning me." She started clearing the dishes. "What do you think?" Thoughts were running through my head, searching for the finish line.

"There were so many things I wanted to do when I lived there that I never got around to," I admitted. "I always wanted to spend the day at the Met. Or take the tram over to Roosevelt Island. I never did make it to the Botanical Gardens. And I've always wanted to visit the Cloisters."

"You've never been up to the Cloisters?" David stared at me. "You've got to be kidding?" The Cloisters sat at the top of Manhattan, a medieval castle on the hills of the Hudson River. I had read about it in a magazine and was fascinated with the artifacts and art it housed, all from the twelfth to fifteenth centuries.

"No," I shook my head. "And I've never been to the Bronx Zoo either."

"What the hell did you do when you lived there?" He leaned back for Angelina to place a dish of fruit in front of him.

"Worked." I got up to help Angelina with the coffee.

"It's settled, then," David announced. "Pack a bag and go."

"Are you sure?"

"Positive," they answered in unison.

"It's not forever," I insisted.

"Of course not," Angelina took the pot of coffee from me and gave me a hug. "But you need some time to breathe."

Rena

The Fifth Goddess

"What did you enjoy most about The Cloisters, Rena?" I sat on the leather couch picking the cuticle on my middle finger.

"I like the fact that there is so much history there." I put my finger in my mouth and bit off a hard piece of skin. "Think about it. That castle was built from remnants of medieval structures that are hundreds of years old."

"Why is that important to you?" Jennifer's strawberry blond hair was wiry, the short curls tight against her scalp, like an Airedale.

"I don't know." I scratched my ankle with my sneaker and the laces came undone. I retied the bow and resumed chewing my finger. Jennifer noticed me gnawing at my nail bed. I gave the cuticle a final tweak, forced my hands into my lap, and continued. "I've been doing a lot of thinking lately. About where I come from, where I'm going. Why I'm here. I don't know what my history is going to be."

"It's a little tough for you to be in possession of that information, right?" she laughed. I squished the chenille pillow, hugging it against my stomach.

"Maybe. But I don't want it to be the same history as my parents. Or my grandparents."

"What do you want to be different?" She wore a sapphire blue sweater. It matched her eyes. I stared at the miniature Japanese water fountain sitting atop a marble pedestal on the other side of her living room.

"I just want to be happy." I averted my eyes from her gaze.

"What's going to make you happy?" Jennifer leaned forward, resting her arms on the tops of her thighs. She wore the same spicy perfume she had the day I found her.

"I don't know." I sighed.

I had met Jennifer last week while we both gazed at an Italian fresco inside the Cloisters. The strokes in the painting were so delicate. It was hard to believe someone could have painted it the first time, much less spent the tedious hours necessary to transfer it to America.

"I wish I could paint like that," I had said to her as she stood staring at the wall. She wore jeans and a light green windbreaker and her tiny wrist bones stuck out from under the elastic of the cuffs.

"How do you know you can't?" she smiled, the freckles on her cheeks wrinkling. The warm scent of her Opium perfume made me feel safe.

"What is it you do?" she asked.

"Nothing right now." I locked my eyes on the fresco. I had no job—no identity. Her face held a puzzled expression, one eyebrow arched, the other sedately rounded. "It's a long story," I laughed. "I'm trying to figure out what I want to do with my life."

"I know that feeling," she nodded. We moved from the fresco and began walking through the museum. I was amazed at the intricate tapestries and the artfully crafted stained glass.

"My husband died on his motorcycle fifteen years ago," she confessed. I was silent. "My son was nine. I was a stay-at-home mom, long before it was acceptable," she laughed. "Back then it was all about having your career, climbing up the corporate ladder, making as much money as the men."

We headed outside to the herb garden on the ground floor and found an empty white bench. The trees of Ft. Tryon Park surrounded the castle, their leaves rustling with the onset of autumn. Gold and orange and maroon. The wind blew slightly, enough to make both of us zip our jackets.

"Joe left enough money for us to live on for a while," she removed a cigarette from her backpack. "You're not supposed to smoke out here," she glanced around. "But I'm just dying." A young couple sat kissing on a bench in the corner. Other than that, we were alone. "Would you like one?" She held the pack to me. We lit up and pufffed in silence for a minute.

"Anyway, I decided to go back to school," she flicked her ash into the dirt. "Am I boring you?"

"No," I shook my head and took a hit from my Marlboro Light.

"I already had an undergraduate degree in social work, so I decided to get my Master's. Then it kind of snowballed." She put the backpack in between her legs on the cement. "I ended up getting my Ph.D. after my son graduated from high school."

"So you're a doctor?"

"I have a Ph.D. in psychology." I watched her exhale a smoke ring.

"What did you do your dissertation on?"

"The effects of non-verbal communication on children, specifically from their parents." She stubbed the butt out in the dirt of a potted plant and wrapped it in a tissue. "It's my dirty habit," she explained. "No one else should have to deal with it." She held out the tissue and I placed my butt next to hers.

"What exactly does that mean?" I asked.

"Basically, I tried to prove that the non-verbal messages communicated from a parent to a child contribute more to the child's mental health than messages that are spoken."

"Did you succeed?"

"I guess so," her glossy pink lips stretched in a grin revealing a couple of crooked teeth. "They gave me my degree. But it sure was a long haul."

"So what do you do now?"

"I do group counseling for a couple of private substance abuse clinics." She shook her bag and extracted a box of Tic-Tacs, offering me one. "And I have my own practice. I love it." The mint cleared my sinuses and removed the sticky taste of tar from my tongue. She glanced at her watch and stood up. "I really need to get going. My son is bringing the grandchildren over for dinner and I haven't even shopped yet." She looked toward the river. "I just needed some quiet time." Turning back to me, she held out her hand.

"Jennifer Mandeville." I shook it.

"Rena Sutcliffe."

"It was nice meeting you." She swung the pack over her shoulder and pulled her arm through the other strap. "Enjoy the rest of the museum. Check out the Fuentiduena Chapel if you haven't seen it yet. It's amazing." She walked toward the door, her tennis shoes lightly skimming the concrete. I sat on the bench, feeling peaceful, bathed in a soft mist of Opium. I stayed to watch the sun set over the Palisades.

But that night I couldn't sleep. I kept waking up, interrupted by the struggle being waged between my conscious and unconscious. I felt the two parts of me warring, one wanting to stay in control, the other begging for release. When I awoke, I felt like I'd been in the ring with Evander Holyfield, bruised and weary.

I searched David's apartment for the white pages and in a sleepy stupor looked up Jennifer's number. I left a message for her and went back to bed. The phone rang while I was still sleeping. "Rena?" Her voice was clear and soft on the other end. "Are you OK?"

"No," I had whispered. And we made an appointment for today. A force like a magnet pulled me toward her apartment, my intellect making excuses why I should turn around and go home. But I fought it like I had the first day I went to St. Nicholas'.

The warm scent of Jennifer's fragrance brought me back to her apartment, and I realized she was holding a steaming cup of coffee out to me. I took the mug from her and blew on it for a minute before taking a sip.

"Sometimes it's necessary to figure out what's making you unhappy before you can find your path." She looked at me expectantly, waiting for a response. I spent the next few hours telling her everything I just told you.

Jennifer sat quietly as the water gurgled over miniature trees in the fountain. "I don't get it," I was frustrated. "I've been practicing yoga for two years. I've read dozens of books, trying to figure out what it is that will make this feeling disappear. And I feel more lost now than I did when I quit my job."

"There is an old Sufi story that tells of a man crawling around in the dirt outside his hut." Jennifer picked through the candy dish on the end table and selected a butterscotch.

"A stranger comes by and asks him what he is doing. The man replies that he is looking for a lost key. The stranger offers to help and searches the ground with him." She unwrapped the candy and popped into her mouth.

"After a while, having found nothing, he asks the man where the key was lost. 'In my hut,' he replies. 'Then why are you looking out here?' asks the stranger. 'Because out here is more light.'"

"What's a Sufi?" I asked.

"Sufi is a name that was given to a group of mystics who lived in ancient Persia," she twisted the plastic butterscotch wrapper and looked at me. "But the point of the story is that we often spend a lifetime searching outside for the answers because we're afraid of the dark." I struggled to understand.

"There is no reason to be afraid." Her words wrapped around me like a melodious hug. "I understand it's frustrating, but it's part of the process."

"I'm beginning to miss some things about the job," I confessed, ignoring her remark. "I enjoyed the money. I want to travel more and I don't know of any other career that I'm qualified for that pays that kind of money." I took a deep breath. "I also don't want to go back." Jennifer set the candy wrapper on the table next to her chair.

"Carl Jung said that it is totally normal to experience dichotomized feelings like that, Rena." She tapped her long fingernails together. "The problem is that it's human instinct to choose one over the other because we can't stand the discomfort of not knowing. Jung believed that if we allow ourselves to sit in the discomfort, not choosing one or the other just for the sake of choosing, that a third alternative will present itself." The tapping stopped. "A gift that is bestowed upon us for our patience."

"I don't know." I dug around the soft skin below my thumbnail.

"Why did you call me?" she asked.

"I didn't know what else to do. No one in my family ever went to a psychiatrist. But I can't stand feeling like this."

"And do you think therapy can help?"

"I really don't know."

"I appreciate your honesty," she chuckled and got up to close the window against the chill that was seeping into the room. "A lot of people use therapy as a Band-Aid. They're going through a situation at work or in a relationship and they can't figure out how to resolve it." She sat back down and crossed her legs. "And there's nothing wrong with that. But your situation is different."

"What do you mean?"

"You're ready to take the next step. You have a longing that I don't think you've even admitted to yourself." Something inside me twitched. "I think we can do some good work together." Attempting to process her words made my head hurt. "What you're talking about doing is finding enlightenment, Rena. That's a long journey and one that entails a cleaning, if you will, of the grime that covers the window of your soul."

"What grime?" I crossed my arms over my chest.

"The grime that has been forming your entire life. Beliefs and perceptions that have been created based on outside information shared with you by your family, friends, the media. But that's not the knowledge you possess in your heart." She tucked her hands under the hem of her sweater. "We integrate these facts into our belief system, but just because they are facts doesn't mean it is the truth."

"I don't understand."

"Man," Kali pulled her fingers through her hair, knotted strands falling at her feet. "I don't think this is a good idea."

"That's only because you're afraid of pain," Kuan Yin removed Kali's hand from her hair. "But there is nothing to fear."

"I agree with Kali," Inanna paced, weaving in between her three sisters. "She's trusting this woman blindly. The last time she did that was with that woman from the support group and where did it get her?" Inanna couldn't stay still. "What's the point? What could she possibly gain from therapy?"

"More than you, in all of your intelligence, can comprehend," Kuan Yin lightly stroked Kali's head. "Rena wasn't ready to learn the truth when she went to St. Nicholas'. But she has spent years veiling herself, forgetting what her soul knows to be true. That peace only comes from being united with God. Jennifer can help her to remember." Erishkigal was huddled next to Kali's feet.

"I don't want to," she sobbed, her shoulders heaving involuntarily. "It will hurt too much."

"Pain is not a bad thing." Kuan Yin pressed her palms together and bowed daintily to each of her sisters. "It's not eternal, but transformational. The pain is what will reunite her with God, ending the separation."

"I don't understand," Kali shrugged and moved away.

"You don't need to," Kuan Yin smiled. "You only need to have faith." She looked at Inanna, knowing that together, the two of them would be stronger than Kali and Erishkigal. "It's the only way for you to get the rest of your belongings back, you know."

"Really?" Inanna's hands moved from her head to her ears to her neck.

"If Rena doesn't continue her journey of self-discovery, they will be forever lost to you."

"You better not be yanking my chain, KY," she shook her index finger at Kuan Yin. "This isn't a three-day weekend we're talking about here. This is going to be years of work." Kuan Yin nodded, grateful that her sister understood.

"No fair!" Kali yelled. "If you convince her, I'm going to have no say."

"Nor me," Erishkigal chimed in.

"I know," Kuan Yin grinned.

"I'm sorry," Jennifer smiled. "Maybe I'm throwing too much at you right now. You've shared a lot with me today and I'm sure it was pretty painful." I nodded. "Why don't we make an appointment for next week?" I noticed the sun was gone, no rays streaming in the window. A pot of African violets rested in a clay pot on the sill, their flowers slowly folding in on themselves.

"I don't know." I closed my eyes and felt the moisture looking for a way out. "I thought quitting my job was enough. I expected to be hit by a lightning bolt that told me what I needed to do. But I haven't found the answer."

"Do you believe it's there?" Jennifer asked.
I nodded, the tears no longer private.

The Fifth Goddess

Post Script

Fellow traveler,

In the world of mythology, Inanna, the Sumerian Goddess of Wisdom, travels to the Great Below to visit her sister, Erishkigal, the Sumerian Goddess of the Underworld. At each of the seven gates to hell, Inanna is stripped of one of her possessions. First her crown, then her earrings, necklace, breastplate, shoes, belt, and finally, her cloak—until she is standing naked at the gates of hell. As the myth goes, Erishkigal murders her sister, jealous at Inanna's ability to live above and resentful at having to live her life below. Eventually, Inanna is resurrected and ascends back to earth. And as she passes back through each of the seven gates, her belongings are returned to her.

Psychologically, Inanna's symbolic death and eventual ascent represent the journey of self-discovery. Those who choose this path descend to the darkest depths of their beings, often enduring incredible emotional pain caused by releasing beliefs, people, and situations that no longer serve their higher selves. In Inanna's mythology, this releasing is represented by the loss of possessions.

For those courageous enough to make the trip, the magical gift of this sacrifice is the awareness of their TRUTH. This realization is what allows them to rise from those depths, stronger and wiser for having had the courage to withstand the pain necessary to complete the journey. And the gifts they receive from having completed the journey are more than they could have possibly imagined. As Rena learned to make choices that honored herself, Inanna was rewarded with the return of her belongings—well, some of them, anyway.

"But wait!" you say. When *The Fifth Goddess* ends, Inanna is still missing her breastplate, necklace, earrings, and crown. Does she get them back? How? You'll have to read the sequel to find out.

In the meantime, if you would like to have additional information on Erishkigal—the Sumerian Goddess of the Underworld, Kali—the Hindu Goddess of Destruction, Inanna—the Sumerian Goddess of Wisdom (a.k.a. Goddess of Heaven and Earth) or Kuan Yin—the Chinese Goddess of Compassion, you can visit my website at www.fifthgoddess.com for a description of each and a complete list of tomes that inspired me in the writing of this book. Or, you can send a self-addressed stamped envelope to me at: P.O. Box 14, Atlantic Highlands, NJ 07716.

Jai sri sat guru maharaj ki.
May the light of truth overcome all darkness.

Namaste,
Staci Backauskas
Atlantic Highlands, New Jersey
October 6, 1999

P.S. The password to get into the "Talk to Your Goddess" secret page on my website is Durga-Ma.

MORE FROM JAI CREATIONS

To order additional copies of The Fifth Goddess, you may

- Call toll free 877-291-4212 to order by Visa or MasterCard
- Go to www.fifthgoddess.com and order over our secure server
- Postal orders can be sent to: Jai Creations, P.O. Box 14, Atlantic Highlands, NJ 07716 Tel: (732) 291-4212 with either a check, money order, or credit card authorization.

Join our mailing list! Keep updated on new titles and receive a FREE copy of The Fifth Goddess newsletter! Please fill out the following:

Name: _____

Address: _____

City: _____ *ST/Prov:* ____ *Postal Code:* _____

Country: _____

Telephone (_____) _____

E-Mail address: _____

The price of the book is $14.95 US or $20.95 Canadian

Sales Tax: Please add 6% sales tax for books shipped to New Jersey addresses.

Shipping: $4.00 for US Priority Mail — 2 to 3 day delivery

Payment: Check ☐ Credit Card: Visa ☐ MasterCard ☐ Checks must be in US dollars and drawn on a US bank.

Card Number: _____

Name on Card: _____ *Exp. Date:* _____

The Fifth Goddess

The Fifth Goddess

This book was designed by Michael Höhne
in Adobe Garamond and Myriad Tilt and Letraset Bergell types,
and produced with Apple Macintosh and QuarkXPress.

The Fifth Goddess

The Fifth Goddess